THE FUTURE: CENTURY 23

Adventure in an Inconvenient Future

By
Don Green

Library of Congress Control Number: 2014912549

ISBN: 13: 978-1500399047
CreateSpace Independent Publishing Platform, North Charleston, S.C.

Author:: Donald R. Green
       18200 Woodinville-Snohomish Rd. N.E.
       Apt 315
       Woodinville, WA 98072
       U.S.A.

To my dear wife, Mary, who encouraged me, supported my preoccupation with writing this book, and read and critiqued the first draft of my manuscript.

Two of the scientific designs described in this story were the result of the author's best efforts in research, computations, and in some cases, experiments with some success. **But these designs are not in any way guaranteed to be accurate, or feasible. They should not be used without first carefully checking the theory, engineering, and practicality.** If the reader decides to try developing these designs, he or she should be sure to read the complete story. To make the story as realistic as possible, the designs changed, as the development work progressed in the story, just as happens in real-life research and development.

ACKNOWLEDGEMENTS

I am grateful for the fine editing of the first drafts, and helpful suggestions provided by Frances Dayee, professional editor. Critiques by her Kenmore, WA Writing Workshop were extremely helpful, especially those from writers who were frequent attendees: Jerry Ellis, Donna Glasscock, John Wilde, and Janet Peacey.

I also appreciate the instruction I received as a student from Simon Johnson, English Professor Emeritus, Oregon State University, in his 2009 creative writing class.

Photographs on the cover were used under the following permissions:

Three pictures depicting horse transportation: permission purchased from dollarphotoclub.com.

Car by Mariordo Mario Roberto Duran Ortiz; Ship by Matt H. Wade; both permitted under the Creative Commons Attribution-Share Alike 3.0 Unsupported license.

Truck by Cheney Ashley; Bullet Train by Siemens; Plow by Joevillers; all are in the public domain.

Airliner by Arcturus; permission under the terms of the GNU Free Documentation License.

The use of these photographs does not claim, suggest, or imply that any or all of the original photograph copyright holders endorse this book, any of its contents, or its author.

PROLOGUE
Decline into Century 23 - Background of the Story

It had been more than sixteen decades since The Darkening, but it was still a destructive force in the 23rd century.

Serious trouble started in 2058 when massive catastrophes brewing for years suddenly began to explode at an alarming rate. Global warming had already caused sea levels to rise enough to wipe out all small, low-lying, coastal towns. Heavy construction machinery, used to build dikes and seawalls around major coastal cities, burned huge amounts of petroleum fuel. This caused a surge in the millions of tons of greenhouse gasses, already being poured into the atmosphere and added to the already rampant global warming. World population was north of nine billion. Numerous countries previously classed as "third world" had become affluent. Much of their population owned cars and trucks, and contributed greenhouse gasses. Global warming was spawning the most destructive droughts, floods, snowstorms, tornados and hurricanes in history, and their destructive power was rapidly getting worse.

Great shortages began in about 2060 when the earth's deposits of oil, natural gas, wood, and coal had been nearly depleted. Prices rocketed upward to levels few people could afford. Oil was the first and worst shortage. For more than 130 years prior to 2060, oil had been the main fuel used for transportation, farming, and heavy equipment, as well as a base material from which fertilizer, plastics, and other products were made. Just before the shortage, while oil was still affordable, world consumption was two hundred million barrels per day and climbing. Scientists warned that oil reserves would soon be depleted, but governments influenced by powerful interests profiting from the rampant usage, wouldn't acknowledge the looming shortage. Governments refused to fund intensive research and development to produce sustainable propulsion methods that didn't require oil. Their mantra was: "Industries will develop anything that is needed." But industries weren't interested in developing anything not absolutely guaranteed to be profitable within a year or two, and propaganda from oil interests said there wouldn't be an oil shortage any time soon. They were wrong.

After oil became scarce, natural gas was pressed into service as engine fuel, but with heavy usage it was soon depleted.

Coal and wood were depleted when, in addition to their traditional heating, industrial and construction applications, they were used to fuel steam and hot-air (Stirling) engines for transportation and farming.

Alternative fuels were hastily produced with government subsidies in response to political pressures from those who profited from them. However, one of these fuels, alcohol, was made from precious food crops such as corn and sugar cane. There were food shortages, and more fuel was required to produce, refine, and deliver the alternative fuels than they replaced. Using any of the alternative fuels produced carbon dioxide greenhouse gas. Alcohol as well as the other alternative fuels soon dropped out of vogue.

Electric propulsion of vehicles and farm equipment was popular for a short time. However, the sudden demand for billions of batteries, and many terawatts (millions of megawatts) of additional electrical power, soon depleted special materials such as rare earths used in batteries, generators, and solar cells. Most of the meager remaining deposits of these materials were located in China and Africa. Prices skyrocketed and battery-powered vehicles became impractical. By the time industry was convinced there would be immediate profits from alternative propulsion methods, it was too late to complete development in time to avoid the exploding final catastrophes.

The lack of affordable propulsion for trucks and tractors, added to catastrophic droughts from global warming, food production dropped sharply. By the end of 2065, one-third of the world population had starved to death. There were monstrous worldwide anti-government riots and brutal wars between nations desperately trying to gain control of dwindling fuel and food sources. The total combined effect of these catastrophes was the death of three-fourths of the world population in only a few years.

Refusal of governments to head off the looming problems was the main cause of the catastrophes. However, during the riots, governments shifted the blame away from themselves with propaganda claiming scientists had caused the catastrophes by inventing devices that led to rapid oil consumption, pollution and weapons of mass destruction. A majority of the people bought it. They didn't understand science, and were convinced that it was a "black art" that would cause even more trouble in the future. Some religions were strongly anti-science, and added to the anti-science pressure. In 2068, in response to public pressure, a law was enacted banning new advanced scientific research, prescribing a penalty of death for violators. This discouraged even small engineering improvements since there was a danger that officials, who knew little about science, would adjudge the improvements to be illegal advanced science.

Prohibition of new science was designated "The Darkening" by intellectuals because it pulled a suffocating black cloak over needed development. Later "The Darkening" became the term most people understood to mean the years after 2068, even though few fully understood its implications.

During the many years of chaos that followed the catastrophes, local, state, and national governments collapsed and were replaced by smaller entities called "Tribes," and "Multi-Tribe Cooperatives," often simply called "Cooperatives". These groups were politically modern, and retained many of the characteristics of the previous governments. A number of laws from the old legal systems, including the death penalty for anyone caught doing new scientific work, were carried over into the tribal laws.

In the 23rd century, pre-Darkening technologies, such as computers, telephones, holovision (holographic 3-D television) and automobiles, are permitted. However, only a few automobiles are in use, and only by very wealthy persons and companies that can afford scarce, expensive fuel or propulsion batteries. The minimum daily wage for a worker in 2231 is 100-credits. A loaf of bread costs six credits. Gasoline and diesel cost over 195-credits per gallon. Batteries for electric automobiles cost 400,000-credits each.

Due to the 75-percent population loss during the 21st century catastrophes, people have a much better life in 2231 than they would have had 165 years earlier. The specter of starvation no longer stalks the average person. However, the increasing population, and The Darkening's suffocation of progress, are soon going to cause food and power shortages unless someone violates the anti-science laws and develops new renewable-power methods

CHAPTER 1
THE COTTAGE

Bob Parker, and his wife, Audrey, moved into a 200-year old stone cottage in mid September 2231. Rumors about some of its earlier occupants flew around town like autumn leaves in a strong wind. Previous occupants were supposed to have disappeared for weeks at a time without being seen leaving or returning. It was said that strange lights sometimes appeared on the property at night

Audrey was a thirty-two year old writer and had a passion for antiques, especially if there was an intriguing story about them. She had wanted the old cottage for years. Living in it opened the possibility of learning more about its mysterious past. Her imagination was in hyper-drive: perhaps there were secret markings under wallpaper or long-undiscovered clues hidden in nooks and crannies of the house itself.

The cottage sat on an 80-acre plot of land 1-1/2 miles west of Stoneville, a small town where Bob and Audrey grew up. There was a tool shed and a barn on the property. Most of the land was covered with orchard grass. However, there was a curious circular patch of thick vine maple brush at the bottom of a small hill near the west edge of the property. A dirt road bordering the front of the property provided a fast route to Bob's blacksmith shop located on the west edge of Stoneville.

Most members of Bob and Audrey's Tribe lived in Stoneville and its surrounding area in the western part of Waidor, a tribal cooperative of 53-tribes. This cooperative covered an area previously occupied by former states called Washington, Idaho and Oregon in what had been the United States of America. Greensville, 35miles to the East of Stoneville, was a larger town that provided good access to unusual goods and services. Special supplies for Bob's blacksmith shop were available there.

One morning, several days after moving into the cottage, Bob came into the kitchen for breakfast. Audrey was opening mail laid out on one end of the table. Her forehead rumpled and her lips tightened into a thin line as she read an official-looking letter. Looking up she said, "Our insurance company has finally decided how much they'll pay on the surgery and hospitalization I had last July. It's just awful. We'll have to pay 100,000-credits more than we expected, and the hospital is demanding that we pay it off at six percent interest over a five year period."

Bob's brow furrowed and his face blanched. "My God. Those payments, added to our other monthly expenses, will break us. I'll have to find a way to bring in more income, or our 70,000-credit savings will be eaten up and we'll lose this house in three or four years. I wish we hadn't bought it."

Tears came into Audrey's eyes. "It's all my fault for having been so damn sick and wanting this house. I'll look for a job in town."

"Don't blame yourself—it was just bad luck. I don't think it's a good idea for you to get a job so soon after recovering from such a serious illness. I'm afraid you'll have a relapse."

"I appreciate your concern, but I had completely recovered by early September, and I feel just fine. We've got to find a way to get more income. Maybe I could sell some writing or take in sewing."

"No. I can work Saturdays. I've got plenty of customers wanting blacksmith services, and I'm pretty sure I can make enough . . ."

"You're already putting in long hours. You'll make yourself sick."

"Nah. I can do a lot more than . . ."

Bob was interrupted by his wrist telephone vibrating. A formal text message locked into it said:

> "Mr. Robert Parker: you must appear for jury duty at the Tribal District Five Courthouse at 9 a.m., November 1st, 2231. If for any reason you cannot attend, you must contact the Courthouse Clerk

in reply to this message and explain. If you are not excused, failure to appear will result in a severe penalty. This message will remain in your telephone's memory until you delete it. Say "finished" to unlock your phone and confirm that you have read the message."

Bob said, "Finished. Delete last message."

"What was that?" Audrey asked.

"A jury duty notice for November 1st. What trial do you think it's for?" Bob said, looking perplexed.

"I'm not sure, but I'd guess it's for the science guy who was shown on the holovison news a couple of weeks ago when he was arrested. That's the only crime committed in this tribal region lately that's big enough to justify a jury trial."

"You must mean James Maxwell, the guy who was caught doing illegal science experiments?"

"Yeah, that's the one. If he's found guilty, he'll get the death penalty."

"Poor bastard, I feel sorry for him. But damn it, I've got a business to run, and I don't have time to sit on a jury all day. The pay for jury duty isn't nearly what I can make in the shop. What was Maxwell doing that got him into such trouble?"

"If I remember right, research on something called 'Ball Lightning' as a method to store energy from a renewable energy source to power automobiles."

Bob looked puzzled. "What's wrong with that? I think everyone in the world is tired of this damned horse and buggy travel we've been stuck with since all the fuels were depleted."

"Hold that thought for a minute. I want to see if there's anything on the news about an upcoming trial. You may be getting called for a much shorter trial—perhaps only a domestic dispute, robbery or something."

"Okay."

Audrey spoke loudly, "Holovision on—news channel 2," accessing a holographic television that was based on technology developed just before The Darkening.

Immediately, a large part of one kitchen wall lit up with an ultra high-resolution, three-dimensional holographic image of the morning news broadcast. The image in full color looked as though the viewer was seeing the original scenes through a large picture window.

"Energy conservation mode."

The resolution and brightness decreased.

"Show content," Audrey said. A small rectangular area appeared at the bottom of the screen with a list of the upcoming news stories. She searched through the list. "Oh darn, they aren't covering anything about a trial." Then she loudly said, "Holovision off," and added "Now what was your question?"

"Why should anyone be punished so severely for trying to do research on something that might be an improvement over our horse and buggy methods of travel?"

"That's just the law. I want to attend Maxwell's trial to see if I can learn more about the anti-science law's history. It might be something I could write about."

*   *   *

In the evening Bob decided to move boxes of keepsakes, and other seldom-used items, into the attic. He pulled on a rope, that lowered a drop-down stairway from the hallway ceiling, and plugged one end of an electrical cord, that had a light on the other end, into a hallway outlet. Trailing the cord behind him, he climbed the steep stairway into the attic and hung the light on a nail sticking out of a bare rafter. Bob had previously had only a cursory look at the attic with the realtors flashlight during pre-purchase inspection of the house.

The attic was floored with rough lumber. There was height enough for Bob to stand under the centerline of the simple, single-ridge roof. However, the downward slope of the roof left only a foot of clearance over the floor at the outer edges. The last 1-1/2 feet at the attic's edges were not floored, and the attic's bare floor joists were exposed there. This left hollow spaces between the joists. Under the joists, the ceiling of the downstairs room provided a weak floor across the bottom of the spaces, and Bob decided to store small boxes there to leave more room on the attic floor for large, heavy boxes.

Bob carried a load of small boxes into the attic. As he started to place one of the boxes far back in a hollow space, he saw a small, brown, partially hidden leather-bound chest.. The buildup of dust and spider webs on it showed that it hadn't been touched for many years.

Just then, Audrey came into the attic carrying several small boxes.

"Hmm, I wonder what this is," Bob said, as he lay down on the floor, wriggled under the slope of the roof toward the edge, stretched out his arm, brushed away spider webs, and pulled the chest from its hiding place.

"It looks very old, Bob. I went to an antique auction last year and saw a similar chest that dated back to 2048. The auctioneer said antique chests like that one haven't been made since the severe shortages in 2060. He wanted 1,400-credits for it."

"Hmm. Then this chest is probably valuable, so I shouldn't force the lock. I'll try to pick the lock or use a bore-scope to design a key."

"Oh Bob, is there any way you can open it tonight?"

"Not without possibly damaging the chest. It probably just contains old letters and such.."

"This is so exciting—I can hardly wait to see what's inside," Audrey said as she reflected on the reason she was so intensely attracted by the cottage.

CHAPTER 2
THE OPENING

Bob carried the chest downstairs and placed it on the kitchen table. Audrey peered at it as if it were a fish and she a hungry cat. "Let's open it."

"If you insist. I'll ride into town and get my lock-picking tools from the shop."

While Bob was in the bathroom washing the cobwebs and dust off his hands, Audrey pulled a hairpin from her hair. She straightened it and bent one end to form a short tab. Inserting the tab-end into the chest's keyhole, she turned the hairpin back and forth while moving it in and out. Suddenly, the catch on the chest opened with a loud "clack."

Bob, returning from the bathroom, heard the "clack." His eyes widened and his mouth dropped open as he realized Audrey had unlocked the chest.

"That was easy, Bob. How come you thought you'd need special tools?"

"I was busy thinking about more important things, like how to arrange all that stuff in the attic. Besides, the only reason you got it open was beginner's luck."

Audrey contentedly chuckled. "Oh, you just don't want to admit that I'm smarter than you."

"I'll let you believe that if you wish. But if all I had to think about was what holovision programs to watch tonight, I would've opened the chest even faster than you did."

"WHAT HOLOVISION TO WATCH TONIGHT! I'll have you know that..."

The house's computer heard Audrey shout "Holovision," and "Tonight." It turned the holovision on, lighting up one wall of the kitchen, and turned off the kitchen light.

"Damn. Dumb computer. Holovision off. Light on," Audrey said grumpily.

"Oh Audrey, I was joking. I know you work hard planning and preparing meals, getting groceries, taking care of our finances, and the many other things you do around here."

"Well, all right. I guess I was overly sensitive because I really had been thinking about what holovison to watch. Now, let's see what's in the chest. I'm dying with curiosity."

"Aw, there won't be anything of value in it. Let's wait until tomorrow.

"BOB!"

"Don't blow a gasket, I was just teasing."

Audrey opened the lid slowly because she didn't want to disturb the chest's contents, especially if there were spiders that might have crawled in through the keyhole. She turned the chest slightly so Bob could better see inside. On top of the contents was a crude, hand-drawn map.

Bob picked it up for a closer look and said, "What do you suppose this is?"

"It looks like it might be a treasure map." Audrey moved closer to Bob so she could see it better. "In fact, it looks like it could be a map for something on our property." Pointing, she continued, "See, here's the house, and this patch labeled 'vine-maple patch' looks like that brushy patch by the little hill Northwest of the house. And look at this 'X' mark labeled 'Entrance' in the midst of the vine maple ."

"Entrance to what?"

"How should I know? It just says 'Entrance'."

"I haven't noticed anything out there other than a plain old patch of brush."

"Let's go out and look it over, Bob. Whatever the 'Entrance' is, it must've been important to be located in such a hidden place."

"It's too dark to go stumbling around in the brush tonight. Whatever it is, it'll still be there in the morning. Let's look over the other stuff in the chest. It might tell us more about the 'X'."

Bob carefully removed a small item, a polished, black, rectangular locket about 3/4-inch square and 1/8-inch thick. It had a tiny hole centered in one end, and a quarter-inch black window centered on top. Attached to one end was a fine chain that could be worn around the owner's neck.

"Let's dump all the stuff out on the table and see what we've got," Audrey said impatiently. She turned the chest over and dumped its contents onto the table. Several brittle, yellowed, old newspaper clippings shattered into pieces when three small notebooks dropped out of the chest on top of them.

"Oh, Audrey, look what you've done. These old clippings are ruined."

"That's no problem, I can tape them back together."

"Well, good luck with that. There are lots of pieces, and they're fragile.

"It'll be fun, like putting a jigsaw puzzle together."

"Okay, have fun trying to do that without further damaging the pieces," Bob said as he fondled the locket. "I wonder what this is. There doesn't appear to be any way to open it." He turned the table lamp on and moved the locket close to better examine it. When the locket was a few inches from the lamp, a beam of light shot out of the tiny hole on one end. Startled, Bob dropped it. When it landed on the table, the light beam went out.

"Crap! I hope I didn't break it."

He picked the locket up and, as it neared the lamp, the beam again shot out of the hole. This time, the beam was directed at the wall. Expressions of intense interest crept onto Bob and Audrey's faces.. Projected on the wall was a circular logo. Curved around it were strange words of an ancient, dead language: "SECRETUS SOCIETUS ARS." Inside the circle were strange symbols. Below the circle a title in English said, "A True History, and Remedy for some Consequences of The Shortages and The Darkening." Text followed in the form of a personal letter. Bob held the locket near the light, while Audrey stood close to the wall and read the letter aloud.

"Dear Great, Great, Great Grandson,

I am the last remaining member of SSA, which was a secret society of scientists. At 95 years old, I don't expect to live much longer. If you are willing and able, the map and notebooks included in the chest with this locket will help you undo some of the damage resulting from the great catastrophes, actions of greedy, powerful men, and government bungling of 2050 through 2068.

The notebooks contain notes on scientific work that I have done on a new method for propelling vehicles. This method requires only some of the most abundant materials on earth, and can run on solar thermal energy alone, so it doesn't require fuel or batteries. If you are not interested, or not able to finish developing this method, please seek out a brilliant friend who has an interest in science, and who can be trusted to keep this information secret until the time is right to reveal it.

The fact that you are reading this means that you have come of age, and an attorney has given you an envelope containing clues about the location of the chest, and how to activate this locket.

To keep these out of the hands of unauthorized persons, I based the clues on family lore that only you would understand. It also means that you had enough curiosity and interest to pursue knowledge that had no immediate monetary payoff. I hope that by the time you read this, there is no longer a death penalty for performing scientific work. However, until you know for sure, do not share any of what you are about to learn with anyone except, perhaps, a trusted friend who is interested and will keep your secret.

Since you are reading this, you know that light powers the locket, and when you remove it from bright light, it turns off. However, you do not yet know how to navigate its contents.

When you activate the locket by placing it in bright light, the projected image returns to the page you were viewing previously. Press the upper right corner to advance to the next page, or the upper left corner to go back a page. Press both the upper corners simultaneously to return to the beginning of the text. If you press them both again, it will return to the page you were previously reading.

Good Luck,

Your Great, Great, Great Grandfather,
James Boyle"

Bob squeezed the upper right corner of the locket, advancing one page at a time, and the projected image advanced through the first three files, which were dated 2060, 2065 and 2068. They described a detailed history of the great catastrophes, between 2050 and 2068, showing conclusively why responsibility for them rested squarely on the shoulders of governments and powerful, greedy men rather than on science and scientists.

The fourth and last file was dated 2162. Bob said, "Look at the date on this file. It was produced 94 years later than the previous file. There must have been more than one generation involved in reporting these eyewitness accounts over such a large span of time. Perhaps the author of this file was the grandson referred to in the letter, or maybe the grandson's grandson."

The file said:

"The majority of people in 2162 have come to realize that in 2068 the public was duped, and that science is a benefit maligned by long-ago governments.

But now, the scientific infrastructure is gone. There are no science teachers or scientists working openly. Most of the scientific textbooks and reference materials were destroyed after the darkening, and only a few widely scattered, secret science hobbyists still have scientific books and knowledge.

Even today there are pockets of population who refuse to give up their religious, or almost religious, science-hating beliefs. At the time of this writing, the death penalty is still the law for anyone caught dabbling in advanced science. This hatred of science has been exacerbated by wide, long-term contamination of much farmland resulting from the past use of atomic weapons. Contamination is expected to prevent growing food crops on that land for at least 10,000-years.

I don't know a single person today who will openly admit having an interest in science. I have to sneak to and from my scientific work before daylight and after dark to avoid discovery. My disappearances in the daytime have made the towns-people suspicious. They are spreading fantastic rumors about me.

-Robert Henry"

After Audrey read the files out loud, Bob said, "I wonder where the last author went to disappear in the daytime. He must have had a laboratory somewhere, but there doesn't appear to be anything like that nearby, so even at night he should have been seen going along the road to and from his laboratory."

Bob opened one of the notebooks from the chest. It was filled with strange symbols and hand-written notes describing concepts that neither Bob nor Audrey could understand. The other notebooks were similarly incomprehensible to them, even though they studied them for at least another hour.

Finally, Bob said, "I'd like to ask our best friend, Doug Murphy, to come over tomorrow night and look at this stuff with us. Is that okay with you? I'm sure he'd keep our secret."

"But, he's only a farmer. What dos he know about science?"

"He's really smart in solving mathematical problems. I've gotten help from him several times on difficult geometry and trigonometry problems I've had in machining jobs. And consider how much he's improved the crop yields on his 170 acres compared to comparable farms. He might have some idea about what these mysterious symbols and notes mean."

"It's okay with me if you ask him. His house is only a five-minute walk from here, and I trust him."

CHAPTER 3
SECRETS AND THE SNOOP

The next morning, Bob was in a rush to get to his shop. Some of his customers' jobs were behind schedule. He didn't have time to go to Doug's that morning, so he went after work. Doug was still out in the field plowing, so Bob left a note inside a small note box beside Doug's front door. The note said:

"Audrey and I found something we'd like to show you if you can come over this evening.

- Bob"

When Bob got home, Audrey was climbing down from the barn's hayloft after throwing hay into the feed trough. Bob removed the saddle and bridal from the horse by the watering trough. As he entered the barn, he asked Audrey if she'd figured out anything more about the contents of the chest.

"No. I taped the old news article fragments together. Some pieces had disintegrated to powder, but the ones I managed to piece together covered some of the information covered in the locket files."

"Was there any clue as to the meaning of the 'X' marked 'Entrance' on the map?"

"I didn't find any. I went to the vine maple patch, but all I could see was a pile of rocks barely visible in the middle. It's going to be difficult to get through all that brush, and it'll take some heavy digging to see if there's anything under the rocks."

The horse trotted into the barn and over to the feed trough. Bob and Audrey left the barn. Just as they were approaching their house Morton Snood rode up on horseback.

"Hi. What's this about something you found?" Snood said, leaning forward in his saddle and peering at Bob.

Bob's face reddened. "What find?"

"The one you asked Doug to come over and inspect with you."

"How do you know about that?"

"I stopped by Doug's house a few minutes ago, and I couldn't help seeing your note when I knocked on the front door."

"Whadaya mean, 'couldn't help seeing my note?' It was behind the little door on the note box that was closed."

"I was going to leave a note myself, so I opened the door to get the note pad."

Bob was upset that Snood knew about the find, but relieved that Doug hadn't revealed the information and betrayed his confidence. Snood was well-known for being a blabbermouth, as well as nosey and meddlesome, so Bob's mind raced to come up with a plausible story that would be boring enough to discourage Snood's interest...

"Oh, that old thing. It's just an old chest full of keepsakes my uncle left me. I thought Doug might get a kick out of seeing what my uncle's life was like on the Kansas farm where he worked. Doug knew my uncle and is interested in trivia about farming."

"Oh. I've got to get home for dinner. See you later."

When Morton Snood was no longer within earshot, Audrey said, "It's a shame you had to lie—but I'm glad you did. That nosey blabbermouth would have spread our business all over Stoneville. The notebooks in the chest have a lot of odd symbols. They must be what scientific work looks like since the locket said the notebooks deal with that. Even though we didn't write them, we could get into serious trouble for having them."

"Yeah. In hindsight, I wish I hadn't left the note for Doug, but I didn't think anyone else would be looking in his box this late in the day."

After dinner, Bob and Audrey cleared the kitchen table, wiped it clean, and carefully laid out the chest's contents on it.

There was a knock at the front door. As Bob came out of the kitchen, he could see Doug through the window. He turned toward Audrey, who was in the kitchen, and said, "It's Doug."

When Bob opened the door, Doug looked puzzled. "Why do you look so relieved? Were you expecting an axe murderer?"

"No, I was afraid Morton Snood had returned. He saw the note I left you, and came right over here asking questions this afternoon."

Doug chuckled. "Oh, that's worse than an axe murderer. I hope you were able to redirect his nose."

"Yeah, but I lied to him. I couldn't think of any truth about our find that sounded boring enough to wave him off. I told him that it was an old chest filled with boring keepsakes from my farm-worker uncle, and I thought you'd be interested in them.

"By the way, Snood said he left a note in your little box."

"No, he didn't"

"That's what I thought. He must have been snooping, as usual, and lied to me to cover it up."

Bob explained how he had discovered the chest, and showed Doug the map and notebooks laid out on the table.

"So what are they?" Doug asked.

"We aren't sure. As you can see, the map is marked with a an "X" called 'Entrance,' but we don't know what it means."

Then Bob and Audrey told Doug about the locket files, and described text giving eyewitness accounts about factors that caused the "Great Shortages" and the "The Darkening." They also told him about the text that said the notebooks were scientific, and a possible method of using direct solar energy to power vehicles.

Their concentration was broken by a knock at the door.

Doug said, "Maybe you'd better cover this up."

Bob said, "No. I'll just get rid of whoever it is. They won't be able to see this stuff from the front door."

As Bob entered the living room he said, "Oh Hell, It's Snood."

"Yes, what is it, Morton?" Bob said as he opened the door

"I saw Doug Murphy coming over here, and I wondered what was going on?"

"As I told you earlier, he's looking at some of my Uncle's memorabilia related to his farm work."

"Do you mind if I come in and look too."

"Yes, I mind. It's private and I'll only show it to Doug, my closest friend."

"Well, I thought I was your friend too."

"Morton, you're one nosey son-of-a-bitch. You lied to me about leaving Doug a note, so it's obvious you were just snooping in his note box.. Now, I'm telling you this for your own good: People don't like to be snooped on and pinned down like this. Now go mind your own business."

Bob closed the door, and a short time later he heard Morton ride off at a gallop.

Bob returned to the table, and they continued to pore over the papers and notebooks. Doug studied two of the notebooks and some of the papers, especially the map, with great interest.

"I have no idea what this map is; it could show where something valuable is located," Doug said with a distant look in his eyes. Then he continued, "The hand-written text in the notebooks appears to be notes from a scientific project the author was working on in secret after the beginning of great shortages in 2060. He saw the public's wrath building, and predicted the consequences of the government efforts to blame the world's problems on advances in science; he predicted 'The Darkening' that occurred in 2068."

Bob said, "That's interesting. Do you see anything that appears valuable in the notebooks?"

"I can't tell for sure yet. In addition to the text, many strange symbols are used in equations that I don't understand. I'm extremely interested in these notebooks. They do indeed look scientific—I would've studied science in school if it'd been allowed. I'd like to study the notebooks a little longer."

"Sure, go ahead."

Doug continued to inspect the notebooks for more than an hour. Bob and Audrey retired to the living room, and watched their small (48 inch) holovision set in there, rather than standing around looking over Doug's shoulder. Finally, Doug called to them.

Pointing to one of the books, Doug said, "If I correctly understand the notes, I agree that the author was apparently working on an alternative method for directly gathering, storing, and applying solar energy to propel automobiles and other mobile machines. His notes said that these devices, unlike present-day methods, could be constructed from plentiful materials and wouldn't require any fuel for operation."

"Holy smoke! That confirms what we understood the locket text to say, and it's just what the world needs today," Bob said, jerking his right hand up and down for emphasis.

"But working on it would be awfully dangerous since it's scientific," Audrey added.

Doug said, "I can't understand the equations and the author's analyses, but there may be enough here to allow you to duplicate his work. If I'm right, you might be able to get incredibly wealthy from devices based on this information. But you'd have to figure out how to build and market them without being caught. You'd first have to figure out how to learn enough science to understand the notebooks. However, before you pour funds and time into it based on what I've said, keep in mind that I don't know enough to thoroughly evaluate what I've seen."

Bob thought for a moment, then said, "I think we should go ahead with this. It could solve our financial difficulties. Our savings will probably be gone anyway before we get our hospital bill paid off. We've got enough credits in the online bank to get started, and maybe even complete the work. Would you like to get in on this as a partner?" Bob asked.

"Do you mean you want to include me as a full partner?"

"Of course, Doug, we'd be fools not to let you in on this. We need your intelligence and your help, both physically and financially. It would probably be too much for Audrey and me to handle alone. However, don't forget that the work could be dangerous; it could cost us our lives if we're discovered."

"I know, but I'd like to be in on it. Great rewards require great risks. We'll just have to be careful. If we're successful, it could bring us more wealth than we ever dreamed possible. Besides, I'm really curious about this, and I believe modern public opinion is leaning more toward the potential benefits of science rather than the risks of progress. We might find a way to get the law changed in favor of science before we're found out."

Audrey's brow furrowed, and her voice was high pitched as she said, "My God, if we're caught, it'll mean death for all of us."

Bob thought for a moment, then said, "We could learn enough to interpret the notebooks without much risk. If we find the information has a lot of potential, we could take a little more risk, secretly building and testing a prototype. Then, if it works, we could work hard to get the anti-science law changed if it hasn't already been eliminated by then. It could solve all our financial problems for the rest of our lives."

"Besides, it would be a hell of a ride. I believe we'll be able to find a way to do the work under cover so we don't get caught," Doug added.

Both men were lost in thought for a few minutes, then Bob asked Doug, "What do you make of the 'X' and 'Entrance' markings on the map?"

"The word, 'Entrance,' implies an opening that leads to some kind of place that you can go into, so it probably isn't buried treasure. The fact that it's inside a patch of vine maple brush, and hasn't been noticed by any of us, may mean it was purposely hidden. Tomorrow is Saturday, and there won't be many people on the road, so we could go inside the brush patch then for a close look at location 'X.'" Doug thought for a moment, then continued, "I have a few animals to feed and cows to milk tomorrow morning. I'll come over here right after that."

"Okay. Audrey and I'll get started first thing in the morning. Join us when you can," Bob remarked.

Audrey said, "I can hardly wait—it may give us more clues about the mysteries flying around town about our cottage."

Bob carefully placed the notebooks, papers, locket, and map back into the chest, closed it, and placed it in a cabinet. Doug was just getting ready to leave when someone knocked on the door.

Bob said, "I wonder who that could be this late at night?"

All of the windows, including the door window, had been electronically made opaque at nightfall, so Bob couldn't see who was at the door. He tried to look nonchalant after he opened the door, but felt a stabbing shock in his gut as he said, "Hello Sheriff. What brings you out this time of night?"

"Oh, probably nothing. Morton Snood said he thought you were acting suspiciously when he stopped by earlier. He said he thought you might be 'up to no good,' so I'm obligated to check it out."

"Crap! He dropped by uninvited and wanted to intrude on my visit with Doug Murphy. I essentially told him to get lost, and I guess it made him mad."

"I thought it might be something like that. He told me you had some kind of chest, and you wouldn't let him see what's in it."

"Yeah, it's a chest full of memorabilia from my farmhand uncle who recently died: a locket, some old paper clippings, diaries written in some kind of shorthand, and such. I asked Doug to see if he could help me try to interpret it."

"May I see it?"

Bob's heart skipped a beat as he thought: oh my God, we've had it! But it'll be better to comply with the sheriff's request, rather than arouse his suspicions by refusing. He probably doesn't have enough background to realize that the chest's contents might be scientific, and we can claim ignorance if he does figure it out.

"Sure," Bob said, as he led the sheriff into the kitchen and got the chest. He struggled to keep his hands from shaking as he placed it on the table. When he opened it, the map was on top.

The sheriff pointed to the map. "What's this."

Bob felt his underarms getting wet. He hoped he wasn't sweating anywhere that showed.

"That's a plot layout for a fruit cellar that never got built." Bob picked up the map to reveal the locket. He held the locket with his hand cupped behind it to shield it from the light as he showed it to the sheriff. "And this is an old onyx locket my uncle inherited from his mother."

"Okay, I've seen enough, Bob. Sorry to have bothered you. I should have known better than to listen to that busybody, Snood. You should have that locket appraised. It might be valuable."

Bob returned the locket and map to the chest as he chuckled nervously and said, "Thanks for the advice, Sheriff. I may just do that. Don't worry about the intrusion. I know you have to investigate suspicious activities, like looking at old lockets and such."

The sheriff smiled as he left. "Let me know if that nosey old bastard bothers you again, and I'll go look for 'suspicious activities' at his house."

Much relieved, Bob followed the sheriff to the door and said, "So long, Sheriff, I'll see you later." As the sheriff rode away Bob thought: much, much later, I hope.

Now that the immediate danger of having their secret discovered had passed, Bob's knees were wobbly. He felt weak and sank into a chair. Audrey and Doug did the same.

"Good God," Audrey said, "I thought for sure our secret was going to be discovered. Some people still resent science, and..."

Bob finished her sentence. "We'd have been in terrible trouble if the sheriff had known what he was looking at.."

After a pause to compose his thoughts, Bob continued. "But I still think we'll have a good chance of getting the anti-science laws changed if we can convince the public there's enough benefit. I believe things have really calmed down during the 163 years since The Darkening. People I've talked to say they wish they had a more convenient, faster method than horses for transportation, hauling and farm work. We might be able to get enough signatures right away on a petition for an initiative to make scientific investigation legal. It's not illegal to try getting the law changed, but if we take that approach we'll have to do it without revealing that we've been studying or thinking in depth about advanced science."

"The truth probably lies somewhere between getting into terrible trouble, and being able to easily get signatures on a petition," Doug said. "People are impatient. They don't appreciate how much work it takes to develop new science. They'd expect it to happen overnight, and would be angry when it wasn't. If we can't get the law changed, and someone finds out what we're doing, we'll be prosecuted. Finding a way to secretly learn enough science to understand the notebooks will take a long time. There'll be plenty of time to think about ways to get the anti-science law changed before we are ready to risk building hardware. We'd better wait until we've done enough work, to be sure the methods described in the notebooks are worthwhile, before we attempt to change the law. If we circulate petitions now, it could stir up suspicions that could get us caught while we are trying to secretly evaluate the methods."

Doug headed for the door. "I'll see you in the morning and help you search for the 'Entrance.' I wonder if it really is just a door to an old fruit cellar."

CHAPTER 4
ENTRANCE

Bob and Audrey had barely finished breakfast when there was a knock at the front door. Bob opened the door and said, "Hi Doug. You're early."

"Yeah. I'm excited about what we might find, and I woke up earlier than usual this morning."

"I'll get my coat and gloves. Audrey, are you coming with us?"

"Absolutely."

They went to Bob's shed to get two shovels and a pick, then hurried out to the vine maple brush patch. The brush was six to eight feet tall in a roughly circular area about 100-ft. in diameter. It was centered at the bottom of a small hill rising at a steep slope to a height of 200-ft. Except for the brush-covered area, the hill was covered with orchard grass that had turned tan. The location marked "X" on the map looked like a perfect site for the entrance to a fruit cellar that might have been dug into the bottom of the hill, but it was inconveniently far from the house.

As they studied the brush patch, Doug said, "Even though the leaves are dropping off for winter, the brush is so thick that I can't see anything except what may be a pile of rocks in the middle."

"Yeah. That's the same thing I decided when I came out here yesterday," Audrey said. Then she continued, "I think we'll have to cut a path to get in there and see what's at the 'X'."

"Okay, but we'll have to make sure that the path isn't visible from the road, or Snood'll see it and come snooping."

Just then, Bob saw the sheriff riding along the road and dropped the shovel he was carrying. "Quick, Audrey, Doug, drop your tools."

Doug and Audrey complied. "What's the matter?" Audrey asked.

"The sheriff is coming up the road, but I don't think he's seen us yet. If he comes over we'll just tell him we're looking to see if the fruit cellar was ever built."

Audrey looked at Bob and said, "Why do you suppose he's out this early?"

"I have no idea. Maybe someone called him. Walk with me as if we're just out for a stroll. Maybe we'll get far enough away from these tools that the sheriff won't see them if he decides to come talk to us. That'll be better than explaining why we are getting ready to dig something up in the vine maple patch."

They walked toward the cottage, and the sheriff continued along the road. He saw the them and waved as he passed. When the sheriff disappeared over a rise in the road, the three adventurers went to the tool shed, got some brush cutting tools, and quickly returned to the brush patch, They picked up their picks and shovels, and began circling around the brushy area.

Doug said, "Perhaps we should thin the brush just enough in a narrow path that we can force our way through to the rock pile?" Then he added, "The brush is growing in a rocky patch of ground, which could explain why it was left brushy instead of being cleared for plowing."

"Okay. Where should we start thinning?" Bob asked

"If we start the path somewhere past the widest part of the brush circle, it shouldn't be obvious to passers-by on the road."

When they were just past the bottom of the hill, Doug said, "It looks as if someone cut or thinned a path through here in the past. The brush has mostly grown back, but doesn't look quite as old and mature here."

"You're right, and whoever did it obviously didn't want it to be seen from the road. It must lead to something more important than a fruit cellar," Audrey said excitedly.

The men set to work cutting, while Audrey hid the clippings out of the way under the unclipped brush on both sides of the path They took pains to make the thinning look random, and tapered the amount of thinning on both sides so it blended in with the denser brush and left no sharp lines of demarcation. Finally they reached the rock pile and were surprised to see that the apparent pile was actually a stack of rocks carefully placed in a four-foot high indent into the hillside. More rocks had been piled outside of the stack to give the illusion of a random pile. Bob and Doug excitedly thinned a small area of brush around the rock pile to make a place for rocks they were going to remove, then furiously tore into the pile. Both men were sweating profusely when they suddenly stopped.

Bob said, "Great God!"

Audrey said, "Wow."

A rock bounced down the pile's backside making a clatter that sounded like it was echoing in a chamber much larger than a fruit cellar. A small, black opening had appeared at the top of the pile.

Bob and Doug were spurred to an even more intense pace by the anticipation of finding out what had been hidden here for perhaps 200-years. They soon had enough of the rocks removed that they could climb into the four-foot high entrance. However, it was so dark inside they could only see about 30-feet into what opened out into a seven-foot high by five-foot wide tunnel.

"Oh hell," Bob said, "it only looks like an old mine."

"Don't give up so easily. Now that we've come this far, we should at least explore it," Doug remarked.

"Yeah. After all that work you should at least see why the previous owner was so secretive about it," Audrey added.

Doug said, "He may have just blocked the entrance to keep kids and animals out of it. I've never heard of diamonds or gold being mined around here."

"How about silver?" Bob asked.

"Naw. Do you have a flashlight?"

"Yeah. I wish I'd brought it, but I didn't expect to find a tunnel"

"We'd better get it."

Audrey said, "I'll get it. You guys should rest after all that hard work removing the rocks."

As Audrey headed for the house, Bob said, "Doug, what do you think is in the tunnel."

"It could be money worth millions from a long ago robbery."

"Perhaps, but paper money from 200-years ago is worthless since the original government no longer exists, and all transactions are now electronic. Besides, it's illegal to own any of that old money."

"Well, at least the tunnel will make a good fruit cellar, even if it is too far from the house."

Audrey returned with the flashlight and handed it to Bob as they entered the tunnel. Many cobwebs hung down inside the entrance.

Audrey went in a short distance, then began shuddering. "My God. Spiders! I'm not going in there unless you spray the place," and she left.

Bob furiously brushed cobwebs away. "I hate these damned things sticking to my face." A cold chill went down his back as he said, "Nothing worse than getting a spider in your eye, or down your neck."

"I hate 'em too. Keep your mouth closed—I would especially hate getting one in my mouth. I'm glad you have the flashlight. That means you get to go first."

"I'll be glad to give you the flashlight."

"No, that's okay."

"Damn."

"Oh, don't be such a baby. Anything that doesn't bite won't hurt you."

"I worry about the ones that do bite."

"Only the big, hairy ones bite."

"Damn."

"Just kidding. I've only seen a couple of two-inch photophobic cave spiders. They look fearsome, but they're harmless and only bite when provoked. Their bite isn't lethal."

"That doesn't help much."

Bob and Doug walked down, up, and around bends for about half an hour, finally coming to the tunnel's end and saw remnants of coal, a few small chunks littering the tunnel floor. Water dripped from the ceiling, and the damp, cold atmosphere smelled like creosote or tar.

"Doug, what's that smell?"

"It's what coal smells like in an enclosed space."

"That tears it. All of our work has been for naught. Our 'treasure' is just a few lumps of coal. There is no Santa Claus."

Doug chuckled. "Maybe there is a Santa Clause, but you've been naughty instead of nice."

"Maybe this coal mine could be worked again. Coal is in short supply, and we could make a fortune."

"The vein of coal wouldn't have petered out like this at the end of the dig if there were more coal ahead. I'm sure the original owner would have used instruments to determine whether the vein continued from here."

As the disappointed men started walking back toward entrance, the light emitting diodes in the flashlight began to dim.

"Crap, Doug! The batteries are running down."

"Don't you have spares?"

"No—at 35 Credits each, they're too expensive to keep extras on hand, and they don't last like they did in the old days. They run down in a year or two, even if they aren't used."

Ten minutes later, the flashlight had dimmed to a dull glow. A few minutes after that, the men were immersed in total blackness.

"Good God, Doug. How'll we find our way out?"

"How can we go wrong? We'll just follow the tunnel back the way we came in."

"I sure hope you're right," Bob said as he broke out in a cold sweat.

CHAPTER 5
ANOTHER DISCOVERY

Bob and Doug felt their way back along the tunnel wall like blind men. After they'd stumbled along for what seemed much longer than a half-hour, Doug said, "Something's wrong. We should have come to the entrance by now, or at least be able to see some light at the end of the tunnel."

"Yeah. I was just thinking the same thing."

"I don't mind admitting that I'm scared as hell. I just hope we can find our way out."

"I'm scared too, but we mustn't panic. That's the worst thing we could do right now.."

"I agree, but it's hard to keep it together."

"Okay, I ..."

Bob cut his statement short as his voice suddenly echoed differently.

"It sounds like we've entered a large open space. We definitely didn't pass this on our way in," Doug said with a tremor in his voice.

"Oh my God. That could mean we're on the edge of a deep drop-off!"

"Okay, lets carefully feel our way forward to see if we can find a way out."

The men made their way along the wall in the total blackness, carefully testing the floor ahead before each step to make sure there wasn't a drop-off. They'd only gone a short distance when Bob said, "I've found something. It feels like a set of shelves." After a minute or so, Bob continued, "There are several objects on the shelves I can't identify. Here's some kind of object with what feels like a small metal box with something on the side—I think it's a crank."

Doug shouted, "Don't..."

Before Doug could finish his sentence, a bright light suddenly revealed they were in a large cavern.

Bob said, "Wow, it's a hand-cranked flashlight! What were you going to say?"

"I was afraid you might have found a dynamite detonator, and I didn't want you to turn the crank until we felt around to see if it was connected to anything."

"Oh."

Bob stopped cranking, and the flashlight kept running. It had a windup spring-driven motor powering a miniature generator.

"This kind of flashlight was available before The Darkening," Doug said. "They haven't made them since the materials for generators became so expensive."

Bob cranked until the flashlight spring was fully wound up"

Aiming the light all around, Bob said, "My God. It's a big cavern with stone walls, floor, and ceiling! Unlike the end of the coal tunnel, it's dry in here. It must be about 50-ft wide, 60- or 70-ft long, and 15 ft high. And just look at all these shelves and tables loaded with some kind of equipment."

"It looks scientific—like it was built before the darkening," Doug said, "but I'm not sure. I'll bet we can get a better idea of what it is by studying the notebooks we found in the mystery chest."

As they looked around the walls of the chamber, they spotted large bookshelves filled with books, and began looking at them. Bob paused every few minutes to wind the flashlight.

"Doug, I think these books deal with the same kind of subject matter contained in the notebooks. Some of the mathematical equations in them look similar to stuff you showed me in one of the notebooks."

Doug looked thoughtful, then said, "I believe these books are valuable. Science textbooks are virtually non-existent now."

"Hmm, that's true. I'll bet we could get a fortune for them."

"Yeah, if we could figure out how to sell them without getting tangled up with the law. Here are textbooks titled 'Fundamentals of Thermodynamics' and 'Elements of Scientific Mathematics.' There appear to be a lot of elementary science books as well as advanced ones. I believe we may be able to learn enough from these books to understand the stuff in the notebooks."

"Okay, Doug, but which books should we start with? There must be several hundred here. It'd take a long time to study all of them."

"I heard about something called 'thermodynamics' that's involved in engineering dealing with generation, storage, and application of energy. Remember that passage in one of the notebooks I told you and Audrey about. It said the author was working on a new way to collect and store solar energy for vehicle propulsion. This cavern must be the laboratory he set up to work on his invention. If we can learn enough from the textbooks he left here, we might be able to finish his work. That could be interesting and far more valuable than the gold or jewels we'd hoped to find."

"Okay, but we'd better find our way out of here or we won't live long enough to even try that. I don't see any way out except the way we came in. Let's retrace our steps. At least now, we have light."

Bob wound the flashlight up again and the men left the cavern. They walked back a short distance until they came to a place where the tunnel they were in branched off the main tunnel.

"Now I see what happened." Doug said. "This side-tunnel branches and forms a narrow 'Y,' with the foot of the 'Y' pointing in the direction we were traveling toward the end of the main tunnel. We were so focused on what was straight ahead, when we were hurrying to see what was at the end, we missed seeing the side branch."

"I hope all we have to do is go up the other branch of the "Y" to get back to the surface."

"Right."

After a five-minute walk, the men were back at the entrance. They crouched down, exited through the tunnel entrance, forced their way through the thinned corridor in the vine maple, and returned to Bob's house.

Audrey was resting in an overstuffed chair. "Okay, guys, what did you find?"

Bob couldn't resist the urge to tease her. "Not much," he said.

"Come on, give! I'm dying to know what it is."

With a feigned look of disappointment, Bob said, "It's the entrance to an old exhausted coal mine."

"No buried treasure or gold mine?"

"I'm afraid not."

Audrey's shoulders and face drooped. "I guess that's about what we expected. At least the old chest may be worth something"

Then Bob allowed his face to brighten, and said excitedly, "But a side-tunnel leads to a large, underground cavern containing a laboratory filled with a treasure trove of scientific textbooks and wonderful things. Some past scientist must've established a secret laboratory there after 'The Darkening'. The books and equipment are probably worth a small fortune if we could sell them, but I don't know how to legally do that right now."

Doug thought for a moment, then said, "I feel that instead of taking a risk trying to sell this stuff, we ought to see what we can learn from the books and notebooks, then determine what kind of energy related device we might be able to develop using our new knowledge and laboratory. This could bring us many more credits than just trying to sell the books."

Bob said, "Developing such a device sounds like a lot of work. It would take a long time, and would probably require a lot of expensive materials."

Audrey added, "And it might not work at all. Neither of you is a scientist."

"I don't mean to brag," Doug said, "but I think I can quickly learn what we need to know from all those cavern textbooks. Bob has the machining equipment and skill needed to build any devices we need. It seems to me that we're in a perfect position to take advantage of this trove of scientific knowledge, and develop something the world has badly needed since the time of the shortages. It could bring us wealth beyond any we've ever dreamed of if we can figure out how to exploit it"

"Don't forget that it's like playing with dynamite—it could cost us our lives, " Audrey said, looking perplexed.

Bob said. "The stuff we found will be at least as valuable in a year or so, if we decide to try selling it, and we should try to take maximum advantage of our find. The anti-science law might be repealed by the time we figure it all out, and that could mean the end of our financial difficulties."

A dark expression crept onto all their faces when Doug said, "But what if we're caught before the law gets changed?"

No one said anything for several minutes. Then Bob said, "We'll have plenty of time to think it over before deciding. I have to report for jury duty the day after tomorrow."

CHAPTER 6
MAXWELL'S TRIAL

Bob reported for jury duty on Monday. Even though only a week had passed since he was notified, so much had happened that it seemed longer. Audrey had decided to attend. Doug decided to launch into studying books from the cavern rather than going to the trial.

Preliminary and evidentiary hearings had been completed, and the Judge decided there was basis for a trial. Bob was chosen from the jury pool during the "voir dire" conducted by the prosecution and defense attorneys. When the jury filed in, the courtroom was packed and buzzing with excitement.

The juror sitting next to Bob whispered, "My name's Flynn. What's yours?"

The men shook hands as Bob said, "Parker. Glad to meet you."

"With the courtroom so full, it's a good thing we have reserved seats."

Bob chuckled. He was about to say he agreed, but the courtroom suddenly became quiet. The defendant, a distinguished 45ish-looking man with brown hair graying at the temples, was led in and seated beside the defense attorney. A tearful woman was sitting behind him in the front row of the spectator's section.

"Poor woman. That's Maxwell's wife. I've seen her on holovision news," Flynn whispered to Bob.

The bailiff stood up and said, "Hear ye, hear ye, the court shall come to order. All rise."

Everyone stood. The judge, wearing a black robe, briskly entered and sat behind a lofty bench that elevated him far above the rest of the court.

The bailiff said, "You may be seated."

There was a rustle of clothing as everyone, except Maxwell and his attorney sat down.

The bailiff said, "Case number 91530, James Maxwell versus Waidor, Tribe-Five, First-Level Council concerning violation of the anti-science laws, the honorable Judge Myron Black presiding."

Looking at Maxwell, the judge asked, " How do you plead?".

Maxwell's attorney said, "Donner for the defense, your honor. Mr. Maxwell pleads not guilty."

There was a buzz of quiet conversation throughout the courtroom. The judge slammed his gavel down and said, "Order in the court." The buzz stopped, and he continued, "The defendant may be seated."

Maxwell and Donner sat down, then the judge said, "The prosecution may present its case."

"Roper for the prosecution, your honor. Mr. Maxwell was caught red-handed producing ball lightning in his workshop for the purpose of scientific research into the nature of this phenomenon. I have irrefutable evidence in a photograph, which I now submit as exhibit 'A.' I also have a holographic video on a memory cube, which I now submit as exhibit 'B.' Mr. Maxwell blatantly and maliciously violated penal code section S-51355, which has been in effect since December 2068. That law prohibits attempts to advance the black arts of advanced science, and prescribes the death penalty for doing so."

Maxwell's wife burst into tears, but tried to stifle her sobs with a handkerchief. However, she could still be heard. The judge slammed his gavel down and said, "Order!" Her sobs got even louder, and the judge said, "Bailiff, help that woman into the hallway. She may watch the proceedings on the hallway video monitor, but she is barred from the courtroom for the remainder of the trial."

The bailiff took Mrs. Maxwell by the arm and helped her leave. When the door closed, the judge said, "You may continue presenting your case."

"This is a simple, straightforward case that should quickly result in a guilty verdict," Mr. Roper said. "I now wish to play the holographic video from exhibit 'B,'"

The judge said, "Proceed.

The bailiff retrieved exhibit B, a molecular-memory cube that was about 1/4 inch on each side. He dropped the cube into a spherical electronic instrument, about the size of an apple, on a small stand beside his chair. A large, thin screen lowered down from the ceiling across the room from the jury, and a three dimensional holographic video appeared. It showed the inside of Maxwell's workshop, as if looking through a window. Maxwell was generating Ball Lightning with a machine that had an external array of slender tubes running at many different angles. The tubes were so cold they had a thin layer of frost on them. Fog formed in the space inside the array and around the tubes. It drifted outward between the tubes, looking like smoke, where it disappeared in thin wisps. Roper explained that the tubes were cooled to a temperature at which they became super-conductive. High- and low-voltage high-current capacitor banks, and a rack of digital instruments could be seen in the background. The holographic video showed Maxwell generating a sizzling, glowing, 6-inch, blue sphere of Ball Lightning that seemed to squeeze through the spaces between the tubes and float across the room.

After about three minutes, the prosecuting attorney said, "That's enough. Turn it off. I believe I've presented enough evidence for a conviction. The prosecution rests."

Donner jumped to his feet and said, "I object to the entire video shown as exhibit 'B' on the basis that it is illegal to spy on people, and that video made with a clandestine camera certainly constitutes spying."

"Exhibit 'B' was obtained legally under a warrant with cause," Roper said emphatically.

"Objection overruled. Mr. Donner, you may present your defense," the judge said.

Donner remained standing and said, "There's no question that Mr. Maxwell was experimenting with the advanced science of Ball Lightning."

Muttering arose from the spectators. It appeared to Bob that the defense attorney had lost his mind, as well as the case, right then and there. However, Donner continued, "I'll show that penal code section S-51355 was founded on a faulty basis and is therefore not valid. On this basis, Mr. Maxwell should be found not guilty."

As murmuring went up from the spectators, Bob leaned over and whispered to Flynn. "Donner has really chosen a long-shot."

Flynn replied, "What other choice does he have? If Maxwell is found guilty, I believe the best he could expect, even with leniency from the judge, is life in prison."

The judge loudly banged his gavel. "Order, order in the court. If there is any more noise from the spectators, I'll clear the courtroom. Jurors five and six, you are not to speak to each other or anyone else during the trial until you are in the jury room. Is that clear?"

Bob and Flynn both answered, "Yes. Sorry, your honor."

The judge turned to the attorney and said, "I have my doubts about the validity of your defense, Mr. Donner, but the law grants you the right to be heard, and I'm obliged to hear your arguments. You may continue."

Donner reddened, and asked, "What is the basis of your doubts, Judge?"

"The fact that you are apparently hoping to change a well established law in this court."

"Isn't it a fact that the law, as well as the defendant, will be on trial here, and if the jury arrives at a verdict of 'innocent,' wouldn't it challenge that law?"

"Yes, but it's not possible to get the law changed in this court. Since the only decision to be made here is whether the defendant violated the *existing* law, I don't see how the jury can arrive at a verdict of innocent.. However, I suppose the publicity about such a defense might stimulate action to later change the law in a higher court," the judge said, glancing at a reporter who was recording a holographic news video of the trial.

The camera, that had been pointed at the judge, swung toward Donner as he said, "All right, then I intend to proceed. I call as my first witness, History Professor Marvin Brussel, of Wasingtonia University."

An older man with a deeply lined face and white hair, walked briskly down the aisle, stepped into the witness box, and was sworn in. Wearing a black suit, white shirt, and black tie, he looked every bit the professional expert that he was.

Donner said, "Professor, do you believe the science prohibition law is based upon true facts?"

"No."

"Why not?"

"My research has shown that the true cause of the catastrophes of 2050 through 2068 and beyond was not science or scientists as was claimed in the basis for prohibiting scientific work. The ignorance and greed of powerful men, corporations, and long-ago governments caused the catastrophes by failing to vigorously sponsor research into new kinds of renewable energy sources before it was too late. Let me explain."

The professor then presented the true history and documentation from the past that supported his statement.

Roper jumped to his feet and said in a loud voice. "Your honor, I object. The defense is just putting up a smoke screen—I fail to see the relevance of all of this in the present case, which is based only on whether the existing law was violated, not whether the law is valid. This is not the time or place to argue its validity."

Before Donner could respond, the Judge said, "Objection overruled, pending clarification. Stop objecting based on relevance, Mr. Roper. I will decide the relevancy of any or all of this testimony when I've heard enough testimony. Go on Professor."

After a few more minutes of testimony, Roper again jumped to his feet. "You honor . . . "

The judge interrupted. "Mr. Roper, I thought I told you to stop objecting until I have had a chance to determine relevancy. Overruled. Please continue, Professor."

It was obvious that the judge intended to let Donner present his argument while the news camera recorded it. Roper reddened and sat down. Professor Brussel continued the history, including a description of the great catastrophes leading up to enactment of science prohibition.

"But, were things really that bad?" Donner asked. "Life doesn't seem so bad today,"

Professor Brussel composed his thoughts for a moment, then said, "At first, it was as if the biblical horsemen of the apocalypse had been released upon the earth. The catastrophes reduced the world population so much that there is now enough electrical power from old wind generators, solar and hydroelectric sources to meet basic needs. That's why things aren't so bad today. However, we only have enough of this equipment still running today because it has been preserved by extensive maintenance and recycling. Our forefathers made this possible by writing detailed maintenance manuals. But, the scarcity and cost of special materials means it won't be economically feasible to produce new electrical power sources. In a few more years our population will increase to a point where there won't be enough old renewable electric power equipment to go around. When that happens, the world will once again be plunged into chaos as energy prices go crazy, and populations clamor for power..."

Donner interrupted. "But, professor, is electrical power really that essential?"

"What would you suggest people use for light and heat in the winter? Petroleum, natural gas, coal and wood are scarce, and prohibitively expensive. Vegetable oil or animal fat, such as tallow, would be expensive and more of these materials would be required than can be produced using horse-drawn farm equipment. Whale oil is no longer an option since whales were hunted to extinction a hundred years ago. And how would wrist telephones and other electronics be operated? How would food be cooked?"

Donner looked at the news camera as he smiled and said, "Very well, Professor, continue."

"Let's see, where was I? Oh, yes, obtaining special materials to build the present types of power generating equipment and batteries, by recycling trace amounts contained in worn-out equipment, is too expensive. Without scientific development of new methods, there'll be no chance of building enough affordable equipment to produce renewable power, or producing light-weight, high-capacity batteries for powering vehicles and farm equipment. Not only is science prohibition based on false information, it's destroying our future."

Roper jumped to his feet and said, "Your honor . . . "

The judge said, "All right, objection sustained. I've heard enough to strike all of the defense testimony so far. This is not a trial about the validity of S-51355, but only whether it has been violated."

Then Donner said, "That's all I have, your honor."

The judge said, "It's getting late. Court is adjourned until 9 a.m. tomorrow," then he slammed his gavel on the bench signaling the end of the day's session.

The reporter picked up his equipment and left to generate the news Donner hoped would, in the long run, save Maxwell..

CHAPTER 7
DECISION

The next morning, after the judge and bailiff's trial opening ritual, prosecutor Roper stood up and, looking at the holovision news camera said, "I have proved Mr. Maxwell's guilt beyond any doubt. The prosecution rests."

The Judge then said, "Mr. Donner, do you have anything further?"

The newsman focused his holovision camera on Donner, who then stood and said, "No, your honor, I have proved that S-51355 is an unjust law that is based upon the faulty premise that scientific research is harmful, and I've shown that S-51355 is destroying our future. The jury surely won't arrive at a verdict of guilty calling for the execution of a man based on that unjust law. The defense rests."

The judge then said, "We will take a recess and re-convene at one o'clock." Then, he banged his gavel, and the courtroom cleared.

That afternoon, when the bailiff brought the court to order and said, "All rise," he announced the title of the trial and identified the judge.

The judge took his place and said, "You may be seated. Prosecution, you may present your summary."

Roper presented a clear summary of his main points. He emphasized to the jury that the case was about the defendant breaking the existing law, not whether the law was fair.

The judge then called on Donner, who presented an emotional, clear summary citing the evidence Professor Brussel presented showing that S-51355 wasn't valid. He also pointed out the seriousness and consequences for all mankind, as well as for Maxwell, if the jury were to convict him based on this law.

The judge then instructed the jury, emphasizing that this lower court didn't have the authority to change the law, but must decide only on whether the existing law had been violated. Then he directed them to the jury room for deliberations. The thirteen jurors filed into a small, stuffy room, which contained a long table with chairs around it. There was also a ten-drawer cabinet at one end.

A lively discussion about the case began immediately after the bailiff left and closed the door, and everyone was seated around the jury table. A gavel lay on one end of the table. The person sitting nearest the gavel used it to rap on the table, and everyone quieted down.

The gavel holder said, "My name is Alicia. We must select a foreman. If you have served on a jury before, raise your hand."

Five of the thirteen jurors, including Alicia, raised their hands.

"Who has been a juror on a serious felony trial?"

Only Alicia and one other person raised her hand. Alicia asked the other person, "What is your name?"

"Marcianna."

Alicia said, "Thank you, Marcianna. Because of the seriousness of this trial, I propose that we elect either Marcianna or me as foreman. All in favor of doing that please raise your hand."

Ten persons raised a hand.

"The proposal is accepted. We'll vote for foreman by secret ballot on slips of paper," Alicia said, as she retrieved two bundles of paper slips and pencils from a drawer in the cabinet, and passed them down each side of the table. "Each of you take a pencil and paper. We'll also probably be voting guilty or not guilty several times by secret ballot this afternoon, so take several of the slips.. A vote for guilty will probably mean the death penalty, and to be accepted it'll have to be unanimous. There may be disagreements and arguments that'll change opinions, so we'll vote whenever three or more of you request it. Write your choice for foreman, fold the paper, and place it in the basket."

Alecia retrieved a woven dark brown reed basket from the drawer and passed it around the table. When the basket came back to her, she unfolded the slips. It was no surprise that, everyone had voted for her to be the foreman.

It didn't take long to arrive at a guilty, or not guilty, decision. Everyone was in agreement that the defense had proven its case about anti-science law, S-51355 being unjust. However, they also agreed that they were bound by the existing law, so the verdict was a reluctant, but unanimous, "guilty."

The foreman called the bailiff and told him they had a verdict. The judge and bailiff re-convened the court, and the jury filed in, depressed that they had to return a "guilty" verdict based on the unjust law that had stymied progress for so long. Then the bailiff called the court to order.

"Foreman, read your verdict," the judge said with a stern expression on his face.

The newsman swung his camera around from the judge to focus on the jury.

Alicia read from a form "In the matter of case 91530, Waidor, Tribe-Five, First-Level Council versus James Maxwell, we reluctlantly find the defendant guilty. So say we all."

The courtroom erupted in pandemonium.

The judge pounded his gavel so hard that Bob thought it would split the bench. "Order, order in the court. Order! Order!"

The hubbub quieted down and the judge looked at the jury as he said, "I'm sorry you had to reach a guilty verdict. I know it was based on a law that I believe, from what we have heard during this trial, is unjust. However, we have no choice. The law is the law. Perhaps the law will be changed as news about this trial get out and more people become aware of the damage S-51355 is causing."

The courtroom became uncharacteristically quiet. Except for occasional stifled coughs, and a slight rustle of clothing, everyone seemed to be holding his or her breath waiting for the penalty to be announced. Someone dropped a pencil. The noise of it hitting the floor sounded loud in the oppressive silence.

The judge said, "Nevertheless, I have no choice but to impose the penalty of death to be carried out by instantaneous laser incineration after a period of one year. This will give the defendant time to get his affairs in order and submit any appeals he wishes to initiate."

Hearing the penalty, the spectators groaned.

"This case is complete, and court is adjourned 'sine die.' Sheriff, take the prisoner into custody," the judge said as he rapped the bench with his gavel.

Maxwell was lead out through a side door by the sheriff. Bob joined Audrey, who had been sitting in the spectator's section, and they filed out through the main door with the rest of the spectators. They passed Maxwell's wife on a Bench in the hallway across from a video monitor on which she had been permitted to watch the trial. She was quietly sobbing. Maxwell's attorney was sitting on the bench beside her, and a woman, who appeared to be her friend, was sitting on the other side trying to comfort her.

The attorney patted Mrs. Maxwell on the shoulder as he said, "We'll certainly file an appeal with one of the Superior Continental Courts. I feel confident they will grant us a hearing in the Supreme Continental Court to get S-51355 overturned based on this case."

Mrs. Maxwell managed to stifle her sobs long enough to say, "B-but that'll take many months, and my husband will be in prison. And it may not succeed . . ."

When Bob and Audrey were well past that wrenching scene, Audrey said, "Poor woman."

Bob thought for a moment, then said, "Yeah. That damn law is stupid, and it should be changed."

CHAPTER 8
THE SHOP

Two days later Bob was in his blacksmith shop making a part to replace a broken plow blade support for Doug. He placed one end of a steel bar into brightly glowing coals in the forge. When the end of the bar was red-hot, he grasped the other end with a pair of tongs, held the hot end against a large anvil, and began expertly hammering it into the curved shape of the blade-support. Each blow rang out loudly, echoing through the shop.

Even though it was a cool day, and Bob was wearing a sleeveless vest, his bare muscular arms and mop of black hair glistened with sweat in the yellow light from the coals in the forge. After he'd worked the metal for a few minutes, the glowing red hot end had dimmed. Bob thrust the end of the bar back into the coals for re-heating. Reaching overhead, he pulled on a rope hanging from a large bellows mounted flat on the ceiling. Air rushed up through an opening in the bottom of the forge, and the coals immediately sprung to life, glowing bright yellow, producing white sparks that shot upward a few inches like miniature fireworks before falling back into the forge.

Yellow light from the coals penetrated deeply into the dimness of the large shop building, illuminating dingy walls that had been darkened by years of smoke from the forge. Electric lights were kept turned off as much as possible to cut down on expensive electricity.

Bob could handle basic mathematics, such as geometry and trigonometry needed by a machinist. He had trouble with advanced theoretical concepts and higher mathematics, but this was no problem in the profession he had chosen. After working for a year as a blacksmith's apprentice, two years as a machinist's apprentice, and one year as a journeyman machinist, he could design and build any kind of mechanical device.

When Bob set up his own business, he decided that a blacksmith shop would have a broader base of customers than a machine shop in the Stoneville farming community. A lot of horse-shoeing and farm equipment repairs were needed.

Most of his shop floor was compacted soil mixed with a binder. His forge was the centerpiece of the shop. However, there was also an array of precision machining and welding equipment on a 20-foot by 40-foot section of concrete floor in one corner of the shop, and he could build almost anything, even if it required extremely precise metal work.

A large double-door at the front of the shop opened onto a street. Bob's 6'3" silhouette, back lighted by the bright glow of the forge, was an impressive sight for passers-by looking in through the doorway. Street traffic was mostly horseback riders and horse-drawn buggies or wagons. An occasional gas-electric hybrid or all-electric car passed by, but they were rare and always driven by a chauffer or an extremely wealthy person. Bicycles were rarely seen.

*   *   *

Late in the day Bob's friend, Doug Murphy, walked into the shop. Doug was 34 years old, slender build, and only 5' 7" tall. However, he was wiry, strong for his size, suntanned from working outdoor, and handsome with blue eyes and thick, wavy, reddish hair. Earlier in life, Doug had been interested in engineering, but learned it was mundane and low paying since it dealt only with known methods to make extremely small incremental improvements, in equipment or structures. There was a danger that too much improvement could be interpreted as advanced science and have deadly consequences for the engineer. Doug could have done well in a business, such as retailing, financial markets, or politics, but he considered them boring. Farming gave him a chance to experiment with new methods for growing crops. During food shortages after *The Darkening*, this kind of experimentation had been proclaimed non-scientific by the courts, so it was safe for the experimenter. It's amazing how rapidly laws that might improve short food supplies were passed by hungry legislators.

Doug had successfully maintained high quality while improving yields up to 200 percent and shortening growing time. He made an average profit of about 400-credits a day, four times the average wage of a laborer, and had become well off, if not downright wealthy. Because of the earlier severe worldwide shortages, food prices were still high and farming was more lucrative than many other professions.

As he approached Bob, Doug said, "Hey 'old pal', how are you coming on the replacement part for my plow?"

"I'm working on it, but I still have a little more work to finish. Maxwell's trial, put me behind. Then, it took me a couple of days to find the steel from which to make your part. You know how scarce and expensive it is these days. I finally found an old piece of machinery that I could cannibalize. I didn't think you'd want to pay for virgin steel."

"Okay. Thanks for saving me credits. At the price of steel, I don't know how the guys driving cars can afford to buy them. And the price of gas: 195 credits per gallon."

Bob frowned and said, "Yeah. I guess car owners have more wealth than sense. Cars, especially electric ones, are more of a status symbol than practical transportation. A battery alone costs 400,000-credits. I earn better than average wages, and I'd have to work about five years to earn that much. With our financial difficulties, I couldn't save that much in a hundred years."

"Financial difficulties?"

"Yeah. Our insurance company decided on a much lower payout for Audrey's surgery and hospitalization than we expected, and we have to pay the balance. I'll have to work extra hours or find some other source of income to make up the difference. I'd sure like to find a way to 'strike it rich.'"

"Gosh, Bob, I'm sorry to hear that. I'd be glad to loan you some credits."

"No, I don't want to borrow any more credits, especially not from a friend. I've got lots of work to do, so I guess I'd better get back at it."

"How soon can you finish repairing my plow?"

"I should be able to get it done by tomorrow morning."

"By the way, have you and Audrey decided whether you want to go ahead with a project to see what we can do with the stuff we found in the cavern?"

"Yes. We think it'll be worth the risk. How about you?"

"I've been thinking about it too. It's fascinating, and I'm all for it. But we'll have to be extremely careful. Remember what happened to Maxwell."

"Okay let's do it."

As Doug left, Bob pulled the metal bar from the forge and resumed hammering the red hot end into the final shape for the plow's blade support. With each intense, ringing blow, sparks shot outward from under the hammer. Finally, Bob held the bar up and turned it over as he inspected its shape. Satisfied, he plunged it into a tub of water, causing a loud boiling and hissing sound, producing a swirling, convulsing cloud of steam shooting upward.

It was nearly dark when Bob stepped out the front door into the cool evening air. He was relieved to be away from the hot forge as he locked the door and walked around to the rear of the shop where his horse stood in a corral. After retrieving a saddle and bridle from a cabinet on the outside of the shop's back wall, he saddled his horse and began the 1-1/2-mile ride home.

When Bob arrived, he removed the horse's saddle and bridle. While the horse drank from a watering trough, Bob went into the barn. Audrey was throwing hay down from the loft into the feed trough as she usually did when Bob was expected home. The horse came trotting into the barn and began contentedly munching hay. Bob and Audrey left together and closed the barn door for the night.

When they entered the back door of the stone cottage, they were greeted by the wonderful aroma of something simmering on the electric range.

"Wow, Audrey, that smells wonderful. What is it?"

"Beef stew."

"Oh boy, my favorite! I Love you!" Bob exclaimed. Then he took Audrey in his arms and kissed her.

Then Audrey said in a girlish tone of voice, "Oh, I'll bet you say that to all the girls."

"Only when they make beef stew for me," Bob said as he patted Audrey gently on her seat.

CHAPTER 9
CAUGHT!

For more than a week following Maxwell's trial, Bob had gone about his normal daily routine to catch up on his customers' backlog. However, he was consumed with curiosity. He and Doug decided to inspect the underground cavern with homemade torches. The cavern was in solid rock, so there was no chance of moisture or explosive gas seeping into it as there was at the end of the coal tunnel. With the broader illumination, they were astonished to see the amount and sophistication of laboratory equipment on tables and shelves in the cavern.

"There had to be more than one person involved in all of this," Doug said.

"Yeah. Since the files in the locket were produced over a span of more than 100-years, the work had to have been passed from generation to generation, and perhaps shared with others outside the family. I wonder how many of these scientists were members of the secret science society. Maybe the notebooks will tell us more about them."

"This cavern is a wonderful place to work. It's dry, and doesn't smell bad like the end of the main tunnel. But we need a better way to light it. Torches are too temporary."

Bob stared off into space as he said, "I'm having second thoughts about going through with this after thinking about Maxwell's trial. My God, death by instant incineration!"

"Yes, but think of the huge payoff if we are successful. Besides, according to the news, the anti-science law may be overturned."

"But we can't be sure. Maybe we should wait and see if it gets overturned before we launch our project."

"If we wait until it's legal, some big, wealthy company may develop the same kind of device before we can get it off the ground. Besides, if we're careful no one will find out what we are doing here in our secret cavern."

As the men continued to explore, they came across a gasoline generator. The exhaust pipe from the generator exited through the ceiling of the cavern.

Bob said, "I've only seen one other gas-powered generator in my life. They've been scarce since the price of special materials and gasoline got so high."

"Let's try to start it."

"No. The gasoline will have gone bad long ago, and it would only foul the engine."

"Well, let's buy a gallon of gas and try it."

"How would we explain needing gas at 195 credits per gallon when we don't have a car or gasoline powered equipment? Besides, even with an efficient muffler the exhaust would be vented outside and would make some noise. It would increase the chance of someone finding this place," Bob said. Then he added, "We can't depend on this generator for lights."

"Maybe we could run underground wires out here from your house to power the lights."

Bob thought for a moment then said, "I hate to be a killjoy, but that wouldn't work."

"Why not?"

"Because the trench we'd have to dig would leave a scar on the ground that would raise questions from people like Snood, and it might lead them to this cavern.. Besides, copper wire is very expensive, and it'd be hard to explain why we need it. It's not something normally used in blacksmith work."

"We could plow an area, bury the wire at night, then disk and harrow the ground to make it all look uniform."

"But that still would require hundreds of feet of wire that we don't have—and, we couldn't get the disking and harrowing done until the next day.

"If I line the plow furrows up with the direction of the trench, we can place the trench between furrows and it won't be visible from the road.

"Okay, and I might be able to find some wire in an abandoned industrial site; there are plenty of those around. In fact, the steel I got for your plow part came from a machine in the old abandoned mill just East of Stoneville. I didn't notice if there was any wiring left. It might've already been scavenged, but it's worth a try."

"What if the mill's owner comes while you're removing the wire?"

"Don't worry. I checked on the ownership before I scavenged the steel for your plow part. No one admits to owning the mill. The ground around it was contaminated with lead and cadmium long ago. The clean-up cost was more than the value of the site. No one wanted it after the original owner abandoned it. I'll check tomorrow to see if there is any wire."

The men extinguished their torches as they neared the tunnel entrance. Exiting into the night, they stumbled through the thinned vine maple path in the darkness.

"I'll let you know tomorrow what I find out," Bob said as he headed for his house.

"Okay. I'll see you then."

After work the next day, Bob rode his horse out to the old mill. At the edge of the mill site was a large, weathered, old sign: Danger—Property Contaminated. Bob believed the sign was why equipment in the mill hadn't been scavenged for materials years earlier. Apparently no one else had checked the tribal records thoroughly enough to learn the inside of the building was not contaminated.

Looking around in the building, Bob was amazed to see how much insulated wiring was there and how easily most of it could be removed. As was so often the case in rough, industrial buildings, there was no ceiling or inside wall sheeting. Bare rafters, frame studs, and wiring were all exposed.

He said to himself, "Wow, what a break! I'll bring some tools back here on Saturday and get the wire we need,"

*   *   *

Saturday, Bob packed a few tools into his horse-drawn cart and went to the old mill. After removing about 100-ft of wire, he rolled it into a coil and took it outside to throw it into the cart. Just as he got outside he heard a familiar voice say, "What are you doing, Bob?" Surprised, Bob struggled to keep his voice steady and at a normal pitch as he said, "Oh, hello Sheriff."

"I was riding by, and I saw your cart out front. What are you doing?"

"Salvaging wire."

"Then I'll have to put you in jail for stealing. I'm sorry I have to lock you up, but I have to do my duty. The law is about the only thing I know, and I need this job."

"I know, Sheriff, I wouldn't expect you to do anything less if you believe I've committed a crime."

"I've known you a long time and I know you're not a bad sort. I'll do everything I can within the law to help you."

"Thanks, Sheriff."

"It wouldn't be so bad if copper wasn't so expensive."

"But this was 'in-place' copper that no one else seemed to want. I suppose others were afraid of the contamination"

"So why were you willing to risk being contaminated?"

Bob thought for a minute, then decided not to share his knowledge that the contamination was only on the ground outside the old mill. "I guess I was just stupid enough to take the risk. I don't understand why salvaging the wire is illegal. I thought it would be all right since no one claims to own this mill anymore."

"Well, Bob, you thought wrong. What do you need wire for anyway?"

Bob's knees went weak, and his mind raced. He was hardly aware of what he was saying as he stammered, "I – I want to put an electric light in my barn, and new wire is too expensive."

"Come along, and bring that coil of wire. It's evidence. I'll let Audrey know you're in jail."

Bob's knees felt weak, and he could barely walk. He placed the wire in the cart and, after three tries, he managed to get up into the cart's seat. Racing through his mind was the thought that if his true purpose for gathering the wire were found out, it might mean death for himself, and perhaps Doug and Audrey.

He hoped that Audrey, if asked, would claim ignorance of his reason for wanting the wire so it wouldn't conflict with the explanation he had just given the sheriff.

CHAPTER 10
BAD NEWS, GOOD NEWS

It was late afternoon when Audrey heard a knock at the door. When she opened the door, Sheriff Lock was standing there, hat in hand.

"Come in Sheriff."

"I'm afraid I have some bad news, Audrey."

"Oh my God, has something happened to Bob?"

"Don't worry. He's all right, but he's in some trouble."

The sheriff explained Bob's predicament, then asked, "Do you know why Bob wanted the wire?"

Audrey hadn't thought of a good cover story, so she said, "I have no idea. He doesn't always tell me what he's thinking."

"Okay, Audrey. He's going to be in jail, at least for a while, until I sort things out. You may visit him tomorrow morning if you wish. You'll have to make arrangements to pick up his horse and cart; I had several side trips to make on the way here, so I couldn't bring them with me."

That night, Audrey walked over to Doug's place and told him about her conversation with the sheriff.

Doug reddened as he said, "My God, I hope Bob didn't tell him the true reason he needs the wire."

"I don't think he would've."

"Did the sheriff go out and look at the vine maple patch?"

"No."

"Then, you're probably right."

"Doug, I'd better not spend much time here—the sheriff might be watching you too. I have an excuse for coming here tonight; may I borrow one of your horses to go see Bob and get our horse and cart tomorrow morning?"

"Yes, of course."

Doug and Audrey went out to the barn and saddled the horse.

As she left, Audrey said loudly, in case the sheriff was hiding in the darkness, "Good night, Doug. Thanks for lending me your horse. I'll return it tomorrow after I pick up Bob's horse and cart."

"Good night, Audrey. Sorry to hear about Bob's trouble."

When she was a little way down the road, Audrey thought she heard hoof-beats behind her. She stopped, but heard nothing, so decided her mind was playing tricks on her. However, after she entered her barn, she heard a horse canter by on the road. She went to the barn door to look out, but the moon had gone behind a cloud and it was too dark to see the nightrider.

"Good God, I wonder if that was the sheriff?" Audrey said to herself.

The next morning, when Audrey arrived at the jail, Sheriff Lock met her in the spacious front office.

The sheriff said, "You may visit Bob for one hour. The visit will take place at this table," he said, pointing at a large table in the middle of the room. "You will sit across from Bob. No touching or handing him anything. If you violate any of the rules, the visit will be terminated immediately. Is that clear?

"Yes."

"Do you have any questions?"

"No."

After letting Bob out of his cell, Sheriff Lock sat at his desk near an end wall. Bob went to the table where Audrey was sitting with her back toward the sheriff. As Bob sat down, she placed a finger on her lips, signaling Bob not to speak.

"Bob, what happened? Why were you taking wire? The sheriff asked me, but I didn't know."

Then, for the sheriff's benefit, she added in a voice that she made sound as if she were almost sobbing, "You never tell me anything!"

Bob related the "light for the barn" story. Then he asked, "How did you come here?"

"I borrowed Doug's horse. While I was there, I asked him if he knew why you wanted the wire. He didn't know either, so I guess I'm not the only one you never tell anything."

Now that vital information had been exchanged, the couple launched into small talk. After a time, the sheriff said, "Visiting time is over. Remember, no contact with the prisoner, and that includes kissing."

Audrey and Bob threw kisses to each other across the table. The sheriff put Bob back in his cell as Audrey left. Outside,

Audrey found their horse still hitched to the cart. She led the horse to a watering trough, and it drank with intense thirst.

"Crap! Poor horse." Audrey muttered. "They could at least have given you some water."

After tying a lead-rope from Doug's horse to the back of the cart, Audrey drove the cart to his farm. Doug was far out in one of his fields plowing. Audrey waved, then removed the saddle and bridle from his horse, put them away in his barn, and released the horse into the barnyard.

Upon arriving home, Audrey unhitched her horse from the cart and threw hay down into the feed trough. The horse ate greedily. It evidently hadn't been fed since the previous morning. Then Audrey walked into the kitchen as she had done so many times with Bob after feeding the horse. She suddenly felt sharply alone and sobbed as she sunk down onto a kitchen chair.

"O-Oh God. I wonder if he will be in prison for a long time?"

*   *   *

While he was eating breakfast the next morning, Bob heard the sheriff on the telephone.

"Hello, prosecutor's office? I wish to speak to Mr. Roper." After a brief pause, he continued. "This is Sheriff Lock. I have a fellow locked up here that I caught salvaging wire out of the old contaminated mill. No one claims to own the mill, and I'm not sure what the law is in this case. I've known the prisoner for a long time, and as far as I know, he's never broken the law. I consider him a friend, and I'm wondering if you could expedite the hearing to determine if he has to go to trial."

After a short time listening to the Roper's reply, the sheriff said, "A six month backlog? The prisoner is Stoneville's only blacksmith and he'll be sorely missed during his incarceration."

The sheriff again paused to listen.

"Okay, sir, I'll tell him."

The sheriff walked over to Bob's cell. "The prosecutor said that he'll do the best he can to expedite your hearing, but a number of serious criminal trials have already been scheduled. The court's schedule is overbooked for at least six months. He advises you to get a lawyer and submit a written brief requesting that you be released on bail while you await your hearing."

"Thanks, Sheriff. I can't afford bail, and if I have to remain locked up I'll lose thousands in earnings from my shop. This puts me in a severe bind."

Later that morning, Audrey came to the jail to visit Bob. She and Bob had just sat down across from each other at the visitor's table when the sheriff's telephone rang.

"Yes, this is Sheriff Lock." After listening for a moment, he said, "Okay, I'll ask him."

The sheriff placed the phone on his desk, and approached Bob and Audrey.

"Bob, a murderer who was supposed to go on trial tomorrow hanged himself. His attorney's next trial was originally scheduled a week from now. The attorney was asked to go ahead with it tomorrow, but said he can't be ready on such short notice, and he needs two days to prepare. The other attorney in town originally had a trial scheduled two weeks from now, and he can't be ready any sooner than week from now. So the court's calendar is clear tomorrow and the next day. You can have your hearing anytime during the next two days if you can get an attorney and be ready that soon."

Bob thought for a moment. "Audrey, do you think you can get an attorney to take my case right away?"

"I'll sure try."

Bob's face brightened as he said, "Well, Sheriff, tell the prosecutor to schedule us for the day after tomorrow. If Audrey can persuade an attorney to work my hearing into his schedule right away, he'll have a day to prepare "

"Okay, Bob, but if you're not ready to go by then, you'll have to pay the court costs anyway."

"How much?"

"About 200-credits per day."

"Well, that'd be considerably less than either the bail fee or the earnings I'd lose by missing six months of work."

The sheriff returned to the phone. "Okay, Sir, we're good to go the day after tomorrow."

The sheriff put Bob back in his cell, and Audrey hurriedly left to find an attorney.

CHAPTER 11
THE ATTORNEYS

With only two lawyers in town, and both of them busy, Audrey knew it was going to be hard to get one in time. However, she hoped they might be able to work Bob into their schedule because surely a hearing would be much simpler than a full trial and would require less work. She decided to visit the lawyers in person, rather than telephoning them, because she felt face-to-face they would be less likely to refuse her. If she had to travel to the next town, Greensville, she might not get back until after dark Even riding hard, it would take 4 to 4-1/2 hours on horseback each way for the 35-mile trip. There were frequent robberies and murders along that road, especially at night.

Audrey rushed to the nearest local lawyer's office. He was swamped, preparing for the trial that had been moved up due to the suicide. By that time, it was noon. Breathlessly rushing to the other lawyer's office, Audrey was greeted by a sign in the front door window: OUT TO LUNCH. Audrey thought: oh my God, I wonder when he'll be back? She hurried to the only restaurant in town, hoping the attorney would be there. Inside was a well-dressed man eating lunch at a table near the front.

Audrey went over to him. "Pardon me sir, are you an attorney?"

"No. I'm an online banker."

"Thank you. Sorry to have disturbed you."

Audrey walked a short distance toward the door, then stood trying to decide what to do. Her heart ached as she realized that the attorney might have gone home for lunch, and she didn't know where he lived. The first pangs of panic made her break out in a sweat. She was afraid that if he weren't available, it would be too late make a round trip to Greensville by the time she found him. With their tight finances, and Bob not able to earn any credits right now, she didn't want to pay for an overnight stay in a Greensville hotel and livery charges for her horse. Audrey's face was flushed, and tears rolled down her cheeks. The waitress came over and asked, "Are you all right?"

"No. I need to immediately find the attorney whose office is across the street, and I don't know where he's gone for lunch."

"Oh. I can help you. He usually eats lunch at the boarding house"

"Thank you very much."

Audrey rushed to the boarding house. Several persons were sitting around a table in the dining room eating lunch.

"Which one of you is an attorney?" Audrey asked in her most winning voice.

A well-dressed man said, "I am."

"May I speak to you about taking a case?"

"Can it wait until I've finished my lunch?"

"No. It's urgent."

"It sounds like something that will require immediate action."

"Yes, my husband has been arrested, and his hearing is day after tomorrow."

"Well, I'm sorry, Ma'am, but I can't take the case. I had a murder trial coming up in a couple of weeks, and it's been rescheduled a week sooner than I expected. I hardly have time to eat. Now, please excuse me while I finish my lunch."

Audrey was surprised that instead of being upset, she was somewhat relieved. At least now, she knew what to do next. She'd head for Greensville and look for an attorney there before they all closed for the day.

After letting her horse, Nellie, drink from a town watering trough, Audrey set out on the trip to Greensville. She urged Nellie to a canter, but when the horse began breathing hard, she let her trot for about 15 minutes to recover, then again urged her to a canter. She repeated this cycle time after time to cover the distance as quickly as possible. The trot was a lot harder ride, and Audrey would have liked to go at a canter or full gallop all the way. However, at that speed the horse wouldn't have lasted more than a couple of miles before collapsing. Audrey daydreamed about how it would be to exchange horses at a gallop every couple of miles like Pony Express riders did in the distant past. Then she could have made the trip in just over an hour.

It was 4:30-p.m. when Audrey rode into Greensville. She hurried into a store and asked the clerk where attorneys' offices were located. The town was large enough that there were four attorneys.

Audrey found the first office. It had a sign hanging over the entrance, "Richard P. Dawson, Attorney". Inside, a receptionist and several waiting clients were in the outer office. Audrey approached the receptionist. "I have an urgent case. Do you think Mr. Dawson could do anything on it right away."

"I'm sorry, Ma'am, but all these people have urgent cases. It would be at least several weeks before he could get to your case."

"But my case is just a pre-trial hearing."

"Sorry, but he wouldn't even have enough time for that."

It was now 4:45-p.m., and attorney's offices usually closed at 5 p.m. Audrey's face was flushed from exertion and frustration as she rushed out and rode Nellie at a gallop to the next attorney's office. There was a sign in the window that said, "Closed." Without dismounting, she rode at a gallop to the next office. It was now 4:50 p.m. She rushed into that office, and saw that it was full of waiting people. Without saying anything to the receptionist, she rushed into the inner office where the attorney was in conference with a client. By this time, sweat was running down her red face.

"Excuse me, Sir, but I'm desperate."

Then she blurted out a description of Bob's plight in one long sentence, and asked the attorney if he could possibly take the case.

"No! I wouldn't work with such an impolite, inconsiderate client even if I had time."

"But, please, Sir, I'm desperate, and I've ridden a long way to see you."

"Get Out!"

"But…"

"GET OUT!"

With tears streaming down her red, sweat-stained face, Audrey rushed out and rode Nellie at a gallop to the last attorney's office. Her heart was pounding. The town clock was striking 5 p.m. as she dismounted. A man in a fine three-piece suit was coming out of the office. Audrey rushed up to him.

"Please, Sir, are you the attorney?"

"Yes, I'm Mr. Stone, but my office is closed."

"Oh, no. Please God, no." Audrey's knees gave way and she crumpled to the sidewalk sobbing.

"Good God, woman, what's wrong."

"I've—been riding—all day—trying…" Audrey took a couple of deep breaths and continued, " to find an attorney—to help us.."

"What can I do for you?"

Audrey, heard sympathy in the attorney's voice. She thought: perhaps here is at least a tiny ray of hope. She calmed herself and stood up. Wiping her eyes, she apologized and told him about Bob's plight and her trying day. "Please, sir, can you take our case? The hearing is the day after tomorrow."

"No, Ma'am. I have several urgent cases that require all my attention."

Audrey blanched and looked like she was going into shock. She teetered like she was going to collapse again. The attorney looked alarmed. He grabbed Audrey's arm to steady her and said, "If you will settle for a student just finishing his last year of schooling for a law degree, I can lend you my intern to handle your husband's hearing. He's a rule-nine intern, and very bright. I'm confident he could do a good job for you."

When Audrey heard these words, the first encouraging ones she had heard all day, some of the color returned to her face. She wiped away her tears and asked, "What's a rule nine intern?"

"An intern who's finished most of his formal training, has been recommended by several senior lawyers, and has passed a rigorous examination."

"Do you think he can do as well as a fully certified attorney?"

"Yes. In fact, I'm confident he'll do better than most experienced attorneys. He's brilliant."

"Oh, thank you, Sir. We'll be glad to have him. What's his name?"

"Jason Bright."

Then Mr. Stone unlocked his office and invited Audrey in. He seated her across from him at his desk, and assembled writing materials.

"Now give me the details and I'll pass them on to Jason tonight."

Audrey gave Mr. Stone a brief summary of what had happened, and he took notes. After she finished, he asked, "Where can Jason contact you tomorrow morning?"

"At my home. Here, I'll write down the address."

"Okay, Mrs, Parker. Write it here on the bottom of my notes. I'll jot down some instructions to Jason, then I'll phone him to pick them up here together with my notes on what you told me. I'd take them to him, but I'm already late for an appointment."

"Oh, I'll take them to him," Audrey offered.

"No. His place is hard to find. It'll be better to have him pick them up."

Audrey handed Mr. Stone back his notes with her address, then thanked him profusely. As she was leaving, Stone was hurriedly jotting notes on a new page. He told her he was instructing Jason to contact her in the morning for further details, then interview Bob and prepare for the hearing that was the day after tomorrow.

When she got outside, Audrey realized that she hadn't asked Stone how much this would cost, but it didn't matter; Bob needed an attorney at any reasonable cost. This was the only chance to get Bob out of jail early and back to work. She thought: it's a good thing I decided to visit this attorney in person. I don't think he would've helped me if I'd telephoned.

It was after five-thirty, and Audrey realized she couldn't get very far before dark. She reconsidered staying in one of the Greensville hotels overnight. However, the unnecessary expense, and the thought that she might not be home when Jason Bright arrived, made her decide to return home immediately even though darkness would overtake her.

Audrey got into Nellie's saddle ready to leave, but suddenly felt weak, shaky and dizzy. She hadn't let down from the stress or eaten anything all day. Now she realized she was probably suffering from exhaustion and lack of food, and could faint along the way if she didn't eat. She rode to "The Country Kitchen," a restaurant she'd passed it earlier. It was small and clean, with large, clean front windows through which tables with blue and white, checkered tablecloths could be seen. It looked like it would have good home-style food. Audrey hated to take the time, or spend the credits, but she had to have food. She ordered a glass of milk, a bowl of split-pea soup, and a roast beef sandwich to go.

"You look like you've had a rough day," the waitress said.

"Yes. I've had to ride hard most of the day, and I haven't had anything to eat since this morning."

"Oh. I'll bring the milk and soup right away."

"Thank you. Please wrap the sandwich to go."

After Audrey had the soup and milk, she felt much better. When she got the sandwich, she paid the bill, hurried outside, and led her horse to a nearby watering trough. While Nellie drank, Audrey partially unwrapped the sandwich and began eating it. After the horse finished drinking, it nosed over toward the sandwich.

"Sorry old girl, this isn't for you. I should've asked where to get some feed for you."

Audrey re-wrapped the remainder of her sandwich, and rushed back to the Country Kitchen. She asked the waitress where she might get her horse fed, and was directed to the nearest livery stable. At the stable, she was shocked at the cost of feed, but knew Nellie needed to be fed before the long trip home. While Nellie happily munched on her feed, Audrey finished her sandwich.

As Audrey started home, a sliver of crescent moon shown down from a darkening sky. In spite of the late hour, Audrey didn't feel that she could ride her already tired horse hard. Letting Nellie just plod along made Audrey feel uneasy—she'd heard about a rider being attacked and robbed on this road just a couple of weeks earlier. To make matters worse, Audrey heard the hoof-beats of a rider approaching at a canter in the darkness behind her.

CHAPTER 12
INTERN AND THE JUDGE

Audrey was alarmed, as hoof-beats got closer in the darkness behind her. She wanted to spur Nellie to at least a canter, but worried her tired horse might not be able to carry her all the way home if she pushed her too hard. She considered getting off the road, but decided not to risk having her horse step into a hole and break a leg in the darkness. She hoped the mystery rider was just an ordinary citizen trapped into riding at night. Sweeping her hair up on top of her head, she pulled her hat down over it as low as she could, and hoped that the rider passing in the darkness wouldn't notice she was a woman. The rider overtook her, slowed, and rode beside her. Her earlier hope that she could remain anonymous was shattered as the rider said, "Hi. What brings you out on the road at this hour?"

Audrey tried to make her voice deep in an attempt to sound like a man. "I had some urgent business I had to take care of."

"Oh, you're a woman!"

Although terrified, Audrey managed to keep her voice steady and confident. "Okay, you found me out. Why are you out tonight?"

"I'm a legal intern. My boss wants me in Stoneville early in the morning to prepare for a hearing. I have to be ready by the day after tomorrow, so I need to get an early morning start interviewing the defendant."

Audrey gasped with relief as she realized the irony of her situation, and shakily said, "Thank goodness!"

"Are you all right, Ma'am?"

"OH, YES! I'm SO relieved to learn who you are."

The man answered in a questioning tone, "I guess I'm honored?"

"I didn't mean it that way. First of all, I was afraid you might be a danger to me . . . "

"Oh God, I never would . . ."

"Let me finish. Mainly, I'm relieved that you're the intern who's going to handle my husband's case. I'm Audrey Parker."

"Glad to meet you. My name is Jason Bright."

"Your boss said you were bright. I hope he meant it in more ways than just your name. How have your grades been in law school?"

"I'm at the top of my graduating class."

"Are client-intern conversations confidential just as they are with a certified attorney?"

"Yes, when an intern is acting as the client's attorney as in our case."

Satisfied that the information would be kept secret, Audrey explained Bob's wire stealing situation to Jason during their long trip, including all the details. However, she gave him the "barn light" story. She didn't yet have enough confidence in him to reveal the dangerous secrets of the cavern.

It was about midnight as they approached Stoneville.

Audrey asked, "Where are you staying tonight?"

"I can't afford a hotel room. I hoped to find a pile of hay on which I could bed down. However, it's too dark to see into the fields, so I'll just throw my bedroll on the ground somewhere for the night."

"You don't have to do that, Mr. Bright. You're welcome to sleep on the hay in our barn tonight, and you can feed and water your horse at our place."

"Thank you, Ma'am"

They arrived at the Parkers' barn a short time later. Audrey threw hay into the feed trough, while Jason removed the horses' saddles and bridles.

As Audrey started for the house, she said, "Thanks for coming to help us, Mr. Bright. I'll have breakfast ready around seven o'clock. You're invited to join me, and you may use the bathroom if you wish. We have hot water and a good shaving mirror."

"Thank you, Mrs. Parker. I'll be glad to take you up on that."

*   *   *

Audrey sleepily pulled herself out of bed at 5:30 a.m. so she could finish in the bathroom and have breakfast started by the time Jason came to the house. He came from the barn at 6:30-looking disheveled and unshaven, with a single strand of hay in his hair. His appearance made Audrey want to laugh, but she didn't know Jason well enough to know how he'd react, so she kept a straight face.

"Good morning, Mr. Bright. The bathroom is the first door on the right down the hall. Let me know about 10 minutes before you're ready for breakfast, and I'll have it ready."

"Thank you, Mrs. Parker. I really appreciate your hospitality."

"It's the least I can do for the man who's going to save my husband. Just call me Audrey."

"Okay, Mrs. Par . . . I mean, Audrey. Just call me Jason."

After breakfast, Audrey and Jason saddled their horses and headed for the jail. The sheriff looked surprised when he saw Audrey with a stranger that was probably Bob's lawyer.

"Well, Mrs. Parker, I see you found someone. Are you sure he's a lawyer? He looks young enough to be in high school." The sheriff grinned with his mouth derisively drawn up in one corner.

Jason's face reddened, and Audrey shot back, "I think he'll surprise you."

The sheriff frowned and said, "I don't like surprises," then he searched Jason and let him take a pencil and notepad into Bob's holding cell on one side of the front office/visiting room. Audrey was required to stay outside the cell, but she stood close to the bars so she could hear as the two men quietly talked. Sheriff Lock returned to his desk about 30-feet away at the end of the room.

After the conference was over, Audrey invited Jason to continue sleeping in her barn, eat her homemade meals, and use the kitchen table for any study and writing he had to do.

*   *   *

The next day, Audrey and Jason entered the courtroom as soon as the doors opened. Jason sat at the table for the defense, and Audrey sat behind him in the same place Mrs. Maxwell sat during her husband's trial. A short time later, Sheriff Lock entered through a side door with Bob in handcuffs. The sheriff removed the cuffs and directed Bob to sit beside Jason Audrey leaned over the front spectator section's railing and hugged Bob.

The sheriff, sitting nearby, rushed over and pulled them apart. "None of that. Contact with the prisoner is prohibited."

There was a small commotion in the courtroom as spectators turned to see the prosecuting attorney enter from the rear of the room and walk briskly to the table for the prosecution.

Jason said, "Oh no. It's a woman prosecutor. I thought it would be Mr. Roper."

Audrey asked, "What's wrong with that?"

"From what I've seen, women prosecutors are fierce adversaries. Winning the trial is like their cub, and they're the mother bear protecting it."

 The bailiff stood up. "Order! All rise."

Everyone stood, and the judge, wearing a black robe, briskly entered through a side door looking official and ominous.

The judge sat down and said, "Be seated."

The bailiff announced, "This district court is now in session, with Judge Myron Black presiding over the evidentiary hearing in the matter of the District versus Robert Parker who is accused of theft."

The bailiff read the detailed charges, and the judge asked Bob if he had legal representation.

Bob said, "Yes, your honor."

Jason stood and said, "Jason Bright for the defense, your honor."

"You look awfully young, son. Have you been certified to practice law in our district?"

"No, your honor. I'm an intern with a law firm, and I'm finishing my last year of law school."

"Then, you cannot represent Mr. Parker in this case."

Audrey gasped, blanched, and slumped in her chair. However, Jason stood resolutely in the aisle beside the defense table and addressed the judge in a strong, unshaken voice.

"Your honor, Mr. Parker would be permitted to act as his own defense attorney if he wished to do so, is that correct?"

"Yes, Mr. Bright, but…"

"And he can grant me his power of attorney, is that correct?"

"Yes, but…"

Jason opened his mouth to speak again, but the judge pounded his gavel. "Young man, don't interrupt me. This is my courtroom, and when I'm speaking, you be quiet. Do you understand?"

"Yes, your honor. I apologize."

After a respectful pause, Jason said, "With Mr. Parker's power of attorney, I can act on his behalf in legal matters. Also, I am a rule nine intern under the supervision of a senior attorney in my law firm."

The judge thought for a moment, then said, "I see where you are going with this, and I think it will set a dangerous precedent. I don't want to be the one to set such a precedent."

"Your honor, you will not have to set the precedent in this matter. In the case of Vicar vs. Kinney in February of 2205 in this very district, Kinney was represented by a rule nine law intern to whom Kinney granted power of attorney."

"I'm not familiar with that case Mr. Bright. We will have a 1-hour recess while I take this under advisement. Court is adjourned until 10:30-a.m."

When the court re-convened, the judge said, "You are right, Mr. Bright. With Mr. Parker's power of attorney, and being a rule nine intern, you may represent him in this court. However, you must present the court with properly executed documentation showing that you do indeed have Mr. Parker's power of attorney, and that you are a rule nine intern."

"Thank you, your honor. I have a copy of my rule nine certification. In addition, I drew up the proper paperwork for power of attorney last night, and Mr. Parker only needs to sign it."

"All right. But Mr. Parker, before you sign let me make it clear that you will be settling for a less than duly certified attorney who has not passed the bar examination. Regardless of that, any decisions I make will be final and binding. In addition, you had better be sure that you can trust this young man. Power of attorney can have far reaching consequences. It could mean that he will have control of all your assets, could sell your house, drain your online account, and so on. Are you sure you want to go through with this?"

Bob thought for a moment, then said, "Yes, your honor. From what I've seen, Mr. Bright is honest, truly cares what happens to me, and is skilled in law. My wife and I have discussed this, and she agrees with me."

As Bob signed the Power Of Attorney papers, Jason said, "I'm pleased that you and Audrey trust me. However, I want you to know that you're protected. I've written the agreement so that I have only a limited power of attorney. It only applies to this hearing."

Jason handed the judge one copy of the papers, handed Bob another copy, and kept one copy for himself.

As the judge looked at the papers, his eyes widened, and he revealed just a hint of a smile. "I must say, Mr. Bright, that you are much sharper than most interns I've known. What grades have you made in school?"

"Straight A's, your honor."

"I'm not surprised. We'll break for lunch and re-convene here for the hearing at 1 p.m."

Sheriff Lock took Bob back to the jail to have lunch. Jason and Audrey left for the restaurant where Audrey had learned the location of the "too busy to help" attorney at lunchtime only two days earlier. So much had happened since then, it seemed to Audrey as if it had been two weeks ago. She was exhausted, her face was drawn and pale, and she looked as if she might pass out.

"Mrs. Pa . . . I mean Audrey, are you all right?"

"Yes, Jason, I'll make it, but I don't feel very well. I guess all the traveling, missed sleep, and stress have taken their toll. I think I'll feel better after I've eaten."

Jason offered Audrey his arm to steady her as they slowly walked the short distance to the restaurant. On the way, Jason patted her hand. "Audrey, you remind me of my mother who died when I was 12."

When they arrived at the restaurant, Jason settled Audrey at a table, summoned the waitress, and asked her to bring a bowl of beef stew immediately. After Audrey had eaten some of the stew, her color returned and she looked like she felt better. Then the waitress took their orders for the rest of lunch.

"Jason, I can't thank you enough for your help. We are so lucky to have such a brilliant, caring person helping us."

"I'm happy to do it. It's the reason I went into law. Besides, this is excellent practice for me. I only hope I can do it well enough to win Bob's freedom."

"From what I've seen I don't have any doubt that you will do at least as well as a full-fledged attorney, and probably better than most. By the way, do you have any idea of how much your firm will charge us?"

"I don't get paid for my work as an intern. It's just an opportunity for me to get experience, so I don't think they'll charge you much, if anything."

"Oh, Jason. You not getting paid doesn't sound fair. We'll pay you something."

"No. It wouldn't be ethical for me to get paid if my employer gets nothing."

"At least I'll pay for any of your restaurant meals while you're here."

"Thank you. I don't have many credits saved yet."

After lunch, Jason and Audrey walked briskly to the courthouse, the hearing, and a good or bad outcome that would strongly affect both their futures.

CHAPTER 13
THE HEARING

The bailiff announced, "Order in the court. All rise," whereupon everyone in the courtroom stood.

Then the judge walked in, sat down, and said, "Be seated."

The rest of the preliminary procedure was the same as before, except the judge asked, "Is the prosecution ready to proceed?"

The woman Jason had earlier described as being a fierce opponent stood and said, "Martina Grand, attorney for the prosecution your honor. Yes, I am ready.".

The judge said, "Mr. Parker, how do you plead?"

Jason stood and said, "Not guilty, your honor."

The Judge then looked at the prosecuting attorney. "What is the evidence against this defendant?"

"He was caught red-handed stealing wire from an abandoned mill, your honor."

Jason stood and loudly said, "Motion to suppress."

"On what grounds?"

"The mill property does not have anyone who claims to be its owner, and therefore the property is in the category of a natural resource. Under laws in effect since shortly after the onset of shortages in 2050, anyone extracting minerals from unclaimed land owns the rights to such minerals. Copper is a mineral. Therefore, Mr. Parker owns the copper wire he extracted from the mill and it is not true that he was stealing it."

Eyes of the spectators in the courtroom widened, and whispers could be heard. The judge slammed his gavel. "Order in the court!" The spectators quieted.

The prosecuting attorney jumped to her feet. Her face and ears were red. "But, the mineral rights law of 2050 certainly meant minerals taken from the ground, not wire from a building. In addition, the mill is contaminated with cadmium and lead, so the wire constitutes a hazard to the public," she said in a loud, agitated tone of voice.

Jason fired back. "There is nothing in the 2050-law that says the minerals must come from the ground. It just says the minerals must come from either property for which the person removing them has mineral rights, or from property that has no claimant. The mill is certainly property, it has no claimant, and there are no mineral rights filed on it. Now, in regard to the contamination, only the ground outside the mill is contaminated, and none of the materials inside the mill are contaminated."

The judge thought for a moment. "That's quite a stretch, young man. I will take this under advisement. Court is adjourned until 9 a.m. tomorrow at which time I'll give you my decision."

Audrey hurried over to Bob, and hugged and kissed him.

The sheriff winked at the couple as he loudly said, "Ma'am, you are not to have any contact with the defendant.." Then he pulled Bob away.

Audrey reluctantly released Bob. The sheriff handcuffed him, then lead him out through the side door of the courtroom. Jason escorted Audrey to their horses and they left.

When they arrived home, Jason said, "Audrey, you go into the house and rest. I'll feed and water the horses, then I'll prepare dinner. I want you to rest all evening – you've been through a rough couple of days."

"But, Jason..."

"I won't take 'no' for an answer."

"All right."

Audrey went into the house while Jason removed the saddles and bridles. The horses went to the watering trough. Jason threw hay into the feed trough. It made a swishing sound loud enough for the horses to hear. When the horses had finished drinking they immediately trotted into the barn, began eating, and Jason closed the door.

When Jason got to the house, Audrey was already in the kitchen preparing dinner.

"Audrey, I told you . . ."

"No, Jason. I rested for a little while, and now I feel fine. I want you to spend your time getting ready for tomorrow's hearing."

"Don't worry, Audrey, I have a photographic memory. All the material I've studied in law school, or anywhere else, is instantly available to me. I've organized the pertinent material for this case in my mind, so there's really nothing more that I can do until I hear further arguments the prosecutor might present. When I hear her arguments, I can bring out material in our favor, and hopefully win the case."

"Oh Jason, how did we get so lucky to get you to be our advocate."

"Audrey, I'll peel the potatoes."

*   *   *

The next morning, Jason and Audrey entered the courtroom a little before nine. Everything at first proceeded just as it had on the previous morning. However, this time after the judge said, "Be seated," he addressed the entire court rather than the prosecution or the defense.

"I have reviewed the pertinent laws, and have found they are exactly as Mr. Bright said yesterday during his defense. However, they are subject to interpretation of what is meant by 'property.' This is controversial, and I struggled with it late into the night."

All hope drained from Audrey's face, and she blanched.

The judge continued speaking. "I have decided the mill building falls under the definition meant by 'property' within the original author's intention when he wrote the 2050-mineral rights law. Furthermore, I checked on the contamination and found it is, as Mr. Bright described, all outside of the mill building. Therefore, there was no crime and the evidence is suppressed. Unless there is further evidence of a crime, the case is dismissed without prejudice. Does the prosecution have any further evidence?"

The prosecutor looked down and said, "No, your honor."

The judge paused, then said, "Mr. Parker, you are free to go. Sheriff Lock, you are to return tools and materials you confiscated as evidence from Mr. Parker during the arrest."

Audrey let out a yip as she got up and ran to Bob and Jason. Bob looked surprised as Audrey threw her arms around Jason and said, "Thank you! Thank you! Thank you!"

Bob appeared dazed, and seemed not to have quite grasped the fact that he'd gone from prisoner to free man in the past few seconds. He appeared to be mulling the events of the past few minutes over in his mind. Suddenly, he stood and threw his arms around Jason and Audrey in a group hug. "Thanks, Mr. Bright. You were amazing!"

Tears of gratitude and relief streamed down Audrey's face, and she held onto Bob's muscular arm as they followed Jason out of the courtroom. As they left, the defense attorney for the next case was entering the courtroom.

Approaching their horses, Audrey said, "Jason, please come home with us and rest. I'll fix us a nice dinner – that's the least I can do for you after what you've done for us."

"No, I've got to get back to the firm. We've got a big case coming up, and I have to help with the preparation. Just seeing your happy faces is enough reward for me. It reminds me why I went into law. Even though my firm doesn't pay me, this case is bound to hit the news and help establish my reputation as a legal advocate. That's a huge benefit for me. Thanks for trusting me to represent you."

Bob and Audrey bid Jason goodbye as he rode away, then rode double on their horse home to get the cart. Audrey rode on the cart's seat with Bob as he drove to the sheriff's office to pick up the confiscated tools and wire. When they arrived home again, Bob dropped off Audrey and the wire he'd been caught harvesting, then said, "I'm going to get Doug to help me quickly salvage the rest of the wire we need. When news from my trial reaches the street, the old mill will be mobbed with people grabbing wire and anything else that's salvageable."

"I could come along and help."

"No. I only have enough tools for two, and Doug's stronger and more experienced in this sort of thing. I think he'll be faster."

"Okay. I'll prepare some lunch for you and Doug."

"No, I want to drive the cart straight from Doug's to the mill as fast as I can."

With that, Bob whipped the horse into a fast canter and didn't slow down until he drove into Doug's driveway.

When Doug opened the door, his jaw dropped open and his eyes widened. "I didn't expect to see you out of jail this soon. Did you break out?"

"No. I was acquitted."

"I'm sorry I wasn't at the trial. But I knew I couldn't do you any good there, and I could contribute more by working on our project. I've made good progress studying the books from the cavern. Tell me what happened at the trial."

Bob said, "I'll explain later. There's no time right now. If we want electric lights in the cavern, I'll need your help salvaging more wire from the old mill. We'll have to work fast before the news of my acquittal hits the streets. After that, everybody in this territory will descend on the mill and take everything that's worth anything."

"Okay. Shall we meet here right after lunch?" Doug asked.

"No, we should go to the mill right now."

"Okay, I'll saddle my horse and meet you there."

"No, that'll take too long. Just ride with me in the cart."

Doug climbed into the cart's passenger seat, and Bob urged the horse to a gallop. On the way to the mill, Bob explained about how Jason Bright expertly handled the trial and got an acquittal on the basis of mineral rights laws from the 2050's. When they arrived at the mill, there was a horse tied outside.

"Oh crap, Doug. I hope whoever is in there hasn't gotten all the wire."

CHAPTER 14
WIRE

When Bob and Doug carried wire removal tools into the mill they found a man looking intently at one of the large machines.

"Hello," Bob said in a loud voice.

The man jumped. "Holy Crap! You startled me. Oh—it's you—I was at your trial, and I was glad you won."

"Thanks."

"Well, I've got to go. See you later."

As the mystery man rode away, Bob said, "We'd better work fast. He's probably the harbinger of hoards of scavengers."

Bob and Doug tore out the longest continuous lengths of wire cable, and looped each length into a skein for easy transport. The cable comprised two insulated wires and one bare wire in a plastic sheath. Doug found a small device that had a factory tag spot-welded onto it as was the custom for equipment manufactured during the 21st and 22nd centuries. It said:

Vacuum Pump, Model 5413
60-Hz, 120-Volts, 10-Amperes
August 5, 2190
Industrial Supply Co.
Area 5, Waidor

He squatted down to read the tag, then looked up at Bob as he said, "One of the science books I've read told of scientific uses for vacuum pumps. We should take it."

"Okay, but we'll have to hurry. We don't want to get caught with something that could be used in scientific applications. I hear what sounds like a lot of horses in the distance, and I'll bet they're coming here"

Doug quickly removed three of the four large screws holding the pump to the floor, but he couldn't budge the fourth one. The horsemen were getting closer.

"Here, let me try," Bob said.

Doug stepped back and handed Bob the wrench. Bob strained hard on the wrench. It deformed the metal and rounded off the hexagonal head of the bolt. Bob ran out to get a pipe wrench from his toolbox. He returned breathless, and said, "Doug, I saw a bunch of horsemen coming at a gallop, and they are less than a half-mile away. They'll be here in about a minute. Shall we just leave this pump?"

"No. It could be vital to us in the future. Let's not leave until we have it. If we're carrying it out after the riders get here, we can keep the tag covered so no one knows what it is. I'll take our skeins of wire out and tie them down in the cart while you're getting the pump."

Doug left with the wire as Bob clamped the pipe wrench onto the bolt head and twisted it with all his might. There was a snap as the head and part of the bolt broke off. Bob heard the horsemen getting close as he lifted the pump free and rushed out to the cart. Doug had just finished tying the wire down. Bob was careful to position the pump near a skein of wire so the tag could not easily be seen

Ten men on horses galloped into the clearing around the mill, followed by a man driving two horses pulling a wagon. The hoof-beats sounded like thunder. Bob didn't bother to tie the pump down. Instead, he and Doug climbed onto the seat of the cart.

Bob said, "Let's get out of here."

He drove the cart away as the horsemen rushed into the mill. When the cart was out of sight from the mill, Bob stopped and tied the pump down. On the way home, the two men discussed who the ten horsemen might be, and whether they might have been a threat. Bob lamented about not having enough time to salvage more materials from the mill.

"Well, I'm thankful we at least got a vacuum pump and the wire we needed," Doug said. "Why was that damn pump mounting bolt so hard to get out?"

"It must have rusted into the threads of a steel backing plate under the floor," Bob surmised.

When they arrived at Bob's house, he said, "We need to measure how much wire we have. I hope we have at least one continuous piece that will reach from the house to the tunnel."

"Why continuous? Can't we splice pieces together?"

"Yeah, we could. But copper wire rapidly corrodes underground if exposed to moisture. A makeshift splice cover, like tape, would probably leak   I believe unbroken plastic cable covering and insulation on the wire will protect it underground for a long time."

Doug and Bob measured the distance from the house to the tunnel. It was 400-feet. Then they unrolled the skeins of cable out into the field behind Bob's house to measure the lengths and inspect the cable covering.

They had just finished determining that the longest piece was 465-feet long, when Snood rode up in front of Bob's house.

"Crap, doesn't that guy ever give up?" Doug said with a disgusted look on his face.

"No, he's like chewing gum on your shoe. No matter how much you scrape, there always seems to be some left. I'll go out front and get rid of…   Oh hell, here he comes. Hello, Morton."

"Hi guys. Whatcha doin?"

Bob said, "Measuring wire for installing a light in my barn."

"That looks like an awful lot of wire for that little job."

Doug said, "I'm thinking about installing a light in my barn too."

"It looks like you guys have a lot more wire there than you'll need. Can I have some of it?"

Bob's face contorted and got red. He almost shouted as he said, "Hell no. Go get your own. We got this from the old mill."

"But the mill is contaminated."

"No. Haven't you heard? Only the ground outside the mill is contaminated."

"Well, either you give me some wire, or I'm going to tell the sheriff you are up to no good."

"Go ahead."

"I'll bet he'll be very interested when I tell him you stole that wire out of the old mill."

Bob and Doug looked at each other and smiled. Then Bob said, "Go ahead and tell the sheriff. Now get off my land and don't come back."

Snood left in a "huff."

"Why did you do him the favor of telling him the mill isn't contaminated?" Doug asked,

"That was no favor. He'll go clear out there, and those ten guys will have nearly finished looting the place. He'll be lucky if there are even any walls left."

As Bob and Doug inspected the cable covering for any cracks or holes, Bob said, "I'd like to be a fly on the wall when Snood reports us to the sheriff. Snood must not have been at my trial since he apparently didn't know that the mill is fair game for scavengers."

"Why do you suppose he wasn't at the trial?"

"It came up so suddenly he must not have heard about it.

"If Snood whines to the sheriff about the amount of wire we got, the sheriff could feel obligated to check more carefully into what we're doing."

"I don't think so. Snood hasn't had a good track record reporting our 'suspicious' activities to the sheriff."

"I hope you're right."

CHAPTER 15
BURIAL

For a few days, Bob, Audrey, and Doug engaged only in their normal routines. In the unlikely event that Snood did manage to convince the sheriff that something illegitimate might be going on, neither the sheriff nor Snood would see anything suspicious. Bob worked two days installing a light fixture high on a wall in his barn, and running a cable underground from it to a switch he installed on a wall in the house. However, he left the final hookup of the wires to the switch and light until he could obtain suitable connectors.

The next day, Doug came over to Bob and Audrey's house. After exchanging pleasantries, Doug said, "I'm anxious to go ahead on our science project."

"Me too," Bob replied. "I think we've waited long enough. The underground cable I installed to my barn left an obvious path of disturbed earth. When will you plow the ground to hide our installation of wire to the cavern?"

"As soon as you build the equipment, I'll plow the area from your house to the brush patch. The furrows will be parallel to the proposed cavern wire-path which will be far back from the road and nearly parallel to it. You'll need to make a pivoted slot-trencher attachment that'll fit between the two inside blades of my plow. When I've plowed the area over to the proposed path of the wire, I'll pivot the trencher down into digging position and make a single plowing-trenching pass between the house and brush patch. Then I'll plow the rest of the area. The trench to the brush patch will be well hidden between two furrows. We can lay the wire into the trench at night and cover it with dirt. Early the next morning I'll use my disk and harrow to smooth the surface and obliterate any signs of the underground wire trench."

"Won't the disk cut the wire?"

"No. The disk doesn't cut that deep."

"What should the dimensions of the trench be?"

"It only needs to be about two-inches wide, and one or two-feet deep."

Bob thought for a minute, then said, "We'll need a cover story about why I need my land plowed. What do you suggest?"

"I could use my potato planter and plant seed potatoes Then we could walk between the rows and no one would notice our footprints. Potatoes are not planted very deep, so my planter won't disturb the wire. The plants will quickly grow foliage that covers close to the ground as well as growing outward and upward well over a foot."

"Okay, Potatoes it is."

"While you're building the trenching attachment, I'll continue studying the math and science books."

"How well are you understanding those books?"

"I'm finding it easy to understand the elementary science books, and I've made good progress in them. The math books are harder, especially the advanced ones, but math will be essential for understanding the more advanced science books. I've finished my Fall plowing and planting, so I've got some time right now to spend on reading. I'd better go. See ya later."

Bob smiled as he said, "You'll have plenty of time for reading before we can bury the wire. I've fallen behind schedule on jobs I've promised customers. I'll have to build the trencher later between my other jobs."

*　　　*　　　*

Two weeks later, Bob had finished building the trenching attachment. He took it to Doug's house and installed it on the plow. Doug anxiously tried it out by plowing and trenching a 20-ft. length in his nearby field. It worked perfectly, leaving a neat, narrow slot in the earth just wide enough to accommodate the cable between the inner two plowed furrows left by his four-blade tandem plow.

"Wow, Bob, this thing works even better than I thought it would."

"Yeah, I'm surprised myself. I thought it'd take a lot more fiddling around redesigning and rebuilding."

The men were still looking, pleased with their handiwork when a look of disgust suddenly came over Doug's face. "Oh crap, there's Morton Snood riding along the road. If he comes over here, he's going to see the attachment and want to know all about it."

"Hell! — Oh, thank God, he's going on past. I guess plowing doesn't look interesting enough for him to come snooping."

"We'd better fill in this test trench right away."

"Okay, Doug. While you're doing that, I'll go into town and buy some seed potatoes."

"No, this is the wrong time of year for planting them. They have to be planted about a week before the last 28-degree freeze for this area in about mid-January. I suggest that you purchase them about mid-December. That's early enough that they won't be sold out, but not so early as to raise questions."

"Okay, but that means we won't have a cover crop tall enough to hide the surface scar left by the trench until early March."

"Remember, the disking and harrowing will leave a smooth, uniform looking field."

"Okay, but our footprints will make an obvious path across the smooth surface from my house to the brush patch."

"Hmm. Good point. We can make random footprints all over the place so no obvious path stands out for a few trips to the cavern. It's going to take a long time for me to learn enough from all of the books. Until the potato plants are tall enough to provide cover, I'll keep the books I'm studying in my house."

"But that'll be risky."

"Not as risky as having my footprints from many trips to the brush patch stand out."

"When do you plan to plow and make the trench?"

"It's too late to start today, but I'd better do it soon. It's already getting late in the year to plow for some winter crops. If I do it now, people will think I'm preparing the soil for a winter or early spring crop. If I wait too long, the soil could freeze. Seeing me struggle to plow frozen soil could raise questions."

Late the next morning, Doug began plowing. Thanks to his 4-furrow tandem plow, it only took part of a day to finish, including the special slot trench for the wire. That night, Doug and Bob worked together in the moonlight, and soon had the wire laid into the slot from the house to the entrance of the thinned path in the brush patch. They shoveled and packed dirt back into the trench, then set about extending the trench along the thinned path through the brush to the tunnel entrance with a pick and narrow shovel. Weaving the trench around the remaining vine maple plants in the path was time consuming. It was dawn by the time they laid the last of the wire in the trench through the brush and replaced the dirt. When they were preparing to leave, they heard hoof-beats approaching on the road. Bob peeked out through the edge of the brush. Bob whispered, "Crap on a crutch, it's Morton Snood. Doesn't that guy ever sleep?"

The hoof-beats stopped, and Bob could see Snood staring at the plowed patch from the road.

CHAPTER 16
NUTS AND POTATOES

Snood sat on his horse for at least five minutes peering at the plowed area. Bob and Doug watched in horror from the brush patch, hardly daring to breath. Finally, Snood rode on.

"Good God, Doug, do you suppose he saw where we covered the trench between the furrows?"

"No, I don't think so. If he'd noticed it, he would've dismounted and gone over for a better look. The disturbed soil between the furrows in the middle of the plowed area isn't obvious from the road."

"But what about the rolled up end of the wire where it comes out of the ground beside the house?"

"If he saw the roll, he probably thought it was just surplus barn-light wire dropped on the ground."

"I hope you're right. We'd better finish running this wire into the tunnel before anyone else comes along."

After Snood left, Doug finished unrolling the last of the wire from the trench into the tunnel and said, "The wire only reaches about 10-ft. inside the tunnel; it isn't long enough to reach the cavern."

"Don't worry. We have plenty of shorter pieces that can be spliced inside the tunnel to make the cable long enough."

"I thought you used the shorter pieces for your barn light."

"No. It didn't take all of them."

"How do you plan to do the splices?"

"I'd like to use ceramic wire nuts. They make an excellent, insulated connections. But I don't know how I can get enough of them without raising questions. I don't normally use them in my blacksmith jobs."

"Yeah. If word gets around, and Snood finds out, he might make the connection between the large amount of wire he saw, and the excessive number of wire nuts."

"I'll buy them in Greensville. It's not likely that anyone from Stoneville will be there, and it's far enough away that word isn't likely to get back to Snood.

" In case someone asks, you'd better have a cover story for the reason you bought them in Greensville, and why you need them."

"The reason for buying them in Greensville is easy—things are cheaper there. The reason for needing them is trickier. I will need a few to connect the ends of the barn light cable to the light fixture and switch in the house. But that won't justify the number I'll need for slicing wires together in the tunnel and connecting the cavern wiring. Perhaps I could make trivets out of left-over scraps of metal and use ceramic nuts for feet."

"Why not send Audrey for the wire nuts?"

"It's too dangerous on the road, especially for a woman alone. Besides, I need to see the sizes and styles of available wire nuts to select the best ones for our application."

Having finished stringing the wire into the tunnel, Bob and Doug left. When Bob got to his house, he began digging a shallow trench the last few feet, the plow couldn't get, from the house-end of the covered trench to the house. Someone rode up in front of his house.

"I wonder who that is." Bob said to himself.

He stopped digging and walked to the front just as the Morton Snood was walking up the porch steps.

"Good God, Snood, don't you have anything to do besides pester me?"

"I'm retired, and I have lots of time, so I perform a community service keeping track of things going on around here, especially if they look like 'funny-business.' Why are you so secretive about what you are doing?"

"I just don't like to have people nosing into my business. It's perfectly normal to want privacy—most people do. Why can't you understand that?"

"Well, I believe it's everyone's duty to be observant and report any activities that they feel might be suspicious. We only have one sheriff, and he can't keep track of everything."

Bob was careful not to show any sign of amusement as he said, "Speaking of that, what did the sheriff say when you told him about the wire you thought I stole from the old mill?"

"Oh, he said he knew all about it and that you'd been tried and acquitted for that. Then he made me take him to my house, and he rummaged through my stuff. He found a gallon can of gas I use as a solvent, and wanted to know all about why I had it. You'd almost think he was punishing me for something, but I can't imagine what."

Bob stifled a laugh, and did his best not to smile. "Did you consider that it might be for wasting his time?"

"When did I ever do that?"

"When you've made a lot of false accusations."

"No, I've never make any accusations—I just report any strange activities I've observed."

"For God's sake, Snood. Don't you realize reporting activities you consider strange implies an accusation, and by law the sheriff is obliged to investigate it?"

"Oh."

"What did you come here for?"

"I was just curious why you plowed your field this time of year."

"It's really none of your business, but I am getting it ready for planting potatoes in January. Now if you don't mind, I have better things to do than stand here satisfying your curiosity."

"All right."

Snood mounted his horse and rode away. Bob decided to finish extending the trench the last few feet to the house at night to avoid prying eyes, so he went into the house through the front door.

Audrey was preparing dinner. "What did Snood want?"

Bob related the particulars, then said, "I'll finish extending the end of the cavern trench to the house, lay the end of the wire into it and under the house's foundation, and back-fill the dirt tonight so the wire will be out of sight."

Then he told Audrey about the sheriff's response to Snood's earlier suspicions. Bob was finally able to release the laughter he'd suppressed earlier, and he shared a jolly round of laughter with Audrey. Bob's dark tension, caused by Snood's visit, disappeared like the rain when the sun comes out after a spring storm.

*   *   *

Early Saturday morning, Audrey packed Bob a lunch and he set out on the 35-mile ride to Greensville. As he was passing the old mill, he noticed a rider about 500-yards behind him. He rode up to the old mill and went in so the rider would pass. He was impressed by the amount of salvaging that had been done. The rider didn't go past, but stopped at the mill and came in.

"Hello, Parker. What are you doing?"

Anger well up in Bob's chest and throat. He had fantasies of strangling Snood, or beating him to a pulp.

"I might ask you the same, Snood. Were you following me?"

"I'm just here to look around," Snood said in an innocent tone of voice.

Bob stomped out of the mill and headed back toward home. When he was safely out of Snood's sight, he took a roundabout route back toward Greensville through some fields, and didn't return to the road until he was well past the mill. He had to ride slowly over the rough ground so his horse wouldn't step into a hole. Snood's interference had cost Bob a precious hour. Bob thought, Snood is just like a leach—once he gets attached, he won't let go until he draws blood.

Bob arrived at Greensville about 1 p.m. and stopped at the Country Kitchen restaurant to ask directions to the electrical supply store. When he got to the store, he asked the clerk for ceramic wire nuts and was relieved when the clerk replied, "What size and style?" and not "Sorry, we're out of them." Bob purchased the nuts and put them in his pocket, so he appeared to be empty handed on his ride home.

When he arrived home, Audrey looked shocked as she asked, "Didn't you get them?"

Bob, seeing an opportunity to tease her, put on his most sorrowful face as he said, "No, none of the stores had any."

Audrey's face reddened as she said, "Well, I'm not going into the tunnel or the chamber until you have cleaned out all of the awful spiders and spider-webs in there, and have proper lighting so I can see any cave-dwelling creatures that might crawl on me."

Bob immediately pulled some of the wire nuts out of his pocket and said, "I was just kidding, Dear. I got all we'll need and a few extras so I can to build some smokescreen trivets."

Audrey's face got even redder. "You'd better quit teasing me like that or someday I won't believe you when you are serious. You've heard of the 'boy who cried wolf', haven't you?"

"I'm sorry, but you're such an easy target that I couldn't resist."

There was a knock at the door. Bob placed the wire nuts back in his pocket and went to the door. It was Sheriff Lock.

CHAPTER 17
LET THERE BE LIGHT

Bob said, "Hi Sheriff, what brings you out here this evening?"

"I just wanted to ask you if Snood has been bothering you."

Bob thought it seemed unlikely that the sheriff would take the time to come all the way out here just to see whether Snood was being a pest. Did the sheriff suspect something? With intense effort, Bob recovered quickly from these disturbing thoughts and answered in a confident voice.

"Only a little. I asked him if he didn't have anything else to do besides nose into other people's business. He said he hasn't had much to do since retiring, so he's helping you do your job."

The veins stood out on the sheriff's forehead, and his face turned a deep shade of red.

"So that old weasel thinks I need help to do my job? He's wasted too many people's time, including mine. I guess he didn't get the message from my thorough search of his house— I'll have to be more direct "

Bob laughed. "Maybe you could tie a string onto him dragging a tin can rattling along the ground behind him. That always works to get rid of stray dogs when they hang around causing problems."

As the sheriff turned to go, he said, "You're a very patient man, Bob. If I'd been in your shoes I think I would've punched Snood's lights out by now."

*   *   *

After building the trencher, doing the "potato patch" plowing and trenching, running wire to the cavern, then disking and harrowing, Bob and Doug were behind in their blacksmith and farm work. They didn't dare get too far behind; if Snood heard Bob's customers complain about late deliveries, and noticed a lack of progress on Doug's farm, he would might become suspicious. Then he might be one step closer to determining there was "funny-business" afoot.

Bob and Doug worked hard for three weeks to catch up on all their blacksmith and farm work. By then, it was early December, the slowest time of the year for Bob's blacksmith business. He hadn't had any more visits from Morton Snood, so after building two trivets as a smokescreen to justify purchasing the ceramic wire nuts, he felt that he could finish connecting the barn light and wiring the cavern.

Bob had previously run the cavern wire under the foundation and left the end of it coiled under the house. Audrey offered to help, but knowing her aversion to darkness and things that crawl around under the house and in the tunnel, Bob told her that it was a "one-man job." He crawled under the house and attached the cavern wire as a tap, branching off the wire that went underground to the barn. Then he ran a wire from the barn light switch to a breaker in the house's electrical input box, connected one end of the barn light cable to the switch, and the other end to the barn light. The next evening he turned on the barn light power, which also put power on the cavern tap wire. When he saw that the barn light was on, he took a light bulb out to the tunnel to test the circuit there. When he touched the wires to the base and center button of the bulb, the tunnel was bathed in bright light: the circuit was good. Bob returned to his house, switched off power to the circuit, then returned to the tunnel and spliced the six remaining rolls of wire onto the end of the wire from the house. Now it was more than long enough to reach into the cavern.

It was a relief to work in the tunnel where neither Snood nor the sheriff could see him. Bob connected the power wire from the house to the existing cavern light circuit after disconnecting it from the gasoline generator. He also installed an electrical outlet receptacle in the cavern.

The next night, Bob went to Doug's house.

"What brings you over this evening, Bob?"

"I've finished the wiring in the cavern. We have light and outlet receptacles for plugging in a reading lamp, power tools and instrumentation. Have you learned enough to understand the stuff in the notebooks?"

"I've learned all of the math and science in the elementary books, and started reading more advanced books. However, the advanced material is difficult and has slowed my progress. I partially understand the notebooks, but I'm going to have to learn a lot more."

"Well, tell me what you can."

"Just as we thought earlier, the notebooks are a record of work that was starting in the late 2050's to develop methods for gathering and storing solar energy. This work was based on a new kind of *portable* solar energy storage device for powering cars, trucks and farm machinery. All of the materials in the device is still plentiful and relatively inexpensive, unlike materials used in batteries."

Bob's grinned broadly as he said, "Great! An affordable new kind of solar energy storage device for powering cars, trucks and tractors! That's just the kind of thing we need! I think everyone in the world is sick of having to use animals for transportation, farming and hauling. Just think of how much faster you could plow your fields with a tractor." Then he frowned as he said, "Working on this is sure gong to be dangerous. Remember James Maxwell's trial? Good Lord, execution by instant incineration . . ."

Doug thought for a few seconds. "Yeah, but the payoff could be huge if it works. I think we should continue. Now that we can work in the cavern, there's virtually no chance we'll be caught. And remember, Maxwell's lawyer is still trying to get science prohibition law overturned. We've got plenty of time for that to happen—I have to learn a lot more before I can understand the details of our project   It'll probably take me a couple of years to learn enough."

"I agree. It'll be worth the risk. Perhaps we can find someone else interested in science to help us speed things up. The author of the locket files thought he was the last surviving member of the Secret Science Society, but I wonder if there were sections he didn't know about that might still be active."

"If there are, it would be nearly impossible to find them. That's why they were called the *Secret* Science Society. Even if we did find a branch that still exists, we couldn't be sure it wasn't a 'Judas goat'."

"What's a 'Judas goat'?"

"That's a goat trained to walk up a ramp leading to a slaughtering station. Sheep follow the goat, and when the goat gets to the slaughtering station, it's permitted to go through unharmed. The sheep aren't so lucky."

"We should keep our eyes open for leads to the science society anyway. If we could bring in a third man with the proper scientific skills, he could contribute a lot." Bob paused, then said, "I'm sorry I can't contribute more to understanding the theoretical stuff. I'm just not skilled in that area. But when we need to build equipment, I'm your man."

"I know, Bob. Don't feel bad. When the time comes, I'll be leaning heavily on you to build the equipment. However, I agree that we sure could use another theoretician with whom I could bounce ideas back and forth."

CHAPTER 18
THIRD "MAN"

For the next six months, it appeared to any outside observers that Bob, Doug and Audrey were performing only their normal activities. In reality, they were also engaging in a great deal of activity related to their newfound interest in science. Audrey was reading math and science books Doug had finished studying. Bob was vicariously learning some of the science as he listened to Audrey discussing her newly learned knowledge with Doug.

One night, Audrey said, "Doug, I'm finding this material a lot easier to learn than I thought it would be."

"Yes, I think you have a real talent for it."

Bob looked thoughtful. "By golly, Doug, it sounds like we may have the third 'man' to help us in our research."

They all laughed, at the thought of feminine Audrey being called a man. However, the men were surprised that Audrey was actually learning the material faster than Doug. Until now, neither Audrey nor the two men had realized that she might be a genius. The answer to that question was not yet clear; she had been getting help from Doug on the material she was studying. At the rate she was going, she would soon catch up with Doug, and her rate of learning unassisted would then become apparent. When that time came, it wouldn't be wise to risk transporting the books back and forth every day between Doug's and Audrey's houses. The study sessions would be moved to the safety of the cavern now that it was lighted.

Bob had mixed feelings about Audrey's newfound talent. He was happy that Audrey would add "man" power to the project, but he was apprehensive about having the status quo of his happy home upset by her new interests.

Bob was brilliant at making things, and he knew how to make them lightweight as well as strong. But, he had little talent for higher mathematics and scientific theory. He was beginning to feel jealous of the close intellectual relationship between Audrey and Doug. This jealousy was getting stronger as Audrey and Doug got into the more advanced material, which Bob could no longer follow by listening to the discussions. Bob's feelings of jealousy and being left out were slowly becoming almost unbearable after Audrey and Doug, moved their studies to the cavern.

*   *   *

One night, about a year later, Bob was feeling especially vulnerable. He'd been working long hours seven days a week in the blacksmith shop. Things hadn't gone well for him in the shop that day. His face was pale, and his eyes were droopy with dark circles under them.

After dinner, Audrey said, "I'm going out to the cavern to discuss something with Doug. The theoretical material has gotten extremely difficult, and we need to discuss it to make sure we understand it correctly. Are you coming?"

"No. I can't understand anything you two say in those discussions. You're sure going out there a lot to see Doug. This is the second time this week. Why in the Hell do you have to go out there so much? Can't you two study here? And why do *you* need to know *all* this stuff anyway?"

"Bob, you know it's not safe to be carrying those books back and forth every day so we can both study them, or for Doug and me to be seen spending too much time at each other's house. The vehicle propulsion energy storage device appears to be based on optics, radiant energy, and heat transfer among other things. We need to understand these before we can design the device. Are you jealous?"

"Oh Audrey, I'm so dumb, and Doug's so smart. I can't understand all that theoretical stuff and be of any help. I don't know how you can love me."

"Bob Parker, you're a genius at building things. Have you forgotten what I went through to get you a lawyer when you were arrested? How can you doubt that I love you?"

As he thought about her statement, his face brightened and regained some of its normal color.

"I guess I was just being paranoid. It was a tough day at the shop. I made a mistake and so badly ruined a part that I can't even salvage the steel from it. I felt stupid, but I guess I'm a fairly decent blacksmith. That's the first time in several years that I've made such a bad mistake."

"Well, no wonder you were so down. Will you have to 'eat' the cost of the steel?"

"Yes, and it'll leave almost no profit for all my labor on that job."

"Oh honey, I'm so sorry. But don't let one incident like that get you down—you're the best blacksmith I know. Now, there's something Doug was struggling with, and I'm not sure I understand it either. I really must go to the cavern and discuss it with him to see whether we can figure it out. Will you be okay?"

"Oh, of course. Go out to your love nest! I'm just kidding. I know you love me, and I'm feeling better."

"I'll be back as soon as we figure out this theoretical 'Gordian Knot.'"

When Audrey got to the cavern, Doug was sitting, poring over a book that was lying on the table. A reading lamp was just to the left of the book. Audrey sat in a chair on Doug's left, and moved the lamp so she could see the book too. Doug looked at Audrey with deep, sad eyes. His face was drawn, and he was sweating, even though the cavern was cool.

"Oh God, Audrey, I'm exhausted from working in my fields today, and I'm not understanding the theoretical stuff about entropy, enthalpy, and Fourier transforms."

"I know how you feel. I've been struggling with them too; Fourier transforms are so counter-intuitive. I think I understand them, but I'm not sure. It'll probably help our understanding if we discuss them."

*   *   *

A short time after Audrey left, Bob started worrying again about Audrey and Doug spending so much time together. He decided to go to the cavern and peek in on them to reassure himself. Just as Bob arrived at the cavern entrance, Audrey was explaining her understanding of the theories to Doug, but Doug was looking at her face more than he was looking at the book, and he had far away look in his eyes. Audrey looked up and said, "Doug, where is your mind?"

Suddenly, Doug placed his left arm around her, and his right hand under her dress on the inside of her bare thigh just above her knee and said, "Oh, Audrey, I've fallen in love with you," and he leaned over to kiss her.

CHAPTER 19
OH MY GOD!

Audrey shouted, "STOP," as she grabbed Doug's wrist and threw his hand off her leg. At the same time, she turned her head so he couldn't complete his intended kiss. As the situation sunk in she thought, Oh my God! Here's a handsome, intelligent man who feels that I'm irresistible. After a moment of shock and skyrockets going off in her head, she regained a tentative grip on sanity and forced her mind back to reality.

She felt flattered to be desired by Doug, but at the same time she was deeply insulted and angered by him flagrantly taking such liberties with obvious sexual implications. However, with the good of the project in mind, Audrey controlled her shock and anger as she said, "No Doug! I'm married to Bob, I love him, and I wouldn't think of betraying him   You're a very desirable man, and you'll make some lucky woman a wonderful husband, but there's no way you and I can be romantically involved. We have to work together to unravel the Gordian Knots in these theories we're studying, but I hope you understand that I am absolutely not available romantically."

Doug said, "Oh God, I'm so sorry. I guess my exhaustion, and the difficulty I'm having with this theory, have turned my mind to putty. Please forgive me. I hope you can forget this ever happened. I guess I'd better go home and get a good night's sleep before I tackle these theories again."

*   *   *

Audrey and Doug had their backs to the cavern entrance. Bob had quietly entered the cavern and witnessed Audrey's rejection of Doug's advances. Bob crept a short distance back along the tunnel out of sight, but close enough to hear Audrey if Doug didn't stop; Bob knew she'd be angry if she found out he'd had been spying on her. After a few minutes, Audrey and Doug's conversation indicated that they were about to leave. Bob rushed home and quickly launched into vigorously sweeping the kitchen floor, a normal effort that would provide an innocent reason why his heart was pounding and he was breathing harder than usual.

As Audrey entered the kitchen, she said, "Hi honey. Did you miss me?"

"No. You weren't gone very long. What happened?"

"Oh, nothing. Doug was too tired to concentrate tonight. We'll take up our discussion again tomorrow."

*   *   *

A year went by as Doug and Audrey studied hard and covered the most applicable material in the cavern textbooks. They got past the uncomfortable memory of Doug's indiscretion, and there were no more romantic advances, much to Audrey's relief. They had become good friends as well as a powerful research team. Together they were able to quickly understand optics, thermodynamics, and properties of materials needed for gathering and storing solar energy. They determined that the notebooks contained enough details for an extremely high temperature solar heat-energy storage device. There was also enough information on applying it to Stirling heat engines and vehicle propulsion that it could be used as a basis for their solar car design.

One night when Audrey and Doug were working in the cavern, and Bob was washing the dinner dishes, there was a knock at the front door. When Bob opened the door, he was irritated to see Morton Snood.

"Well what do *you* want?"

"That doesn't sound very friendly to someone who's going to do you a favor."

"Favor?"

"Yes. I was riding by and I noticed you left your barn light on. Because of the high price of electricity, I thought you would want to turn it off right away."

Bob thought, Oh crap, I never did install a separate switch for the cavern light.

"Well thank you, Morton. I'll turn it off immediately."

Bob closed the door, then turned off the wall switch for the barn and cavern lights. He realized that the cavern would be plunged into blackness, but he knew that Snood would be watching, and would snoop further if the barn light stayed on.

When the cavern suddenly became pitch black, Doug and Audrey found the wind-up flashlight on its shelf and used it to find their way outdoors. As they were approaching the edge of the brushy patch, just before they turned off the flashlight, Snood was beginning his ride home. He halted his horse, turned, and returned to Bob's house.

Audrey whispered to Doug, "I hear hoof-beats. Do you suppose the rider saw our light?"

"It's entirely possible. We'd better return to the cavern and hide for a while."

The two turned off the flashlight, stumbled back through the darkness on the thinned path through the brush, and felt their way into the tunnel where they again could safely turn on the flashlight.

Snood knocked on Bob's front door.

Bob's forehead wrinkled in disgust as he said, "Again? What is it this time, Snood."

"I thought I'd do you another favor and let you know that someone is messing around in that brush patch west of your house. They had a flashlight, but turned it off when they heard my horse."

Bob wanted to kill Snood, but he managed to restrain himself. He knew it was probably Audrey and Doug, and thought for a frantic moment about how to explain the light. Then he thought of a tribe of people, called "The Wanderers," who were homeless and wandered the countryside, camping overnight wherever they could. They usually asked permission to camp on someone's property. It was rumored that if the landowner refused permission, he would sometimes disappear. It was also a popular rumor that persons intruding on The Wanderers' camp at night would be robbed or worse.

"Thank you Snood. The Wanderers asked me if they could camp out there tonight and, well, you know how they are. I didn't dare refuse."

"Oh, okay. I have a pressing matter I have to take care of in town. See you later."

Snood rushed off the porch, jumped on his horse, and rode off at a full gallop. Bob watched from the front porch. After Snood had gone over the rise in the road, and his horse's hoof-beats could no longer be heard, Bob turned the barn light back on, and the cavern was again bathed in light.

Audrey and Doug soon showed up at the house.

"I'll bet you wonder what happened," Bob said as the pair came in.

"Yes, we certainly do," Audrey said. "Was it a power failure?"

Bob related the story about the double dose of "help" Snood gave him. Then told how he had "tied a tin can to Snood's tail" with the story about The Wanderers camping near the brush. The three had a good, rollicking laugh about Snood being scared out of his wits and galloping off to what he thought was a much less dangerous location.

When the laughter subsided, Bob said, "I'll install a switch so we can turn the barn light on and off separately when the barn/cavern power is on. I should have done it earlier, but I've been hesitant to purchase any more electrical equipment for fear it would raise questions."

The next day, Bob went into Stoneville to purchase a light switch at the hardware supply company. Just as the switch was placed on the counter, Morton Snood entered and looked over Bob's shoulder.

"What're you buying?"

"Damn it, Snood. What did I tell you about nosing into other people's business all the time?"

The supply clerk, knowing of Snood's reputation for snooping, decided to have a little fun.

"Bob, didn't you tell me that you were going to use the switch to remotely detonate a bomb under some nosey guy's house?"

Snood looked shocked, and quickly left the supply building. Bob couldn't believe that Snood had swallowed the clerk's statement as the truth. He knew Snood would go straight to the sheriff, and the last thing Bob wanted right now was the sheriff's attention.

As Bob turned to run after Snood, the clerk said, "Holy crap, I'm sorry. I didn't think he'd take me seriously."

Bob caught Snood just as he was mounting his horse. "Mortimer, wait. The clerk was pulling your leg. Don't you remember telling me about my Barn light being left on?"

"Yes."

"Well, I had forgotten to turn it off in the house when I got back that night. I decided that it would be better to have a switch in the barn as well as in the house so I can turn the light off as I'm leaving the barn. That's why I'm buying a switch."

"Oh. Well, the way you've been treating me, I wouldn't doubt that you'd put a bomb under my house."

Bob thought Snood sure got that right. But he remembered how bad it would be to have a visit from the sheriff right now, and forced himself to say, "I'm sorry. I'll try to be more civil to you. But it does irritate me when you snoop into my business at every turn." The little voice in Bob's mind said, "Boy, what an under-statement that was."

Snood rode off and Bob went back into the supply store to finish his purchase. As Bob approached the counter, the clerk said, "Again I apologize. I never dreamed he'd believe me."

"Yeah, most people would've seen right through the joke. But I've been giving Snood a bad time lately about nosing into my business so much, and I guess his conscience overpowered reason."

"I heard that he has a bad reputation for being nosey"

"Yeah, the poor bastard can't help it. He doesn't even realize that he's doing it."

Bob completed the transaction, and left for home. As he rode along, he thought, I sure hope I calmed Snood down enough that he won't go to the sheriff.

CHAPTER 20
INTERPRETING THE NOTEBOOKS

When Bob got home, he immediately installed the light switch in his barn. Just as he was finishing, someone walked in, boots clunking on the wooden floor behind him. Bob jumped, spun around wide-eyed, and saw it was only Doug and Audrey.

Doug chuckled and said, "Expecting an axe murderer?"

"Worse. I was afraid it was the sheriff, or Morton Snood again."

Then Bob told Doug and Audrey about the incident with Snood at the hardware supply company.

Doug said, "I sure wish we could unhook that snoop from our business."

"Me too! But what brings you over here this time of day? You're usually working in your fields."

"We want to bring you up to date on the project."

"Okay, go ahead."

"Not here. These barn walls are thin, and you never know where the 'axe murderer' might be lurking."

They went to the house and sat around the kitchen table.

"Audrey and I have figured the rest of the details in the notebooks. It's really big—just as we expected from our initial impression two years ago, it's exactly what the world needs today! And the details explain the hardware in the cavern," Doug said excitedly

Bob looked perplexed. "I thought you told me last year that it would take a couple more years to understand enough of the details."

"Yes, but that was before Audrey discovered some books, called 'Schaum's Outlines', in the cavern. They are concise, clear explanations, for several levels of physics and thermodynamics, including down-to-earth examples. They summarized many of the things we needed to learn, and that sped things up."

Bob's face brightened. He leaned toward Doug. "Yes, go on."

Doug said, "Now that we've learned enough to interpret the notebooks, we can design equipment and a lot of work is going to fall on your shoulders. We'll need you to build equipment we need to finish development work started by the notebook's authors."

"But what are the notebook details you figured out?"

"In a nutshell, it's what we suspected earlier: it's a new method for gathering, storing and applying solar heat energy to propel vehicles."

"We knew that last year, so what's new?"

"Now we know exactly what the device is, how it works, and enough of the science behind it that we believe we can design the propulsion system."

"For God's sake, tell me the details!"

"Well, give me a chance. Don't be so impatient."

"Okay, I'm sorry. It's taken a long time to get to this point, and I'm dying with curiosity."

"Solar heat is stored in a solid cylinder, called a 'core,' at a white hot temperature, about 3,600-degrees Fahrenheit. Many horsepower-hours of heat energy can be stored in a relatively lightweight core."

"How are you going to get solar heat into the core?"

"A 20-foot diameter solar furnace mirror will focus the sun's rays onto a small spot on the core. Focusing the mirror through a quartz window onto the end of the storage core will raise the core to the needed temperature."

"Why quartz instead of glass?"

"Quartz will withstand much higher temperatures and thermal shock than glass."

"What material can be used for the core that's not too scarce, heavy, or expensive, and will withstand that kind of temperature? I know tungsten is okay at high temperatures, but it's heavy and has low heat retention, so it would take a really large, heavy piece to store much heat. Also, it's scarce and far too expensive."

Audrey spoke up. "The perfect material is carbon in the form of a large chunk of solid graphite. It has a reasonably high thermal conductivity, and its strength and heat capacity increase as it gets hotter. Furthermore, carbon is one of the most abundant elements on earth."

"What are heat capacity and thermal conductivity?"

"Heat capacity determines the amount of heat energy a piece of material contains at a particular temperature It's the same thing you called 'heat retention.' Thermal conductivity determines how fast you can remove heat from the surface. High thermal conductivity means the surface temperature of the core will not drop too much when heat is rapidly extracted from it during high power demand for rapid acceleration or uphill travel in a car."

"I don't have enough theoretical background to understand more than part of what you said. But I'm familiar with graphite, and I haven't noticed it has particularly high heat retention."

"As I mentioned, graphite's heat capacity is higher at high temperatures. At red heat and above, graphite has to be protected from the air or it will burn like charcoal, so you probably haven't had any experience with it white hot. We'll have to protect the core by surrounding it with a vacuum or inert gas, like argon, to keep it from burning—we only want to use the heat stored in it like a hot brick in an ancient foot warmer."

"How much white-hot graphite will it take to store enough heat energy to propel a vehicle 200-miles or so?"

"According to the notebooks, about 900-pounds, depending on engine efficiency."

Bob looked worried. "Nine hundred pounds is an awful lot of graphite. I don't know if I can get a piece that big. Even if I can, it may raise questions. I don't know how I can justify it as blacksmith supplies."

Doug said, "I calculated the optimum dimensions of a 900-pound heat energy storage core of high density graphite. It would be a cylinder about 25-inches in diameter and 25-inches long.

Bob thought for a moment. "That's smaller than I expected. I've heard of 25-inch graphite cylinders being used by steel mills as electrodes in their arc melting furnaces. But I'll have to think long and hard, about how to explain needing a piece that large in my shop, in case someone asks. How would you use heat from the core to propel a vehicle? Power a steam engine?"

"No," Audrey said, "Stirling Engines can have an efficiency of about 40-percent, run quietly, and require only heat to make them run. With this solar heat storage device they don't require fuel or emit any exhaust."

"That's all well and good, but wouldn't a white hot core would cool rapidly, even while sitting idle in a container. My guess is that most of the heat would be gone in an hour or so. Besides, the heat radiating from it would melt the container and at least part of the vehicle. It would also fry the passengers."

"That's not a problem. The core will be wrapped in super-insulation."

"What's super-insulation?"

"Many layers of thin foil that are spaced a small distance apart. For best results, the insulation-wrapped core would be enclosed in a vacuum. However, the enclosure can be filled with argon gas that won't react with graphite, and has a low thermal conductivity. Argon would be safer than a vacuum since it would keep air out of the enclosure much longer in case of a pinhole leak."

"What material would you use for the foil? Tungsten?"

"No. We'd use thin, flexible, graphite foil gasket material. It's made from graphite fibers using a process similar to that for making paper. Graphite foil is far less expensive than tungsten, and it won't chemically react with the graphite core at high temperatures."

"How do you get the heat from the core to the engine?"

"We believe the core itself can be used as the hot zone receiving gas from the cold end of the engine's displacer. Argon or other inert gas in the vessel containing the foil and core would serve as the working gas for the engine. Argon is not a very good conductor of heat, but with properly designed fins on the core for transfer of heat to the gas, that shouldn't be a problem."

"So, do you want me to build a Stirling engine?" Bob asked.

"No, we found one in the cavern, along with a small prototype storage core."

"Why not just use that core instead of building a new one?"

"Because it is too small for propelling a vehicle very far, and it was designed for only electrical heating. Considering the cost and limited availability of electrical power, we believe direct solar heating is the best way to go."

"If I can get the graphite and foil, I'll build the storage device, but you'll have to design it. I hope procuring such a large amount of these unusual materials won't get me into trouble."

CHAPTER 21
THE CORE

As Doug and Audrey designed the heat storage core, they often called Bob out to the cavern to consult on whether building certain design features were possible. Six weeks later, Bob found Audrey sitting in the kitchen when he got home from work. He asked, "How come you're not in the cavern?"

"Doug and I have finished designing the core. We'll go over the design with you this evening so you can start building the equipment."

"That's good news. After Doug told me how Schaum's Outlines helped to understand the notebooks, I thought the design would be completed quickly. But it has taken so long I began wondering if you were ever going to finish it."

"It was more difficult than we anticipated. We had to learn more about optics to come up with the best method for absorbing solar energy into the core. Also, we had to learn more about mechanical engineering and heat transfer to design the core supports, and the fins for transferring heat from the core to the engine's working gas."

That evening, when Bob and Audrey entered the cavern, Doug was studying a book on radiant heat transfer and thinking about a design for the core's super-insulation. He put down the book, and the trio went over to a table where a large drawing of the core was laid out. The drawing had a side view, end view, and cross sections. Bob was used to reading design drawings, so he immediately recognized several unusual features in the core design. He asked, "What is this deep, cone-shaped cavity on one end of the core?"

With pride in her voice, Audrey said, "I designed that. It has the correct apex angle to make it a perfect blackbody that absorbs all the sunlight focused into it. None is reflected."

"And what are all these fine grooves, running lengthwise the full length of the core, located all around the circumference?"

"You are looking at it the wrong way," Doug said, "The ribs formed *between* the grooves are the important feature. They are fins for rapidly transferring heat from the hot core to argon working gas. A close-fitting hollow graphite cylinder will be slipped over the outside of the ribs. This assembly will be surrounded by the super insulation and contained in an outer shell filled with argon working gas which will flow in at one end of the core, then pass down through the grooves between the ribs and out the other end of the core to the hot end of the displacer. This is a rough design. We have to do a lot more work on specific design details, so the design may change, but this will get us started so we can order the materials we'll need."

Bob thought for a moment, then said, "Shall we order the 25 inch diameter graphite right now?"

Doug smiled and said, "That'd be a good idea. Even though we haven't finished all the design details, it may take months to get the graphite here. We'd better order it now so it'll be here when we need it."

The next day, while Bob was at work, Audrey s searched the World Wide Network for information on sources of large graphite cylinders. The Network had been maintained since the darkening, but only a few small improvements had been made since that time. Engineers who could have made large improvements were fearful of being accused of working on advanced science. After searching for almost an hour, Audrey found one supplier who made electrodes for the few steel mills that were still in business. When Bob got home from the shop, Audrey said, "The good news is that I was able to find a supplier for the graphite."

"What's the bad news?"

"It costs 50-credits per pound."

"Oh crap! That means 900-pounds'll cost 45,000-credits, and we'll have to buy about the same amount for the hollow outer cylinder if it has to be machined from a solid cylinder. At that price, the heat storage cores might not be affordable for most people, and we sure can't afford to buy that much graphite right now."

Audrey and Bob walked over to Doug's place.

When Doug answered the door, Audrey brought him up to date on the graphite procurement, ending with Bob's concern about the storage cores being too expensive.

Doug asked, "What are the present applications for large graphite cylinders?"

"I only found mention of its use in steel mills."

"How many?"

"Five, world-wide."

"Then I wouldn't worry about the price knocking our device out of the market for energy storage in vehicles. Remember that batteries for car propulsion cost 400,000-credits. Our energy storage devices, at a material cost of a little more than 90,000-credits for the two cylinders, should be attractive for even the moderately well off as well as the rich. As more people buy solar powered cars, the economy of higher sales volume will lower their cost, allowing more people to buy them, reducing the cost even more, and so on. Solar powered cars would greatly expand the market for graphite. Since carbon is plentiful and relatively cheap, most of the cost to make graphite is for labor and compressing and heating the carbon. The economy of scale should reduce the cost of graphite as widespread demand ramps up."

Audrey thought for a moment, then she said, "But that doesn't help us with the cost of graphite for our prototype. Ninety thousand credits for the two cylinders is more than we can afford."

"Don't forget that we're partners. I expect to pay half of the costs."

"Well, even 45,000-would be beyond our means."

"Okay, since you and Bob are paying all the electric bill for lighting the cavern, and Bob lost several day's work when he was arrested for salvaging wire, how about if I toss in 70,000, and you two toss in 20,000?"

"We can handle that."

"Then it's settled."

The next morning, Audrey again accessed the Network to find the location and telephone number of the graphite manufacturers' outlets. She was appalled that the only outlets were located over 3000-miles away in a tribal co-op on the other end of the continent.

Wagons 48 to 60-feet long, articulated in four or five places and pulled by 20-horses or mules, were used for long-haul mainline loads of freight. Coast-to-coast shipping was a massive effort requiring 31 to 93 days, depending on whether the customer chose express or standard shipping. During bad weather, shipping took even longer.

Express shipping required a change of drivers and animals every 8 hours, day and night for continuous travel. Standard shipping required the drivers and animals to work 4 hours before a rest stop for food and water, then work another 4 hours before an overnight rest This mode of shipping cost more than twice as much as standard shipping.

The cost of standard shipping for the two 900-pound cylinders from the graphite outlet to Greensville was 11,000-credits. Greensville was the town closest to Stoneville for receiving mainline freight.

When Bob arrived home from work that evening, Audrey told him what she found out. His forehead furrowed as he sunk heavily onto a kitchen chair. "Oh God. We really can't afford to pay 5500 for half the shipping as well as 20,000 on the Graphite. Also, it's going to be difficult and dangerous to load and unload two 900-pound pieces of graphite onto Doug's hay wagon in Greensville without proper equipment."

"Don't worry. I went over to Doug's and told him we couldn't afford to pay our 5,500-credit share of the shipping. He said he'd cover it for now, and we can reimburse him later when we can afford it.

"Audrey, I hate to be any more indebted to Doug."

"Well, if we want to continue with the project, I don't see that we have any other choice."

"You're right, but that doesn't make it any more acceptable."

"Doug said he's confident you can solve the loading and unloading problem."

"I'm not as confident as he is. I have a chain hoist that'll handle the weight, but it has to be hung from something higher than the wagon and will support 900-pounds. Now that I think about it, how are we going to get the heavy core through the brush patch and into the cavern?"

"I don't know, Dear, but I'm sure you'll come up with something."

"I sure hope so."

CHAPTER 22
GRAPHITE

Audrey telephoned Electrodes Inc. and asked if they could supply two 25-inch lengths of graphite. One was to be a 24-inch diameter solid cylinder. The other was to be a hollow cylinder with an outside diameter of approximately 26 inches and an inside diameter of 24-inches closely fit to slip over the solid cylinder. She requested they be delivered to the freight terminal in Greensville. The salesman said they could neither produce hollow cylinders, nor hold to an accuracy required for a close fit of the solid cylinder inside a hollow one, but that a nearby machine shop, Eastern Machining Inc., could machine the cylinders to the desired final dimensions and accuracies.

Audrey ordered two solid cylinders, both 25-inches long, one 24-1/2 inches in diameter and the other 26 inches in diameter. The oversized 24-1/2 inch cylinder diameter was to allow machining it to an accurate final diameter of 24-inches. She instructed the salesman not to ship the cylinders until she made some arrangements and got back to him. He said, "Okay, but I'll have to ship by the day after tomorrow. We can't allow material to accumulate in our shipping department."

Next, she telephoned the Greensville freight terminal.

"Hello. What kind of equipment do you have for loading a 900-pound solid cylinder and a 145 pound hollow cylinder, both 2 feet long and a couple of feet in diameter, from your loading dock to a wagon?"

"What kind of material are they?"

Audrey had anticipated this question.

"Granite."

"What are you going to use it for?"

Audrey hadn't expected this question from a freight terminal. She paused for a moment to think, then said, "Sculpting."

"What are you going to sculpt?"

"Look, I'm in a hurry and I don't have time to answer endless questions. Now, what about your equipment?"

"We have a hand-operated hydraulic forklift."

"Okay, thank you."

After having so many uncomfortable questions from the freight terminal, she decided not to call the machine shop until it was necessary. When Bob came home after work, Audrey greeted him, with a big smile on her face, saying, "Hi, Honey. Guess what I found out today."

"Tell me. I'm not good at guessing games."

Audrey told Bob about placing an order for the graphite, and her conversation with the freight terminal clerk.

Bob looked pleased. "Now I won't have to worry about how to load the cylinders onto Doug's wagon at the Greensville freight terminal. I reinforced a high crossbeam in the shop today so it'll support a chain hoist lifting the heavy load here. Now all I have to do is figure out how to bore out the larger cylinder so it'll fit closely over the ribs on the core."

Audrey thought for a moment, then said, "I found a machine shop located near Electrodes Inc. that can bore out the large cylinder, but I didn't call them. They might ask questions, so I thought I'd better wait until I talked to you to see if it was necessary to have them do the work. If we want them to do the work, I'll have to arrange that tomorrow. Otherwise, Electrodes Inc. will ship both solid graphite cylinders to us day after tomorrow."

"Let's have the machine shop do the boring if it's not too expensive. I don't have a lathe large enough, so I was considering trying to build a large special purpose lathe just to machine the final inside diameter. That would take a lot of time, and there would be a risk of ruining the graphite."

The next day, Audrey telephoned Eastern Machining Company and got an estimate on the cost for boring out the center of the larger graphite cylinder to make it into a 25 inch long by 26 inch outside diameter tube with a one-inch wall thickness. She remembered what Bob had said about having to build a special lathe, to bore out the larger cylinder, so she also got a cost estimate for turning the *outside* diameter of the smaller solid cylinder to closely fit the 24 inch inside diameter of the outer tube.

When Bob got home that night, Audrey looked sad as she said, "You'd better sit down – I have some bad news."

"What now?"

"Eastern Machining wants 1000-credits to hollow out the outer cylinder."

"Well, that's 500-credits for our half of the cost, and I think we can afford it. Besides, It'll reduce the weight enough to reduce the shipping cost by 3,300-to 5500-credits, so it'll more than pay for itself."

"They wanted another 950-credits to machine the solid core cylinder's diameter to fit inside the outer cylinder."

"Oh, damn. I wish you hadn't revealed that the solid cylinder has to closely fit inside the hollow cylinder. It may raise questions that will be hard to answer."

"But I thought you would have to build a special lathe to handle a solid cylinder that large."

"That's true for boring one out. However, for an outside diameter I can easily build a hand-operated adapter to rotate the solid cylinder at the correct height and move it left and right under a fly-cutter on my milling machine to cut the diameter down to a perfect fit."

"I'm sorry. I hope my revealing that much of our design doesn't cause us trouble."

"Me too. But that's water under the bridge. Go ahead and ask Eastern Machining to bore out the outer cylinder, but not machine the inner one."

The next day, Audrey asked Electrodes Inc to send both cylinders to Eastern Machining so they could be shipped together after the larger one was bored out. Everything seemed to be going so well, she could hardly believe it.

Next, she telephoned Eastern Machining..

"This is Mrs. Parker. I got an estimate from you for the cost of ..."

"Oh yes, Mrs. Parker I remember our conversation. You want a 26-inch diameter solid cylinder hollowed out to make a 24-inch inside diameter tube, and another solid cylinder machined to fit inside the first one. May I ask what you are going to use them for?"

Audrey's pulse quickened and her face felt hot as she remembered Bob's distress, and her feelings of guilt, about revealing too much. "I'm sorry, I misunderstood what my husband wanted. We only want the larger cylinder bored out." Struggling to explain the cylinders' use, she remembered reading about graphite furnaces for melting high temperature metals, and said, "It's for a high-temperature inert-gas filled furnace for melting metals to make high temperature castings. My husband is going to carve a crucible from the solid cylinder, so you won't have to do any machining on it. I'm having both cylinders sent to you from Electrodes Inc. so they can be shipped to us together."

"Oh. Okay, Ma'am. We'll start on it as soon as we receive the material from Electrodes Inc. I'll need your shipping address, credit account number, and the number of your authorization certificate."

"Authorization certificate?"

"Yes. Large pieces of graphite are classified as unusual material, and our tribal cooperative requires an authorization certificate number before we ship to ensure that they are not being used for scientific or other illegitimate activities."

Audrey's heart leapt, her face got hot, and she felt a cold chill run down her back as she said, "I – I don't know my husband's authorization number."

The clerk at Eastern Machining Inc. said, "That's okay, Ma'am, many of the tribal cooperatives don't require authorization certificates, so your husband may not have one. However, our tribal cooperative manufactures many special materials, so you'll need a certificate. You can obtain one by getting a blank form from your tribal clerk and filling it in, stating what business your husband is in, and why he needs the special material, then having your local sheriff or judge sign it."

Sheriff or Judge! Audrey felt like she'd been hit in the stomach. "Oh. I—I'll have to call you back."

CHAPTER 23
TROUBLE

Audrey was frustrated and exasperated from this yet another unexpected roadblock. She stomped back and forth from the living room to the kitchen, growling and banging her right fist into her cupped left hand pretending that it was the faces of those responsible for her frustration. When Bob got home, Audrey told him what had happened. Bob sunk onto a chair, and the two of them stared at the wall in a black cloud of gloom.

Neither Bob nor Audrey got up when there was a knock at the door. They were so depressed they didn't care, even if it were the sheriff or Snood,.

"Come in, " Bob said gloomily.

Doug opened the door and asked, "What's the matter?"

Bob told him about the required certificate and approvals. Doug sat and the three of them despondently tried to think of a non-incriminating way to approach the judge or sheriff.

Finally, Audrey said, "Today I had to explain away the mistake I made yesterday asking Eastern Machining if they could machine the inner cylinder." Then she explained to Bob and Doug her lie about using the graphite to build a furnace and crucible. "I had to come up with it on the spur of the moment. It's the first thing that popped into my head, and I don't know how viable that story will be. Someone could notice that the part Bob makes is nothing like a crucible."

"Your lie sounds believable," Bob said. "I don't think either the judge or the sheriff has any idea what a crucible looks like. Besides, when I have machined the core to the proper diameter, cut grooves into it, and fitted it into the outer cylinder, I'll haul both of them to the secret cavern. They won't be in my shop very long. After I've moved them, I can tell anyone who asks about them that the outer cylinder cracked, and I couldn't afford another one. What do you think, Doug?"

"I agree. If we can't think of a better idea, let's go with Audrey's."

For another hour they tried to think of a better justification for the certificate, but nothing better came to mind.

The next day, Audrey got a blank certificate from the tribal clerk, filled it out, got Bob's signature, then went to see the judge. She thought the judge would be less likely than the sheriff to go to Bob's shop and see what he was building. She had to wait a couple of hours before the judge was available to sign, then he was in a hurry to go to lunch. He didn't ask any hard questions before he signed the certificate. Audrey had filled in the "purpose" line on the certificate as: "Special Materials for Blacksmith Applications," so it would cover any other special materials that might be needed for the project in the future She was pleasantly surprised that she didn't even have to tell the "Furnace and Crucible" story to the judge.

Relieved, Audrey left the courthouse. While riding home, she called Eastern Machining on her wrist telephone, and gave them the shipping address, credit account numbers, and certificate information needed to authorize shipment. She then called Electrodes Inc., completed the sale, and told them to ship both cylinders to Eastern Machining as soon as possible.

By this time, it was early afternoon. Her ordeal was over—for now. She congratulated herself on a job well done, and relaxed at her kitchen table with a refreshing cup of tea.

*   *   *

Fourteen weeks later, the Greensville freight terminal called at 11:30 a.m. Audrey answered. The caller said, "Ma'am, two large cylinders addressed to Bob Parker have arrived. When you called about our heavy-load handling equipment, didn't you tell me they are supposed to be granite?"

"Yes."

"I wonder if your supplier screwed up. These are the funniest looking granite I've ever seen."

"It's a special granite that's much softer and easier to sculpt."

"Oh, okay. What do you want me to do with them?"

"Just hold them. My husband and a helper will be there tonight or tomorrow to pick them up."

Audrey immediately phoned Bob at the shop, then Doug, saying, "The 'granite' has arrived."

Audrey, Bob and Doug had planned every detail for transporting the graphite cylinders, including using the code name, "granite." Bob had reinforced Doug's hay wagon for carrying the heavy load. As Doug and Bob finished hitching two horses to the wagon and loading it with hay, Audrey arrived bringing four packed lunches. Doug fetched a rifle from the house and tucked it into the hay.

Audrey looked puzzled. "What are the hay and rifle for?"

"The hay may be useful for hiding the 'granite'. Besides, we can feed some to the horses, and use the rest of it for a mattress tonight. The rifle is 'just in case'."

"Good thinking. Best of luck on the trip."

It was 12:30 p.m. by the time the two men had lunch and left for Greensville. Bob rode his horse. At a slow walk the horse was much smoother riding than the heavily reinforced wagon. Doug was driving the wagon as it rattled through Stoneville. Although the wagon seat was spring mounted, Doug was constantly jostled up and down by the heavily reinforced wagon's springs. The men knew that it would take about nine hours to get the wagon to Greensville, so they'd come prepared to spend the night along the road. They stopped at 6 o'clock to rest, feed the horses, and eat a lunch.

"Gosh, Bob," Doug said between bites of sandwich, "I sure wish I could find a woman as good as Audrey. I need a wife."

Bob's mind flashed back to the night in the cavern when Doug made a pass at Audrey. His pulse quickened, but he fought giving any outward signs of his intense jealousy. It was important to maintain a good working relationship with Doug so they could finish the project in which they had invested so much time and treasure. "Yeah, I'm lucky, and I know it. I'd do anything necessary to keep from losing her, including mayhem."

When they'd finished eating and got up to go, Doug suddenly grimaced, grabbed his back, and didn't straighten up completely.

"What's wrong?"

"Jostling up and down in that damn wagon seat is starting to get to my back."

"Let me drive your team while you lie on the hay. We can tie a lead from my horse to the back of the wagon."

"Thanks. I appreciate it."

By ten o'clock that night they were about four miles from Greensville.

"Hey Doug, let's bed down here for the night," Bob said. "It's no use going into town until tomorrow morning."

"I agree. I'm tired of bouncing up and down in this wagon, and I'm ready for a good night's sleep."

The men took care of the horses, then bedded down in the hay. At about 1 a.m., Bob was awakened by the hoof beats of at least four horses cantering along the road. Bob poked Doug to wake him..

"W-What's the matter?"

"Listen."

"I wonder who's out here this time of night."

"It could be a gang of robbers. Be quiet," Bob whispered."

Doug scrambled to the front of the wagon and pulled the rifle from the hay. "It's probably just a group of travelers, but I came prepared—just in case."

CHAPTER 24
"GRANITE"

The hoof beats on the road got louder, and just as they were approaching the location where Doug and Bob had left the road for the night, a bright moon broke out of the clouds. The four riders halted their horses. One man said to the others, "Well, would you look at that. A wagon and three horses. That'd make a pretty good night's haul."

Another man said, "Yeah. At least we'd have something to show for all of our riding tonight."

The four rode toward the wagon. Suddenly, Doug stepped down from his hiding place behind the hay, and vigorously cocked his rifle, making a loud click – clack sound. This sound, universally recognized by anyone familiar with guns, caused the men to abruptly halt their horses.

Doug said in a loud voice, "Don't make a move. You men had best turn around and be on your way."

The four riders stared at Doug for a moment, then the leader said, "You'd better drop your rifle. There are four of us, and we're all armed. You couldn't shoot us all before one of us dropped you."

"Well, first of all, none of you have your gun drawn, and second, I could drop two of you before you could draw and take aim. Also, I have a partner, and he has a 45 caliber automatic hand gun. He could drop at least one of you before any of you could shoot him. So which three of you want to die for three mangy old horses and a beat up wagon-load of hay?"

"I don't believe you have a partner."

"Say hello, Bob."

"Hi. I'll bet I could get two of 'em, Doug."

"Okay, I'll take the front two, and you take the other two. Whatta ya say, gentlemen? Do you want to live or die? Any sudden moves and we'll assume you chose die."

Silence hung in the night air like a thick fog. Doug's rifle was pointed directly at the leader.

Finally, the leader said, "C'mon men, this broken down old crap of a wagon, and those mangy old horses aren't worth the effort of driving them out of here. Let's get back on our way."

As the hoof beats faded into the distance, Doug's knees felt weak, and he shuffled over to Bob."

"Doug, I didn't know you were a magician."

"Magician?"

"Yes, the non-existent hand gun you created for me out of thin air."

"Pretty good bluff, huh?"

"Yeah, I'm sure glad you're a fast thinker."

"There's only one thing wrong now"

"What?"

"Running that bluff scared the crap out of me. My knees are too shaky to get back up on the hay. Give me a boost."

"I'll do better than that," Bob said as he swept Doug up in his arms and effortlessly threw him up on the hay."

The men rested until daybreak but after the excitement, and knowing that the bandits could return, neither slept. They hitched the horses to the wagon and arrived at the Country Kitchen restaurant in Greensville at 7 a.m. After a hearty breakfast, both men felt refreshed as they took the horses to the town's watering trough, then drove the wagon to the freight terminal.

At the terminal, they pulled the wagon up beside the loading dock, pitched the hay away from the wagon's stake-side nearest the dock, then removed that side to reveal the flat bed.

The station agent heard the commotion and came out. "What are you guys doing?"

"I'm Bob Parker, and we're here to pick up the granite cylinders you called my wife about yesterday."

"Oh, okay. You may use the hand-operated forklift over there. The cylinders are mounted on a shipping pallet, so it should be easy to load them onto your wagon."

Bob and Doug had no trouble loading the cylinders. They replaced the stake-side of the wagon and covered the cylinders with hay.

They got most of the way home by late afternoon, and stopped about three miles short of Stoneville to eat the last two sandwiches Audrey'd packed. They decided to wait there until a few hours after sunset so they could come into town under cover of darkness. As they were eating, a horseman appeared in the distance. Bob jumped down off the wagon and walked around it to make sure the hay was covering the cylinders on all sides as well as on top.

Suddenly, Bob stopped and called out. "Doug, we have a hole through the hay here."

Doug quickly carried hay from the front of the load, and forced it down into the hole.

The rider, approaching at a canter, closed in rapidly. "Well, hello, guys."

"Hello, Snood."

CHAPTER 25
HAY--SNOOD

Snood looked puzzled. "How come you're hauling hay clear out here?"

Neither Bob nor Doug was prepared to answer the question. They hadn't expected to encounter Snood. Since Bob had a certificate authorizing the graphite, he considered telling Snood the "furnace" story, but then Snood would probably snoop around even more.

After a pause, Doug said, "We heard about a hay wagon overturning, and the owner abandoning the load of hay on the side of the road, so we went out and got it."

"Oh. I see you're eating sandwiches. Why are you eating here? You're almost home."

Bob remembered how effective his story about "The Wanderers" had been in getting rid of Snood. "We had to get away from a couple of highway robbers a little way back and didn't get time to eat, so we're starved."

Snood looked alarmed. "Robbers?"

"Yes. They seem to be prowling around out here looking for easy pickings."

"How did you get away from them?"

"Here, I'll show you," Doug said as he reached for his rifle. "Click-clack."

"Oh, a gun! I just remembered I'm late for an appointment."

Snood whirled his horse around and rode off at a gallop toward town.

When Snood got far enough away, Bob and Doug discussed whether to take the graphite to the shop immediately. Since Snood had already seen them hauling the load toward town, it might not make much difference. They decided that late night, with darkness and deserted streets, would be better since it would avoid questions about why they were bringing a load of hay to the blacksmith shop.

At about 2 a.m. the men awoke on their bed of hay, hitched the horses onto the wagon, and Doug drove it to the shop followed by Bob on his horse. However, as they arrived in the darkness they could barely make out the silhouette of a horse tied in the park across the street from the shop, and someone sitting slumped on a bench there. Another person, apparently startled by the sound of the wagon, was running away from the bench and deep into the park..

"Doug, what do you think that's all about?"

"I don't know, but we'd better check it out before we put this load in your shop."

Doug halted the wagon. Bob got off of his horse and tied it to the wagon. He walked over to the man on the bench. It was Morton Snood, unconscious, but breathing. There was a yard-long piece of tree limb laying on the ground beside the bench, and a lump forming on Snood's head.

Doug leaned forward in the wagon seat and yelled, "Who's that on the bench?"

"It's Snood. He's unconscious. He was probably suspicious, and was waiting here to see if we came to the shop tonight. The guy we saw running away probably sneaked up behind him and knocked him out, perhaps intending to rob him. It serves Snood right for being such a snoop. I'll telephone for an ambulance wagon while you move this load into the shop."

"Don't you think you should stay with Snood?"

"No. You aren't supposed to move an injured person, especially when they are unconscious. There's nothing we can do for him but call an ambulance. We need to get our load out of sight before people arrive, or it could raise questions that would be hard to answer."

Bob took his horse over to the shop and opened the large front door. Then while putting his horse in the corral behind the shop, he used his wrist telephone to call for the ambulance. Doug expertly backed the wagon into the shop, commanding the horses, "Back, back, back . . ." When the wagon was inside, Doug unhitched the horses and put them in the corral with Bob's horse.

Bob hooked the chain hoist to the shipping pallet with a cable sling and started hoisting the cylinders off the hay wagon. He wanted to get the pallet out of sight before the ambulance arrived.

Doug rushed into the shop, locking the front double doors behind him. "My God, Bob, kill the light. It looks like Snood is waking up. He was moving and rubbing his head. I hope he didn't see anything."

The two breathlessly stood in the darkness hoping they wouldn't hear a knock at the door. The pallet and its precious cargo hung precariously in the air several feet above the wagon. A few minutes later, they heard a light tapping. Doug whispered, "Shall we open the door a crack to see who it is?"

"I guess so," Bob whispered.

There was more tapping. Bob opened one of the double doors a crack, fearing it might be Snood. "Well, there's no one at the door, and Snood isn't on the bench. We'd better call and cancel the ambulance wagon."

"That wouldn't do any good. They're already on their way by now.."

Bob and Doug went outside, closed the door and walked around the shop to see what was causing the sound. A light breeze was causing a bush limb to tap on the building. The joke nature played on them with this harmless bush limb, that had caused them so much panic minutes earlier, made the men chuckle.

As they went back around toward the shop's front door, the men saw the ambulance wagon stop in front of the park bench. Bob hurried over to the ambulance. "Sorry, boys, Mr. Snood regained consciousness and walked away a few minutes ago." The ambulance driver uttered a few choice profanities and left.

Now that all the interlopers were gone, Doug ran to retrieve his horses while Bob opened the double doors. The men quickly hitched the horses to the wagon and pulled it out of the shop, parking it a short distance away. After they were back in the shop with the doors locked, they laid some boards on the shop's dirt floor to make a solid walkway. Then they lowered the pallet of graphite cylinders onto a heavy-duty handcart, pulled it along the boards into a back corner of the shop, and tied a heavy tarp over it. By this time, both of them were sweating profusely.

"Well, we did it," Bob said triumphantly.

"Yeah, we sure did. Let's go home."

Bob had just locked the shop doors behind them when a voice emerged from the darkness. "What are you two doing out here this time of night?" Sheriff Lock asked.

CHAPTER 26
TANGLED WEB

Hearing the sheriff's voice, Bob felt a jolt go through his body. His heart leaped in his chest. "I – I . . ." he stammered,

Doug jumped into the conversation. "Bob helped me pick up a load of hay that had been spilled and abandoned along the road between here and Greensville, and we stopped by Bob's shop on our way home to check on something. What brings you out here this late, Sheriff?"

"Morton Snood pounded on my door and said that he'd been attacked and knocked unconscious just across the street. He thought it might be robbers, but didn't see who it was. He insisted that I investigate immediately. Did you see anything suspicious?"

Doug said, "Yes. When we arrived a little while ago, we saw Snood slumped on the park bench across the street, and someone running away through the park. Snood was unconscious, and we telephoned for an ambulance."

"Why didn't you immediately report this incident to me?"

"We felt that it was more important to call for the ambulance. By the time we got off the telephone, Snood had regained consciousness and left. We didn't see anyone else around. Knowing Snood, we figured he'd report it to you immediately."

"Why didn't one of you stay with Snood when he was unconscious?"

"He was resting comfortably on the bench, and wasn't bleeding. We know that an injured person shouldn't be moved by someone that has no medical training, so there was nothing more we could do for him until the ambulance arrived. We went to the shop to see if anyone had broken in, but we kept an eye on Snood. He'd already left by the time the ambulance got here. There wasn't any evidence of the shop having been broken into. Was anything stolen from Snood?"

"That's the strange thing. Nothing was taken from Snood. You must have scared the robber off before he could get anything."

"Yeah, I guess that's probably it."

"Well, call me if you remember anything else you think I should know."

"Okay, Sheriff."

After the sheriff left, Bob said, "I'm sure glad you answered the sheriff's questions. I was so rattled I couldn't think straight."

"I could see that. Let's go home before anything else happens."

"I'm sorry you had to add more to our big tangled web of lies."

"I didn't really lie about anything except the reasons for our actions, and there's no way for anyone to know I lied as long as we stay consistent in our story."

Bob tied a lead rope from his horse to the back of the wagon so he could ride in the wagon seat beside Doug and discuss their plans.

Bob said, "I think it would be wise to keep shop visitors from seeing what I'm machining."

"How do you plan to do that?"

"I could drape heavy tarpaulins around the work area."

"I don't think that would work. It would be too easy for someone like Snood to lift the tarp up for a peek. How about building an inside room, and putting in a lockable door?"

"Lumber's too expensive."

"Maybe we could salvage some from the old mill."

*　　　*　　　*

The next morning, Bob and Doug went to the old mill with the hay wagon and some tools. Windows and much of the exterior lumber had already been scavenged. However, most of the flooring and some of the framing and outer plywood sub-walls were still intact. The men spent two long days removing plywood, flooring, 2 X 12 joists, 2 X 4 framing lumber, and an interior door, and hauling them to the blacksmith shop.

Snood had recovered nicely; his encounter with the robber in the park evidently hadn't slowed him down. As Bob and Doug were getting the last of the lumber they needed, Snood came into the old mill saying, "Hi guys. I saw your wagon outside. What are you going to do with all that lumber?"

"It's none of your business. I'm sick of having you snoop into everything I do, " Bob replied in a testy tone of voice.

Red faced, Snood stomped out of the mill and Doug asked, "Are you sure that was the right way to respond? That jerk is apt to go to the sheriff again."

"Oh, I don't think he will. He knows that salvaging stuff from the mill is legal now. Besides, I believe the sheriff is tired of all Snood's meddling, and needless trouble-making. I decided not to make up a cover story this time—I'm afraid I'm going to slip and get caught in the web we've already spun. We've told so many lies that I hardly know what's true any more."

For the next month, Bob worked on customers' jobs during normal business hours, and build a lockable, windowless, inner room along one inside wall of the blacksmith shop during evenings and weekends. He found out why not all the lumber had been scavenged from the mill: it was so old and brittle that it was hard to drive nails into it. The nails tended either to bend or to split the wood.

The room had a wood floor to support the precision machining equipment, and reinforced ceiling joists strong enough to support the chain hoist and its heavy load. Doug helped when he could, but it was the beginning of the busy season on his farm. When the room was finished, Doug helped Bob move the milling machine and lathe, from the concrete floor in the corner of the shop, onto the wooden floor in the inner room. Then they moved the graphite cylinders from under their tarp into the room and locked the door.

Although Bob was already exhausted from doing all the extra work on top of his regular job, he immediately started building the special attachment that would allow him to use his milling machine to cut and groove the solid inner core cylinder to the proper outside configuration.

By the time he finished building the attachment outside his normal working hours, Bob was beyond exhaustion. One morning, Audrey saw him stagger on his way out of the house on his way to work. He looked pale and drawn.

"Bob Parker, you're ill. Get back in here. I'm putting you to bed and calling the doctor."

"But, I've got to keep the customers' machining jobs caught up so I can work on the heat storage core."

"Look at you. If you keep driving yourself like this, you may permanently damage your health, or go to sleep operating a machine and lose an arm, a hand, or worse. Now, get back in here!"

Bob started to turn around, but lost consciousness and fell to the floor. When he woke, he was in bed. The doctor was bending over him listening to his heart with a stethoscope. Doug and Audrey were standing nearby looking worried.

"Well, Doctor, what's wrong with him?"

"Mrs. Parker, as nearly as I can tell, he's suffering from extreme exhaustion. He'll need bed rest for several days. His heart doesn't appear to have been damaged, but I'll draw some blood and have the enzymes analyzed to determine for sure."

Bob, now awake enough to understand what was being said, declared, "Doctor, I can't take time off from my work. I'm behind in my promised completion dates as it is."

"Mr. Parker, I think your customers will understand when they find out you're sick. If you don't rest and recover, you might seriously damage your heart and be an invalid the rest of your life."

Doug said, "Good God, Bob, stay in bed and recover."

"Yes. We and the community need you in good health," Audrey added.

"But . . ." Bob started to object.

"Please, Dear," Audrey said in a quavering voice.

"Oh—okay, if you insist," Bob said reluctantly.

After the doctor and Doug left, Audrey burst into tears. "I – I thought I was going to lose you. Please take care of yourself—for me."

During the next three days Audrey took care of Bob, babying him and doing everything she could except spoon feed him. She would have done that too if he hadn't objected. Every day, Bob started to get up to go to work, but Audrey persuaded him to stay in bed, reminding him about what the Doctor had said about the danger of permanent disability. On the fourth day, the Doctor's report came by mail. The blood work showed there hadn't been any heart damage. When Bob read it, there was no holding him back. He jumped out of bed, had breakfast and headed for work.

As he finished breakfast, he told Audrey, "While I was lying in bed all those days, I had a chance to plan how I'm going to get the heavy cylinders through the brush and into the cavern."

"How?"

"I'll tell you later. Right now I've got to catch up on my work," he said as he hurried out the back door.

For the next two weeks, Bob concentrated on getting his normal blacksmith work back on schedule. As the Doctor had predicted, Bob's customers forgave him for being a few days late on his promised delivery dates. When Bob had gotten his regular work back on schedule, he began machining the heat storage core.

Late one night, Bob was working in the new inner machining room with the door closed. He was putting the finishing touches on machining the solid core cylinder. The lights were off in the rest of the shop, so it looked completely dark from the outside. The sheriff was passing by on his final patrol of the night. He knocked, then pounded on the front door. Bob couldn't hear the knocking and pounding over the noise of the machine.

CHAPTER 27
RAILROAD

Early the next morning, sheriff Lock knocked on the front door of Bob and Audrey's cottage. When Bob opened the door, the sheriff said, "I'm on my morning patrol, and I want to ask you a question. Late last night I heard a machine running in your shop. That seemed strange because it looked dark inside. I knocked, but no one answered. The door was locked, and I didn't see any sign of a break-in. It was so late I decided not to telephone you. Were you working last night?"

Bob thought for a moment organizing plausible answers to the question and several others he thought would be coming. Then he said, "Yes."

"I thought it might be something like that. I'm glad I didn't phone your house that late at night and wake Audrey. I figured the machine noise kept you from hearing me pounding on the door. What were you working on that late without lights?"

"I'm building a high temperature inert gas filled furnace and crucible for casting high temperature metals. I was working in the inside room that I built. It saves heat in the winter, and keeps out heat from the forge in the summer. The room has a light, so I turn the lights off in the main part of the shop to conserve electricity."

Bob was terrified that the sheriff would not accept his explanation and would probe deeper. He hated to add any more lies to the already huge tangled web.

"Okay, Bob."

"Thank you, sheriff, I appreciate your concern."

As the sheriff left, Bob wanted to shout, "He bought it! Thank God he bought it." Instead, he quietly closed the door..

Audrey wandered into the living room in her bathrobe. "I heard the sheriff's voice. What did he want this early in the morning?"

Bob described his conversation with the sheriff, then felt relief as he was finally able to vocally express his jubilation. "Thank God he bought it!"

Audrey looked perplexed. "What are you going to do if he goes back past the shop this evening and wants to see what you're making?"

"No problem. I've finished machining the core, and I plan to move it and the outer cylinder to the cavern as soon as I build equipment for moving them through the path of thinned brush. This equipment will look ordinary to a casual observer, so I can build most of it in the main part of the shop. I'll hide the graphite cylinders under a tightly tied-on tarpaulin in a back corner of the inner room until I've completed the moving equipment."

"Oh, that's right, you mentioned earlier you'd thought of a way to move the cylinders through the brush. What is it?"

"I'll build a small, narrow railway using heavy-wall pipe for rails and supporting structure. It'll be in sections that can be bolted together on support legs high enough that brush in the thinned path can be bent up around both sides. That way, the brush won't have to be cut or broken. I'll build a small, heavy duty railroad cart to carry the cylinders. At the tunnel-entrance end of the track I'll install an elevated turntable, on the same level as the track, that will allow us to turn the cart 90-degrees to line up with a ramp down into the tunnel entrance. From there, we can use pry-bars to push the cart and steer it in the cavern."

"That sounds like it might work, but the cart and load of graphite cylinders will be awfully heavy. The solid core cylinder weighs 900-pounds, and the hollow cylinder weighs about 140-pounds. How much do you think the cart will weigh? Will pry-bars work for moving it?"

"I estimate the cart at about 275 pounds. That'll make a total of 1,315 pounds. The lathe in my shop weighs about 1500-pounds, and we used pry bars to slide it along boards laid on the floor. I believe the same technique will work for sliding the cylinders from the wagon bed onto the cart, and for moving the cart along boards in the tunnel."

"Oh. I can see that you've thought this through."

"I've tried, but a lot of things could go wrong."

*　　　*　　　*

During the next five weeks, Bob worked at night and on weekends to build the sections of track, supporting structures, railroad cart, and turntable. When all was ready, he stopped at

Doug's house after work. "Could you bring your hay wagon to the blacksmith shop after dinner? I've finished building the equipment to move the graphite into the cavern."

"That's good news. But this time of year it'll still be daylight after dinner."

"That's okay. The equipment doesn't look unusual, so we can openly haul it to my house at dusk rather than waiting for total darkness. If anyone asks about it, I'll say that I built it as a hobby to entertain my nieces and nephews when they come for visits. That way, after using it for its real purpose, I could set it up behind my house to store it."

After dinner, Doug and Bob arrived at the shop as planned. Doug backed his wagon in through the double doors. Then the two started loading the railroad equipment onto the wagon. Just as they were loading the last piece, the sheriff came into the shop and asked, "What's all this stuff?"

Bob was glad that he'd thought of a good cover story, and he confidently told it to the sheriff.

"That seems like a lot of work to put into a kids toy," the sheriff said, drawing one corner of his mouth up and shaking his head.

"I had fun building it."

The sheriff left, muttering, "Boy, some people have strange ideas about what's fun."

Doug and Bob drove the wagon out and locked the shop. It was dark by the time Doug arrived beside the brush patch. However, a full moon gave enough light for the men to do the work. Doug and Bob quickly unloaded the miniature railroad equipment, starting with the turntable on its stand. They installed the turntable in front of the tunnel entrance It was difficult getting the turntable and sections of track through the remaining brush in the thinned path. Every clump of vine maple had to be bent over far enough that items could be lifted past it, and then had to be repositioned around the sides to look as undisturbed as possible. Finally, the men quickly bolted together all the elevated track sections from the turntable back to just inside the outer edge of the brush patch. An off-ramp into the tunnel was attached to one side of the turntable. Doug placed boards along the tunnel floor from the bottom of the ramp, then he and Bob moved the cart from the wagon onto the tracks. The railway was ready for action, but by now it was nearly dawn.

It was essential to get the cylinders into the tunnel before daylight, and Bob decided there was not enough remaining nighttime to haul them from the shop to the brush patch. The railroad track was black and well hidden by the brush, so after pulling a few vine maples outward and over the outer end to camouflage the track, it could be safely left in place. However, if anyone came to Bob's house expecting to see the miniature railroad, it would be hard to explain where it was without revealing the secret of the brush patch. In the remaining time before dawn, Doug drove the wagon to the road. Bob and Doug raked the surface of the potato patch dirt to erase the tracks made by the horses and wagon. The sun was just peeking over the distant, purple mountains, and reflecting off a few puffy pink clouds when Bob and Doug finished. It was Sunday, and both men were looking forward to taking the day off for a much-needed rest.

Just as Bob and Doug finished putting the rakes away in Bob's shed, they heard a voice from the direction of the road.

"What are you two up to now?"

They spun around. It was Morton Snood sitting on a horse, leaning forward in his saddle and peering at them.

CHAPTER 28
OUT OF SIGHT

Not knowing how much Snood had seen, Bob was shocked and flustered.

Doug immediately answered. "Not that it's any of your business, but we were just getting a shovel to dig up one of Bob's potato plants to see if the they're ready for harvest. Now why don't you go on and mind your own business?"

Snood's face flushed and contorted with anger. He gave his horse a hard kick and rode off at a gallop toward Stoneville.

Bob looked at Doug and asked, "Do you think that nosey old bastard saw what we were really doing?"

"I don't know. Let's hope not, or he could come back out here with the sheriff. I'd better dig up one of the plants nearest the road just in case."

Because of Snood's intrusion, Bob decided to wait an extra day before moving the graphite cylinders into the tunnel. However, he made this decision with great trepidation since it meant he'd have to leave the railway components hidden in the brush patch instead of placing them out in the open behind his house. If the sheriff came by expecting to see the railway set up for Bob's nephews, it would be hard to explain why it was nowhere in sight. Bob thought: I wish the sheriff hadn't seen the components at the shop. Then he came up with at least a weak excuse to explain the missing railroad. He decided to say that the kids couldn't wait for a visit to his house, so he shipped the railroad to them. He hoped he wouldn't have to use the excuse, since it would mean spinning more lies, a potential death trap that was already getting out of hand.

*   *   *

Two days went by without incident, and it was time to transport the cylinders into the tunnel out of sight. Bob decided to cover them in the wagon with a load of hay, and move them during darkness in the wee hours of the morning. He mounted the cylinders on their original shipping pallet, with the hollow cylinder slipped over the solid one to protect its fragile ribbed surface.

Bob and Doug arrived at the shop about 2 a.m., backed the wagon in through the double front doors, then unhitched the horses and took them around to the rear of the shop where they couldn't be seen from the road. They brought the pallet of graphite on a hand-cart to the rear of the wagon. While Doug pitched hay from the middle of the wagon toward both ends, Bob used the chain hoist to lift the pallet with its 1,315-pound load from the hand-cart. He and Doug moved the hand cart, then pushed the wagon under the load, lowered the load, and covered it with hay. Doug brought the horses around, hitched them to the wagon, and drove out of the shop. Bob locked the shop and joined Doug in the wagon seat.

After the twenty-minute trip to the brush patch, Doug stopped the wagon so the pallet of cylinders was near the outside end of the miniature railroad track. While he blocked the wagon's wheels and tossed hay off the cylinders to both ends of the wagon, Bob moved the railroad cart onto the end of the track, then blocked the cart's wheels so it wouldn't move while the pallet was being slid onto it. The men used pry bars to slide the heavily loaded pallet inch-by-inch off the wagon onto the cart. When the cylinder pallet was on the cart, Bob unblocked the cart's wheels, and easily pushed it along the track to the turntable. Everything went exceptionally well for a while, but then, trouble! The turntable wouldn't turn more than about 20-degrees, even with both men pulling on it. The turntable had to be rotated 90-degrees to line up with ramp into the tunnel.

"Crap, Bob. What's wrong?"

"It's stuck."

"I can see that. I mean why is it stuck?"

"I don't know. I the turntable has a well-greased bronze sleeve-bearing, and a polished, greased thrust bearing, so it should turn easily."

"My God, I hope we can get this load into the tunnel before daybreak."

The men pulled and yanked on the turntable for ten minutes trying to turn it. Finally, with sweat running down their faces and dripping off their chins, Bob said, "I'll go get a pry bar."

Bob hurried to the wagon and retrieved one of the wooden pry bars. Back at the turntable, he slipped one end of the bar between two beams in the turntable's rotor frame. Both men pulled with all their might. Nothing. They gathered all their strength, and yanked and pulled as hard as they could. The wooden bar snapped and they both tumbled backward, landing in the surrounding vine maple brush. By this time, they were so exhausted and discouraged that they turned off their flashlights and sat dejectedly on a rock pile near the tunnel entrance. At that moment, another flashlight approached, and they heard a feminine voice.

"Hi guys. I just wanted to see how you're doing. I expected you to be finished by now."

Bob said, "The damn turntable's stuck. No matter what we do, we just can't get it to turn more than 20-degrees. We sure don't want to leave the cylinders out here after daylight."

"Here, let me try to see what's wrong," Audrey said.

"Go ahead if you want to, but I don't think it's anything you can see. There's probably something wrong inside the bearing," Bob replied in a depressed tone of voice.

Audrey shined her flashlight around on the turntable structure and carefully looked it over. She was able to force her head and slender torso through a small opening in the framework and look underneath the backside of the turntable assembly. She said, "Oh, here's the trouble."

The men simultaneously exclaimed, "Huh?" as they jumped to their feet, beads of sweat rolling down their faces."

"There's a vine maple sticking up between one of the turntable's braces and the support frame," Audrey said as she forced her hand forward and re-positioned the offending wood away from the sticking point.

After Audrey pulled herself out of the opening, she said, "Okay, try it now."

The turntable easily turned through its entire 90-degree range of rotation.

Bob looked admiringly at his wife who had, in less than five minutes, solved the problem he and Doug had been struggling with for most of an hour. Relieved, the three broke out in laughter.

Bob said, "Thanks, dear. I guess we were too focused on the possible mechanical problems." Then he lined the cart up with the tunnel entrance ramp and tied a rope around a board on the back of the shipping pallet and a cross-piece on the cart. He wrapped three turns of the rope around a cross brace of the turntable support structure to serve as a brake. Doug held the rope and played out slack while Bob pushed the cart onto the ramp. The 1,315-pound cart, restrained by the rope, gradually rolled down the ramp, and out onto the boards in the tunnel.

Audrey chortled jokingly. "Well, thanks to me, you've finally gotten our cargo where it belongs. If I hadn't come along, I'll bet you two would've been here into next week"

Bob chuckled as he shot back. "Oh we would've gotten it. We just weren't trying very hard."

Doug was also in a jovial mood. "I'm afraid she's got us Bob. Let's face it, we were trying to solve the problem by brute force, and we damn near killed ourselves trying."

It was dawn by the time the trio emerged from the vine-maple brush patch. The horses, still hitched to the wagon, were waiting at the end of the thinned path. Doug removed the blocks from the wheels, drove the wagon back to the road, and parked it. Hoof beats could be heard in the distance along the road. Bob and Audrey ran and got rakes from the shed to smooth the tracks in the potato patch. The hoof beats were approaching fast, and even with Doug's help there wouldn't be enough time to complete the smoothing job before the rider got there.

CHAPTER 29
VESSEL AND FOIL

Bob, Doug and Audrey raked furiously trying to cover the wagon tracks. When the rider was close enough to see what was going on, they forced themselves to slow down and rake at a normal speed. As the rider approached, they could see that it wasn't anyone they knew. He tipped his hat, and they waved back. When he was out of hearing range Audrey, struck by the irony of what had just happened, began to giggle. Bob grinned, then chuckled. Audrey leaned on her rake, opened her mouth, threw her head back, and roared with laughter. Then Bob started laughing. Doug joined in, and all three began laughing uncontrollably, steadying themselves on their rakes to keep from falling over. Tears streamed down their cheeks. The tension they'd felt minutes earlier was completely released. Finally, wiping away tears, Audrey said, "C'mon, let's get this finished before anyone else comes along.".

Doug drove the wagonload of cover-hay to his home while Audrey and Bob finished the smoothing job and returned rakes to the shed. They were weak with relief from having gotten their precious, dangerous cargo hidden without being seen. Bob said his muscles ached from his earlier application of brute force to the stuck turntable. By that time it was 5:30 a.m. and he took a four-hour nap before going to work at the shop. As he left, Audrey reminded him of the three-days he recently lost from exhaustion, and begged him not to work into the night.

"Don't worry, dear, I'll only be working on customers' jobs today," Bob said as he closed the door behind him.

Bob saddled his horse and rode to the shop. For the rest of the day and into the evening, he worked exclusively on projects for his customers. A lot of farm equipment needed repairing, and the jobs were pouring in. Many parts were no longer available and had to be custom built.

Maintenance and manufacturing manuals available for all equipment and components facilitated repair work, and even fabrication of parts for complex equipment. The manuals were published in a massive government effort shortly after the darkening. They were originally intended to assist prosecutors to distinguish between existing technology and new science in trials of persons suspected of working on new advanced science. However, the greatest benefit of the manuals was to enable future manufacture and maintenance of devices that existed up to the darkening. If not for the manuals, the world would probably have fallen completely back into the dark ages since there wouldn't have been manufacturing or repair guides for complex equipment, or a standard for new versus old science. Everyone would have been afraid maintenance or manufacturing efforts might be interpreted as new science. As long as persons doing this work followed the processes and procedures described in the manuals, they were safe.

After three weeks of long hours, intense effort, and ignoring Audrey's admonitions to not work so late, Bob had caught up on his work and could again build parts for the portable energy storage device. He began building a gas-tight vessel to be filled with argon gas to house the graphite heat-storage core and its surrounding layers of graphite foil super-insulation

* * *

While Bob was catching up on his customer work, Audrey was busy designing items for the project so she could procure the materials. She was having trouble deciding how much flexible, leather-like graphite foil to purchase for the insulation wrap. Her computations showed that 300-layers of foil, each layer separated from its neighboring layers by about five times the thickness of writing paper, would be excellent insulation wrapped in a space about 7-1/2 inches thick. However, it would require nearly a mile of foil. Purchasing that much would almost certainly raise hard-to-answer questions.

Audrey discussed the insulation with Doug, and they decided to reduce the insulation to 100-layers of foil. Although this would result in a higher heat leakage rate, it seemed a reasonable compromise between heat leakage and cost for a quick demonstration. Any long trips in the solar heat powered car would be taken immediately after the core was fully heated. That way, not enough heat would leak out through the insulation before the trip to appreciably reduce the range. Audrey calculated that the rate of heat leakage, even at the maximum core temperature, would be insignificant compared to the rate of heat usage by the engine during the trip.

One hundred layers would require about 1,200-feet (0.23-mile) of foil, an amount that wouldn't be as costly or as likely to raise hard-to-answer questions. The prime goal was to complete development of the prototype solar powered car without the scientific work being discovered, and before running out of credits.

Audrey began working to procure the foil.

The customer service clerk asked, "What thickness, width, and length do you want?"

"Five-thousandths of an inch thick by 30-inches wide, and 1,200-feet long."

"What are you going to use so much of this material for?"

"My husband has a blacksmith shop. He needs to make high temperature gaskets."

"We can't supply that length of foil in one continuous strip. It's made from short graphite fibers bound together in a process much like making paper. Our equipment limits the continuous length to 300-feet. Would four 300-foot rolls and one 50-foot roll work?"

"But that will mean losing some material at the end of each roll if there is not enough end-material to make a whole gasket."

"What size gaskets?"

Audrey hadn't expected this question, and became flustered. But she quickly gathered her wits. "They'll be various sizes depending on the customers' needs."

"Would the multiple rolls be acceptable if we give you five extra feet free of charge to compensate for roll ends?"

"Yes. Thank you."

"Then, we'll start working the material into our production schedule as soon as we receive payment. The normal price is 15-credits per foot, but in this quantity we'll only charge you nine credits per foot for a total of 10,800-credits."

This was a much higher price than Audrey had expected. It took her breath away. She was speechless for a few seconds. Then she said, "That's more than my husband authorized."

"We've never sold a batch this large before, and we may be able to do better on the price. Please wait while I talk to my supervisor."

In a few minutes, the clerk returned and said, "Since it's such a large batch, we can offer it to you for 6 credits per foot for a total of 7,200-credits. That price per foot will only apply to a batch of 1200-feet or more, and we reserve the right to increase the price for future batches."

Audrey decided to ask Doug if he could cover this much cost, so she said, "That seems quite reasonable, but let me get back to you"

"One other thing. Because of the quantity, we can't deliver right away. We don't normally supply batches that large. We believe it will take about five weeks to work it into our production. Is this a problem?"

Audrey thought for a moment. She knew Bob would have to build some kind of device to dimple the foil, pressing little peaks in it to separate the layers. Then she said, "It won't be a problem if you can give us at least a small amount right away so my husband can test the gasket cutters he's making and start cutting a few gaskets."

"Would an immediate ten-foot sample of 20-inch wide foil meet your husband's needs during the delay?"

"Yes."

After hanging up the phone, Audrey walked to Doug's house. He was using a horse-drawn rake to make long furrows of newly cut hay ready for pickup. She walked into the field, waved Doug down, and asked, "Can you afford 7,200-credits for foil?"

Doug's eyes widened, his brow furrowed, and his mouth turned down at the corners. Seeing his reaction, Audrey feared the worst.

CHAPTER 30
ONWARD

Audrey could tell that Doug was struggling with the thought of investing another 7,500 credits in the project.

"My God, Audrey, I already spent 81,000-credits getting the graphite here. We're spending credits like drunks in a casino. I didn't expect to have to spend a lot more right away."

"For crying out loud, Doug, I got the best deal I could. At first, they wanted 10,800-credits for the foil."

"Okay, okay, don't get mad. I'm just feeling the pinch of lower income from not getting farm work done during all the studying and designing I did in the cavern.

"I miss-spoke. I should have asked if you could afford 3,750-credits for half of the cost. Bob's business has been good recently. In fact, he had to quit working on the solar powered car for a few weeks to catch up on jobs for his customers. We should be able to pay half of the foil cost."

"Okay, I can afford half. But, I'm worried about how much more this is going to cost before we have a working prototype. We still have to obtain or build a car to demonstrate the energy storage device and Stirling engine. I suppose we could just demonstrate them in a stationary test rack, but that wouldn't reach a large number of people in a short enough time to have the impact we need. Driving a solar powered car around in different towns would be much better. Our only chance we have to avoid prosecution for violating the anti-science law is for a large segment of the population to want one of these cars."

"Don't worry about getting a car in which to demonstrate our solar propulsion system. I inherited an old car from my Grandfather many years ago, but I was never able to drive it because gas was too expensive. It's covered with a tarp, and buried under the junk in our shed. Bob wanted me to get rid of it to make room for things that are stored in our hayloft, but it was my grandfather's favorite toy, and it's my only remembrance of him."

"That's a big relief! But why didn't you tell me about that earlier? I've been worried about how much a car might cost, even if we built it ourselves."

"Sorry. I've been so preoccupied with the first part of the project that I didn't think to mention the car to you sooner. It's very old, but it's in good shape since all the materials that would have deteriorated, like neoprene and rubber, were treated with preservatives before I got it."

When she got home, Audrey ordered the graphite foil, then started designing supports to hold the heat storage core centered within the containment vessel. These had to be rods or tubes strong enough to support more than 900-pounds and withstand additional forces due to bouncing up and down on the road. In addition, the supports had to have low thermal conductivity so they wouldn't drain heat from the core. They also had to withstand 3,600 degrees Fahrenheit. Audrey was stumped about what material to use, so she went to the cavern library for some intense study.

*   *   *

A few weeks later, Bob had nearly finished the containment vessel. Now he wanted two short pieces of stainless steel: a heavy wall pipe, and a rod to try an idea he had for a heat exchanger to transfer heat from the storage core to the engine's working gas. He would have asked Audrey to order them, but she was still busy trying to find a material for the core supports. Rather than overload her with another procurement job, or hand it to Doug who was busy with his farm work, Bob decided to procure the stainless steel himself.

He found that the cost per foot of new stainless steel pipe was even more expensive than solid rod. That gave him an idea. He searched the net and found a naval scrap-metal yard specializing in salvage from old engine-propelled ships, dating back almost 200-years to when diesel and coal were still relatively available. After the Great Shortages and The Darkening, ships using diesel and coal power were obsolete and had to be converted to sail-power similar to pre- 20th century ships.

Bob called the naval scrap-metal yard. "I'm interested in your stainless steel shafts. Do you have any 2-1/4 inch and 1-7/8 inch in diameter?"

"Yes."

"What is the price of shortest length of 2-1/4 inch diameter you have?"

"We have a 10-foot length that I can let you have for 10,000-credits."

Bob knew that even salvaged stainless would be expensive, but this was much more than he'd expected. He began to sweat.

"That seems like a lot of credits for scrap metal."

"These shafts are like new. They're polished for smooth running in bearings, and they have a diameter accuracy within one thousandth of an inch."

"Do you have any rough, less accurate shafts that are cheaper?"

"What are you going to use them for?"

There it was, the inevitable "what for" question everyone always seemed to ask. It made Bob angry.

"It's none of your business. Do you want to sell me some material or not?"

"Sorry, sir, I just wanted to get a feel for how smooth and accurate you need the diameter to be. I guess I should have asked the question that way."

Bob, hearing the man's polite apology, immediately cooled down. "I'm going to make a heavy wall pipe out by boring out the 2-1/4 inch rod, and make a solid cylindrical part by machining the other rod."

"Then I've got a good deal for you. We have rough 2-1/4 inch schedule-80 heavy-wall stainless pipe, and rough 1-7/8 inch stainless rod that I can let you have for 250-credits a foot and 140-credits a foot, respectively, and I can cut them to any length you want."

"That's more like it. I'm surprised those weren't listed on the net."

"Just an oversight in this month's posting. Now, how much do you want, where do I send it, and how are you going to pay for it?"

Bob ordered two feet each of the rod pipe and rod, and charged it to his on-line credit account.

*   *   *

Meanwhile, Audrey pored over books in the cavern library. She finally chose a material she thought would work for core support tubes. Vitreous carbon, a glasslike form of carbon, had all the right properties: strength at high temperatures, had low thermal conductivity, and would block radiant heat loss if the tube's hollow center were filled with foil super-insulation. Even though vitreous carbon was brittle, she felt that with thick enough sections it would be strong enough to resist breakage. She returned to her computer, found a supplier on the network, and ordered ten tubes (including one extra).

Audrey had located and purchased most of the items and materials needed for the project, but when she got to the quartz window for the solar energy injection port, she was completely stymied. After working without success for two weeks trying to find one, she got together with Bob and Doug.

"Guys, I'm at a dead end on the quartz window. We may have to give up on the idea of direct solar recharging the heat storage core."

Bob looked perplexed. "If we do that, we might as well have just performed a static demonstration using the electrically heated core we found in the cavern and saved ourselves most of the work."

Doug and Audrey both tried to speak at once. Doug won. "No. The device in the cavern is too small, it doesn't have adequate insulation, and it wouldn't impress the public fast enough to save our necks."

CHAPTER 31
STOVES AND CHANGES

Audrey tried without success for several more days to find a quartz window. Finally, she shifted her network search criterion from "Quartz" to "High Temperature Windows."

Immediately, a number of categories popped up. One was stove windows. Audrey remembered seeing a stove in a rich man's home when she was a little girl. There was a large, heat-resistant window in the stove's door through which red and yellow flames could be seen cheerily dancing over the fuel. Due to the shortage and high cost of wood and coal, such stoves were now seldom found in homes. She searched for stove windows, and found only one supplier. With a limited market and no competitive manufacturers, the price for the new windows was thousands of credits, so she changed the search criterion to "used stoves." She was excited to find a woodstove listed at a local junkyard.

Audrey's heart pounded as she telephoned. "I'm interested in the woodstove you have listed on your network site."

"I'm sorry. The stove sat here for a long time without being sold, so we sent it to a scrap metal company just yesterday. I wish you'd called earlier"

"I do too. Did it have a large window in the door?"

"Yes. What did you want the stove for."

Oops! There was the "what for" question again. If she got snippy and refused to answer the clerk, she might not get an answer to a question she needed to ask. Audrey thought hard for a good explanation, and mentally chastised herself for not thinking about it before she called. Finally, she said, "I want to use it for a decorative planter in my flower garden. What scrap metal yard did you sell it to?"

"Marlin's in Greensville."

"Okay, thanks."

Audrey telephoned Marlin's. "I'm interested in a woodstove you got in yesterday. Do you still have it?"

"I'm not sure. Let me check whether it has been crushed for melting."

Audrey's heart was pounding and her face felt hot as she waited for news she feared would be bad.

Finally, after what seemed like a day or two, the clerk returned. "The stove hasn't been crushed yet."

"Would you sell it to me?"

"Yes."

After negotiating a price, Audrey said, "Please hold it for me. I'll leave immediately to come for it."

Audrey planned to remove the window and carry it back in a saddlebag, leaving the rest of the stove in the scrap metal yard. After gathering up a few tools, she left a note for Bob, saddled her horse, strapped on saddlebags, and left for Greensville.

Five hours later, Audrey arrived at Marlin's. She anxiously went to the pile of items where the stove was located. Thankfully, the stove was on the outside of the pile. However, Audrey was appalled at what she saw. The stove's window was missing! At Marlin's office, she fought to calm herself as she asked the clerk, "Where's the window from the stove?"

"Usually, glass windows are removed from scrap metal items before they're shipped to us."

Suddenly, it dawned on Audrey what had happened. Her face and ears felt hot, and she could feel pounding pressure in the blood vessels on her forehead. "That stupid worker I talked to at the junkyard! I asked him if the stove had a window, and he said yes. He didn't have the presence of mind to tell me that it had been removed before the stove was shipped in the load of scrap metal, and I stupidly didn't ask"

Muttering "Stupid! Stupid! Stupid! . . ." to herself, Audrey began her long return trip home.

The day was surrendering to darkness by the time Audrey got home. Bob had prepared dinner, and was keeping it hot for her. He took Audrey into his arms and kissed her. "You've had quite a trip. Are you tired dear?"

"Tired doesn't begin to describe it. I'm totally exhausted, partly because of getting so mad. Thanks for having dinner ready. Otherwise, I probably would've just fallen into bed without any."

"Why were you mad?"

Audrey told Bob about stove windows and the junkyard worker's stupidity—and her own for not at least asking if the window was still in the stove before she left for Greensville that morning.

"I was so excited, about finding something that should work for the solar window, that I didn't ask all the questions I should have."

"Well, we're learning as we go. It isn't practical to think of every single thing before getting into a project. I used to try to plan projects that way, but it took three times as much planning, and I still missed some things. It's a lot faster to quickly plan a rough outline and some of the details, then be flexible and figure some things out as you go."

"I suppose you're right. But I still feel stupid for not asking more about the window before traveling all that distance."

"I hate to tell you this, dear, but I've found some serious flaws in the heat storage unit design you and Doug came up with. I think I have solutions for them, but I imagine you're too tired to think about it now, and we'll need to bring Doug in on it too. I'll discuss it with you two in the morning."

"Good. I'm just too exhausted tonight."

*   *   *

It was 8 a.m. when Audrey awoke, even though she'd gone to bed at 8:30-the night before. When she came into the kitchen, Bob and Doug were sitting at the table.

"Well, hello sleepy head," Bob said. "I was beginning to wonder if you were still alive."

The two men chuckled, but Audrey, who hadn't had her coffee yet, failed to see the humor. She grumpily muttered to herself as she poured a cup of coffee and sipped a little. Bob had prepared breakfast, and the pleasant aroma of coffee, bacon, pancakes, and maple-flavored syrup permeated the kitchen.

Sunlight streamed in through the window, producing a golden rectangle of light on the floor and filling the room with a warm radiance. Audrey's mood shifted as she drank her coffee in the cheerful kitchen surroundings. She put pancakes on her plate and sat beside Bob.

Speaking with an attitude of authority, Bob said, "I'm sorry to tell you two this, but I've found a couple of serious errors in the design of the heat storage device."

Audrey looked curious, and Doug asked, "How so? We were careful with the mechanical and thermal theory in the design. Where do you think we went wrong?"

"Did you consider details of the solar charging, or how you would transfer of heat from the core to the working gas in the Stirling engine?"

Doug looked puzzled. "Yes, of course. But we haven't designed all of the parts for those functions yet."

"What does that have to do with the core design?" Audrey asked. " I designed a conical black-body solar absorption cavity in one end of the core, and you've already machined it."

"Yes, but did you think about how you would get sunlight into the cavity?"

"Of course. We'll focus a large dish-shaped solar furnace mirror into the cavity through the solar window."

"But what about the super insulation over the core?"

"We will just provide a hole in it for the focused sunlight to enter through."

"And what will happen after the core is white-hot, and the sunlight is removed?"

"Good God!" Audrey said. "The stored heat will be rapidly lost by radiation outward through the insulation hole after the core is charged and the storage unit is removed from the solar furnace. I was focused on so many other problems that I didn't think of that."

"I've come up with a design change that has a plug of insulation inside the containment vessel that can be moved into the hole after the core is charged."

Bob paused to let that thought sink in, then continued, "Now, what about the transfer of heat from the heat storage core to the working gas for the Stirling engine?"

Doug answered. "We've already realized that our earlier thoughts about using the ribbed core surface won't work because we don't have a good way to channel the gas past the ribs and still independently isolate gas pressure and flow to each of the four cylinders in the engine. We plan to make the sidewall of the super insulation movable. This way, the insulation can be retracted to allow radiant heat from the white-hot core to shine onto the inside of the containment vessel wall. Working gas for each cylinder of the engine will pass through one of four independent sections of tubing welded to the outside of the hot vessel wall. In this way, heat radiating from the core will heat the working gas for each cylinder, independently increasing its pressure."

"But what about the core support tubes that have to penetrate through the insulation?" Bob asked.

Doug thought for a few minutes about Bob's statement, then exclaimed, "Oh crap! They'll pin the insulation in place—it won't be movable. We didn't think of that aspect. I guess we were too focused on the theory and not enough on the practicality."

Bob smiled and said, "Here's a design change I think will solve that problem. I've been thinking about a cylindrical device I call an 'Extractor,' or 'Heat Exchanger' that can be inserted to selectable depths into a hole in the center of the heat storage core. In this way, it would absorb heat input at selectable rates and transfer it to the engine's working gas.

"The Extractor would have four independent quarter-round sectors tack-welded together to form a cylinder. Each sector would have an outer shell with internal, lengthwise fins closely fitted around a solid quarter-round center sector. Working gas from the cold side of each of the Stirling engine's four displacer cylinders would flow through a tube into the bottom of a sector shell. It would be heated by flowing through the shell's internal fins up to the top of the shell, then flow back down to the bottom through a hole drilled through the length of the solid center sector. The hot gas would then flow out through a tube to the hot end of the displacer. Working gas heated in this way will expand and push the engine's power piston down, powering the crankshaft one-half revolution. Then the displacer piston reverses, forcing the working gas back through the Extractor. Exiting the Extractor, the gas passes through a regenerator where it deposits some of its heat, then passes through a cooler where it gets cold, contracts, and allows the power piston to move upward completing a full revolution of the crankshaft. With four independent sectors in the heat exchanger, each of the engines four displacer and power cylinders can be timed to contribute power to the crankshaft.

"I guessed that the cylindrical Extractor's outside diameter, and its insertion hole in the core, might be about 2-inches in diameter and 15 inches long, but I don't know enough heat transfer theory to determine how big they need to be for the proper rate of radiant heat transfer."

"But won't the maximum core temperature of 3,600-degrees melt the stainless steel extractor?" Doug asked.

"No. Only enough of the Extractor will be inserted into the hole in the core to establish a balance between the heat input from the hot core, and the heat output to the engine. This will be adjusted to keep the maximum Extractor temperature below 1,200-degrees Fahrenheit, the maximum temperature limit for stainless steel in this application. If it starts getting too hot, the Extractor will be withdrawn far enough to keep its temperature below 1,200. I have a thermocouple instrument we can use to monitor Extractor tip's temperature."

Doug asked for a pencil and paper. He and Audrey began figuring as Bob left for the blacksmith shop.

About a half-hour later, Doug telephoned Bob, and placed the phone on speaker so Audrey could hear too. "Audrey and I calculated the radiant heat transfer from the core to a 2-inch diameter, 15-inch long Extractor. It would be far too low. The Extractor would have to be at least 40-inches in diameter to get about 50-horsepower transferred to the engine working gas at our estimated minimum usable core temperature when the heat storage core's energy is nearly discharged. That's impossible since the core diameter is only 24 inches."

Bob thought about Doug's statement, then said, "I don't want to make the Extractor diameter larger than about four-inches, since boring out the core reduces the amount of graphite and therefore, the storage capacity. When I was kibitzing one of your early study sessions, I heard you say energy is radiated from an object at a rate that depends on its temperature to the fourth power. If we set the minimum allowable core temperature higher than we'd originally planned, we should get a much greater rate of heat transfer to the Extractor. If we do that, will a 4-inch diameter Extractor work?"

"Hold on for a minute while we do some calculations."

A few minutes later, Doug returned to the phone. "You're right. If we assume a minimum usable core temperature of 1,950-degrees Fahrenheit, and 1,200-Fahrenheit or lower for the temperature of a four-inch diameter Extractor inserted 15-inches into the core, we should get a radiant heat energy transfer rate from the core to the extractor equivalent to about 25 horsepower. Although that's below the minimum power level we wanted, it's adequate for the lower limit as the core runs out of heat. We could probably get by with even lower minimum horsepower at core temperatures below 1,950-degrees."

Audrey asked, "Although a four-inch diameter Extractor should work, how are you going to move the Extractor in and out of the core without letting air into the containment vessel? The displacer/engine unit has to remain nearly stationary, and I don't know of any flexible tubing, that will withstand such high temperatures, for connecting it to a movable Extractor."

Bob gathered his wits for a moment, then said, "To move the Extractor in and out of the core, without moving the Extractor or letting air in, we'll move the core instead of the Extractor. I'll build a tubular bellows from thin stainless steel washers welded together on alternating inner and outer edges. This will form an accordion-like tube that can be stretched or compressed like a spring. One end of the bellows will be sealed to the end of the core containment vessel. The other end of the bellows will be sealed to the outer end of the Extractor, so the Extractor will be contained inside the bellows, even when it is fully withdrawn.

"The Extractor can be coupled to the stationary engine/displacer unit with rigid stainless steel pipes, since the Extractor will remain stationary. However, neither the heat storage core nor its container have any rigid external connections, so the core and its container can be moved on rollers forward and backward to insert and withdraw the Extractor in and out of the core."

"But is seems to me that energy would rapidly radiate outward from the white-hot core through the 4-inch access hole through the insulation when the Extractor it is not in use and is pulled completely out of the core."

"I'll fasten a stack of foil super-insulation over the end of the Extractor to prevent radiation loss. Completely withdrawing the Extractor will pull the end-stack of insulation into the Extractor's access hole through the core's insulation."

"It sounds like you've thought this through pretty well. I'm impressed and thankful you were able catch these problems in the design Audrey and I came up with. I guess we were too focused on the theory. "

Doug and Bob ended their phone conversation.

Audrey called the junkyard. "Do you have the window from the stove I talked to you about yesterday?"

CHAPTER 32
AUDREY'S WINDOW

Audrey listened intently as the junkyard man on the phone said, "The window isn't listed in our inventory yet. I'll have to ask the yard woman if we have it. Do you want to hold the phone, or shall I call you back?"

"I'll hold."

A short time later, the man said, "She believes she saved the window. If she did, it'll be in one of the piles of things she removed from items that were scrapped during the past week. She doesn't have time to look for it right now. The piles are at different locations all over the yard, and they haven't been inventoried yet. All of the parts will be inventoried and listed by the end of next week."

"Could I come right away and look for it myself?"

"Yeah. But you'll have to sign an agreement that you won't hold us responsible if you're injured in the yard, and if you break anything, you buy it. Why are you in such a rush?"

"I just want my decorative stove planter to look right, and it won't look as good without the window."

"If you still have the window, how much will you charge for it?"

"Well these windows are pretty scarce."

"Yes, but I only want it for a planter, so I'm not willing to spend a lot. Besides, I don't think there's much call for them since fuel is so expensive."

"Okay. How soon shall we expect you?"

"How much?"

"Oh, I guess I can let it go for 75 credits."

"Seventy five credits! I can't spend that much for just a planter."

"How much can you afford?"

"I think 20-credits would be reasonable."

"I can't let it go for that. How about 30-credits?"

"That sounds reasonable."

"How soon should we expect you?"

"Right away."

Audrey saddled her horse and left for the junkyard.

*　　　*　　　*

Bob needed sheet metal for making the steel accordion-like tubular bellows for containing the Extractor. New stainless steel sheet metal was expensive, so he decided try finding some scrap trimmings. He telephoned the junkyard, and learned they had some available in several thicknesses at a low price. He purchased more than enough stainless sheet scraps to make the bellows.

The clerk said, "Mr. Parker, your wife is here at the yard now. Shall I send the trimmings home with her?"

"Yes, that'd be fine."

Later, Doug came to the blacksmith shop to discuss more details of the design changes with Bob.

"How do you want to proceed?" Doug asked.

"I'll have to order the 4 inch stainless steel pipe and rod for the Extractor. I hope they'll let me return the smaller pipe and rod I ordered when I first decided to try the Extractor idea."

"How're you going to bore the insertion hole in the heat storage core for the Heat Extractor?"

"I'll have to use a drill and several boring heads in my milling machine to bore the hole 4-1/8 inches in diameter."

"Okay. I'll load my wagon with hay to use as a cover, and meet you at 2 a.m. to move the heat storage core back to the shop from the cavern."

"Let's wait 'til tomorrow when there'll be no moon—the darker the better.

"Okay."

Doug left for his farm, and Bob called the naval scrap metal yard to order the larger pipe and rod from which to make the Heat Extractor. He was relieved that they hadn't cut the smaller pipe and rod he'd ordered earlier, so he was able to change the order without any extra charges over those for the larger diameters.

*　　　*　　　*

Audrey sorted through many piles of parts at the local junkyard. Several times, she found plain glass windows, but not the heat-resistant stove window. She was about to give up when the sun broke out from behind the clouds and reflected off something shiny leaning against a pile of stovepipes on the other side of the junkyard. She hurried over to it. From its size, shape and retaining clip marks, she could see it was the stove window, and it was in perfect condition.

Audrey was so excited that she could barely control herself. She grabbed the window and hurried to the office.

Confronting the junkyard man, she said, "You told me this window would be in one of the piles of parts. I finally found it standing all by itself on the ground by some stovepipes. That cost me a lot of time, so I think you should compensate me by reducing the price."

"Mrs. Parker, after I agreed to 30-credits the owner chewed me out for selling the window to you at such a low price, so I'd like to increase it. But a deal is a deal. We'll let you have it for the price I promised you on the phone.

"By the way, your husband phoned in an order for some sheet metal scraps. He wants you to pay for them and bring them home."

Audrey paid for the window and sheet metal, and placed them in her saddlebags. She left the junkyard feeling satisfied for making a good deal on the heat resistant window.

When Bob got home from the shop that evening, Audrey proudly showed him the window.

Bob's eyes widened, and he grinned broadly as he said, "You did it! I was beginning to think you wouldn't be able to find a quartz window."

"Sorry to change materials on you, Dear. As you know, it's a window out of a stove. However, it's not quartz. But since it is made for direct contact with flame, it should withstand plenty of heat."

"Crap, Audrey, I thought stove windows were quartz. Why didn't you get quartz."

"Oh, for crying out loud, Bob. I worked hard for weeks looking for a pure quartz window, and couldn't find any. I believe this stove window is artificial quartz, which is purified silicon dioxide glass similar to natural quartz. Besides, I think a quartz window would have cost us thousands of credits if I could've even found one."

"But... ."

"Shut up, Bob! I worked hard to get this window, and I saved us a lot of credits. The least you can do is test it to see if it'll work. All you have to do is see if it holds up at 1,800-degrees Fahrenheit like quartz. If it doesn't, I'll renew my search, but I'm not sure natural quartz is even available any more. And, by the way, I'm worn out from all the effort of getting this window so you're fixing dinner tonight."

"I'm sorry, Dear, I guess I wasn't thinking. It's just that I'm worried. If we can't find a window that'll work, the whole project will go 'down the drain'. It's no use testing the window before it's installed in the heat storage unit. Since the window is transparent, most of the radiant energy from the sun will pass right through it, and it probably won't get up to 1,800-degrees. We can't be sure how hot it will get until we try solar charging the heat storage unit through it. Besides, if quartz isn't available, the stove window is our only option."

This calmed Audrey a little, but she was still smoldering and muttering to herself as she absent-mindedly started peeling potatoes. She'd evidently forgotten that Bob was supposed to fix dinner.

When the muttering stopped, Bob felt it was safe to speak again. "Doug and I will have to move the heat storage core back to the shop tomorrow night. I hope Snood or the sheriff won't be lurking around."

Just as Bob finished making that remark, there was a knock at the door. Bob and Audrey both jumped. Bob slowly opened the door dreading that it might be Snood or the sheriff. Instead, a stunningly beautiful stranger stood there.

"Robert Parker?"

"Yes."

"I'm Hortense Farb, District Special Materials Control Officer with the Office for Prevention of New Scientific Work.

CHAPTER 33
OFFICIAL SIREN

Bob was flustered by the beauty and potential danger of the woman standing in the doorway,. Evidently, the graphite cylinders and/or foil had attracted the attention of the anti-science government agency. The three scientific conspirators had been doing everything they could to avoid this kind of attention. Bob was speechless. Audrey, on the other hand, seemed prepared.

With a smile and a cordial sweep of her hand, she said, "Please, come in. Shall I call you Miss, Ms., or Mrs. Farb?"

"Miss Farb is fine."

"Please sit down Miss Farb. May I bring you a cup of tea or coffee?"

"Tea would be nice. I've ridden quite a distance today, and I'm parched."

Bob was sweating and half out of his mind with worry. He silently thanked God for Audrey's strength and intelligence, and her apparent ability to handle this situation. He was still unable to speak coherently enough to visit, but he could see that Audrey had a plan. He managed to say, "Stay put, Dear, I'll get the tea." That would give him a chance to recover so he'd be less likely to blither like an idiot and blurt out something incriminating.

When Bob returned, he was carrying a tray with three delicate china cups, a pot of tea, creamer, sugar, sugar-free sweetener, spoons and cookies. He'd calmed considerably and stopped sweating.

"What have you ladies been talking about while I was in the kitchen?"

"Miss Farb's here on an official visit, and she asked about the graphite. I explained about the graphite furnace you were building."

Audrey's mention of graphite stabbed into Bob's stomach like a red-hot poker and he blanched. His worst fears had just been realized. When Bob suddenly became pale, Audrey noticed and quickly added, "I haven't yet told her how buying the graphite nearly wiped out our savings account, and how the graphite cracked and had to be scrapped. I see that it still upsets you to think about it."

"Oh, I'm sorry Mr. and Mrs. Parker. I can see that you've suffered an awful loss. There is just one more question I have to ask: what did you do with the scrap from the ruined graphite?"

Bob felt like he was going to pass out, and was again speechless.

Without hesitation, Audrey said, "Bob broke it into small pieces to use as fuel in the forge. Graphite burns like coke when it's in small enough pieces and gets hot enough. At least we got a small benefit from that horrendous disaster."

"Surely, you haven't burned that much graphite already. I'd like to see the remaining pieces."

At that moment, someone knocked at the door. Bob got up, relieved to be out of Miss Farb's penetrating inquiry, even if only for a minute. It was Doug. Bob stepped outside, and closed the door.

"Bob, you're white as a corpse. What's wrong?"

"Oh God, Doug, my worst nightmare's come true."

Bob explained the situation to Doug, ending with, "And she wants to see the unburned scrap. What am I going to do?"

"You're going to show her the unburned scrap."

"How. I don't have any I can show her."

"Yes, you do. With your Heat Extractor design, we no longer need the hollow outer graphite cylinder. Since it's non-returnable, we may as well use it to prove your point."

"Oh, You're right. But it's not broken up into pieces for burning."

"I'll take care of that. My hay wagon's ready to go, and the outer cylinder isn't too heavy for me to carry. Give me your shop key, and stall the officer as long as you can."

Bob fished the keys out of his pocket, handed them over, and went back inside.

"What was that all about?" Audrey asked.

"Oh, that was the man I sometimes have help me in the shop. He hadn't finished all the work I assigned him, and he wants to finish it this evening."

"Mr. Parker, could we go to your shop right now and see the graphite scrap. I have to get something to eat and find a room for the night."

Audrey must have seen Doug at the door and guessed that he and Bob had formed a plan that would need time to play out. "Oh, Miss Farb, Bob and I were just about to prepare dinner when you arrived, and we'd love to have you join us. We don't have much company dropping in for visits. You could telephone the hotel to make your reservation from here, then you and Bob could go to the shop right after dinner."

"I appreciate the invitation. I've been traveling around from tribe-to-tribe in the Co-op for five days, and it would be nice to have a home-cooked meal for a change. However, Co-op rules prohibit me from accepting anything from persons I'm investigating."

"Well, your horse will have to be fed and watered, and it would save you time and effort to do that here. You must be tired, and we have plenty of hay. Besides, who's to know if you eat dinner here? There wouldn't be any record of it."

"Well... ."

"Oh, come on, it's not going to be a problem."

"Okay, my horse does need hay and water. I'll go take care of him while you two fix dinner."

Bob knew that Doug would be loading the graphite cylinder onto the wagon, which would be visible from the barn, and he said, "Miss Farb, why don't you rest and visit with Audrey. Let me take care of your horse. I know where everything is, and can do it much easier."

"All right. Thank you. I am awfully tired."

Bob lead Miss Farb's horse to the watering trough, then to the barn for some hay. Doug was driving his wagon along the far edge of the potato patch toward the brushy area, and he waved at Bob. Bob thought it's sure a good thing Miss Farb let me take care of her horse. No telling what she would have thought if she'd seen Doug going into the brushy area. I hate it every time I have to add another lie to this web we've woven. Sooner or later we're probably going to get trapped in it.

When Bob got back to the kitchen, he was relieved to see Miss Farb sitting with her back to the window visiting with

Audrey. As Bob sat down, he saw Doug driving his hay wagon rapidly toward the road.

*   *   *

After dinner, Bob and Miss Farb rode to the shop. When they arrived, the lights were on, and they found Doug inside.

Looking at Doug, Bob said, "Did you get finished?"

"Yes, Mr. Parker."

Bob thought Doug's formality was a nice touch in playing the part of a "hired hand."

Then Doug got a good look at Miss Farb. "Holy smoke! Hortense, is that you?

"Yes, but how do you know me?"

"Hortense Farb?"

"Yes. Should I know you?

"I'm Douglass. Douglass Murphy. You were in the sixth grade nineteen-years ago when I was in the seventh. We were in a school play together. You moved away the next year. I had a crush on you, and I always wondered what happened to you."

Hortense's eyes widened, and she flashed a grin revealing white, perfect teeth. "Oh! Doug Murphy! I had a crush on you too. How have you been?"

"Fine. Never better."

Bob was worried. Doug's face and body language had the look of a man who was totally smitten by this slender brunette beauty with fair skin and violet eyes. Even though her long chestnut hair was done up in a bun, and she was dressed in dusty gray riding pants, black boots, soiled leather riding gloves and a tan buckskin jacket, her beauty shone through. Any man walking past her would have stopped in his tracks and turned around for a second look.

The two paused for a long, penetrating look at each other, and Bob's fears began a crescendo that made his heart race. If these two got together, Doug might tell this official siren something that would raise the specter of the death penalty for their scientific work.

"C'mon Doug," Bob said forcefully. "Miss Farb came here for an inspection. We need to finish it so she can get to her hotel."

Bob's fears intensified even more on the way across the shop to the forge. Hortense and Doug couldn't take their eyes off each other. Even though there were pieces of graphite in the forge, Bob was starting to sweat.

"Miss Farb, are you satisfied?" Bob asked.

She glanced at the forge, and said, "Uh huh."

Bob tried to break Doug's trance by asking, "Doug, did you finish the cleanup I assigned you to do?"

"Uh huh."

"Doug. Doug? Hey!"

"Huh?"

"I saw your hay wagon outside."

This briefly brought Doug out of the apparent spell he was under.

"Oh. Oh yeah. My wagon. I thought I might sell some hay to the livery stable, but they're closed now so I'll have to bring it back tomorrow."

Then Doug locked eyes with Miss Farb again.

Bob tried again to bring Doug out of his trance. "Don't you think you should haul your hay home and get it under cover in case it rains tonight?"

"I didn't see a cloud in the sky, and I don't think it's going to rain," Miss Farb said in her musical feminine voice. Then she continued, "Doug, can you come over to my hotel for a visit. I have to leave tomorrow."

Doug looked pleased. "Yes."

Miss Farb appeared almost as smitten with Doug as he was with her. Since she wasn't married, Bob feared she could be longing for a suitable lifetime partner. Being such a beauty, she'd probably been bombarded with offers, but apparently hadn't found anyone that suited her—before now. Bob worried that their mutual attraction, even when they were children, might now blossom into a full-blown romance. He had visions from a myth he'd read in school, about sirens who lured seamen to their death in Homer's *The Odyssey*. Bob was horrified. His brain was on fire, about a four-alarm fire by now, as he said, "But the rain sometimes comes up suddenly. That's a lot of hay. You sure wouldn't want to get it wet. And how about your horses, Doug. They need to be fed and watered."

Doug came out of his trance just long enough to respond. "That's okay, I'll water 'em at the trough here in town, and I've got plenty of hay for them on the wagon."

Desperately trying to think of something else that might divert the potential disaster, Bob said, "But . . ."

Nothing else came to mind, and Bob wished he'd brought Audrey along for backup.

Doug and the Siren left together as a very worried Bob locked the shop and headed home.

CHAPTER 34
ROMANCE

Audrey was in the living room watching holovision when Bob got home. His face was pale, his forehead rumpled with worry.

"You look awful. What happened?" she asked.

Bob explained, ending with, "I'm terrified about what Doug might tell her while he's under Miss Farb's siren spell."

Audrey sighed. "Doug's smart. I don't think you have anything to worry about."

"But I've never seen him like this. He was acting as if he'd been drugged. I'm afraid his brain has turned to putty. There's no telling what he might say."

"Oh, I don't think it'll work that way. After all, they just met, and I don't think he'll get that familiar with her. She'll be moving on tomorrow, and that'll be that."

"Audrey, they knew each other as children, and had crushes on each other. And you know from experience how good looking and charming Doug is."

"What do you mean by 'from experience'?"

"I saw you two in the cavern the night he tried to seduce you."

"What! You spied on us? Don't you trust me? Why didn't you say anything about it? Why didn't you protect me? For all you knew, he could've attacked me."

Bob suddenly realized he'd stepped into it up to his kneecaps. He was so wrapped up in worry about Doug and the siren that he'd revealed the spying that he'd meant to keep secret. In a vain attempt to deflect Audrey's anger, he said, "Well, I stayed within earshot until I was sure you were all right." He thought for a moment, then continued, "Besides, I didn't see a very strong reaction from you. You just gently admonished him and told him how desirable he was."

This didn't have the guilt-shifting, argument-winning effect Bob was hoping for.

"Bob, you idiot, what would you have had me do? Slap him and scream? Pummel him with my fist? How do you think that would've affected our working relationship? Do you think we would have made all this progress on the project if I had done that?"

Bob leaned forward and placed his hand on Audrey's shoulder. "You're right, Dear, I'm sorry."

"You'd better be sorry. By the way, you're sleeping on the couch tonight."

*   *   *

While Bob was having his attitude adjusted by Audrey, Doug and Hortense were having a good visit in the lobby of the hotel. They talked until 4:00-a.m., catching up on each other's lives during the past nineteen-years.

Finally, Hortense glanced at her watch and said, "Oh, look what time it is. I need to get some sleep. In just a few hours, I have to leave for Greensville."

Doug would've liked to share her bed, but he remembered Audrey's rejection, and that women are considerably more fussy about such matters than men are. He tried desperately to think of a way to stay connected to this woman with whom he now felt he was falling in love. Whether from fatigue or poor judgment, he blurted out, "Hortense, I love you. Will you marry me?"

Hortense's eyes widened and her mouth dropped open. After an embarrassing pause, she said, "Doug, although we knew each other as children, and we learned a lot about other during our long visit tonight, we'll need to spend a lot of time together before even considering a lifetime commitment."

Doug looked down at the floor, then back at Hortense. "Do you love me?"

"I like you very much. In fact, so far I like you more than any of the other men who've proposed to me. But I need to know everything about a man before I even consider marrying him. I've always been disappointed in men after getting to know them well. They turn out to be too possessive, too controlling, too selfish, too stupid, have a terrible temper, and so on."

"What can I do to convince you that I'd make you a good husband?"

"Well, for one thing, don't keep any secrets from me. For example, what is Bob Parker up to? His story about trying to build a high temperature furnace sounds fishy, and the whole thing about the graphite cracking and his burning the fragments doesn't ring true. If you lie to me, I'll never trust you."

Every fiber in Doug's body wanted to tell Hortense everything. However, he remembered the death penalty for scientific work, and his better judgment kicked in. He "lied his head off."

"Bob is a fine Blacksmith, and I only work for him when he needs extra help. I really don't know about any other activities he might have."

"You own a farm. Why would you want to do odd jobs for Bob?"

"I can always use extra credits."

"I thought you said you're well off financially."

"Yes, but I'm also ambitious and always willing to earn more credits. That's a good trait for a husband, isn't it?"

"As long as it's not an obsession that would prevent him from having time for his wife."

"How can I court you? You're on the road most of the time."

"That's a good question. Perhaps you could move to Greensville. I'm there most weekends."

"I can't afford to do that. My farm's here, and I'd lose a lot of credits if I sold it now."

"Well, it looks like we're at an impasse. You can't move to Greensville, and I can't move my office here. Greensville's at the hub of my district, so it saves many miles of riding when I perform inspections in the surrounding communities. Now, you really must go. I have to get some sleep."

"Good night, Hortense. Please keep in touch."

"I certainly will."

Doug leaned in for a kiss. Hortense turned her head, offering her cheek. Then she headed up the stairs to her room.

On the way home, Doug wondered whether Hortense really liked him, or if she'd been playing out a diabolical plot to pump information out of him. He hoped he hadn't said too much.

The next morning, Bob stopped at Doug's place before going to the shop. . Doug was in his field cutting hay with a mower pulled by one of his horses. Bob walked briskly into the field and waved Doug down.

"Hi, Bob. You look worried. Is something bothering you?"

"How did it go with Hortense last night?"

"We had a good visit in the hotel lobby."

"Didn't go to her room, huh?"

"Naw. I was afraid to ask. You know how fussy women are about such things. But I asked her to marry me."

"Huh? My God, Doug."

"I know. I was a fool to ask her so soon. But she's going back to Greensville, and I was afraid I'd lose her forever."

"What'd she say?"

"Didn't shut me out completely. She said she likes me, but needs to know me a lot better before considering marriage. I plan to go to see her in Greensville as often as I can."

"Have you considered how being romantically involved with a Special Materials Control Officer might affect our project?"

"I, uh, really didn't give it much thought. I guess I sort of lost my head."

"Well, be careful. A lost head can kill us dead. She may just be pretending to like you so you'll open up to her."

"Don't worry. I didn't tell her anything incriminating last night. I'll be on my guard and extra watchful about what I say to her. I hate to keep anything from her, but she'll never find out anything about the solar car project from me."

"Believe me, I hope that's true. But I don't think you can keep her from finding out if you get too close to her. For God's sake, even one slip could get us killed," Bob said as his stomach began to churn.

*   *   *

During the months that followed, Doug frequently rode to Greensville on weekends to visit Hortense. He often took her to the Country Kitchen restaurant for dinner, went with her to her friends' homes for social evenings, took her to dances, went for long walks with her and had conversations about their hopes, aspirations, philosophies and dreams. Finally, on one of their walks she talked to Doug about her job, and complained about the large number of investigations she had to complete every week, hardly having time to complete any of them properly. Doug was elated that she evidently trusted him enough to open up to him. However, this made it even more difficult for him to keep from telling her his secret. During this time, Doug began calling her "Tensey" as a term of endearment, and she sometimes called him "Dougie."

Square-dancing, a holdover from olden times, had become popular with young adults Doug took Tensey to a square-dance and was pleasantly surprised to see her get a little wild. Up until then, she had been friendly with him, but somewhat reserved and formal. At her friends' homes, her personality really sparkled, and her sense of humor came out to play. She often had everyone laughing. Everyone seemed to like her. Married men and their wives enjoyed her (for different reasons). Men enjoyed looking at her, visiting and flirting. Wives enjoyed chatting with her, and they didn't feel threatened by her; they considered their husbands to be too far below her league to worry.

*   *   *

Five months later, Doug and Tensey were sitting on her couch watching a particularly romantic drama on holovision. The hero of the story was just at the point of making passionate love to the heroine. In the past, Doug had fleetingly hugged Tensey and kissed her hello and goodbye, but now he finally felt courageous enough to attempt a passionate kiss. His heart was pounding in his throat as he remembered how Audrey had rebuffed him when he tried kissing her years earlier, but now he felt that it was time to either move things forward with Tensey, or give up. He leaned in, put his arms around her, and surprised her with a long, gentle kiss. He was relieved when she didn't struggle and resist, but put her arms around him and pulled him closer. When Doug started to pull away, Tensey pulled him in for more. Doug's heart was pounding so hard it felt like it would explode. My God, she liked it, he thought as he penetrated her lips with his tongue. She accepted his tongue, and met it with hers. Doug thought how nasty and unsanitary this would have seemed just a few months ago, but now he couldn't imagine that any part of Tensey was less than perfect. He just wanted to be part of her in every way possible.

He was inhaling part of her breath, and she was inhaling part of his. The pheromones in her breath further aroused him. Doug finally worked up enough courage to place his hand up under Tensey's dress on the inside of her thigh just above her knee. She put her hand on his and pulled it off her thigh. For several long moments Doug looked into Tensey's beautiful violet eyes fearing what she was going to say. She didn't say anything, but continued to hold onto his hand and led him to her bedroom. He removed her clothing and she removed his. Naked, they embraced and got into bed together.

The next morning at breakfast, Doug said, "Tensey, you know I love you. Will you marry me?"

"Oh Doug, I like you a lot. In fact I think I might even love you, but I can't agree to a lifelong commitment to you yet. I have to be completely sure, and it'll take at least a year of being together in all kinds of situations. So far, we've experienced only good times with each other. We need to experience a full range of things together. If you really love me, you'll be willing to wait."

"Of course Dear. I'll wait as long as it takes."

CHAPTER 35
FOIL

Saturday morning, Bob and Audrey were awakened by the telephone. Audrey answered. "Yes, that's my husband. May I give him a message? – Okay."

"Who was that on the phone, Dear."

"The graphite foil we ordered has arrived here at the Stoneville freight terminal." Then, chuckling, Audrey continued, "I guess, now that the graphite is cracked, and you can't build the furnace, you won't need the foil. Shall I send it back?"

This brought on a round of playful tickling that soon developed into passionate lovemaking.

Afterward, the love nest felt warm and cozy as Audrey and Bob snuggled together, completely spent after their intense sexual conflagration, and they both went back to sleep. When Bob awoke, it was ten o'clock. He would have liked to stay in the warm nest a bit longer, but he didn't want to leave the foil exposed at the terminal any longer. After a great deal of internal self-convincing argument, he forced himself to get up and hurriedly dress.

"Sorry to leave right now, dear, but I've got to go into town, pick up the foil, and get it out of sight. I'm sure glad we had it shipped here instead of Greensville—freight offices are only open 'til noon today."

Without eating breakfast, Bob hurried over to Doug's place to borrow horses and a wagon. Doug had already left for a weekend visit with Tensey in Greensville, but Bob had permission to use the horses and wagon any time Doug wasn't using them. The wagon was under the shelter, and still had hay in it.

When Bob arrived at the freight company, he found all the rolls of foil were fastened onto a single shipping pallet. An attached envelope contained an invoice explaining that production had gone faster than anticipated, so the entire foil order had been sent instead of the ten-foot free sample.

The combined weight of all the rolls on the pallet was more than Bob had planned to handle. He hoped he'd be able to unobtrusively place each roll by hand into the wagon, get them to his shop, and carry them in without being seen. Loading the pallet onto the wagon at the freight terminal wasn't a problem; there was a hand-operated forklift on the loading dock. But unloading the heavy pallet was going to require backing the wagon into the shop and lifting the load with the chain hoist. Then, the wagon would have to be pulled out of the shop before the pallet could be lowered onto a handcart. Bob had not thoroughly planned how he might do this in the daytime without being seen. He didn't like planning it "on the fly" since the interior of the shop would be exposed to the street when the large front doors were open, and they couldn't be closed without first unhitching the horses and leading them to the corral behind the shop.

The freight dock, on the other hand, was behind the freight office, and not visible from the street. Bob felt reasonably secure as he used the freight company's forklift to load the pallet onto the wagon.

However, to the ever-vigilant Mortimer Snood, all things were visible—even behind the freight office. Just as Bob was driving the wagon away from the loading dock, Snood rode up on his horse.

"Watcha got there, Bob? I thought it looked like tar paper when I rode past the loading dock earlier this morning."

In his haste to pull hay over the foil, Bob had been sloppy about covering it. He didn't want to add any more strands to the web of lies, but he was flustered by Snood's sudden appearance, and answered, "Yep, you're right, it's rolls of tar paper for roofing."

"Why did you bury it in hay."

"The hay was already on the wagon, and it was a convenient way to keep the shipping pallet from sliding around so much."

Now that the "tar paper" was known, it didn't matter if anyone else saw it. Bob hauled it straight to his shop. Snood followed. Bob backed the wagon into the shop and unhitched the horses. He practically had to run over Snood to lead them outside.

"Aren't you going to unload the wagon?" Snood said, intently peering into the shop.

As Bob locked the shop, he said, "No. It's Saturday. I'm going home for lunch and I probably won't unload today."

Bob hopped up onto one of Doug's horses, and leading the other, rode bareback to Doug's place leaving a disappointed looking Snood behind to wonder about the "tar paper". When Bob arrived at Doug's, he watered and fed the horses.

Sunday evening, when Doug got back from visiting Tensey, Bob told him about his encounter with Snood, and that the "tar paper" would have to be unloaded late at night so no one would wander into the shop, get a close look, and discover it was not really tar paper.

Doug clenched his jaw as he said through his teeth, "Oh! That damn snoop. I'd like to drop him off a cliff. But he'd probably never hit bottom—he'd stop part way down to snoop into something."

That night, Bob used the chain hoist to lift the pallet, pulled the wagon out of the shop and moved the pallet with its load of foil into the inside room. Then he pushed the wagon back into the shop, locked the inside room and the shop, and returned home.

Monday morning, Bob borrowed two of Doug's horses to return the wagon. He had just hitched the horses to the wagon and pulled it out of the shop, when Snood arrived and peered into the shop trying to see the "tar paper." He walked into the shop, but Bob jumped from the wagon seat, grabbed Snood by the arm and said, "Damn it Snood, get out of the way. I have to lock up so I can return this wagon."

The sheriff, making his rounds, saw the entire encounter between the two men and walked over to them. Bob thought, oh crap, I'm in trouble. However, the sheriff took hold of *Snood's* arm and said, "Mortimer, I've warned you several times about harassing people. Come along. I'm going to see that you are checked into a mental institution for an attitude adjustment. I understand they have excellent ways to correct personality problems like yours."

Snood scowled as he said, "What do you mean, 'personality problems.'"

The sheriff didn't answer, but pulled Snood out through the door.

Bob grinned as he said, "Thank you, sheriff."

The "tar paper" was safe.

*　　　*　　　*

During the next five weeks, Bob worked evenings and weekends developing a machine for dimpling the foil. Small bumps made in this way were to keep the layers of foil super-insulation separated by about five times the thickness of a sheet of writing paper. After many trial and error dimpling experiments, and making changes in the machine, Bob succeeded. In the early hours of morning, he transported the foil and dimpling machine under cover of darkness to the cavern. There, he and Doug could work together to feed the foil through the dimpling machine and out onto a long table where it would be carefully rolled up, then later rolled in layers around the heat storage core.

Bob and Doug worked together, for a couple of hours several nights, dimpling over a thousand feet of foil. As they worked, Doug said, "I've had a bad year farming, and my finances are in terrible shape. I sure hope this project doesn't cost a lot more before we finish. In fact, I hope that before long we can get some profit from it."

"I'm afraid we have a lot of work to do before we can make any profit. We'll have to sell the public on the benefits of solar powered cars fast enough that public opinion will help us avoid being prosecuted for doing scientific research."

"Boy, that's a long-shot, and we'll be taking a terrible risk."

"I know, but if we're successful the payoff will be huge, and we'll have contributed something that will benefit mankind. Besides, Maxwell's lawyer may get the anti-science law overturned before we've finished developing our solar car"

"Oh, haven't you heard. Maxwell was executed a year after his trial. His lawyer failed to even get a hearing from the higher court. I saw the execution on holovision one night, and I thought you must have seen it too. They put him in a small, isolated instantaneous laser incineration chamber and closed the door. A few minutes later, a large puff of smoke came out of the chamber's ventilation duct, and a man went into the building with a broom and dustpan to sweep up the ashes. That was the end of Maxwell."

"I guess I missed it. I've been too busy to watch holovision, or even survey the news on my wrist telephone."

Just as they were starting to dimple the last 150-feet of foil, a man's voice said, "What are you two doing?"

Startled, Bob and Doug spun around. The sheriff was standing in the entrance to the cavern.

CHAPTER 36
CAUGHT AGAIN

Bob and Doug blanched at the sight of the sheriff peering into the scientific laboratory they'd tried so hard to keep secret.

"How'd? Why'd? What? How did you get in here?" Doug stammered.

"I walked, of course."

Bob was wide-eyed as he asked, "How did you find this place?"

"A psychiatrist at the asylum called me and said Snood's progress is hampered because he's absolutely convinced that you are doing something illegal. Even though I think Snood is off his rocker, I am required by law to investigate any suspected illegal activity reported by someone like the psychiatrist. Last night I was riding to your house to ask you a few questions. I saw you and Doug in the moonlight, near the brush patch. I didn't have a flashlight, but I tried to follow in the darkness anyway. You disappeared and I couldn't see where you'd gone.

"I came back today, explored, and found a thinned path and miniature railway through the brush. Following the path, I found the tunnel entrance and wondered where it went. But without a flashlight I didn't go in.

"Tonight, I brought a flashlight and watched you two enter the thinned path. Then I followed the path to the tunnel entrance, but you were out of sight by the time I got there. I walked all the way down to the tunnel's end and back again before finding the side tunnel that led me to this cavern.

"I see a lot of what looks like scientific equipment: meters, gauges, electronics, and what's this? Shelves of science books. This is all illegal."

Bob looked stunned, and Doug's face was deathly white.

"I guess we're dead men," Doug said in a weak voice.

The sheriff asked, "Does Audrey know anything about this?"

Bob said, "No. I've kept it from her."

"Then, I'll let her know why you won't be coming home tonight."

*   *   *

The next day Audrey was still in shock after a nearly sleepless night. Adding to her anxiety, the local freight terminal clerk called and told her some black glass tubes had arrived. Audrey was glad the clerk thought the vitreous carbon tubes were only glass, but she could hardly think of what to tell him. If she accepted them, and someone discovered what they really were, she might be implicated in the scientific work. However, if she refused delivery and things worked out later, the tubes wouldn't be available when needed. Also, if she refused them she'd still have to pay for additional expensive shipping to send them back. Finally, Audrey deflected potential blame for scientific work away from herself by saying, "I don't know anything about them, but since my husband ordered them, I'll pick them up right away."

Before leaving for the freight terminal, Audrey called the firm where Jason Bright had worked as an intern, and was told that Jason now had his own law firm. She got the number and telephoned the receptionist at "Bright and Associates."

"Is Mr. Bright there?"

"He's not available right now. May I take a message?"

"This is Audrey Parker. My husband and his friend, Doug Murphy, have been arrested. We desperately need Mr. Bright to represent them. It's literally a matter of life or death!"

"Oh, Mrs. Parker, Jason has spoken about you and your husband often. Your earlier case helped establish his reputation, and Jason is grateful to you for having faith in him while he was only an intern. I'll have him call you in an hour or so when he returns."

Audrey left to pick up the vitreous carbon tubes while waiting for Jason's call. She was thankful that she'd arranged to have the tubes delivered to the local freight terminal, which was only about 20-minutes away, including time to saddle her horse. Since the tubes were only about a foot long, and a little over an inch in diameter, Audrey planned to carry them in her saddlebags. When she arrived at the terminal, the clerk appeared to have trouble finding the tubes, wasting 25 minutes of Audrey's time. After receiving the tubes, she furtively placed them in her saddlebags. She was glad the tubes were small and inconspicuous However, her satisfied state of mind was short-lived. The sheriff was watching the terminal; he'd ordered the clerk to call him if any strange items arrived for Bob.

"Hello, Mrs. Parker. What are those items you put in your saddle bags?"

Audrey spun around, shocked to see the sheriff standing there.

"I – I don't know, sheriff. It's something Bob ordered for the blacksmith shop."

"Well, hand them over. They may be evidence we'll need for the trial."

She thought for a moment, then gave the tubes to the sheriff. "Okay, sheriff. Bob won't be needing them while he's locked up," Audrey said, trying to keep her voice steady and nonchalant, even though her heart was pounding in her throat.

Her wrist telephone silently vibrated signaling an incoming call. She believed it was Jason, but she didn't want to answer in front of the sheriff. She was relieved that the sheriff apparently thought she knew nothing about the scientific work, and she was being careful not to do anything to change that.

On the way home, she accessed her voice mail. Jason's message said. "Mrs. Parker, I'm terribly busy right now, but I'll try to squeeze you in. I can't promise anything, but I'll make some calls and try to postpone some of my cases. I'll call you when I know what I can do for you. If I can't take your case, I'll recommend another excellent attorney."

Audrey shouted at the voice message; "No! No! No! This is life or death. We must have *you*, Jason!"

*   *   *

Doug had called Hortense from the jail to let her know he wouldn't be able to visit her the next weekend. Whether she felt guilt that she might somehow be responsible for Doug's arrest, or felt love, or little of each, she used some of her vacation to come from Greensville and visit Doug in jail.

Doug and Bob had been placed in adjoining cells for serious offenders, located in the rear of the jail building. The cells had only bars between them, so Bob and Doug were able to talk to each other. But they had to whisper and be careful what they said. A deputy often hung around and might overhear them.

Visits with outsiders were conducted at a table in the middle of the large front office where two holding cells for minor offenders were located, and where there was a desk near one wall. The sheriff or a deputy sat at the desk about 20-feet away facing the table, and monitored visits to ensure there was no contact or passing of items between visitors and prisoners. Prisoners and their visitors sat across the table from each other; there was no screen or glass window between them as in larger city jails. Tensey's visit with Doug felt much more intimate than it would have through glass, but they were closely watched. Even though the deputy manning the desk was an older man, somewhat hard of hearing, they spoke in hushed tones and whispers to be sure he couldn't overhear.

Tears came into Tensey's eyes as she leaned forward and whispered, "Oh Doug, I'm so sorry. I've gone over and over the report I turned in during my investigation so long ago, and I couldn't find anything in it that might have aroused suspicion. I've been tortured by thoughts of anything I might have said in the verbal debriefing about it with my boss that might have brought this on. But I don't see how I could've since I knew nothing about the cavern or what you were doing there."

"No, Tensey. You're not responsible for our trouble. It was that damn Snood," Doug whispered.

Then Doug went on to tell how Snood had been responsible for the sheriff's visit and the resulting arrests.

"I'm so relieved to know that I wasn't responsible," Tensey whispered hoarsely, wiping away tears. Then she continued, "I've had time to think about you, and I've decided I love you. But, I'm really mad at you for not telling me what you were doing. I understand why you had to do it, but you got me in trouble with my boss for not finding out what you and Bob were up to."

"I'm sorry. But would you rather I had told you and put your life as well as my own in jeopardy?"

"No. I'd rather you had not been doing anything considered illegal. What were you doing, and why on earth were you doing it?" She whispered.

Doug wondered for a moment if Tensey was working with the law and trying to trap him, but he decided that her tears and her love were genuine.. In a whisper barely audible, even to Tensey, Doug said, "We were developing a solar powered car. It's something badly needed in the world today, and the payoff would've been huge if we could've widely demonstrated it to gain public support before we were arrested. We thought, if enough of the public could see its benefits, its popularity would protect us from prosecution."

"It scares me that I can actually see the logic behind that.

"I'm taking three weeks of vacation so I can stay and help you. If you wish, I'll take care of your livestock and your place, at least for now."

"Thanks, Tensey. I've been worried about how to take care of that. Audrey has been taking care of my farm animals, but she is very upset, and has to deal with getting us legal help, so I didn't want to burden her with it. Where are you staying?"

"At the hotel."

"You can stay at my place. I'll ask the sheriff to give you my key."

"Thanks. That'll save me a lot of credits, and it'll make it easier to take care of the livestock."

"You'll find fresh vegetables in the refrigerator and meat in the freezer. They'll spoil if you don't use them. You may also get vegetables out of my garden if you wish."

"Good. I'll prepare some dinners and share them with you."

"I'd like that. Jail food is awful."

Tensey got the key for Doug's house, and asked the sheriff for permission to bring food to share with Doug during visiting hours. The sheriff said he'd be glad to have her be responsible for any number of meals so he wouldn't have to arrange for them. He asked her to let him know in advance whenever she was going to bring food. She told him that she planned to bring dinner for Doug during evening visiting hours every day.

*   *   *

Early the next morning, while Audrey was brewing coffee, her phone signaled a call. It was Jason Bright.

"Hi, Audrey."

"Oh, Jason, can you help us?"

"I got your message that Bob and Doug are in extremely serious legal trouble. I've managed to shift some of my work load to one of my associates and postpone two cases so I can help you. What happened?"

"They were caught doing scientific work."

"You weren't kidding when you said it was serious! That's about as serious as it gets. I'll leave right away, and see you in a few hours."

"Thank you so much. I can't tell you how thankful I am that you'll be able to help us."

"Well, don't be thankful yet. Let's wait and see if I can keep them from being executed."

"I 'm confident that if anyone can do it, you can."

"But, remember, Audrey, there is still a precedent for the death penalty in such cases."

"Yes, I know. We'd originally thought we'd be able to demonstrate the benefits of the work, and it would rapidly get wide enough public acceptance to protect us from prosecution. But that didn't work. Bob and Doug were caught before they had finished. Incidentally, the law isn't aware that I know anything about the work, but I know a lot and may be able to help you."

"Good. We'll keep that confidential. I'll start now and should arrive at your place around 1 p.m."

True to his word, Jason knocked on Audrey's front door in the early afternoon.

"You made good time. Have you had lunch?" Audrey asked.

"No. I didn't take time to stop."

"C 'mon in. I'll make you lunch while I describe what Bob and Doug were doing that got them into so much trouble."

As Audrey worked on lunch, she summarized everything, from discovery of the notebooks and the work to develop a solar powered car, to Snood's meddling that caused the final arrests by the sheriff.

After lunch, Jason and Audrey went to the jail to see Bob and Doug. Jason asked the sheriff to show him the list of evidence. Glancing through the list, Jason quickly memorized it with his photographic memory.

Tensey was already at the jail visiting Doug. When Audrey and Jason arrived, Bob was brought to the visitor's room. Jason asked Doug to join them and, after a deputy searched Audrey, Jason and Tensey, they all started toward a private interview room for prisoners, their families and their attorneys. Jason turned to Tensey and said, "Miss Farb, this is a private meeting between Audrey, the defendants, and me. You'll have to stay here."

"I don't care if she comes. I trust her," Doug said emphatically.

"No, I won't permit it. We can't trust anyone not directly affected by this case."

Audrey heard her inner voice say, "Tact sure isn't Jason's strong point."

Tensey's face turned red, and tears rolled down her cheeks as Jason led Doug, Bob and Audrey into the interview room and closed the door..

Doug reddened and said, "You are a tactless son of a bitch. She'll feel that we blame her for our trouble. She didn't have anything to do with it. I love her, and I trust her completely."

Jason calmly said, "I'm sorry if I hurt her feelings, but you and Bob are in grave danger and I intend to do everything I can to save you. Is she in love with you?"

"She's taken vacation time from her job to visit me and take care of my livestock."

"But is she in love with you? Are you engaged to her?"

"She said she loves me, but she hasn't yet agreed to marry me."

"Then, we don't dare trust her yet."

CHAPTER 37
PREPARATION FOR THE HEARING

Bob and Doug discussed details of their work on the heat-energy storage device with Jason. They told him about everything in the cavern in a normal voice, but lowered their voices when they told him about the notebooks in case the sheriff could hear them through the door. Although Audrey had participated in the development work, she was quiet since a female voice heard through the door explaining things might implicate her in the crime.

Jason sensed that Bob and Doug considered the notebooks to be a dangerous subject, so he lowered his voice as he said, "The notebooks weren't in the evidence list. Do you know where they are?"

Bob spoke in nearly a whisper as he said, "We haven't revealed the existence of those damn notebooks to the sheriff. We felt they might be even more incriminating than the contents of the cavern. Audrey knows where they are and can show them to you."

Time after time, Jason lowered his voice nearly to a whisper and came back to the topic of the notebooks from which basic technology for the project had come. Finally, Bob asked Jason in a hushed voice, "Why are you concentrating so much on the notebooks?"

"I have an idea, but I'm not sure it'll work. I'll have to see the cavern *and* the notebooks before I can decide."

After discussing the case for a few more minutes, Jason said, "I think we're done here for the time being."

Jason and Audrey left the interview room, and the sheriff put Bob and Doug back in their cells. Before leaving the jail, Jason got permission from the sheriff to visit the cavern, and the sheriff said he'd send a deputy as an escort

As Jason and Audrey arrived back at the stone cottage, Jason asked, "Can you go with me to the cavern and show me the notebooks without making it obvious to the deputy?"

"Yes."

The deputy escort arrived at the cottage about 15 minutes later.

When Audrey, Jason and the deputy got to the tunnel, its entrance was blocked by a crime scene tape that said, "WARNING: CRIME SCENE. UNAUTHORIZED ENTRY PROHIBITED." The deputy broke the tape, and they went to the cavern. Jason was awed by the size of the cavern and the complexity of equipment that had not been removed as evidence by the sheriff.

After he and Audrey had carefully looked at everything, Jason said, "Okay, deputy, we've seen enough here."

As they left the tunnel, the deputy replaced the crime scene tape blocking the tunnel entrance, then headed toward town. Jason and Audrey went to the house where they could discuss the case in private.

When they were safely inside, Jason asked, "Okay, where are the notebooks Bob and Doug told me about?"

Audrey said, "I didn't see them in the cavern where we normally kept them, so they must be hidden where I used to keep them here in my kitchen." Then, she went to her kitchen bookshelf and retrieved a thick binder labeled "200-Famous Recipes." She opened it up, and gasped.

"What's the matter, Audrey?"

"This is full of recipes!"

"So, isn't that what you expect in a cookbook?"

"No. I removed the recipes and placed them in a drawer. Then I hid the notebooks in the binder. My God, I hope the police didn't get them when they collected evidence from the cavern."

"I don't think the police got the notebooks since they were not mentioned in the evidence list."

Audrey reddened and furrowed her forehead as she asked, "Are the notebooks very important to your case?"

"I don't know for sure until I see them, but my entire defense may depend on them."

"Oh my God. Oh my God. Where could they be?" Audrey said as tears came into her eyes.

"Don't panic. We need to have clear heads. The logical thing is to go to the jail and ask Bob and Doug if they put them somewhere."

Audrey and Jason saddled their horses and rode at a gallop to the jail. Jason searched the evidence list to see if he had missed the notebooks. They were not listed. Then Jason asked to see the prisoners.

Audrey started to accompany Jason to the cells in the back of the building, but the sheriff said, "You can't go back there, Mrs Parker. Only the attorney is allowed in the maximum security prison area."

Audrey sat impatiently waiting on a chair in the sheriff's office. Ten minutes later, Jason returned from the rear of the jail building. Audrey followed him as he quickly left.

"Well?" Audrey said when they were safely outside the building.

"Bob was surprised you didn't know where the notebooks would be. He took the them out of your cookbook binder and replaced the recipe pages you had in the drawer."

"But, where did he put the notebooks?"

"He said, he placed them in the 'mystery chest,' whatever that is, where he felt they'd be safer."

"Oh, of course. I know exactly where that is. I'm ashamed that I didn't think of it before. I guess I was just too panicked to think straight when they weren't where I expected to find them."

When Audrey and Jason arrived at the house, Audrey said, "Follow me."

Jason followed as she went to the hallway and climbed the "pull-down" stairway to the attic. Audrey turned on the attic light and retrieved the mystery chest from its hiding place between the attic floor joists just past the edge of the attic flooring.

"That's a good hiding place. I didn't even see it until you pulled it out," Jason said.

"Yes. We think it remained there undetected for almost 70-years after one of this cottage's previous owners hid it."

Jason frowned. "Oh. Only 70-years? Then my idea for the defense won't work."

"If it's old you want, the chest is 200-years old, and some of the stuff in the notebooks was written before the darkening."

"Good. Then it may help us."

"What's your idea?"

"It's too early for me to tell you about it. I don't want you to be disappointed if I decide it won't work. Besides, you might slip while talking to someone, and that could ruin my potential surprise attack on the prosecution."

Audrey carried the chest downstairs and placed it on the kitchen table. Jason watched intently as she opened it.

"What's this?" Jason asked as he picked up the black locket.

"Here, I'll show you," Audrey said as she held the locket close to the lamp.

The message from the locket's original owner was instantly projected on the wall. She quickly showed Jason the files stored in the locket.

"Oh!" Jason exclaimed. "This is extremely interesting, especially the dates on the files and the eyewitness accounts of responsibility for the catastrophes."

"Be careful not to put too much emphasis on responsibility for the catastrophes. It didn't help Maxwell in his trial," Audrey said. Then she briefly described how the judge had instructed the jury that his court couldn't overturn science prohibition, even after the defense attorney had proven science wasn't responsible for catastrophes leading to The Darkening.

Audrey showed Jason the notebooks and explained the general principles that were described in them. Jason smiled, realizing Audrey's deep knowledge of the project, and how "dumb" she had pretended to be whenever the sheriff was nearby.

After looking through the books with Audrey, Jason said, "I need to take these books to my hotel room and memorize some of the pages"

"Memorize them in one night?"

"Yes. Have you forgotten about my photographic memory?"

"Oh, I wasn't thinking." Then she asked, "Have you checked into the hotel yet?"

"No."

"Then I insist that you stay here in our spare bedroom. I'll prepare your meals to save you time, and you can ask me any questions that you might have about the scientific work. Also, I can take care of your horse along with ours."

"Thank you Audrey. Staying here will certainly save time, and I need every advantage I can get. I'm hoping I can win this case in the evidentiary hearing like we did in the wire salvaging case. If I can't, it'll be a complicated case, and it's going to be difficult for me to spend enough time away from my other cases to do a good job on this one. I'll do my best, but I'm not making any promises."

"You're the most brilliant person I know. I'm sure you can do it."

"We'll see."

Jason pored over the notebooks in the living room while Audrey prepared dinner. After Dinner, Jason studied late into the night, and was asleep in an overstuffed chair in the living room with the light still on when Audrey came out of her bedroom in the morning. As soon as he woke up, Jason bombarded Audrey with technical questions that came up while he was studying the notebooks. At about 10-a.m., he finally released her so she could prepare breakfast. She hadn't had her coffee yet, and she felt grumpy, but she did her best to keep from showing it.

About mid-afternoon, the court clerk called and said the pre-trial hearing was to start at 9 a.m. four days later. Jason asked if it could be sooner, but the court's schedule was too full.

When the phone call ended, Jason turned to Audrey. "I'm ready for the hearing, but I can't waste three days just waiting here. I'll have to return to Greensville and work on some of my other cases, then come back here for the hearing."

"Okay, I understand. Again, I'm so grateful to you for going to all this trouble to help us. Is there anything I can do?"

"No. I think I now have an approach that'll work. No guarantees, though."

For the next three days, Audrey was deeply worried. Whenever she visited Bob, she saw Hortense visiting Doug. When visiting hours were over, the two women walked out to their horses at the same time. At first they didn't speak. Even though Audrey knew Snood was mainly responsible, she couldn't help feeling Hortense might be at least partially to blame for Bob and Doug's arrest. However, as she overheard conversations between Doug and Hortense, Audrey began to believe this woman genuinely loved Doug, and would be devastated to think that she had anything to do his arrest. Finally, on the third day as they were leaving, Audrey spoke.

"Nice day today"

After this small weather report, Hortense looked at Audrey, eyes wide. Unexpectedly, she tearfully grabbed Audrey's hand.

"Oh Audrey, I hoped you wouldn't think I had anything to do with the men's arrests. At first I was afraid I might somehow be partially to blame. I worried and worried about it, but I couldn't think of anything I did that would have contributed to the sheriff's discovery. I didn't know anything about the cavern, or what the men were doing there, until I heard about it on the news. Doug and Bob's arrests made me feel awful. Then Doug told me that Snood had caused the trouble, and I realized I didn't have anything to do with it."

Then Tensey took a deep breath and continued, "On top of everything else, I had just gotten word that my mother died. She was the only immediate family I had left. I've felt so alone and depressed that I even considered suicide."

"My God, Tensey, I can't understand why you would ever consider suicide. Why would you do that to Doug. You know he loves you."

"He's the best thing in my life. Now that I've finally found a man that I can love, he's going to be executed. I just can't stand it."

Tensey burst into tears.

"It isn't over until it's over. You don't know our lawyer, Jason Bright. He's brilliant," Audrey said in a reassuring tone.

"But I've heard of other cases like this, and the best outcome that any defendant has gotten is life imprisonment. Most were executed. Oh Audrey… ." Tensey's voice choked up again, and tears rolled down her cheeks.

Audrey, was now totally convinced of Tensey's love for Doug—and her pain. She put her arm around Tensey and said, "There, there now. Why don't you come over and have tea with me tonight?"

Through the sobs, Tensey managed to say, "A-all r-right, that's awfully nice of you."

Tensey wiped her eyes and blew her nose, then said, "Tell me more about Mr. Bright."

As they rode home together, Audrey related how Jason, when he was still only an intern, completely devastate the Prosecuting Attorney's case against a wire theft defendant. She didn't reveal that the defendant was Bob.

Tensey said, "But I just can't shake the thought that no one has ever been able to avoid the death penalty for this crime."

CHAPTER 38
LIFE, IMPRISONMENT, OR DEATH

There was a knock on Audrey's door at 6 a.m. the morning of the hearing. She was pleased that it was Jason. Smiling, she said, "I was worried when you didn't return from Greensville last night."

"My associate had trouble with one of the cases I handed him, and we had to work through the night. I came here as soon as I could, but I didn't get any sleep last night.

"Oh, I'm sorry. Are you going to be all right in court today?"

"I'll have to be. Could I get some breakfast and crash here until 9 o'clock when I have to leave for the hearing?"

"Yes, absolutely. I'll get breakfast started right away."

"One other thing, Audrey, I'll need the notebooks in court today. Would you get them together for me?"

"You still haven't explained how you are going to use the notebooks. Why do you need them if you're trying to prove Bob wasn't doing scientific work? It seems to me you'd want to avoid any mention of them."

"Audrey, I've had a tough 24 hours, and I don't have time or energy to spend telling you about it right now. Please trust me and just do as I ask."

"Of course. By now, I know better than to question your reasoning. I'm sorry."

Audrey prepared breakfast for herself and Jason. After breakfast, he was soon fast asleep on the living room couch. While clearing the breakfast dishes, she looked in the cookbook binder where she thought she had placed the notebooks. They weren't there. She was shocked, and looked everywhere in the house and attic for them; they were nowhere to be found. She thought, oh my God, not again! Frantically, half out of her mind, she again looked in places where she'd already looked. Then, mostly from habit, and without thinking, she frantically rushed to the tunnel. As Audrey ran to the brush patch, Hortense came running from Doug's house through the adjoining field. When Audrey got to the tunnel, she saw the crime scene tape was still intact and realized that she couldn't legally go in. It didn't matter anyway; she remembered that neither she or Jason had returned to the cavern after they'd retrieved the notebooks from the mystery chest.

Breathlessly coming up behind Audrey, Hortense said, "I saw you running. What's wrong?"

"I can't find the notebooks. I can't find the notebooks. I... ."

"I get it. Stop repeating yourself. Are they really that important?"

"Yes. Jason ... Oh my God, Jason ..."

Without finishing her sentence Audrey ran to the house, and Hortense followed. It was plain to see that Audrey was hysterical with worry. When Audrey got to the house, she rushed up to the attic and looked in the chest again. The notebooks hadn't magically materialized there since she had looked there before. She rushed into the living room followed by Tensey. It was now 7 a.m.

"Jason, Jason wake up."

"Huh? What? Is it time to go?"

"No. We've got a serious problem. I can't find the notebooks."

Jason thought for a moment, then said, "Oh My God, I'm sorry. I took them to Greensville. I've been so preoccupied with my other cases the last couple of days, and I was so exhausted, that I forgot them. There isn't time to ride to Greensville and get them before the 9 o'clock hearing. Those books are the entire basis of my defense. How could I have been so stupid? We'll automatically lose if we don't show up for the hearing, and I don't think I can win without the books. I'm terribly sorry, Audrey."

Hortense broke down and sobbed. Between sobs she asked Audrey, "A-are you s-sure Jason is as bright as you said he is?"

Struggling to regain her own composure, Audrey said, "Absolutely. He's under a lot of stress because he's taking care of us along with his already heavy workload. He traveled here last night without getting any sleep. Hortense, pull yourself together. This is a critical time for our men, and they need us to be strong and sharp. Let's try to solve this problem."

After a few minutes thought, Audrey said, "Jason, with your photographic memory, can you remember enough to argue in court for a while without the notebooks?"

"Yes, but I can't stretch that out for long. The judge will require them to be physically entered into evidence."

"How long do you think you can stall by reciting material from the notebooks without actually having them in hand?"

"Maybe an hour. Then I could imply that we left them at your house, and ask for an hour recess to get them. I think the judge would welcome a recess if I can overwhelm him and the prosecuting attorney with a bunch of scientific material they don't understand. The judge may want to confer with a consultant. Altogether, I could probably stall for perhaps a couple of hours."

"Well, as I see it, our only chance is to ride to Greensville and get the notebooks."

"But, that's at least an eight hour round trip."

"Not if we set up a pony express."

"Pony express?"

"Yes. Change horses and riders every few miles so we can travel at a gallop most of the way."

"But how...?"

Audrey looked thoughtful as she said, "A number of riders can ride their horses from here toward Greensville alternating between a cantor and a trot. Each rider will lead a second horse for a mile or two, then quickly change to the second horse and lead the first, and so on, to go faster and cover more distance."

"But, to cover the round-trip distance at a gallop in even a little over two hours, you'd have to already have fresh horses every mile or two from here to Greensville."

"Don't get ahead of me, Jason. That's where you and Hortense come in. Call your associate in Greensville and ask him to get a rider right now to carry the notebooks, riding one horse and leading another, alternating between horses every few miles for maximum speed. Meanwhile Hortense and I'll get a number of riders from here. Hortense, myself, and all the other riders leading their extra horse will start toward Greensville at a canter. The I'll stop a couple of miles from Stoneville, Hortense will go two miles farther, and the others will each stop at a pre-designated positions every couple of miles along the road until the last rider from here meets the one from Greensville. By that time, horses waiting along the road will be rested. From then on, riders can carry the books at a gallop in relays all the way back to me, and I'll deliver the books to you at the courthouse."

"By Jupiter, Audrey, I think that'll work. I'll call my associate right away." When Jason finished his phone call, he rested for a while then left for court.

While Jason was telephoning his associate, Audrey used her wrist telephone to call friends on neighboring farms. It took about forty minutes, but by 8 o'clock, she had enlisted all the riders she felt would be needed. Hortense had saddled their horses, so she and Audrey left immediately and took the first two positions along the road. Their horses would be well rested by the time a rider got to them with the books. Audrey stopped about 2 miles out of town. Hortense positioned herself about 2 miles further down the road. The rest of the riders rode mostly at a cantor, changing horses every one or two miles, until they reached their pre-designated positions every two miles along the road.

* * *

It was 10:30 a.m., and Audrey still couldn't see any sign of an approaching rider. Since the hearing had started at 9 a.m., Audrey was worried that Jason might not be able to stall until the books arrived. She was just beginning to feel panic when in the distance a rider's tiny image appeared, distorted by the heat waves rising from the road in the cool morning air. Audrey mounted her horse. Her heart was pounding in her throat. She wondered if she would get to the courthouse in time. Hortense approached at a maximum gallop. Audrey spurred her horse to a gallop, matching the speed of Hortense's horse, as Hortense handed the bag of books to Audrey. Hortense's horse was breathing hard, was covered with foamy sweat, an had foam dripping from its mouth. It had been driven nearly to death. Audrey urged her horse to a maximum gallop the entire distance to the courthouse. Without even tying her horse to a hitching post, she dismounted and hit the ground running. She burst into the courtroom just in time to hear the judge pound his gavel and say, "The court will come to order. Mr. Bright, you were supposed to fetch the notebooks during the recess. I don't see them. Unless you can produce them right now, I am going to rule in favor of the prosecution."

Audrey rushed to Jason's side, and flopped the books on the table in front of him. The judge again brought his gavel down hard on his bench, and said, "Order in the court. What's .the meaning of this disruption."

Jason, sweating and red faced, suddenly looked relaxed. "These are the notebooks, your honor."

The judge glared at Audrey. "Young lady, sit down and be quiet or I will find you in contempt."

After a few seconds, the judge continued. "Mr. Bright, approach the bench and show me the sections in the notebook you referenced in your presentation."

Jason and the prosecutor came and stood before the judge. Jason held a notebook for the judge and prosecutor to see, and pointed to several pages while speaking quietly.

A buzz of conversation erupted between spectators. At that moment Hortense, who had let her exhausted horse rest a few minutes before finishing the trip into town at a trot, burst red faced and sweating into the courtroom. The judge angrily slammed his gavel down.

"Order. Order in the court."

The courtroom quieted and the attorneys returned to their seats. The judge leafed through the notebook that Jason had handed him, then handed it to the evidence clerk. It was the only piece of evidence for the defense.

Jason and the prosecutor returned to their seats, and the judge summed up the case Jason had presented. "Five pages in the notebook summarize work done by its author. Said pages were dated in the year 2060, eight years before the darkening. They completely described the heat storage device and its use with a Stirling engine for propelling a vehicle. Therefore, the work done by the defendants is not new scientific work, but an application of methods that existed before the darkening. I find no evidence as a basis for prosecution, and this case is dismissed without prejudice."

Audrey and Hortense in unison let out a yip and ran to their men. First, they hugged and kissed them, then they both grabbed

Jason and hugged and kissed him while he turned red. They all left the courtroom together, with Jason in the lead, and each woman hanging tightly onto her man.

From the courthouse, they went to Bob and Audrey's place. Audrey and Hortense prepared a sumptuous lunch and they all laughed and joked together as they ate.

Immediately after lunch, Jason left for Greensville after being thanked profusely, hugged by both men and kissed by both women. Doug and Hortense sat side-by-side on the davenport like lovebirds. They couldn't take their eyes off of each other, and seemed intensely preoccupied. To make matters worse, they kissed each other every few minutes.

Finally, Bob said, "Audrey, why don't I help you clear the lunch dishes?"

"Of course, Dear."

Shortly after Bob and Audrey went onto the kitchen, they heard the front door close.

Audrey looked knowingly at Bob and said, "The lovebirds have flown."

CHAPTER 39
CREDITS, CREDITS

Doug and Hortense were not seen for three days. On the morning of the fourth day, they came to Doug and Audrey's place so Hortense could say goodbye. She had been called back to work, and had to return to Greensville. Doug and "Tensey," as he now called Hortense, looked worn out. Their bloodshot eyes had dark circles under them.

Bob smiled and said, "My God, it looks like you two haven't slept for days." Then he coyly asked, "What have you been doing?"

Doug reddened and smiled. "That'd be telling."

Tensey's face and ears reddened. She smiled, but avoided eye contact with Bob by looking down and studying her hands folded in her lap.

After visiting briefly with Bob and Audrey, Doug and Tensey left to ride to the "Welcome" sign on the outskirts of Stoneville. Then Doug returned to Bob and Audrey's place where Bob was preparing to go to work.

Doug looked concerned as he said, "On the way back from telling Tensey goodbye, I was thinking about our project. Now that it's legal, and details including the tunnel and cavern have gotten into the news, there'll be people snooping around. We need a strong, lockable, steel door on the tunnel entrance, and I think its going to be expensive. I hate to tell you this, but I'm almost broke. We need to think about getting more investors involved in our project."

Bob felt a cold chill. "I guess in the back of my mind I knew we'd exhaust our funds, but I hoped we'd be closer to finishing the project before it happened. We aren't far enough along to demonstrate the solar powered car. If we can't get any investors, I guess we'll have to mortgage the equity in our houses, and my shop."

Audrey said, "I think Bob can build the door without it costing too much. He could use a steel plate I saw at the junkyard. It looked about a quarter inch thick, and four- by six-feet or so in size."

Doug thought for a minute, then said, "That's all well and good, but we're still going to need a lot more credits to finish our project."

*   *   *

Bob built a lockable steel door and installed it on the entrance to the tunnel just in time to keep curiosity seekers out. An increasing number of persons had heard about Bob and Doug's trial, and the news broadcasts included details of the brush patch, secret tunnel, and chamber. People were so intrigued by the mystery and drama that they ignored the "No Trespassing" signs and came onto Bob's property trying to find the tunnel entrance. A few of them found the thinned path through the brush and were kept out of the tunnel only by the door. One of the nosey visitors drove there in a gasoline-powered automobile with a company name and a logo painted on both sides. The company was one of the few automobile manufacturers in the world, and was infamous for stealing technology. Without asking, the driver found the path through the brush, and went to the steel door before Bob got there.

Bob asked, "What are you doing?"

"Satisfying my curiosity."

"Didn't you see the 'No Trespassing' signs?"

"Yes, but I thought they were for the general public, not persons with an engineering interest. It's common courtesy for engineers to share knowledge with each other."

"We've spent a lot of time and credits, and have taken terrible risks to do the engineering to get to this point in our development. We'd be willing to license the technology to you for a price, but we're not giving away any of our technology free."

"Any knowledge you wish to share with us would automatically become our property to use as we please. We wouldn't agree to pay for that. After all, it's only knowledge, and knowledge belongs to everyone. It's the investors that take all the risks and deserve all the profits"

"You've got to be kidding. That attitude is probably one reason so many car manufacturers went broke"

"That's historically the protocol in our company, and we aren't broke yet."

"Well, you don't have much competition since most other car companies went bankrupt. Anyway, we aren't giving away the methods and knowledge we've worked so hard to develop. Now, get off my land!"

"Okay, but if you are not willing to cooperate, we have other ways of getting what we want."

"I've got an 12-gauge pump-action shotgun, and I know how to use it, so I'd better not see any more of you snooping bastards around here trying to steal our work product."

During the next two days, Bob and Doug worked together to clear enough brush so they could keep an eye on the tunnel entrance from both of their houses. Bob installed outside sensor lights over the tunnel entrance and added several more locks to the steel door.

*   *   *

A few days later, it was time to assemble the heat storage device and connect it to the Stirling engine. However, Doug and Bob's credit accounts were too overextended to purchase needed fittings and materials such as stainless steel tubing.

Bob met with Doug and said, "We've arrived at a point where we can't go ahead without financial help. Why don't we ask Tensey to invest?"

"For good reason: A special Materials Inspector isn't paid much—it's a tribal co-op job. Even if she invested her entire online credit account, I doubt if she would have enough to do us any good; we'll need many thousands of credits. Besides, I'm afraid she'll lose respect for me if she learns how broke I am."

"I know about a local venture capitalist, Mr. Vultura. He might be willing to invest."

"Okay, let's arrange to see him."

For the next week, Bob and Doug worked on a presentation they thought might entice the venture capitalist. Doug would make the presentation since he was a more eloquent speaker than Bob, who was happy to just sit in on the meeting and observe.

The big day arrived, and the two men put on their best clothes. Doug made the presentation to Vultura, clearly describing the general features of the heat storage device and how it would be used to power vehicles directly from solar power.

Mr. Vultura listened patiently.

Doug concluded by saying, "As you can see, this solar-powered car will solve one of the leading problems in the world today. It could be huge. What so you think? Are you willing to invest?"

"But you haven't presented your business plan."

"Business plan?"

"Yes. Didn't you prepare a business plan?"

"I'm sorry. We're engineers concentrating on the technical aspects of the project, and we've not had business training.. What's a business plan?"

"Good God, gentlemen, I'm astounded that you don't know. It's a plan that includes a complete analysis of the potential market for your device, shows how it will overcome competition, what the risks are, predicts how many credits it will make, etc. It also must present warrants and describe how you are going to pay me five times the amount I've invested within fifteen months."

"Warrants? Five times the investment in fifteen months?"

"Yes, warrants would guarantee that you will produce 400% profit for me and repay my principal within the allotted time, or ownership of the project and all of the equipment will transfer to me."

"That hardly seems fair. We have years of our lives, and all of our own credits tied up in this. Fifteen months is not very long, considering what we still have to do."

"Yes, but it's my credits at risk. Take it or leave it."

Doug said, "Good day, Mr. Vultura," and the men left Vultura's office much wiser, but thoroughly disappointed with the world of venture capital.

Bob said, "Holy crap, Doug, Vultura will only invest in a sure thing, and he wants the amount he invested, plus four times that much, returned in a short, fixed time that can't be predicted. That kind of investor would only work when we've already demonstrated our solar car. Then we'd only need funding to set up for manufacturing, and we'd be able to estimate the completion date, market and potential profits. Vultura certainly isn't worth a damn for funding our development work."

"Yeah, you're right. His requirements make it too risky for us—not even worth generating a business plan for him. We'd end up paying him a lot of credits if we succeed. He'd be taking almost no risk since he'd have our technology and all of our equipment to sell if we failed to meet the warrants on time."

"Let's try to get an online bank loan using our property as collateral."

"Yeah. It sounds less risky. But I believe the limit for online transactions is 20,000-credits. For the amount we need to borrow, we'll have to meet with a banker in person."

Bob and Doug went to a bank and met with the loan officer, Mr. Grim. They found out that second mortgages, and outright loans with collateral, were similar in nature: 4-3/4% to 5-1/2% interest, and forfeiture of the mortgaged or collateral property if payments weren't made on time during a five or ten year payoff period.

Bob asked Grim to give them privacy so they could discuss the bank's terms.

After Grim left the room, Bob said, "I've heard that Grim is hard nosed and seizes any opportunity he can to foreclose. How certain are you that we will be able to make payments on time, and finish the project before we run out of funds? We could lose everything."

Doug thought for a few minutes, then said, "I believe we have a pretty good chance, but there are many unknowns. We don't know what all we'll need for the project, so I really can't predict how much more it's going to cost. I can't even predict how much more time it's going to take to finish—we don't know what unexpected problems we'll run into. But one thing I can say for certain: if we're successful, this will be huge, and we'll be rich beyond our wildest dreams. And best of all, we won't have to pay the bank 400% of the loan amount in fifteen months. To reduce the monthly payments, we'd better select the ten year option with no penalty for early payoff."

"Okay, I see your point. There'll be a lot of risk, but the rewards could support us for the rest of our lives. We don't have any other sources for funding, so let's make the deal with Grim."

The men invited Grim back into the room. Mortgages had a slightly lower interest rate than a loan, so they chose that option.

A few days later, the online bank credits Bob and Doug needed were activated, and they again set to work on the project. They finished the foil dimpling job that was interrupted when the sheriff caught them. This work had been delayed, not only while the men were in jail, but was further delayed while they had to search for funding and work through the backlog that had built up in their blacksmith and farming businesses.

When the dimpling was finished, they transported the solid graphite cylinder to Bob's shop. While they were traveling to the shop, Bob said, "Boy, it's sure a lot easier to work in the open. I'm kind of glad we were caught. It brought out the fact that this isn't really new scientific work, but only development using existing science."

"Yeah, but we now have a new problem—credits. If we can't make this thing pay off, we'll lose our homes, my farm, and your shop."

With this depressing thought hanging in the air, they rode for a while in silence.

Then Bob changed the subject. "What do you hear from Tensey?"

"Not much. I telephone occasionally, but lately I've been too busy to visit her in Greensville, and I'm worried and depressed about the delays and the financial risks we're taking. It's hard to sound cheerful when I talk to her."

"Maybe you should level with her about our situation and ask her to invest in our project."

"My God, no. I don't want her to think I'm a loser. If she were to invest, and we were unsuccessful, she would lose her entire investment and, even though it would probably be a small amount, it would probably kill any chance I might have with her."

When they arrived at Bob's shop, they unloaded the graphite heat storage core cylinder and set it up on the milling machine so Bob could bore the flat-bottom hole for the Heat Extractor. When they had finished the set-up, Doug said, "I just can't shake the feeling something's missing."

CHAPTER 40
PROBLEMS, PROBLEMS

Bob said, "I know what you mean about something missing. I feel the same way."

Doug thought for a few minutes, then said, "I just figured out what's missing."

"What?"

"Snood! It seems like he ought to be here looking over our shoulders, getting in the way, and making a nuisance of himself."

"You're right. I'm glad the sheriff took him out of circulation."

At that moment, a voice at the entrance of the shop said, "Hello. Is there anyone in here?"

Bob and Doug came out of the inner room where the milling machine and lathe were, and saw Mr. Grim from the bank. "I just wanted to stop by and see how the work is progressing on your project."

"Are you worried? You have our property as collateral."

"I wanted to keep track of your progress. I'm excited about your project—it has great possibilities."

Bob couldn't see any reason to deny Grim access, so he took him into the inner room and showed him the graphite cylinder set up for boring. Grim seemed impressed—by the value of the lathe and large milling machine. Bob felt uneasy about Grim's apparent emphasis on the monetary value of the machines, but chalked it up to him probably being more comfortable with the financial rather than the mechanical and engineering aspects of the project. After looking the shop over, Grimm left.

That afternoon, Bob finished boring the Heat Extractor hole. Doug had left his horses and wagon at the shop. When the work was finished, Bob loaded the graphite cylinder and took it back to the cavern away from prying eyes of industrial spies. Even though the project was now legal, Bob felt it was necessary to protect against theft of the "method and means" until they were patented. Evenings and weekends during the next four weeks,

Bob assembled the heat storage device in the cavern, while Doug and Audrey designed the solar furnace mirror for heating the storage core to a white-hot temperature.

One night, while Bob was working on the device, Doug and Audrey approached him looking worried. "We've got a problem we hope you can help us solve," Audrey said. "We've determined that the solar mirror should be a paraboloid dish 20-feet in diameter, but we don't have any idea how to build it with ordinary equipment. Large mirrors built for astronomical telescopes, require huge facilities and millions of credits to build. We don't have the resources."

Now, Bob looked puzzled. "What's a paraboloid mirror?"

"A concave dish shaped mirror, that has a parabolic cross section, and focuses sunlight shining on it onto a small spot at its focal point like a magnifying glass does. If the dish is large enough, the amount of sunlight focused onto the spot produces intense heat."

Bob thought for a moment, then said, "I recall reading something about liquids when I was trying to learn a bit of science, before I finally gave up. The surface of any liquid in a container, spun around a vertical axis at constant velocity, will form a dish-shaped surface. Reflections from that surface will focus at a distance and magnification that depends on the rotation speed."

"Do you remember where you read it?"

"Umm – yeah. It was in the only book I read—*Elementary Physics.* I got it from a bookshelf here in the cavern."

Going to one of the cavern bookcases, Bob pulled the book off a shelf. Leafing through it he suddenly stopped and said, "Yes, here it is. In fact, here's the formula for the focal length related to rotation speed," and he handed the book to Audrey.

"Oh, this is simple, and it forms a paraboloidal surface," she said, then read the formula out loud. "The focal length in inches is 17,569 divided by the square of the number of revolutions per minute."

Doug performed some computations, then said, "This works out nicely. At a rotation rate of 10-rpm, we would get a focal length of about 14 feet. That's well within our capability."

Audrey said, "There's a liquid plastic that hardens in a few hours after you add a catalyst to it. We could rotate it in a 20-foot diameter tub, forming its surface into a paraboloidal shape until it hardens. Then to make it highly reflective, we could evaporate a thin coating of aluminum onto it."

Bob said, "I've heard about liquid plastics that harden after adding a catalyst, but they are expensive."

They thought about the problem for a few more minutes.

Finally, Doug spoke. "We can greatly reduce the amount of plastic required by shaping the bottom of the rotating tub to be as nearly the desired dish shape as possible so the plastic only has to form a thin layer on the surface to make it a perfect paraboloid during rotation."

Bob said, "I don't think we'll be able to produce a dish-shaped tub bottom because it would have to curve around the circumference as well as along the radius. Curving a sheet of metal in two directions requires special cupping equipment I don't have."

Audrey flapped her arms up and down. She looked like an enthusiastic child with an idea about to pop. "Oh, I know, I know! We can cut long, narrow triangular gores and mount them on parabolic ribs. Even though each gore would curve only in the radial direction, the gores could be sealed together side-by-side in a circle to approximate a dish. There would be only small deviations from a paraboloidal shape near the joints between the gores. The deviations would be filled in by the plastic to form a perfect paraboloid when the tub is spun."

Bob, who had been looking dour, worrying about how he was going to make the vital casting tub, brightened. "By golly, she's right. I can make the ribs and gores out of sheet metal and weld them together. There'll be imperfections, but the liquid plastic will fill them in during spinning and make a perfect paraboloidal surface without requiring too much plastic. Come to think of it, we don't have to cast the entire 20-foot dish at once. We can cast individual gore-shaped sectors that can be mounted side-by-side on a support frame to form a circular dish."

Doug had been calculating while Audrey and Bob had been speaking. "My rough calculations show that it would take about 25 gallons of plastic to coat a 20-foot dish to a depth of 1/8 inch.

Epoxy resin is about the least expensive liquid plastic at around 100-credits per quart. It'll cost about 10,000-credits to coat the dish."

Audrey looked thoughtful. "We'd better try it out on a small scale, say a one foot dish, before we go for broke on a full sized dish." Bob and Doug agreed.

The next day, Bob began working on a one-foot diameter casting-tub, while Audrey ordered a quart of epoxy casting plastic and a ten rpm geared electric motor. Two days later, Bob completed the tub and rotor required for spin-casting the mirror. The electric motor and epoxy arrived from Greensville. After installing the motor and setting the apparatus up in the inner room of the shop, Bob started the tub spinning, mixed the epoxy and catalyst, and poured it into the tub

. Three hours later the epoxy had hardened, and Bob anxiously stopped the spinning so he could examine the resulting surface. Disappointment! The surface was covered with lumps and ripples that spoiled the paraboloidal shape. Bob called Audrey and Doug. They stood looking at the terrible results and wondering what went wrong.

Audrey said, "According to the theory, it should've worked. What'll we do now?"

CHAPTER 41
HALLELUJAH AND AMEN

Audrey and Doug dejectedly studied the lumpy, rippled surface of the small dish-shaped test mirror Bob had made. Finally, Doug said, "I believe these surface ripples, and maybe the bumps, could have been caused by not having the axis of the spinning tub perfectly vertical. That would cause the liquid to flow continuously downhill trying to find its level in the rotating tub." Audrey agreed.

"I measured from the floor to the edge of the tub in four places," Bob said. "The tub was as close to horizontal as I could get it, so its axis of rotation must have been vertical."

"But, the floor may not be perfectly level. I suggest that you place a level on the tub's rotation axel and check the level's vertical indicator bubble."

"I can't do that. The axel is completely covered by the tub, bearing, and gearbox.."

"It's essential that the axel be long enough to stick out so you can get a level on it. Also, I just thought of something else. Is the drive motor geared directly to the axel?"

"Yes."

"Then a lot of vibration may be getting transmitted to the tub. This could cause the liquid to ripple."

"Okay. It looks like I'll have to rebuild the spin-casting system."

"Sorry about that, Bob."

"It's going to be a lot of work to rebuild even this small scale spin-casting equipment. I'll have to install pulleys on the motor and tub axel, use elastic belts between the pulleys, and install anti-vibration mounts on the motor, to cut down on the vibrations transmitted to the tub. I sure wish it wasn't a paraboloidal tub."

"You don't have to build a paraboloidal tub."

"Why not?"

"That's the nice thing about the surface of a spinning liquid. It'll form a paraboloid regardless of the container's shape. In this small size, you could use a flat-bottom pie pan and it won't take much extra plastic to fill the space between the pan bottom and the liquid surface. It should take less than a quart."

Some of the worry wrinkles in Bob's forehead disappeared as he understood Doug's advice. He immediately began building the small test system using the revised design. The belts, pulleys and anti-vibration mounts were available at the local hardware supply company, and Audrey gave Bob her 12-inch pie pan. Then she ordered another quart of Epoxy.

*   *   *

Three days later, Bob finished the small rotational test system. He set it up in the inner room of the shop to spin-cast the mirror surface, then called Doug and Audrey to witness the process so they could help him spot anything that went wrong. When they arrived, he placed the level on the spin axel to demonstrate that it was perfectly vertical, then started the spin and poured in the epoxy. They watched for a while, then left, being careful to tread lightly on the floor to avoid causing vibrations. Three hours later they returned to find the plastic hardened with a surface that was wrinkle free and roughly dish-shaped. However, it was bumpy.

Doug said, "Oh hell. What'll we do now? Bob, do you suppose the axel is no longer vertical?"

Bob again placed the level on the spin axel and inspected the bubble through a magnifying glass.

"It's still vertical. Here, take a look."

Bob held the magnifying glass so the others could see the bubble.

Audrey said, "Well then, the only thing it could be is some characteristic of the plastic itself. I suggest we try polyurethane. The liquid form of it is more viscous than epoxy, and might help dampen out any surface effects that are due to waves. It's more expensive, but it's elastic when it solidifies, and it's a different class of plastic than epoxy, so it might work."

Doug looked thoughtful. "Hmm. Elastic. I don't know if it would withstand vacuum evaporation coating with aluminum. Surfaces get hot during that process. But let's try it. The amount we'll need for a small test shouldn't cost too much."

Bob agreed.

"I read about a thin, aluminum-coated, reflective plastic sheet material called 'Aluminized Mylar,' used for decorations and reflective insulation," Audrey said. "Perhaps we could glue that to the paraboloidal polyurethane surface, rather than vacuum evaporating aluminum onto it."

Bob said, "I don't know anything about Mylar. It's worth a try, but first we have to have a dish surface that doesn't have bumps on it."

Audrey returned home to order the polyurethane and some aluminized Mylar needed for a small-scale test. Polyurethane was listed at 200-credits per quart, double the cost of epoxy. It would cost about 20,000-credits for enough to cast a full-size 20-foot dish. Before ordering even 200-credits worth for a test, Audrey called a meeting with Bob and Doug to discuss the impact of polyurethane's cost on the marketability of full sized mirrors.

Bob said, "The cost of getting enough polyurethane for a full-size mirror would take a large chunk of the credits we got from Grim. Maybe we should consider testing some other plastic."

The three thought for a few minutes, then Doug said, "In a 25 gallon quantity for a 20-foot dish, polyurethane's cost per quart should be lower than for a single quart. And in the volume needed for many mirrors, the cost should be even lower. So it should be affordable for customers purchasing solar powered cars. I think we should go ahead with the small test on polyurethane while we explore other possibilities. It may or may not work, but a cost of 200-credits to find out isn't going to break us."

Audrey and Bob thought for a few minutes, then Bob said, "I can't think of any better alternative right now, and if it works it may be our only chance for success."

Audrey added, "I agree. I'll order enough for the small test."

When ordering the quart of polyurethane, Audrey found out that a 5,000-gallon tank would cost only 100-credits per quart, half the price of the quart she was ordering. This meant that polyurethane for each 20-foot mirror manufactured in quantity would cost an affordable 10,000-credits. While waiting for delivery, Bob worked on customer jobs that had fallen behind schedule, and Doug went back to work on his farm.

*   *   *

Three weeks later, the quart of polyurethane arrived, and the sample of Aluminized Mylar was supposed to arrive a day or so later. Bob managed to break the epoxy out of the pie pan, so it could be re-used for spin-casting the new sample. Audrey and Doug watched, while Bob poured the catalyst-polyurethane mixture into the rotating pie pan. Three hours later, they returned to find a perfect, smooth paraboloidal dish-shaped surface on the solidified plastic.

"Hallelujah," Audrey shouted.

"Amen," Bob shouted.

"Are you having a religious revival meeting?" a voice behind them asked.

They all spun around to see Mr. Grim standing in the doorway of the inner room.

Audrey asked, "Did you receive our loan payment three weeks ago?"

"Yes. I just wanted to see how things are going."

"Our project is right on schedule."

"Good. I'm glad to hear it. By the way, your next payment is due at the end of next week."

"Okay. Thanks for reminding me."

"What brought on the outburst I heard as I was coming in?"

"We just had a breakthrough in solving a troublesome problem," Audrey said, smiling.

Grim leaned forward with great interest. "What was it?"

Doug smiled and said, "I'm sorry, but our work is proprietary, and we can't tell anyone outside our company about it."

"But I lent you credits."

"No, you accepted mortgages on our property for a lot less than it's worth. There's a difference. You have collateral, and you are protected if things don't work out."

As he turned to leave, Mr. Grim reddened and said, "Okay. If you want to play it that way, don't be surprised if I'm hard nosed if you miss a payment.".

After Mr. Grim was out of earshot, Bob said, "So what else is new."

CHAPTER 42
MORE TROUBLE

Bob, Doug and Audrey were ecstatic about their success in spin-casting a perfect dish-shaped paraboloidal surface on plastic in the 12-inch pie pan. When the thin, reflective Mylar sheet arrived, they breathlessly rushed to the blacksmith shop to try gluing the Mylar onto the dish. Before applying the glue, Audrey tested a single triangular gore of the Mylar for fit. When she placed the gore on the surface of the polyurethane dish, two unexpected things happened. The first was a pleasant surprise: Mylar was strongly attracted to the polyurethane mirror's surface by a natural electrostatic charge, so glue, with its possible thickness variation, wasn't necessary. The second surprise was disturbing. The flat triangular Mylar gore rumpled as it pulled into contact with the form's cupped dish-shaped-surface.

"Oh, crap. I didn't think of this," Audrey said in a depressed tone of voice.

"Neither did I," Bob and Doug exclaimed almost in unison.

"The Mylar can't curve in two directions without first being formed into a cupped shape," Bob said. "And we don't have any equipment that'll do that."

They stood around the rumpled reflective gore looking downcast and staring at it as if they were trying to conjure a solution from the gore itself. Five minutes later, Audrey suddenly brightened and said, "I have a simple idea that might fix this."

Both men said, "What?"

"Let's try cutting the gore crosswise to divide the triangle into small several trapezoidal sections. The difference between a straight line, and the cupped surface within each trapezoid, will be smaller than that for a whole triangular gore. The mylar might have just enough elasticity that the small trapezoids would fit tightly against the cupped surface of the dish without wrinkling."

"I don't think that'll work," Doug said in a dismissive tone.

"Well, what have we got to lose? A one-piece triangular gore sure doesn't work. This small Mylar gore didn't cost much, so why not try applying it as several smaller pieces?"

"Oh, all right. It'll be easy to try."

Bob retrieved a scissors and handed it to Audrey. "Okay, knock yourself out."

Audrey cut across the triangle at three locations, making one small triangle from the tip of the original one, and three trapazoidal sections. She carefully laid the pieces end-to-end along a radius of the dish surface to rebuild the original triangular gore, and the pieces settled into tight, smooth contact with the dish-shaped backing. Audrey picked the pie tin up from the spin-cradle, pointed it a little to one side of the door, and asked Bob to turn off the lights. The little reflective gore focused a perfect image of the bright scene, outside the door, on the dark inside wall without any trace of the splits between trapezoids in the triangular gore showing in the image..

"You've done it!" Bob exclaimed.

Doug said, "You were right. It works! Let's complete our little mirror and try to focus an image of the sun with it."

Audrey cut enough gore sectors, cut them into pieces as before, and applied them to the rest of the dish, then went outside where she could point the mirror at the sun. Bob poked a long stick into the focal spot of the gore, and it produced a blindingly bright spot on the stick. Soon the spot began to smoke and, after a time, burst into flame.

"And that's with just this one-foot mirror," Doug said enthusiastically. "Imagine what a 20-foot mirror with 400 times this area would do."

For a short time, Audrey basked in the satisfaction of having bested the men in solving the Mylar-wrinkling problem. After enjoying a few minutes of adulation from the men, she went home confident of success, and ordered enough of the expensive polyurethane and Mylar to build the 20-foot diameter mirror.

Bob and Doug began designing the spin-casting apparatus and adjustable mirror stand for the thousand-pound, 20-foot mirror. They knew that each of the mirror's 63 gore sectors would have to be adjustable so they could be aimed at the overall common focal spot. Also, the entire mirror would have to be re-aimed every few minutes to keep it pointed at the sun throughout the day. To avoid the added expense of motors and sensors for automatically aiming at the sun, they planned to aim the mirror manually using hand-cranked, heavy-duty gearboxes during the initial demonstration of the system.

*   *   *

A month went by. The polyurethane had arrived, but the Mylar had not. Audrey telephoned the supplier. The salesman said that aluminum-coating a continuous 630-foot piece of one-foot wide Mylar was more difficult than anticipated.

Audrey thought for a moment, then asked, "How much of the Mylar have you already produced?"

"We've only been able to produce three 200-foot lengths."

"If you'll throw in a free extra 20-feet to compensate for roll-end losses, and the price is right, I'll accept three 200-foot rolls plus a 50-foot roll instead of a continuous 630-foot roll."

"We'll be glad to do that. Your original order would have cost 6930-credits at 11-credits per foot for the continuous roll. I can let you have three 200-foot rolls plus the 50-foot roll for 3250-credits, so it'll be a much better deal for you."

"I wish you'd told me about the difficulty in producing the long roll when I called a month ago."

"Sorry. We knew it would be difficult, but we didn't know it would be almost impossible with our present equipment. We'd never had a request for a roll that long before. Shall I ship the shorter rolls now?"

"Yes. But since you missed your original delivery date, will you please expedite this shipment at no extra cost?"

"Yes. That's only fair."

*   *   *

Three weeks later, the Mylar had not yet been delivered. Bob had been working hard to meet the promised completion dates for his customers' jobs. However, he managed with Doug's help to build the spin-casting rotary drive and support beam for casting pairs of gore segments for the 20-foot dish shaped mirror. The night they finished, Doug asked, "What are your plans for constructing the mirror?"

"I will spin-cast the mirror in sixty-three individual gore-shaped sectors in triangular tubs having parabolic bottoms. I plan to cast them in thirty-one pairs of ten-foot long tubs, one tub mounted on each end of the support beam. Finally, the sixty-third gore sector will be cast using a counterweight on the other end of the beam for balance. The bottom of each ten-foot gore tub will be a thin sheet attached to parabolic ribs to give it strength and rigidity. Sides of each tub will be temporarily sealed to the bottom with caulk to hold the liquid polyurethane during spin-casting. The sides will be removed after casting each gore to leave a thin gore-shaped sector of paraboloidal mirror attached to its own parabolic tub bottom.

After the plastic solidifies, I will need you and Audrey to cut reflective, triangular Mylar gores into trapezoids and smoothed on to cover each mirror dish sector. While you two are doing that, I will bolt completed sectors side-by-side onto a support frame forming the 20-foot circular dish mirror. I have provided slotted and pivoted support bars on the back of each mirror sector so it can be mounted on the mirror support frame and be individually adjusted to aim at a central focal spot."

"It sounds like a good plan," Doug said as he and Bob left for home.

The next day, the Mylar finally arrived. Audrey and Doug joined Bob at the shop. After Doug and Audrey each stirred up a batch of the plastic with its catalyst, they rapidly poured it into the two casting tubs, starting at the wide end and weaving back and forth as they distributed the liquid evenly as possible along the bottom of each tub. They jumped out of the way and Bob started the support beam spinning up to its final speed of 10-RPM.

With a worried look on his face, Bob said, "Well, that does it. In three hours when this stuff has set, we'll know whether our mirror fabrication method works."

CHAPTER 43
MIRROR, MIRROR

Three hours later, Bob, Doug and Audrey waited impatiently while the spin-casting machine slowed to a stop.

Audrey was the first to speak. "The surface looks good, but we won't know for sure until we've tried focusing sunlight with it. I've made a ten-foot, reflective, triangular Mylar gore and cut it into ten one-foot pieces. Let's take the sides off one of these casting tubs and see if the Mylar pieces can be smoothed onto the polyurethane surface."

Bob was careful not to tear the newly cast dish-shaped gore surface as he removed the sides from one of the ten-foot long casting tubs. Then Audrey laid the Mylar trapezoids end-to-end to cover the triangular surface. When the Mylar was smoothed into contact, it adhered by electrostatic attraction without any wrinkles.

Bob and Doug carried the mirror sector outdoors to the south side of the shop and placed the large end on the ground. Doug balanced the sector and aimed it at the sun, and Bob shoved one end of a long, nearly black stick into the focal spot. The end of the stick looked blindingly white as it entered the intense light at the focal spot of the mirror sector.

"My God, that's intense—look at the blinding light reflected from that black surface."

Doug started to say something, but the blinding white end suddenly burst into intense flames and quickly disintegrated in a cloud of smoke, while most of the stick outside the focal spot was unaffected. Doug, Bob and Audrey were momentarily awe-struck, then burst forth in loud laughter and cheers. They shouted, "It works! It works! Thank God it works!"

"I've got to tell Tensey about our success!" Doug exclaimed as he began to call Greensville on his wrist telephone.

Grim, at the bank on the other end of the block, heard the shouting and came running to see what the excitement was about. As Bob told of their success, Grim passively looked at the smoking end of the stick. Then he said sarcastically, "So you can burn the end of a stick. So what?"

Just then, Doug stopped fiddling with his wrist telephone and turned to the group standing around the mirror sector. "I couldn't reach Tensey," he said, looking disappointed. "I'll try again tonight."

Grim left, and when he was out of hearing range Bob said, "Grim makes me nervous. He's like a vulture perched on a branch, watching and waiting for us to fail so he can devour our property."

Doug thought for a few moments, then said, "He may not have long to wait. We're going through the credits he lent us like water through a large drain pipe, and the work is taking longer than expected."

Audrey reddened and said, "Bob is working as fast as he can. In fact, he's at risk of ruining his health."

"Oh, I'm sorry Audrey, I didn't mean it that way. Instead, I should've said, 'Everything has been more difficult than I expected'."

Doug and Bob carried the mirror sector back into the shop, followed by Audrey. For the remainder of the day, and the next two weeks, Bob and Doug cast a new pair of gore-shaped mirror sectors every three or four hours, from early morning until bedtime. Sixty-three of the sectors were required for the 20-foot mirror. Audrey cut aluminized Mylar triangles, then cut them into trapezoidal pieces and smoothed them on to cover the sector surfaces as the were cast.

On the second evening, between gore casting sessions, Doug finally got a phone call through to Tensey. "It sure was nice to feel successful, for a change, when I was talking to Tensey," Doug said that evening as he, Bob and Audrey rode to the shop together.

Audrey asked, "Why weren't you able to reach her earlier?"

"Her wrist-phone developed a problem and she had to get a new one."

The next day, after ten of the mirror sectors had been completed and covered with reflective Mylar, Bob borrowed Doug's hay wagon and team. He hauled the sectors, together with the support frame and aiming mechanism, to a location near the brush patch where he had prepared a concrete pad for supporting the mirror. Between sector casting sessions, he installed the mirror support frame together with the heavy gearboxes of the aiming mechanism on the pad. Then he mounted the ten sectors on the support frame. Meanwhile, between casting sessions, Doug and Audrey were cutting and applying aluminized Mylar to the sectors. Whenever ten sectors were completed, Bob hauled them to the pad and mounted them on the mirror support frame. After he passed the halfway point, eleven-feet above the ground, Doug and Audrey helped him haul and mount batches of ten mirror sectors as they were completed. The men pointed the mirror support frame with its mounted mirror sectors at the ground so they could safely work from ten-foot stepladders without the danger of accidentally getting into intense focal hot-spot. Audrey handed mirror sectors and bolts up to the men.

When the last mirror sector had been mounted, the men adjusted all the sectors to focus on the mirror's focal area, and tested the hand-cranked gearboxes for adjusting the mirror's azimuth and elevation angles to point it at the sun throughout the day. The gearboxes were heavy-duty with high gear ratios since the engine/ heat-storage-assembly would weigh almost 2,000-pounds in addition to the 1000-pound weight of the mirror.

Next, they installed heavy steel arms connected to the mirror support frame and projecting outward past the focal spot 14-feet in front of the mirror. The arms were to hold the engine/ heat-storage unit at the mirror's focal spot during charging. While installing the arms, Bob and Doug aimed the mirror at the horizon away from the sun so they wouldn't get burned or blinded while working near the focal spot.

When the mirror was completed, Bob and Doug began working on Audrey's old car to convert it for use with the Stirling engine and heat storage device. However, after they had worked on it for only a few days Doug called a meeting.

"We need to buy steel, instruments, cables, and fittings. We're virtually out of credits for the project, and we aren't far enough along to demonstrate the solar powered car. Somehow, we have to get more funding right away or we won't be able to finish."

Bob said, "Audrey and I have been worrying about that too. But what can we do? We've already tried the venture capital route. If we go that way, we'll likely work for another 15 months, then lose everything including our technology by missing payback of the principle plus 400% profit, even if everything works."

Doug looked thoughtful, then said, "But we are closer to being finished now. Maybe we should take a chance on Vultura's offer."

Bob's face contorted as he recalled the painful memory of their meeting with Vultura. "No. I think it would be too risky to count on that much profit in such a short time. It'll probably take us at least a year to finish the development, and another year to get some income from it, even if we just sold licenses for our technology to manufacturers. Even then we couldn't sure they'd buy. Getting a solar-powered car into production for sale to the public would take even longer, and lots of credits we don't have."

Audrey, who had been listening intently said, "Let's at least try out the engine and heat storage system together with our mirror before we go after funding. With the results of a stationary test, we might be able to find an investor less greedy than Vultura."

Doug said, "Okay, that sounds like a good idea. We have all the essentials for a stationary test, and we might be able get funding in time to save us if it's successful."

Audrey's face brightened as she said, "Guys, if you're done with the financial part of the meeting, Bob and I have an announcement."

"What's that," Doug said nonchalantly.

"I'm pregnant!"

Doug looked stunned. A few seconds later he said, in a dour tone of voice, "Congratulations."

"Aren't you happy for us," Bob asked.

"Oh, of course, but I'm worried about the impact on the project. You'll probably be less willing to take financial risks now, and I certainly can't support it alone."

"I don't see it being any more of a problem than it has been. We're already broke; we'll have to get more financing or the project's dead anyway," Bob said incredulously.

The next day, conditions were right to test the solar energy storage device together with the Stirling engine in-place on the mirror support arms.. It was late spring, and early morning clouds had disappeared revealing a bright sun in a cloudless, blue sky.

They mounted the Heat Storage Unit and Heat Extractor/Engine Unit on a small frame. Altogether, this assembly was called "Solar Propulsion Module." Next, they injected helium working gas into the Heat Extractor/Engine Unit, and argon protective gas into the Heat Storage Unit. They brought the Solar Propulsion Module out of the cavern and installed it on the mirror's support arms in preparation for solar charging.

Bob said, "Well, here goes. If these static test results aren't spectacular enough to attract an investor, we may *never* be able to complete this project."

Audrey, Bob and Doug gathered around the mirror. Bob adjusted the mirror to the proper azimuth (compass direction), and Doug adjusted the elevation, to keep the mirror aimed at the sun as it moved across the sky. As the focal spot of the mirror moved onto the solar charging window of the heat storage device, blinding white reflected light appeared in the window. Bob ran to the tool shed to get a pair of acetylene welder's dark goggles. Since he was the only one with eye protection, he would have to call out the elevation adjustments for Doug as they tracked the sun. After 10 a.m. the mirror's elevation changed only slowly, but the azimuth changed rapidly and Bob had to adjust it every few minutes. Audrey went to the house and later brought sandwiches, cold water, and cups to the men. They grabbed bites of food and swigs of water between mirror adjustments. Seven hours passed. The sun was getting low in the sky so the mirror's elevation angle was changing more rapidly. The core was almost fully charged, and the men were getting tired. A half hour later, Doug said, "The sun is low enough in the sky that the energy input from now on will probably be less than the heat lost by radiation out through the window, so we won't gain anything.. I think it's time to lower the module, pull the solar window's radiation shield into place, and perform the engine's test run."

Audrey said, "I'm not feeling very well, so I'll have to go home pretty soon and rest. But I'd sure like to see the test."

"Okay, let's do it," Bob said as he began adjusting the mirror azimuth away from the sun.

Doug lowered the mirror elevation to bring the engine within reach, then pulled the heat shield into place inside the storage unit's solar window. Bob turned the starting crank on the engine. Nothing happened. He cranked until his arm got too tired to continue. The engine wouldn't start! He stepped back and said, "Crap!"

"Here, let me try," Doug said as he grabbed the crank and furiously cranked the engine.

Nothing—the engine wouldn't start.

"Oh God," Audrey said in a timorous tone of voice.

"Damn," Bob said in a shaky voice.

"Yeah," Doug said weakly.

The two exhausted men and Audrey stood looking at the engine for a long time. Finally, Audrey broke down and wept.

"We're going to lose everything," she said between sobs. "Our living expenses alone are soon going to use up our few remaining credits if we can't get more somehow. I thought surely we'd be successful and be able to get some credits from an investor by now."

CHAPTER 44
SUCCESS OR FAILURE?

Audrey had gone into the house to rest. Bob and Doug worked into the night trying to get the engine to run. It was no use. Brute force was not solving the problem, no matter how hard the men cranked. They went over the engine hookup and retightened pipe-fittings, but the engine still wouldn't start.

At about 10-p.m., Doug said, "We're not getting anywhere. It's time to re-evaluate whether we should continue the project."

Bob thought for a few minutes. "If we quit, we're going to lose everything."

"But we're running out of credits, so there's not much reason to continue struggling. We don't even have enough to live on for long."

"Let's talk to Audrey before deciding."

In the house, the men found Audrey rested and feeling much better. They described the struggles with the engine, and shared their thoughts about their situation.

Audrey said, "While I was resting, I thought about our engine problem. The heat storage core gets hot enough that the engine should surely run. You checked all the things you could, and found them normal, so there has to be something we've overlooked.

"I also thought about your conclusions on our financial situation. We need to get at least one more investor so we can finish the project and get some income from it. Without that, there's no way we can make enough to meet our loan payments, make payments on our hospital bill, and still have enough to live on; we're too deeply in debt and we'll lose everything if we don't go ahead. Completing the project, so we can get some income from it, appears to be our only logical course of action. I'll be glad to try figuring out why the engine doesn't run, if you two will go try to get funding from the venture capitalists in Greensville. Maybe one of them will be more reasonable than Vultura."

Bob's shoulders slumped, and he looked at the floor. "I'm exhausted, and I feel that we might just be pouring more work and credits into a black hole."

"Well, look at it this way. If we give up, it's guaranteed that we'll lose everything. If we struggle on until circumstances *force* us to quit, we at least have a chance to succeed. I think things will look brighter after you've had a good night's rest."

*   *   *

The next morning, Bob slept in until 9 a.m. When he awoke, he could hear Doug in the kitchen talking to Audrey. He quickly pulled on his clothes and hurried into the kitchen. A pleasant aroma of coffee filled the warm kitchen.

Audrey and Doug were eating breakfast, and Bob felt a little twinge of jealousy. However, just as he came into the kitchen he overheard Doug talking about his romantic phone calls to Tensey during the past two months.

"I think Tensey loves me, and if I can climb out of this financial hole she might even marry me, " Doug said wistfully.

Bob smiled and asked, "What are you two up to?"

"We've been discussing the trouble we're in," Doug said, "And I think the suggestion Audrey made last night, about seeing venture capitalists in Greensville, is worth a try."

"Yeah, now that I'm rested, I feel better about that than I did last night."

"When do you want to leave for Greensville?"

"As soon as possible."

"Okay, I'll pack a few things and be ready to go when you are."

As Doug got up to leave, Audrey brought Bob a plate of scrambled eggs.

"I'll get my stuff and meet you here," Doug said as he left.

A half hour later, Doug arrived on his horse and the two men left for Greensville. As he and Bob rode side-by-side, they discussed the project, and again concluded there was no way they could continue the project if they couldn't get funding. For about five miles, they were quiet, each lost in his own thoughts. Then Doug said, "Would you mind if I go visit Tensey some evening while we're there?"

"As long as it doesn't interfere with conducting our business. Why should I mind?"

"I thought you might resent being left on your own in the evening with nothing to do, and no one to talk to."

"Of course not. I enjoy my own company just fine. Besides, there are several bars in Greensville, and they might be a good source of information on potential investors. If I know you as well as I think I do, you'll be spending at least one night at Tensey's place, and I'll have our hotel room to myself. But remember, you'll have to be back by 8 a.m. so we'll be able to spend a full day talking to potential investors."

As soon as they got into Greensville, Doug and Bob went to a local bank to ask about possible local investors. The bank wasn't interested in investing, and the loan officer only knew two venture capitalists.

After lunch, the men checked into a hotel, and telephoned both of the venture capitalists to make appointments. One of them was available the next day, but the other one was tied up that day, so Bob and Doug would have to stay an extra day to see him.

Later, in the hotel room, Bob and Doug went over their notes and rehearsed what they were going to say during their presentations. This time, they brought a business plan complete with photos of the equipment, and were much better prepared than they had been when they made their naive presentation to Mr. Vultura. They felt confident that at least one of the Greensville venture capitalists, Mr. Slicke or Mr. Grabner, would give them favorable terms for the privilege of investing in their project. Doug decided not to go see Tensey until they were successful with one of the venture capitalists.

*   *   *

Both men had spent a restless night, tossing and turning.

"I didn't sleep worth a damn last night," Bob said when they got up. "I just couldn't stop thinking about our 2 o'clock meeting with Mr. Slicke this afternoon."

"Me too. I worried about what we are going to say, what questions he might ask, and how important it is for us to get at least one of these guys to invest in our project. Another worry is that we might say something to screw up our presentations."

"I've been thinking the same things. I guess we've been working together long enough that we're getting to be of the same mind like an old married couple."

The men had a good laugh about Bob's remark, relieving some of the tension they were feeling. Then they went to breakfast.

After breakfast, they returned to their room and practiced their presentation, first with one of them playing the part of Mr. Slicke, and the other making the presentation and answering questions, then reversing roles. It became obvious that Doug was better able to cover his nervousness and exude an air of confidence, so he and Bob decided he would make the presentation and Bob would play a supporting role.

Finally, it was lunchtime. Bob said, "Shall we go to lunch?"

"My stomach is tied up in a knot. I don't think I could eat anything."

"I feel the same way. Let's keep working on our presentation and see if we can find any holes in it before we go meet with Slicke."

Over and over, the men went through their presentation looking for any possible flaws. Finally, they felt a surge of panic and a stabbing sensation in their stomachs as they realized it was time to go.

"My God, Bob, I feel weak and shaky."

"Me too. I guess we should've had lunch."

"Yeah, but then in our nervousness, one or both of us might have puked on Slicke's carpet. I don't think that would have inspired him to fund our project."

The absurdity of this picture and the tension they were feeling made both men laugh until tears streamed down their cheeks. This released some of their stress, and they felt more confident as they left for their meeting with Slicke.

At Slicke's office, Doug made a flawless presentation of the project, it's marketability, potential profits, and the obvious benefits to mankind of the resulting product.

When Doug had finished his presentation, Slicke asked, "Do you have a prototype you can demonstrate for me?"

"No. But we are close to having one."

"Your project shows promise. However, there is still a lot of risk since you haven't yet demonstrated that it works. If I were to invest, I would need a warrant that you would return a factor of at least 20-times my investment in two years, or the ownership of the entire project and all the related technology and equipment would transfer to me."

Bob felt like a red-hot knife had just been shoved into his stomach. Then, as he thought about what he and Doug had mused earlier about puking on Slick's rug, he began to laugh. Doug looked at Bob questioningly, and Bob quickly glanced down at the rug. Doug immediately caught on and burst out laughing too. Mr. Slicke looked puzzled.

"What do you two find so funny?"

"Now we can go eat lunch," Doug said as he and Bob departed leaving Slicke sitting behind his desk with a puzzled look on his face.

Body language of the two entrepreneurs showed they felt much more relaxed than they had for the past day and a half. As they ate a hearty lunch, Doug said, "Why do I feel so relaxed? We didn't get our funding."

"Well, making the presentation to Slicke was good practice for the one we'll make tomorrow to Grabner. Surely, he'll be more reasonable than Slicke."

CHAPTER 45
OH TENSEY

When Bob and Doug got back to their hotel room, Bob said, "Are you going to see Tensey tonight?"

"No. I want to wait until we have funding so I'll feel successful. Right now, I feel like a failure."

"Don't beat yourself up. Your presentation was perfect. The reason we didn't get funding is that Slicke is a greedy bastard who doesn't want to take any risk for his ludicrously high profit."

"I suppose you're right, but I just can't shake the feeling that I must've done something wrong."

"No. He probably sensed our desperation for credits, and he thought he could trap us into a deal where he would end up owning everything after we worked another two years with nothing to show for it. That seems to be the way these guys operate."

"Anyway, I just don't feel like facing Tensey right now."

The men felt that they were as well prepared as possible for their presentation to Mr. Grabner. They took naps, went to the hotel bar for sandwiches and a couple of beers, then watched holovision in their room until bedtime.

The next morning, Bob and Doug were both well rested and in a good mood. As they ate breakfast they confidently talked about how they were going to approach Mr. Grabner.

"Surely this time we'll be successful," Bob said, smiling.

"Yeah, this time we've had a lot of practice presenting to these yahoos, and I don't even feel nervous."

When they arrived at Grabner's office, they strode in as two men who had all the confidence in the world. After greeting the venture capitalist with strong handshakes and smiling faces, they all sat down and Doug made his pitch. Grabner listened to a description of the project, then asked, "Do you have a working prototype you can demonstrate?"

"No. But we are just on the verge of getting it to work," Doug said confidently.

Grabner's face took on a grim expression. "I'm sorry, gentlemen, but I only invest in products that have been demonstrated. I'm deluged almost daily with ideas that don't work out."

"But we've demonstrated the solar charging and heat storage device. Engineering calculations show that it will work. We just haven't had time and resources to make the engine run on the stored energy, or install the system into a car. To succeed, we only need credits to continue."

"I'm sorry, gentlemen. Come and see me if and when you are able to demonstrate the entire system."

Bob thought for a moment, then said, "All right, say we were able to demonstrate that the system works perfectly. What kind of warrants would you require?"

"I'd want a return of a factor of four plus the principle on my investment within fifteen months, or the project ownership, including all facilities and equipment, would transfer to me."

"That's the same thing Mr. Vultura wanted."

"Oh, yes, I know Vultura. It sounds like he offered you a pretty standard deal. If you'd known that, you could have saved me some time, and saved yourselves the trip to Greensville. Good day, gentlemen."

When they got back to the hotel room, Bob said, "Are you going to see Tensey tonight?"

"No. It's been more than two months since last time I came for a visit with her, and I'll have to do a lot of explaining. I might have to admit how much trouble we've been having, and I feel too down right now."

After dinner, the men sat in their hotel room and discussed the day's events at length. They concluded that they'd done everything they could within reason, to get funding, and there wasn't much reason to continue the project. Most depressing of all was the impending loss of their homes and property. Bob expressed the seriousness of their situation best when he dejectedly said, "I just don't know how I'm going to make a living without my shop. I wish I'd never found that old chest. And with a baby on the way..." Doug looked at the floor as he said, "Yeah. I'm in the same pickle. Without my farm..."

* * *

The next morning after the initial shock had worn off, and after having had a good night's rest, Doug felt better so he got up early, left a note for Bob, and went to see Tensey. When she opened the door, her gleaming chestnut hair, violet eyes, flawless suntanned face and slender body impressed Doug as much as it had the first time he saw her. He believed her breathtaking beauty might be part of the reason no one had married her. Most guys probably thought she was so far out of their league that it was no use even trying to court her. The ones who did date her probably turned out to be arrogant self-assured slobs whom she found repulsive. Doug gave her a friendly hug as he said, "Oh, Tensey, I'm so glad to see you. How've you been?"

"I've been okay. What brings you here?"

"I had some business here, and I've been wanting to see you. I've missed you terribly."

"Well, I'm glad to see you, and I've missed you a lot too. But why did it take you so long to come see me? It's been way too long."

"I telephoned you, didn't I?"

"Yes, but that's not the same as a visit."

"I've been unbelievably busy working on the solar car project, and trying to keep my farm going. I've been pressed to the wall every day, and just flop into bed exhausted every night. But that will end soon."

"Well, I'm still mad at you for not coming to Greensville to visit me sooner. I thought we had a special friendship."

"It's at least an eight-hour round trip from my place to Greensville, and you can't imagine the hours I've been working."

"In one of your phone calls, you told me you were successful on the project—something about a mirror. You haven't told me anything different since then. How come you still have to work on it so hard? What's going on with the solar car project?"

Doug wanted to tell Tensey everything: the technical and financial difficulties, and failing to finish enough of the project to attract venture capital, but he was terrified that he'd lose her. His heart felt like it was in his throat. He especially didn't want to risk telling her about failure of the static test on the power module, so he just explained that there had been a lot more work to do beyond the mirror development.

"Well, if you loved me as you've claimed, you would've come to visit me no matter how busy you've been," Tensey said, vertical furrows marring her flawless forehead between her eyes. Then she continued, "How'd your business here go?"

"Oh, Okay, I guess," Doug said, reddening and looking at the floor. "But, tell me what you've been doing since I last saw you."

"Just the usual stuff. I've been having to take a lot of Special Materials Inspection trips."

"So why didn't you come to my place for a visit when you were on one of those trips?"

"None of my trips took me close enough."

Doug and Tensey visited for another half-hour, mostly making small talk and filling her in on Bob and Audrey's news, including Audrey's pregnancy. Then Doug said, "Tensey, you know that I love you. Now, seeing you again, I realize how much I want you in my life permanently. I may soon be free to move to Greensville. Many of the farms around here need workers. And even if they are not hiring, I learn fast and I'm sure I could find other kinds of work here. I'd like to court you—I want to marry you, and I'm sure I could make you happy."

"I'd like that, Doug—to be courted, that is. I feel that you are a decent, hard-working man, and I feel that we are good friends. I liked you, even when we were children." Then, in a coquettish way, Tensey added, "But, you'll have to make up for waiting so long to come visit me."

"Oh Tensey, you've made me so happy. I'd go to the ends of the earth for you."

"Whoa, now, I didn't say I'd marry you just yet. The courting has to come first."

"I'm delighted that you'll give me a chance to show you that I'd make you a good husband—because I'm sure I can."

"How soon will you be moving to Greensville?"

This question jarred Doug back to reality. In the excitement of seeing Tensey again, he'd temporarily forgotten his problems. His mind suddenly focused on his failure to get venture capital, and his impending financial doom. However, not wanting to sour his chances with Tensey, he only said, "I've got some problems I have to clear up before I can move, but I can probably do it in a month or two."

Doug's face had changed from total happiness to deep lines of despair.

Tensey was alarmed to see such a sudden change, and asked, "Doug, what's wrong?"

"I have some problems I just thought about, but nothing I can't handle in the long-run."

"Is there any way I can help?"

Doug thought, if I ask her for financial help, and reveal what a "Weak Willy" I am, I'll lose her for sure. No woman wants a weakling for a husband. On her low salary as a Special Materials Control Officer, I'm sure she doesn't have enough credits to finance our project, and even if she did, I wouldn't ask. Then he said, "No. This is something I have to take care of myself."

CHAPTER 46
CREDITS OR FORECLOSURE?

Tensey invited Doug to stay for lunch.

Doug considered for a moment, then said, "Yes. Thank you. May I help?"

"No, but thanks for offering."

Doug sat in the kitchen and visited with Tensey while she prepared lunch.

Watching Tensey in action, Doug was impressed by how organized and efficient she was. They were able to have good visit; Tensey was so practiced at preparing lunch that she hardly had to think about what she was doing. They talked about many personal topics. However, Doug steered the conversations away from any financial matters. He was afraid even general discussions about the economy, investments or cost of living might lead to questions that could force him to either lie, or reveal his weak position. He had already decided that he would *never* lie to Tensey again.

After lunch, Doug helped clear the table. Then he gently hugged Tensey and gave her a long, tender kiss before leaving. He promised to visit her more often.

When Doug got back to the hotel, he and Bob quickly packed and left for home. As they rode, Bob asked, "How did it go with Tensey?"

"She was upset that I hadn't visited her sooner."

"Did you tell her about the problems we are having with the project?"

"No. I hope to convince her to be my wife, and I don't want her to think I'm a weakling and a loser."

"Well, Doug, in my opinion, if she loves you your present situation won't make any difference to her. She knows you're a strong, intelligent man who can overcome any temporary setbacks."

"I hope you're right. That's exactly the kind of woman I want for my wife."

"Well, then, why don't you tell her about our trouble."

"Because, no one is perfect. She seems to be on the fence about marrying me, and my present situation might just tilt her the wrong way. Whether or not she can tolerate losers won't make or break her for me. I just don't want to risk losing her to some other guy who might come along while I'm getting my act together."

*   *   *

When Bob and Doug arrived at Doug's house, they got a bad shock. Nailed on the wall beside Doug's front door was a bright orange notice with big black letters that said,

"NOTICE TO VACATE.

THIS PROPERTY IS TO BE FORECLOSED, AND IT MUST BE VACATED BEFORE FINAL FORECLOSURE 30-DAYS FROM THE DATE SHOWN BELOW. DO NOT REMOVE THIS NOTICE. SUCH REMOVAL IS A FELONY WITH A SEVERE PENALTY."

"Holy crap, Doug. The date on this notice says it was posted today. There's bound to be one on my house, and my shop too. I wonder what happened—I thought we had enough credits left to cover another loan payment."

Bob rode home at a gallop. Sure enough, there was a notice on his front door too. The instant he walked in, Audrey rushed over and tearfully threw her arms around him.

"I-I'm so glad you're home," she sobbed.

"What happened? Why are we being foreclosed?"

"The notice was tacked up today while I was at the market. After paying our medical bill, I didn't have enough credits left in the account to make this month's payment on the second mortgage and buy food, so I chose food. Even though the bank has a legal right to foreclose after only one payment is missed, I didn't think they'd do it. If we can somehow pay the mortgage and late payment penalty before the 'notice of foreclosure sale' is published, we can stop the foreclosure. Were you successful in getting an investor?"

"No. The venture vultures in Greensville are just as greedy as the one here. They asked if we had a working prototype we could demonstrate. Doug and I had to admit that we hadn't successfully demonstrated the prototype yet. That didn't sit well with them. I asked one of the vultures what warrants he would require if we had a demonstration prototype. It turned out that even then, he'd only make a deal in which we'd have less than a 50-50-chance of meeting his terms. We'd likely work for another one or two years for nothing, end up broke, and he'd own everything."

"Oh, Bob, what'll we do when the baby comes. You won't even have your shop. If the bank can't sell the shop right away, or if the new owner doesn't need to hire help, you won't have any way to make a living here," Audrey said as she began to sob again.

Seeing Audrey so distressed, and realizing he didn't know any way out of their terrible predicament, tears came into Bob's eyes. He and Audrey just sat on the living room couch staring at the wall for about an hour. Then, Audrey's expression changed slightly and she said, "I almost forgot to tell you in the midst of all our troubles; I think I've figured out a way to make the Stirling engine run."

"Oh honey, that won't do us any good without funds to finish the project," Bob said, tears again filling his eyes.

Audrey looked down at the floor with tears flowing down her cheeks, and didn't say anything more about her idea.

Audrey and Bob spent a restless night, tossing, turning, and worrying. Finally, they got up and prepared breakfast. The sun shown in the kitchen window, making a golden rectangle on the floor, and the aroma of coffee, bacon, eggs and toast filled the house. During the previous week, this pleasant scene would have cheered them, but now they just picked at their food. The few remaining credits they had were gone. They wouldn't even have a way to buy food unless they were saved by some unlikely miracle. They wouldn't be able to depend on Doug's farm produce, since he would be losing his farm and would also be broke.

After breakfast, Bob went into the living room and sat staring out the window trying to think of a way out of their catastrophic situation. Audrey used her computer to access the net, and looked for any jobs for which she or Bob might be qualified. There were a few engineering jobs. Although Audrey had much of the needed engineering knowledge from her studies in the cavern, she didn't have the required credentials. Blacksmith jobs for Bob were available in other places, but most were in the south-central section of the continent where there were awful tornados, floods, hurricanes and droughts. These were frequent and extremely severe due to global warming which was intense due to atmospheric pollution that was still prevalent, even though the use of fossil fuels had been reduced to almost nothing for more than a hundred years. The release of methane, an even worse greenhouse gas than carbon dioxide, from thawing tundra and evaporating lumps of undersea hydromethane had formed a feedback loop that was still intensifying global warming: more warming caused more release of the gas, which caused more warming, etc.

Audrey went into the living room to join Bob, and saw Doug coming up the front sidewalk. When he got close to the front door, she opened it and said, "Come in to the temple of gloom. Neither of us slept worth a damn last night."

"I know what you mean. I didn't sleep well either. I just kept trying to figure a way out of this mess, and I couldn't think of anything. Have you and Bob come up with any ideas?"

"Nothing that wouldn't mean moving into a much less desirable tribal region. I did see a few job offers for farmhands in Greensville, but they were temporary and didn't pay much. "

Doug sat down and joined in as part of a depressed trio as they dejectedly discussed their situation and tried to find a way to avoid losing everything. It didn't help that they now only had a few weeks either to find a solution, or begin the long process of packing and preparing to move. But move to where?. They considered selling off their personal clothes and furniture, and estimated how many credits they'd get from it. However, the terms of the mortgage had placed a lien on all their furniture and equipment until the final foreclosure settlement, so even that wasn't an option. Second-hand clothes wouldn't bring enough credits to forestall foreclosure. Another possibility they considered was to all move into a cheap apartment together while they tried to find work. At least then, they wouldn't be homeless. The fact that this was the best solution they could think of cast a shadow on their souls and they became even more depressed. To top it all off, a rider dressed in jeans and a pulled-down hat had stopped in front of the house.

"What now," Bob said as he got up to get a better look at who it was. Doug and Bob stood looking out the window as the rider came up the front walk.

Doug exclaimed, "Good God!"

Audrey looked alarmed. "What? What's wrong?"

CHAPTER 47
WHAT'S WRONG?

Doug and Bob didn't answer, so Audrey got up and went over to the window saying, "What's this all about?"

Doug recovered from his initial surprise enough to say, "I saw her just yesterday. She didn't say anything about coming here today. Oh, crap, she probably went to my place and saw the foreclosure notice. I didn't want her to know about my trouble."

"Well, if she loves you, it shouldn't make any difference," Audrey said forcefully.

Doug frowned as he said, "I don't know if she's that tolerant."

"Well, she's let you sleep with her. Morals are a lot looser than they used to be, but I don't think Tensey is the kind that would have slept with you unless she at least liked and trusted you a lot."

There was no more time for discussion. When Audrey opened the door, Hortense looked past her and curtly said, "Doug Murphy, I'm really angry with you."

"Why? What'd I do?"

"It's what you didn't do."

"Tensey, please tell me. I can't stand to have you angry with me."

"You claim you love me, yet you didn't tell me you were in financial trouble."

"I didn't think you would want anything to do with me if you found out what a weak position I was in."

"You didn't trust me?"

"I'd trust you with my life."

"Well, then, you should've trusted me enough to tell me."

"Okay, then, I trust you to not break my heart. Will you marry me?"

"That's not a fair question right now. I like you very much, Doug, but as I told you in Greensville, I want to be courted. We need to be a lot better acquainted before I make a lifetime commitment to you."

"Okay. But it's going to be a while before I can work myself out of this financial mess and move to Greensville to court you."

"Don't worry about that."

"What do you mean?"

"Do you remember when I told you my mother died?"

"No, you didn't tell me that."

"You remember, it was while you were in jail—oh—no, I remember it was Audrey that I told. But that's beside the point.

"Six months before my mother died, she inherited ten million credits from her wealthy, widowed sister who had no other living siblings or children of her own. When Mother died intestate I inherited all of her estate, since my father had passed away, and I was her only living child. However, some of my aunts' other nieces and nephews got together and contested my inheritance in probate. I got Jason Bright to represent me. Since I was inheriting directly from my mother, he was able to wrest the entire fortune away from all those other grabbing hands. They were trying to get it on the basis that it came from our mutual aunt only six months before my mother passed away. I just got the final results of the probate late yesterday afternoon, and I immediately went to my good friend, Mr. Grabner, to discuss investing part of my inheritance with him. I had heard about a number of his successes and the good returns he's gotten for his investors."

Doug got a lopsided smile on his face as Bob said, "Yeah, *really* good returns."

Tensey looked at Doug and continued. "During our discussion, Mr. Grabner told me about two entrepreneurs who attempted to get venture capital yesterday, and how disappointed they looked when he refused. Knowing you and Bob were there on business, I thought it might be you two. I told Grabner of my relationship with you and asked if the entrepreneurs were you and Bob. He said yes, and that he felt bad about having to turn you down. This morning I left Greensville at daybreak to come and offer to invest in your project. Then, I saw the foreclosure notice on your door."

Doug reddened and looked down at the floor as he said said, "Tensey, you might as well know the whole story. We need at least 50,000-credits to pay off our obligation to the bank, plus another 150,000-to finish our project."

"How about if I invest 300,000. That's only 3% of what I inherited, and I think the solar powered car company will need that much by the time it has gotten its product ready to market."

Doug, Bob, and Audrey gasped and their mouths dropped open. The miracle they needed had happened: their financial problems were solved

But Doug put his hand on Tensey's shoulder and said, "We can't take your credits, Tensey Dear. We haven't successfully tested the propulsion system yet."

Audrey and Bob stared daggers at Doug. However, Tensey said, "I don't care. I want to invest in the project anyway. It's something the world needs, and it should be unimaginably profitable if it works. Big profits require big risks. However, I'll want an agreement drawn up that gives each of us one-fourth of any proceeds if the project is successful. I want us to form a company with the four of us as equal partners. Is that acceptable to all of you?"

Audrey and Bob enthusiastically said, "Yes." Then Bob added, "As long as you don't require any unreasonable warrants."

Tensey looked puzzled. "Warrants?"

Bob smiled. "Never mind."

Doug looked thoughtful, then said, "Tensey, if I accept, I hope it won't make you think I'm a gold digger. I'd rather go broke than have you think that."

"No. First of all, you didn't know about my fortune when you asked me to marry you. Knowing all of you as I do, I think it's a good investment. Doug, if you don't want to let me invest, I'll buy you out and invest in the project with Bob and Audrey."

"Okay, how can I refuse an offer like that? Welcome aboard. You're now a partner in our new company, and entitled to one-fourth of the profits—if we ever make any."

Audrey said, "What shall we call the company?"

They all thought for a few minutes, then Bob chuckled and said, "Blacksmith's Downfall?"

Audrey caught the silliness bug and said, "Housewife's Escape?"

Doug said, "Farmer's Bottomless Credits Pit?"

Tensey hadn't caught the silliness. She said, "How about 'Solar Motor Company.'"

They all agreed that "Solar Motor Company" was an excellent name, and the new company was born.

Bob brought out a bottle of wine and said, "I've been saving this for a special occasion, and this certainly qualifies."

Audrey got four glasses out of the cupboard. After Bob poured the wine, Audrey lifted her glass and said, "To success."

The four celebrants clinked their glasses together as they echoed, "To success."

Doug asked Tensey, "Where are you staying tonight?"

"I haven't had time to make arrangements."

"You're welcome to stay at my place."

"Thank you. I'd be delighted, " Tensey said, glancing coquettishly at Doug."

"I hope you two will stay for dinner," Audrey said, glancing at Bob to see if he agreed. Bob gave a nod of approval.

Doug glanced at Tensey, and she nodded. He smiled and said, "We'd love to."

"May I help in the kitchen?" Tensey asked.

"No. Bob will be plenty of help," Audrey said, looking at Bob and motioning toward the kitchen with her eyes. Then she continued, "Let's let these love birds visit while we prepare dinner?"

Audrey and Bob went into the kitchen, while Tensey and Doug visited in the living room. Audrey looked in to ask Tensey if she was allergic to any foods, but the two lovers were locked in a passionate embrace and it would have been difficult to get their attention. Audrey decided she could ask later, and quietly slipped back into the kitchen.

During dinner, Doug and Tensey scarcely took their eyes off each other; they weren't very good conversationalists. After dinner, their conversational skills didn't improve. They seemed preoccupied with their inner thoughts as Doug sat with his arm around Tensey on the sofa. There wasn't room for a sheet of paper between them. Finally, Tensey said, "We really must go. I need to unpack, take a bath and wash off the trail dust."

After Tensey and Doug left, Bob chuckled and said, "I'll bet the bed gets a workout before the bathtub does."

"Oh, Bob, you're awful."

"No, I'm frisky. All the pheromones wafted around here by those two got to me. Let's go to bed early tonight."

"Not unless you take a bath."

"Oh, do I smell bad."

"No, but I'm sure you're 'covered with trail dust, Cowboy'."

"So you're in the mood for a little role playing, huh?" Bob said, with a broad grin.

"Cowboy just home from a long cattle drive?"

"Okay, Cowboy and ravished maiden it is. The pheromones must have gotten to you too."

CHAPTER 48
AUDREY'S IDEA

Audrey had breakfast ready by the time Bob came into the kitchen looking completely relaxed, bathed, and well rested from an early bedtime the night before even though a lot of energy had been spent on role playing and ravishing.

"You look awfully good for someone who just spent the night with a crazed cowpoke," Bob said casting a knowing glance at Audrey.

"Well, the cowpoke doesn't know it, but he was just used by a hot mama who is high on hormones stirred up by pregnancy."

"Oh boy, every night will be a potential happy homecoming for the cowboy. Feel free to use him any time."

"Let's change the subject."

"To what?"

"Business."

"Aw shucks, Ma'am."

"I'm going to call Doug and Tensey to come over so we can talk about how to proceed."

An hour later, Doug and Tensey arrived and sat down around the kitchen table with Bob, while Audrey brought a tray with four cups, napkins, creamer, and a pot of coffee.

As Audrey sat at the table, she said, "We need to shut down the bank's foreclosure proceedings on our property as soon as possible. Tensey, can you immediately advance the 52,000-credits that we need to completely pay off the remainder of Doug's and our mortgages and late payment penalties?"

"Yes, but it may take a few days before the inheritance credits are transferred into my bank. A transfer that large requires a personal visit to the bank by my attorney. However, I have 9,000-credits that I have saved over the years."

Doug looked alarmed. "Oh, Tensey, I don't want to completely drain your account."

Audrey's eyes widened and she said, "If we lose the blacksmith shop, we won't have any way to finish the project. How about this? We could use part of Tensey's savings to bring our payments up to date and pay the late payment and penalty. If her inheritance doesn't come through in a few days, it'll be a month before any more payments are due. Since the probate has already been completed, at least part of Tensey's inheritance should be available before more payments are due, even if the banks holding her inheritance can't release all of it at once to her account."

Tensey sipped her coffee for a few minutes while she thought about Audrey's idea, then said, "Yes, I believe that would work. However, we don't even know if we have a problem yet. I'll telephone my bank this morning and see if they've received the inheritance credits."

Doug said, "I don't want Tensey to invest until we've demonstrated that the engine will run on energy from the heat source."

Bob's forehead wrinkled, and his face reddened. "Now, Doug, we've been through that. If we delay heading off the foreclosure, we may lose everything."

Doug thought for a moment, then said, "Okay. I'm sorry. I guess I'm feeling overly protective of Tensey."

They all were quiet for a few minutes, then Doug asked, "Audrey, you said you had an idea about why the engine wouldn't run on heat from the storage unit before we went to Greensville. What did you figure out?"

"Oh, yes. In the midst of all the emotional turmoil of impending eviction and foreclosures notices, I almost forgot about it. I think I have a simple solution to the problem."

"What is it.?"

"I believe all we have to do is increase the pressure of the working gas in the engine and displacer."

Bob said, "Why should that be necessary? The gas expands when we heat it."

"Yes, but remember the gas-laws from thermodynamics."

Doug thought for a moment, then said, "The pressure after heating is equal to the initial gas pressure times the ratio of its final temperature divided by its initial temperature in degrees Kelvin."

Bob looked puzzled and asked, "But why should a higher initial pressure be better. The initial pressure has no effect on the ratio of final to initial pressure, if the ratio of temperatures is the same."

"Look at it this way. If the initial working-gas pressure is only atmospheric, say about 15 PSI, and the initial and final temperatures are 373 and 1,783 degrees Kelvin respectively, the final pressure after heating will be 69 PSI for a change of only 54 PSI. However, if the initial pressure is 500-PSI with the same initial and final temperatures, the final pressure will be 2,390-PSI pressing down on the power piston for a change of 1890-PSI. This would produce a lot more power from the engine."

Doug exclaimed, "By golly, Audrey, you've got it! I don't know why I didn't think of that. It should work."

Smiling, Audrey said "I sure hope so, because I couldn't think of any other ideas that might make it work."

"I think she's got it. Until now, I was beginning to wonder if we've been wasting our time and credits, " Bob said enthusiastically.

Bob, Doug Audrey and Tensey went to the solar mirror. Tensey and Audrey watched while Bob and Doug filled the engine and displacer with helium at 500-PSI, and made sure the heat storage unit was still filled with argon at slightly above atmospheric pressure. They hauled the Solar Propulsion Module out of the cavern and attached it to the support arms on the mirror. There were clouds over the sun, so a few minutes filled with high anxiety ticked by until the clouds moved on. Bob and Doug cranked their gearboxes to focus the sun onto the charging window of the heat storage core. During the rest of the day, clouds floated across the sun from time to time.

"Damn it, these clouds are slowing the charging process," Doug said in an irritated tone of voice.

"That looks like a serious problem," Tensey said. "There won't always be sun when car owners want to travel, and that could limit your market. Could you supplement the solar charging with some other source of heat?"

Audrey nodded. "Yes. I've been thinking about that. We could use an electrical arc in the core as a supplementary heat source."

"So, why not just always do that instead of using solar heating?"

"Because electricity is expensive."

"Would it be as expensive as gasoline or diesel?"

"No, not nearly as much."

"Then, why not use electricity?"

"It has to do with the efficiency of the engine. At 43% efficiency, the engine converts less than half the heat energy stored in the core to mechanical energy to propel the car. With everyone using that much electricity for all their transportation needs, they would soon exceed the limit of the available supply of electrical power, and the price would increase beyond reach."

"Why not just build more electrical supply capacity?" Tensey asked.

"Because no research into new power production methods has been done since the darkening. Materials used in old-style equipment for producing renewable power are in short supply and extremely expensive," Audrey said.

"Well, how about using electricity just to supplement solar on cloudy days. I think for this project to pay off, we'll need to have some way to at least supplement solar."

"You're right about all this. You have a good head for business. Provision for electrical charging should get our foot in the door with customers who can't always wait for sunny days to travel. It might even bring about modification of the laws passed during the darkening so they will allow *some* research into new power production equipment that doesn't use materials that are in short supply."

Suddenly, the men shouted, "It works, it works!"

The engine had started itself during charging, and was running while still attached to the support arms on the mirror without even being cranked.

Doug got a puzzled expression on his face. "How did this happen? How did the engine start itself?"

Audrey thought for a few moments, then said, "One of the pistons must have been in just the right place so when the gas pressure got high enough, it pushed the piston down, turning the crankshaft, initiating gas flow through the heat exchangers from the displacers, and powering all the pistons. Don't throw the crank away. We can't count on this lucky self-starting happening very often."

The men danced and shouted, excited to see, at long last, the system successfully working for the first time. Giddy with relief, the men withdrew the heat exchanger from the core to stop the engine, and returned the Solar Propulsion Module to the cavern. Tensey said, "Hallelujah," and ran to Doug's house to place a telephone call to her bank. Audrey followed Tensey , but at a much slower pace, because of her pregnancy.

When the men arrived at Doug's house a little later, they found Tensey and Audrey sitting in chairs looking dazed and depressed.

CHAPTER 49
NO CREDITS

Tensey had telephoned her Greensville online bank. What she learned horrified her. The credits from her inheritance had not come through and, even worse, the bank had made a mistake in the previous balance of her electronic credit account. Instead of the 9,000-credits that seemed to be in her account when she checked earlier, she only had a balance of 5,200. She couldn't give the bank any argument about her balance, since she hadn't been keeping a separate record of her deposits and withdrawals. The bank had always been correct in the past, so she had become lax in her book keeping.

When Bob and Doug arrived, and saw the depressed look on Tensey and Audrey's faces, Doug asked, "What's wrong?"

Audrey looked grim, while Tensey burst into tears and described her current financial situation, ending with, "Now I won't be able to invest in the project in time to save it. I'm so sorry."

Bob and Doug sank into chairs and stared at the same wall Tensey and Audrey had appeared to find so fascinating.

After about five minutes, Audrey broke the silence. "Even though you don't have many credits right now, we may be able to save the project. Could you invest 4,200-credits now to cover the overdue payments and penalties?"

"That'll only leave 1,000-credits in my account to cover my rent and living expenses."

"Do you plan to keep your job as District Special Materials Inspector after you inherit all that wealth?"

"No. I was thinking about quitting my job and moving here when I got the inheritance credits."

"Surely the credits will come to your account within the next week or two. Did you find out what was holding it up?"

"Yes. The inheritance has quite a number of stocks and bonds. It's taking time to get them re-issued to me."

"Aren't there any liquid account credits?"

"Only about 5 million. The estate attorney is waiting until he can transfer everything to me at once."

"Why don't you call him and insist on getting the liquid credits right away?"

"I assumed that was not possible."

"I think the delay is possibly just a ploy by your attorney to hang onto the 5 million as long as possible. It doesn't make sense that the liquid credits can not be immediately available, now that probate is finished."

Tensey telephoned the estate attorney and requested immediate transfer of the liquid credits.

After a short time, Tensey put the phone on hold and told her anxious partners, "It'll take about two weeks to transfer the cash credits due to the size of the account."

"How about transfer of a smaller amount?" Audrey asked.

"I asked my attorney if a small amount of credits, say 100,000, could be transferred immediately. He said, 'No, that's against the firm's policy.'"

Tensey switched the telephone's speaker on so the others could hear. Then she said to her attorney, "Do you promise to send at least the cash credits within two weeks. It will cause me severe damage if you don't."

"Yes."

"I have three witnesses here who heard what you said."

"Oh, well Miss. Farb, it might take longer. We can't be exact about such a complicated transfer."

Tensey's face got red. Her mouth pressed into a thin line, hiding her lips completely.

Then she said, "Listen, if you don't get those cash credits to my bank within two weeks, you will cause me grave financial damage. You've been sitting on my inheritance long enough. I have three witnesses that heard you say you could meet my two-week requirement. If you don't do that. I'll sue your butt off."

There was a moment of silence, then the attorney said, "Okay, two weeks."

This was a side of Tensey that none of the others had seen.

Doug said, "Tensey, I admire your spunk."

"That was impressive," Audrey added. "But will you be able to invest the 4,200-right away? I don't think we can forestall foreclosure much longer."

"Yes, I'll do it right away. I'm confident that credits from my inheritance will arrive within two weeks. However, I'm going to cut my expenditures as much as possible in the meantime 'just in case.'"

"I have a suggestion," Audrey said. "Since you are planning to move here anyway, why don't you move in with Doug to save on expenses until your inherited credits are available."

"Audrey!" Bob exclaimed, his facial expression screaming disapproval.

"I was only being practical," Audrey sputtered.

"Okay, it sounds like a good idea if Doug is willing," Tensey said, smiling.

Doug blushed and grinned broadly as he said, "Doug is willing!"

The next morning, Tensey transferred 4200-credits from her account to Bob and Doug's business account. Doug immediately rode to the bank and paid their previous month's delinquent mortgage payments plus the late payment penalties in person so he could get an original written and signed receipt. He saw Mr. Grim looking disappointed watching him pay. Doug stopped by Bob's shop to tell him about Grim's reaction. They had a good laugh together about Grim's greed, and how relieved they were to have escaped foreclosure,

After he arrived home, Doug hitched four horses to his hay wagon in preparation for moving Tensey to his house from Greensville. He placed some hay on the wagon for cushioning glass items, and for feeding the horses during the trip since they would be away for several days. Tensey told Doug she had a lot of furniture, including a piano, and he estimated the weight of all her household goods to be around two tons. Doug hitched four horses to the wagon, and left before noon sitting side-by-side with Tensey in the wagon seat. She had prepared a picnic lunch to share. Although they should easily reach Greensville before dark, Doug took his rifle, "just in case."

Sitting close together on the narrow seat, Doug and Tensey visited about many things, starting with the solar car project and slowly merging into their most intimate thoughts. Confined to this small space in complete privacy, and not able to do much else for many hours, they had conversations much deeper than any they'd had in the past. Finally, they were even discussing their private thoughts about sexual preferences. Although they had slept together, they'd never revealed their deepest, most private thoughts to each other. Doug was amazed at Tensey's range of preferences. He thought, she could have written a supplement to the Kama Sutra. This certainly didn't dampen his desire for this stunningly beautiful woman. He decided he was the luckiest man in the world, and he desperately wanted to marry her. But, he restrained himself from being pushy for fear of seeming too needy.

Doug stopped the wagon in the shade of a tree. Tired of sitting in the wagon seat, Doug and the object of his love spread a clean blanket on a large, mossy log near the wagon, sat down, and balanced their lunch on the blanket between them. They'd eaten about half of the food when they heard the thundering hooves of several horses approaching from Greensville.

Doug told Tensey to get out of sight behind some nearby bushes, then pulled his rifle from the hay under the wagon seat. Standing near the wagon, he cocked the gun and held it across his chest aimed upward with both hands so he could quickly point and fire if necessary. The horsemen were close enough that Doug could see there were four of them, just like the robbers who had accosted him and Bob many months earlier.

CHAPTER 50
OH DOUG, YOU'RE WONDERFUL

The approaching riders didn't have bandannas covering their faces as robbers usually did. However, Doug continued to stand beside the wagon with his rifle at the ready.

The man in the lead ordered the men to halt, and said, "Hello, sir. We're a posse after three bandits who have been robbing people along this road. Have you seen any other riders on the road today?"

"Not a one."

"I see you have a gun. That's a good idea with those guys running loose."

"Thanks. A friend and I had an encounter some time back with bandits on this road at night. But there were four of them."

"Probably the same guys. One of them was killed during a holdup a while ago."

"Oh. Did their victim escape?"

"No. After the man killed one of them, they killed him and his wife. Please keep your eyes open, and report any suspicious groups of riders to the sheriff in Greensville."

After the four riders left, Tensey came out of her hiding place. "You were wise to bring a rifle, Doug. But I wouldn't want you to face off with three gunmen. You'd likely be killed."

"Tensey, I'd give my life to protect you. Besides, I'm pretty good with a gun, and I'm a fast thinker, so I might even be able to trick them and avoid bloodshed—mine *or* theirs."

As they finished eating their lunch, Doug told Tensey about how he and Bob had tricked the four robbers on the trip to pick up graphite in Greensville.

"Oh, Doug, You're wonderful! I feel safe with you."

*   *   *

When Doug and Tensey got to Greensville, they went to the shipping terminal to buy packing boxes, to a grocery store to purchase enough food to last a couple of days, and finally to Tensey's home. She called her landlord and notified him that she was moving out. Then, tired from their trip, Doug and Tensey worked together to get dinner, took a shower and went to bed early. Tensey demonstrated some of the range of preferences she had mentioned to Doug earlier   He was an enthusiastic student.

The next morning, Tensey prepared a sumptuous breakfast: eggs, bacon, pancakes with syrup, coffee and juice. During breakfast, she and Doug shut out the rest of the world and enjoyed a feeling of being together as part of a larger plan in the universe.

For two days, Doug and Tensey packed her things and loaded them onto the wagon, stacking furniture high and tying it on. When they had finished loading, they tied a waterproof tarpaulin over the load.

On the way out of town, they stopped at The Country Kitchen restaurant for lunch and sat facing each other in a booth beside a window. They ordered soup and sandwiches. After they finished eating, Tensey looked wistfully out of the window and quietly shed a few tears.

Doug asked, "What's the matter Dear? Seeing you sad makes me sad too."

"It's just that I'm leaving my nice home, where I've lived for so many years, and this restaurant, where I've eaten so many times. Now, I am here for possibly the last time. Things will never be the same again."

Doug moved over to the Tensey's side of the table, sat beside her, and put his arm around her.

"Oh, sweetheart, I promise you that I will love you and take care of you, and I will do everything in my power to make you happier than you have ever been. Ever!"

"I know, Doug. But I don't deal well with big changes."

"Tensey, you know that life is filled with changes. I promise that if you marry me, I will do everything I can to bring you more happiness than you ever dreamed possible."

Tensey pulled a a dainty, lace-edged handkerchief out of her pocket and dried her eyes. "I know, Doug. But I still can't help feeling sad about leaving this place I have loved for so many years."

Doug chuckled as he said, "Oh, now you're making me jealous of this other love of yours"

Tensey, still drying her tears with the handkerchief, gave a little lilting laugh and said, "Don't worry, I love you more."

"Oh Tensey, that's the first time recently that you've told me you 'love me' instead of you 'like me'."

"Well, it's true. I love you, Doug."

"I'm crazy happy to hear you say those words I've so often hoped to hear."

"Then, I'll say it again. I love you Doug."

The restaurant was getting crowded, and the waitress had been watching the lovebirds "bill and coo". She came over to the booth and grumpily said, "Is there anything else. There are others waiting for the booth." Before Doug or Tensey could answer, she flopped the check down on the table and left.

Tensey chuckled as she said, "Well, so much for nostalgia."

Doug chuckled too as he started to the credit counter to pay. "Does that mean you still love me more than your old home and this restaurant?"

"Perhaps, just a little," Tensey said as she clung tightly to Doug's arm and cast a coquettish glance at his eyes.

At the counter, the waitress entered the charges against Doug's account, then asked, "How much should I enter for the tip?"

"Are you kidding," Doug said as he transferred his password and closed the charge session by holding his wrist telephone near a small icon on the credit device.

*   *   *

With four horses pulling the wagon, they could maintain a trot for many miles. However, Doug held them to a walk to give him more time to visit with Tensey. The wagon had side-view mirrors that were required on all wagons driven in town or on highways. Since the load was much taller than Doug, he kept a close watch in the mirrors for any riders coming up from behind.

About eight-miles out of Greensville, Doug saw three horsemen following. They had come out of some bushes and each man had a bandanna covering his face. Doug urged the horses to a trot. The horsemen sped up. He slowed the horses to a walk. The horsemen did the same. They were apparently trying to size up the situation since the wagon's driver and passengers, such as a shotgun man, couldn't be seen over the tall load.

"Tensey, I don't like this. There are three men following us. I'm going to suddenly whip the horses into a gallop. This'll surprise the men and gain us a little more lead. There are some bushes around a turn just a little way ahead. When we get there, I'll pull the wagon over and stop. Jump off and run as fast as you can behind the bushes far away from the road. I'm going to do the same, but not near you. Do you understand?"

"Yes. But why…?"

"There's no time to explain. Just trust me. Ready?"

"Yes."

Then Doug applied the whip, and the wagon lurched forward. The riders were three hundred yards behind, and didn't accelerate for about six precious seconds. When they did accelerate, Doug and Tensey had gone around the bend. Doug pulled off of the right side of the road, applied the wagon brake, and pulled back hard on the reins. The horses nearly sat down as they rapidly stopped. Tensey jumped off and ran to some thick bushes about 100-yards off the road. Doug grabbed his rifle and dashed behind some bushes well back up the road from where Tensey was hiding. He figured the distance would give him an advantage in a gunfight since rifles are much more accurate that pistols.

The riders came galloping around the bend and stopped behind the wagon, guns drawn. Two of them looked curiously at the tarpaulin cover as the third slowly rode to the front and cautiously peered around the high load at the drivers seat. "I'll be damned. There's no one here. They must have been scared and run off. Well, it's easier 'pickins', and we won't have to waste bullets on 'em."

When Doug heard this, he was convinced this was the gang who'd been robbing and murdering people along this road. There was a loud click-clack as Doug cocked his trusty rifle and shouted, "Drop your guns or I'll drop *you*."

All three of the gunmen pointed in the general direction of the shout. One of the robbers fired, missing Doug by twenty feet. Bang! Click clack. Bang! Two riders dropped off their horses like flies hit by a stream of strong bug spray. Click clack, Bang!, Bang! The third rider fell to the ground. Doug cautiously approached the three outlaws lying crumpled on the ground. Tensey timorously came out of hiding.

"Doug, you're wonderful. You saved us—oh, Doug, you're hurt!"

"Yeah, the last one I shot figured out where I was before I got him. Don't worry, it's only a nick."

"Let me see. Oh, Doug, it tore a big piece of flesh out of your arm! I can't believe you managed to kill all of those awful men. Here, let me bandage your wound."

Tensey took off her shirt, pulled a small pen knife out of her pocket, and cut off one of the sleeves. She pulled a clean handkerchief out of another pocket and made a pad to put pressure on the profusely bleeding wound. Then, she bound the pad tightly in place with her sleeve. When they climbed aboard the wagon, Tensey took up the reins and urged the horses to a trot which she maintained most of the way to Stoneville. Doug looked pale, and had broken out in a cold sweat, but he was able to direct Tensey to the doctor's office. Tensey set the brake, tied the reins to the brake handle, and helped Doug into the office.

The receptionist followed the office's routine, and insisted on a bunch of forms being filled out before the doctor would see Doug. Tensey shouted, "Can't you see that this man is bleeding to death and is going into shock. You get the doctor NOW!"

"But Ma'am, the office policy is... ."

"I SAID NOW!!"

The doctor heard the commotion and came into the waiting room. "What's all the shouting ab. . .."

Tensey said, "Look at this man. He's bleeding to death and your receptionist is a nincomp..."

"Now, Ma'am, there's no reason for accusations, I'm sure things are not as bad as... Oh! Crap! Help me get this man into the examination room. I have to stop the bleeding immediately."

After he located the large vein that was torn, the doctor swabbed the area with alcohol and antibiotics, injected a local anesthetic, and set to work suturing the blood vessel and closing the wound. While the doctor worked, he asked Tensey what happened. After hearing her explanation, he said, "Since this is a gunshot wound, I have to call Sheriff Lock. Please press the button on the intercom."

Audrey pressed the button, and the doctor instructed his receptionist to make the call. Ten minutes later, the sheriff showed up, and asked Tensey what happened. She told the sheriff about the events leading up to the shooting. The sheriff then asked her to describe the men. After hearing the descriptions, he said, "Pending confirmation of their identities, it sounds to me like Doug wiped out the last of the infamous "Sidewinder" gang who've been terrorizing this area. There's a reward for killing or capturing them. I'll ride out there to photograph and identify the bodies."

"Oh Doug, you're wonderful," Tensey said wiping tears from her eyes.

CHAPTER 51
MARRIAGE

Bob helped Tensey move some of her things from the wagon into Doug's house, and the rest into his barn. Doug was still recovering from his gunshot wound. His arm was in a sling, and the doctor had instructed him not to use his arm for a couple of weeks. As the last few items were carried into the barn, the sheriff rode up.

Bob asked, "What's up, sheriff?"

Tensey came out of the barn just in time to hear the sheriff say, "I guess you know Doug's a local hero. I'm here to let him know he needs to activate his 100,000-credit reward account in person at the bank."

Tensey got a dreamy look in her eyes and said, "Oh, isn't Doug wonderful."

Bob reddened, and even the sheriff looked a little embarrassed by this girlish adulation from such a normally reserved woman.

Bob whispered to Tensey, "Get a grip on yourself."

She said, "Thanks for your help moving my stuff, Bob. C'mon sheriff. Let's go give Doug the news."

As he started home, Bob thought, oh, oh, I probably shouldn't have said that. She's too much in love to "get a grip on herself."

After the sheriff left, Tensey kissed Doug all over his face and said, "I love you. Will you marry me?"

Doug shouted, "YAHOO!" Then he added, "I'm so happy. This is my greatest dream. Let's get married right away."

"But, what about your promise to court me?"

"Does defending you from murderers count?"

"Of course. I was only teasing. But I *do* want a big, old-fashioned church wedding. I'll only have one wedding, and I've dreamed of it ever since I was a little girl."

Bob and Audrey helped Doug and Tensey send out invitations and make arrangements for the minister, church, a keyboard musician, flowers, a caterer for the reception, and a wedding cake.

* * *

A month later, an evening rehearsal was held, with Bob as best man, and Audrey as matron-of-honor. Several of Tensey's friends came from Greensville to be bridesmaids, and Jason Bright came to serve as a groomsman.

The wedding was held the next day. Friends and relatives of the couple nearly filled the church. Doug's parents traveled a hundred miles from the Kelso tribal region.

As the church guests were seated, the musician played background music. Then she shifted keys, and modulated to a slow wedding processional. The bridesmaids entered one at a time, slowly stepping down the aisle. Bob's four-year-old nephew entered carrying two rings pinned to a small cushion, and an eight-year-old flower girl, one of Bob's nieces, followed him. The flower girl scattered rose petals in the aisle as she was supposed to, but the ring bearer was distracted by his mother who was sitting a few pews back from the front of the church. He went to her and offered her the rings. When she tried to get him to carry the rings to the altar, he began to cry and loudly said, "No. I don't want to. I want mamma. I have to pee." The mother took him by the hand, and led him to the altar. The minister, who was standing in front of the altar, whispered something to her, and she handed the pillow bearing the rings to the best man. Red faced, and with the congregation snickering, the mother lead her child up a side-aisle and out of the sanctuary.

Suddenly, the keyboard modulated into a bridal wedding march. A slender vision in a beautiful ankle-length light blue gown and white veil appeared in the doorway. Since both of her parents had passed away, she was escorted holding onto the arm of one of her father's brothers. The beautiful vision, and her escort, slowly walked down the aisle to a position beside Doug..

The ceremony, started with the minister asking, "Who gives this woman to marry this man?"

Tensey's uncle said, "I do," then sat in a front pew.

The minister read the great love chapter from the bible, First Corinthians:13, and spoke about the importance of remembering the advice given there, especially the part about patience and kindness. Then, while Tensey looked at Doug adoringly, he shakily recited vows he had written. Tensey recited her vows in a strong, steady voice while Doug looked at her and held her hands in his.

Then the minister instructed Doug and Tensey to exchange rings, and say "With this ring I unite with you," as they each placed a ring on the finger of the other.

When that was done, the minister smiled and said, "I now pronounce you lifetime partners." Then, looking at Doug, he said, "You may now kiss the bride." Doug lifted Tensey's veil revealing her violet eyes and such beauty that, added to the stress of the wedding, made his knees shake violently and his face blanch. Bob could see Doug's situation, and grasped his arm to steady him. Gazing into Tensey's eyes, Doug fought off unconsciousness, then gradually pulled his arm free from Bob's grasp. He put his arms around Tensey and kissed her.

Although he'd never admit it to Audrey, Bob felt a little woozy himself. Tensey's already striking beauty had been enhanced by makeup tastefully applied by one of her bridesmaids who was a renowned makeup artist with a modeling agency.

The happy couple walked rapidly back along the aisle to the familiar strains of a lively recessional. A voice in Doug's head said, "Thank God that's over. I'm lucky I didn't keel over and make a fool of myself. But I'm glad it made Tensey happy."

A voice in Tensey's head said, "That was so beautiful. It was just as I had imagined it during all these years."

Doug and Tensey had discussed where to go on their honeymoon, and decided home was the best option for now. They planned to take a more extensive honeymoon after solar-powered cars became available and long distance travel was easier and safer. Doug had hired a carriage and driver to take him and his bride to his house.

*   *   *

A week later, Doug and Tensey finally "came up for air" and went to visit Doug and Audrey.

Doug said, "What have you been up to?"

"We've got some great news to share," Bob said excitedly.

"What?"

"While you two were incognito last week, Audrey and I set up some equipment and performed a static test to measure the engine/heat storage assembly's power output."

"Was it satisfactory?"

"More than satisfactory. We got a peak output of nearly 100-horsepower."

"How did you do the tests? There hasn't been much sun."

"While you were moving, getting settled, and getting ready for your wedding, I finished modifications so the heat storage core can be heated with an internal electric arc. We didn't bother with solar heating for the tests."

"Wow, that's great news. I can hardly wait to try the solar propulsion system in a car."

"Me too. Let's get the car to the shop so I can start installing the system."

At the shed, Doug and Bob removed the tarp that had been covering the car for so many years. The car was supported on blocks to keep the tires off the shed's dirt floor. Bob used a small air compressor to pump up the tires, which were flat since the car was unused for such a long time. While the compressor was doing its work, Doug asked, "How come the gaskets, tires and hoses aren't rotted like old rubber objects I've had around the house?"

"Because the gaskets are carbon composites that don't deteriorate, and the tires, hoses and other pliable items aren't rubber, they're neoprene. A super-preservative coating for neoprene was developed just prior to the darkening, and Audrey's grandfather must have applied a lot of it 47 years ago when he decided to store the car."

"Oh. So the car is only 47 years old?"

"It's 54 years old. Audrey's wealthy great-grandfather gave a lot of credits and the car, to his son for his 18th birthday. The son only drove it five years before most of his wealth was gone. Gas was so expensive he could no longer afford it."

Bob and Doug jacked the car up and removed the blocks, then pushed the car out of the shed.

As they stood looking at the car, Bob said, "I've been so busy with other things, I haven't planned the installation of our propulsion system. I don't know where it would be best to do the work. We'll need equipment I have at the shop, but it might be better to stay closer to home where we can keep an eye on things in case that car company spy comes back again."

"I think it'd be better to work at the shop. You'd be closer to your tools, welder, and heavy lifting equipment. The car can be locked in the shop, and now we can afford to hire a night watchman, especially when the rest of Tensey's inheritance arrives at her bank. We can easily haul the engine/storage unit assembly from the cavern to the car when the time comes to install it."

"Okay, the shop it is," Bob said, grinning broadly.

"I'll let Tensey know I'm leaving, and I'll get a couple of my horses and rigging to pull the car to your shop."

Doug and Tensey returned with the horses and found Audrey and Bob sitting inside the car looking over the controls.

Tensey appeared to be excited about something. "I just received confirmation that 5 million credits from my inheritance has finally arrived at my bank!" she said with a big smile, then continued, "And also in the electronic mail were the incorporation papers we had Jason draw up for us. I printed them out. All we have to do is sign them in front of a notary, and we will officially be the 'Solar Motor Company'. If we sign the papers and set up a company account, I'll deposit 500,000-credits in it today. We can pay off the balance of Bob and Doug's mortgages, and have plenty to run the company for a while."

Her announcement first caused stunned silence, then boisterous, exuberant cheers from Bob and Audrey. Doug was mysteriously subdued.

"What's the matter, Doug," Bob asked. "Aren't you happy about this?"

"Yeah, but the mail also included notification that my reward credits have been deposited in my account."

"Why is that a bad thing?"

"It's only a piddling 100,000-credits."

"What do you mean 'piddling'? I can remember when we were about to lose everything for want of only 4,200."

"Compared to Tensey's fortune, it's insignificant."

Tensey looked perplexed. "Douglas Murphy, did you think I was marrying you for your wealth?"

:"Well, no, but others will think I was marrying you for *yours*."

"Oh, that's disgusting. Remember, I proposed to *you*."

"But, I proposed to you first."

"But you didn't know anything about my inheritance the three times you proposed to me before I proposed to you."

Bob and Audrey had been suppressing snickers, and finally could hold back no more. They burst out in uproarious laughter.

Doug said, "Why are you laughing about our problems?"

Stifling his laughter, Bob said, "Do you two realize how ridiculous you sound? You have both had good fortune beyond belief, and you're arguing about it instead of enjoying it."

Tensey and Doug looked at each other, then burst out laughing. The four laughed together until tears were rolling down their cheeks and their sides ached.

Just then, they saw someone getting off his horse in front of the house.

CHAPTER 52
SUCCESS AND FAILURE

Bob and Doug went outside to meet the stranger. As they got closer, they recognized Mr. Vultura, the venture capitalist.

"What do *you* want?" Bob growled.

"I heard that your test of the solar heat storage and engine system was successful."

"How did you find out about that?"

"We venture capitalists have our sources."

"Well, it's really none of your business, but yes, we were tremendously successful beyond our wildest dreams," Bob said, exaggerating to vindictively rub Vultura's nose in it.

"I'm ready to invest if you need capital."

"Forget it. We don't need you any more."

"Oh. Might I ask why?"

"No. Maybe your 'sources' can tell you."

Bob's tone of voice and body language made it clear that vultures were not welcome, so Vultura turned around and left without another word.

"Do you think you should have been so abrupt with Vultura? We might need him in the future. You never know what might happen," Doug said, worry showing in his voice.

"I'd hate to allow that vulture to invest in our company under any circumstances."

"Yeah. I suppose you're right. Guys like him only invest in sure things and get a huge profit, while the guys like us who invent and develop the miracles often barely make wages if we're successful, and lose our shirts if we're not. Besides, we have our own capital now."

After lunch, Doug and Bob hitched the horses to the car. Bob steered while Doug walked in front and lead the horses. When they got to the shop, Doug unhitched the horses, and Bob reached in through the car window to steer while both men pushed the car backward into the shop.

Meanwhile, Audrey and Tensey placed an advertisement online for a night watchman. They immediately began getting responses and checking references. Interviews were planned for the next day when Doug and Bob could participate in the selection process.

The four Solar Motor Company partners, Bob, Audrey, Doug and Tensey, interviewed potential watchmen all of the next day. Finally, they chose a man with impeccable credentials on his training, character and past employment record, and who had bulging muscles that would intimidate any potential intruders. The man also had a "Sharpshooter" medal from his military service, and a permit to carry a 45 caliber Magnum automatic handgun.

*   *   *

During the next four weeks, Bob designed and fabricated all the parts and equipment he'd need to install the Solar Propulsion System in the car. He removed the car's existing gasoline engine and fuel tank, and made fixtures to allow easy removal and re-installation of the Solar Propulsion System on the mirror's support arms so they could quickly pick it up for solar charging, then return it to the car.

This work was taking most of Bob's time, and his customers were complaining about their jobs not being completed on time. Doug was helping Bob a lot, and missing soil preparation and planting deadlines on the farm.

One night, Bob went over to Doug's house to discuss what to do about falling behind in their blacksmith and farm work. Tensey had already gone over to Audrey's for a visit. The men considered abandoning the blacksmith and farm work altogether, but decided it was premature to let those businesses decline, considering they hadn't yet demonstrated the complete solar powered car.

"Doug, for the past month we've been primarily living on credits, drawn from the company's account. I need to hire someone to work on my outside customer jobs so I can concentrate on our project."

"I've been thinking the same thing. I need to hire someone to help with my farm work. Under the present laws, our company can deduct pay-outs, such as wages for employees, from its tribal and co-op taxes. I suggest that we have our company formally pay ourselves and our wives regular wages, and hire shop and farm help. This'll give our company tax advantages on what we pay outside workers."

"Okay, let's do it."

"I suggest that we have a partner's meeting and elect Tensey Chief Financial Officer, if she's willing."

"Partner's meeting?"

"Yes, the four of us."

"I thought we were the board of directors."

"Yes, as owners, we are also considered the board."

Bob stroked his chin as he said, "I hadn't thought about this, but sure, why not. It's a good idea. Tensey could keep track of our financial records and make the tax reports. Audrey couldn't do it. She'll be too busy helping us on the project, and taking care of the baby when it arrives. She could be our secretary, and record the minutes of our board meetings if she'll accept that position."

"Okay, I agree. Let's ask our wives."

The next morning, a meeting of the Solar Motor Company board was convened. Tensey and Audrey were nominated as the Chief Financial Officer (CFO) and Executive Secretary positions. When they accepted, they were elected unanimously. Bob and Doug were elected as the Chief Executive Officer (CEO) and President, respectively.

Tensey and Audrey, advertised for the blacksmith and farm helpers their husbands needed. Bob and Doug looked over resumes and contacted references before making their final selections from the applicants. They decided on two good men who went to work immediately. It was a tremendous relief for Bob and Doug, and they could now work on the Solar Motor Company's solar powered car project during normal working hours while keeping the blacksmith shop and farm going. The remaining mechanical work on the project now went ahead at full-speed.

* * *

With Doug's help, Bob quickly finished the remaining work needed to prepare the car for installation of the Solar Propulsion System. They hauled the System from the cavern to the shop, and furiously launched into the installation. It only took a week to finish. A few small modifications were necessary, but Bob quickly dispatched them in another week.

One day, when they had run into a particularly sticky little mechanical problem, Doug watched Bob quickly and efficiently solve it and fabricate a needed part . Doug looked admiringly at Bob and said, "My God, Bob, you're a genius."

"Aw, now Doug, if you keep looking at me like that, I'll have to ask you to marry me."

"If you'd put on a dress, weren't so ugly, and we weren't both already married, I might say yes."

"Good God, I hope not. You're not my idea of a perfect woman."

Work on this phase was nearing completion, and both men were feeling the stress and worry about whether the upcoming test of the complete solar powered car would be successful. During the next two days they put the finishing touches on the solar car, and it was ready to test.

Doug stood outside the shop door looking up at the cloudy, overcast sky. "Damn. It's no use hauling the car up to the solar mirror today. We'll have to use the internal electrical arc to heat the storage core."

Bob connected his 6 kW welder to the internal carbon arc electrode, and manipulated the control handle on a rod that connected to the internal electrode inside the outer shell of the heat storage device through a sliding rotary seal. The electrode was manipulated to contact, then withdrawn a short distance from the graphite core. An eerie blue light shown through the solar charging window as the arc sputtered to life. During the next four hours, the men waited impatiently while the core to reached a quarter of its maximum heat charge.

Finally, Bob said, "Damn it, I wish this welder had more power. I can't wait any longer. Let's road test this baby."

"I was just thinking the same thing. But shouldn't we get Audrey and Tensey so they can see the inaugural run of the car?"

No. The car'll almost certainly have bugs that need to be fixed before it'll run right. It'll probably take a lot of time and they'd just be standing around and waiting. Besides, this is just an initial test, not a run. Let's go! I can't stand to wait any longer."

Bob opened the front doors of the shop and got behind the wheel accompanied by Doug in the passenger seat. Slowly, Bob pressed down on the pedal that inserted the heat exchanger into the cavity in the storage core. Nothing happened.

Looking perplexed, Bob said, "My God, it doesn't work!" as he withdrew the heat exchanger.

Doug looked alarmed. "What do you mean, 'It doesn't work'?"

CHAPTER 53
LEARNING

"I inserted the heat exchanger into the hot core, and nothing happened, except the heat exchanger began to overheat," Bob said, agitation showing in his voice.

The men sat in the car thinking about what might be wrong. Then, Doug said, "Oh crap! We got so excited that we forgot about the most elementary step in getting the engine to run."

"What is it?"

"We forgot to crank it."

"Holy crap, you're right," Bob said, slapping his forehead in disgust.

Doug got out of the car and cranked the engine a couple of turns. It started up, and Bob had to remember to pull the exchanger part of the way out of the core to keep the engine from running too fast and damaging itself.

"Well, we're off to a brilliant start," Doug said as he got back into to car.

"Yeah, a couple of regular geniuses," Bob said as he pushed down the clutch and put the car in gear. Having never driven a car before, he let the clutch out too fast and killed the engine.

"What happened," Doug asked impatiently.

"I don't know."

"I suppose I'll have to crank the damn thing again."

"Yeah. I'm beginning to wish I'd taken time to install the electric starter from the original gas-powered version of the car. But the battery wasn't any good and I didn't know how much a new one would cost, or whether we could even find one. They are pretty hard to find these days."

"Okay, let's try again. This time, I'll stay out until you learn how to drive this thing," Doug said as he got out to crank the engine again.

"Oh my God," Bob said as he yanked his foot off of the heat exchanger pedal, "I forgot to withdraw the heat exchanger clear out while the engine wasn't running. It's gotten nearly up to its maximum temperature limit. Quick, crank the engine to cool the exchanger off before it melts."

Doug turned the crank, and the engine quickly raced up to its maximum speed and began to go beyond. The normally almost silent engine was making some loud clacking, swishing, and roaring noises. Bob put the car in gear and let out the clutch to slow the engine. The car lurched forward, digging ruts in the dirt floor, as an astonished Doug jumped out of the way, then was showered with dirt. The car carried its shocked driver out onto the street. He swerved, skidding into alignment with the street, and lurched from side to side several hundred feet along the street before he had the presence of mind to push on the brake. He got the car stopped, but forgot to press the clutch and killed the engine again. By this time, Doug was running down the street toward the car, and soon caught up with it. When he arrived, he found a befuddled Bob sitting and staring straight ahead as if afraid to move.

"Bob. Bob."

"Huh?"

"Pull the heat exchanger out of the core if you haven't already done it."

"Huh?— Oh, Okay," Bob said in a dreamlike tone of voice as he pressed on the heat exchanger control pedal in a direction that inserted the exchanger further into the core.

"No! No! My God, take your foot off of it," Doug shouted.

"Huh? Oh. Oh yeah," Bob said as he responded to Doug's instructions. Then he came out of his dream state and continued, "Dammit, Doug, the heat exchanger was already withdrawn before I left the shop. The pedal was at its negative limit. My little surprise excursion onto the street was powered exclusively by heat that was stored in the overheated heat exchanger.

By this time, Bob had completely recovered from his shock, and could function again. "Good grief, Doug, what have you been doing. You look like you've rolled in a dust pile."

"Yeah, I was just so happy to see this damn thing work that I lay down on the shop floor and rolled around."

Both men laughed.

Finally, looking more thoughtful, Doug asked, "What do you think went wrong?"

"I'm not sure, but I think I'll have to engage the clutch more slowly. I thought that would cause it to wear out fast, but slipping the clutch while getting underway seems to be the only way to keep from killing the engine or ripping the back tires off."

"That seems reasonable. And I'd suggest inserting the heat exchanger slowly so the engine power level is more appropriate for slow acceleration."

"I agree. Crank the engine, and we'll give it another try."

"Okay, but do something more than just depress the clutch. Take the car out of gear this time. You damn near ran over me last time. By the way, I'm going to let you drive the car solo until you learn how to control it."

"I understand. It's a good thing it's Sunday, and there weren't many horses and wagons on the street today. Otherwise, I might have wiped out a few."

Doug cranked the engine to life again, then Bob put the car in gear and slowly let out the clutch while slowly pressing the heat exchanger insertion pedal. Bob accelerated to about 15 MPH, but swerved from side to side down the street as he over-controlled the car. He headed out of Stoneville, barely missing a wagon that was coming into town. The wagon driver shook his fist and shouted something, but Bob was too preoccupied to hear him. Finally, Bob got to his house and was able to pull into his own driveway, take the car out of gear, and brake smoothly to a stop. Doug soon arrived on his horse at a gallop. Bob got out of the car, but crumpled to the ground.

"What's the matter, Bob, are you injured?"

"No, I'm just weak in the knees."

Audrey looked out the window, and saw Bob crumple. She rushed out and said, "Oh honey, what's the matter, are you hurt?"

"No, just chicken. That was one scary ride."

Audrey said, "You guys got the car working!" as she and Doug helped Bob to his feet.

Tensey came running over from Doug's place. When she got close enough she shouted, "Oh hallelujah! It works. Did you drive all the way here from the shop?"

"Yes. Oh my God, the shop! I left it hanging wide open! We hadn't planned to drive this far," Bob said, looking like he'd just chopped off one of his fingers.

"Don't worry, I closed and locked the door before I got on my horse," Doug said reassuringly.

"Thank God. I just visualized getting back to the shop and finding the place completely robbed of everything that could be carried off."

Finally, with all the immediate concerns taken care of, and the initial shock and awe somewhat abated, the four Solar Motor Company owners laughed and joked together about Bob's hair-raising trip as he described every moment of it. Then he offered to take them all on an inaugural ride. They all generously said they'd wait so he alone could enjoy the car while learning to drive it. They also said they were "Grateful, er, that is, not angry that Bob hadn't taken them along on his first run."

Tensey said, "If these cars are so hard to start and control, I wonder if anyone will want to buy them?"

Bob thought for a moment, then said, "I think most people will be able to quickly learn how to drive one. Besides, there are a number of refinements that I'll make, like electric starting, automatic insertion and withdrawal of the heat exchanger to maintain it at a safe temperature, and better gauging to monitor the heat exchanger and core temperatures, to name a few. Then the car will be a lot easier to drive."

"Won't the battery for electric starting be too expensive?" Tensey asked.

"No. A battery for starting the engine is much smaller than a car propulsion battery, and it can be made from cheaper materials."

The four friends went into Bob and Audrey's house, and had lunch around the kitchen table.

Bob got a far away look in his eyes. Audrey asked, "Where did you go? You don't seem to be here with us."

"I was just thinking that this is the very table where we dumped out the contents of the mystery chest so long ago. Little did we dream then how many trials, tribulations, and adventures were in store for us."

All of them looked down at the table, then Tensey said, "Yes, but there's still more to come—we have to demonstrate solar charging, now that the heat storage power module is installed in the car, and we'll have to market solar cars to get any payback."

CHAPTER 54
PUBLIC ATTENTION

The morning dawned sunny and bright, perfect for solar charging. Bob drove the car to the mirror for the first complete test of removing Solar Propulsion System, solar charging it and replacing it in the car. While Audrey and Tensey watched, Bob unplugged the instrument cable, and disconnected the heat exchanger control cable. Doug hooked the support arms from the mirror onto the engine/heat storage assembly. He released clamps that held the assembly in place, and lifted it free from the car, disengaging the engine-to-transmission drive gear in the process. Bob and Doug cranked the azimuth and elevation controls to lift the assembly and place the solar focal spot on the heat storage charging window.

Audrey said, "Lifting the entire Solar Propulsion System for charging is awkward. I think it could be done more easily using a system of mirrors to re-direct the focal spot down to storage unit in the car. Then nothing would have to be removed from the car during solar charging."

"I like that idea. Why didn't you and Doug design it that way in the first place?" Bob asked.

"It'll be more expensive. Also, some energy will be lost in each reflection, so it would require a larger paraboloidal mirror. We thought this added expense should be postponed until after the initial demonstrations."

"Oh."

Eight hours later, Bob and Doug lowered the Solar Propulsion System, reinstalled it in the car. Bob took it for a test drive and it worked perfectly. However, Bob soon returned and shakily got out of the car.

"More narrow escapes?" Audrey asked.

"Yeah. But they weren't quite as narrow as last time. I think I'm getting the hang of driving this thing."

*　　　*　　　*

During the next week, Bob practiced driving the car on back roads that were seldom used. When he'd gotten sufficiently good at it, he taught Doug how to drive. On sunny days, the core could be solar-charged to full capacity, so power for practice drives on those days was free.

Word had gotten around Stoneville, and people often waited, or had picnics, along the road near Bob's house hoping to see the strange, silent car go by on one of its practice runs. As time went on, word spread far and wide to other towns, and visitors came and asked to see the car. Some were amazed at how low the estimated price was, and wanted to purchase a car immediately. They were disappointed when they were told it would be a while before the cars would be on the market.

Bob, Audrey and Doug were still making design changes, and Bob was implementing them. One day, Doug and Bob were working together in the shop to build and install an automatic heat exchanger regulator that would insert the heat exchanger only far enough into the storage core to provide the engine power demanded by the driver. This would keep the heat exchanger from overheating. Just as they finished, Doug said, "I think setting up a factory to manufacture these cars and solar charging stations would be difficult and extremely expensive. It would take more credits than Tensey's entire inheritance. Maybe we ought to consider licensing our solar car to an existing car company."

"That sounds like a good idea, if we can keep the company from stealing our technology instead of paying us for the license."

"I've heard of a tribal co-op office that grants a document, called a 'Patent,' that protects you from having others steal your invention. They aren't very busy. I've never known anyone who's gotten a patent. I suppose they are rare these days; there's always a risk of a new invention being adjudged new science rather than engineering."

"How can anyone invent something new without applying science?"

"Patents these days are invariably for small engineering rearrangements of existing designs."

"Getting a patent sounds like a good idea since our trial already established in court that development of our solar car was engineering and not new science. But I don't have any idea of how to get a patent."

"I'll bet Jason Bright could help us, or point us toward someone who could."

"Let's get together with Audrey and Tensey, and call him."

They drove to Bob's place, called Tensey, and joined Audrey so they could all have a meeting, then participate in a telephone conference. The women both agreed that a patent should be obtained. Bob telephoned Jason Bright and put the phone on speaker mode. Jason was familiar with patent procedure, but cautioned them that it was a long, expensive process. It required a special artist to make drawings illustrating the invention. These had to be drawn in a special style that would meet restrictive patent office requirements.

Jason instructed the inventors to describe their work in formal notebooks to log their invention and describe how they developed it. Each page had to be numbered, dated and signed by the inventors and two outside witnesses. Bob, Audrey, and Doug were taken aback by the notebook requirement; they hadn't written about their work in notebooks. They had only made design drawings from which Bob could work as he machined and assembled items. Jason's advise was to describe all their development work, including experiments, with all good and bad results, in notebooks as soon as possible, and carefully preserve the existing old notebooks used in Bob and Doug's trial. Then he gave them contact information for an attorney who specialized in patents.

After they ended the telephone conference, Doug drove the car into town to purchase notebooks with numbered pages. Bob went along to guard the car while Doug was in the stationery store. When Doug came out of the store, he found Bob and the car surrounded by curious onlookers who were amazed to see a car from so long ago that was still on the road. The trunk space had been replaced with a strange, large cylinder that had a small, round rear window. Through the window the onlookers could see a glow radiating from red-hot, high-strength "Thornel" graphite binding threads, that looped through the outer surface of the movable insulation plug, holding the insulation together.

"Coming through, coming through," Doug said as he tried to force his way to the car.

One particularly burly man pushed him back and said, "Wait your turn."

Bob saw what was happening and, since he had installed a battery during the upgrades, he could now honk the horn. This startled the crowd, who had seldom heard a horn, and never so close. They scurried backward, and Doug quickly made his way to the car and got in. He gradually drove away, being careful to avoid running over any toes, then silently accelerated.

Someone in the crowd said, "Listen how silent it is. It must be electric."

Someone else said, "They must be billionaires."

Doug and Bob laughed about the comments as they reached 25 mph and headed home. They were especially gratified to know their solar cars would soon be within the financial reach of most people in the crowd, non of whom were billionaires.

*   *   *

During the next two weeks, Bob, Doug and Audrey took turns writing in two 150-page notebooks Doug had purchased. They filled the books with details of the solar powered car, design and process for making the solar mirror, how to use the mirror in recharging the heat-energy storage unit, etc. Doug, Audrey and Bob signed as the inventors. They had Tensey and Sheriff Lock sign as witnesses on each page. Then, Audrey called the patent attorney and arranged for herself, Bob, Doug and Tensey to meet him in his Greensville office. By this time, Bob had determined that the car had a range of about 200-miles on a full charge, so he decided to drive it to the attorney's office.

The next morning they all got into the car. Bob was driving, Audrey was in the front passenger seat, and Doug and Tensey sat in the back seat, as they sped off toward the attorney's office at the breakneck-speed of 35 mph. The car would have gone much faster, but new asphalt was scarce and expensive. There was no longer enough recycled asphalt to go around, and there were graveled sections with potholes at random intervals along the paved road. Rapidly slowing to 5 mph or less before hitting the bumps was essential to avoid the risk of damaging the prototype heat storage unit. In spite of frequent slow-downs, the trip took only a little over an hour rather than four hours it usually required on horseback.

"Wow, that was incredible. So much better than horseback," Tensey said enthusiastically as they entered Greensville. "I think these cars will sell."

They went directly to the patent attorney's office. After they explained the solar car and process for making the recharging mirror, Bob asked, "How long will it take to get a patent."

The attorney looked thoughtful, then said, "At least a year."

"A Year? Good God, we need to start manufacturing these sooner than that so we can begin recouping the credits we've invested. We at least need the ability to safely license the technology to manufacturers."

"Well, Mr. Parker, it takes at least a month or two for someone to complete a patent search to satisfy me on whether there is prior art. Then it takes at least a month for a patent art specialist to make the needed drawings. The co-op's patent office requires another 9- to11-months to work through its backlog to your application. Then it takes the tribal co-op's sole patent attorney several months to work through your application and perform the literature search and inquiries to satisfy himself that your invention is novel and can be patented. If you want to risk it, you can register for a quick patent pending status, and go ahead with product sales or licensing before the formal patent is issued."

"Why would that be risky?"

"If for any reason your patent doesn't go through, your technology would be out there and exposed for anyone to copy. Also, if you sell some cars or licenses, and they infringe on someone else's patent, you could be sued and forced to pay compensation."

Audrey, Bob, Tensey and Doug left the room and conferred quietly among themselves, then they returned and Bob said, "We'd like to apply for both a patent and 'patent pending' status."

"Okay. I will require a 1000-credit deposit to get started, and you will be charged 300-credits per hour for my time. However, my assistant will do most of the work; his time is billed at only 75 credits per hour. You will have to get your construction drawings to me soon. Since you are in a hurry, I will engage a patent artist to start making the stylized drawings before I complete the patent search for prior art. I will need copies of your notebooks right away."

"Doug said, "We have our notebooks along. Can you have your office make copies of the pages right now? We don't want to release the originals."

"That's wise. I'll have my secretary make copies if you'll take me out for a ride in your car."

Bob took the patent attorney for a demonstration ride in the car. He stopped by Jason Bright's office and included him in the ride. Doug, Audrey, and Tensey stood waiting on the sidewalk.

When Bob drove past Mr. Grabner's office, several doors away, Grabner must have seen the car streak past; he stuck his head out to look down the street, recognized Doug, and quickly walked over to him. Grabner bent slightly forward at the waist with his hands clasped together and said, "Hello Mr. Murphy. It looks like you have a demonstration prototype you can show me. Are you still looking for an investor?"

"No," Doug said coldly.

"Tensey looked embarrassed. "Oh, now Doug, we may need more capital."

"Yes, but Grabner requires warrants that probably would result in us losing our shirts."

"Doug, Mr. Grabner is my old friend, and I don't appreciate you talking about him that way."

Mr. Grabner reddened, looked down at the sidewalk, and said, "I can offer you much better terms now that I've seen your car work."

Just then, Bob returned with the two attorneys. When Bob stopped, the attorneys got out of the car raving about what a wonderful, quiet, comfortable, fast machine it was. Each said he'd like to be among the first customers to buy one

When Bob joined the group, Grabner directed his pitch to Bob. It was obvious that he very much wanted a piece of Solar Motor Company.

Bob looked disgusted and said, "You wouldn't invest when we needed credits, and now we don't need you."

Grabner's face reddened again.

Tensey's eyes flashed and her face became red as she said, "Now, just a minute, guys, remember that I'm Chief Financial Officer. We all have a say in this, and we may need a huge amount of capital if we build a manufacturing plant to turn out a lot of these cars. If we do that, we'll need venture capital from several sources. Let's think before we turn anyone down."

Audrey said, "I agree with Tensey."

Doug and Bob thought over what Tensey and Audrey had said, then Bob gruffly said, "We'll think about it."

Mr. Grabner's color returned to its normal pallor.

Jason, who'd been standing nearby, said, "If you need a large investment, you should decide whether you want venture capital, or an initial public offering (IPO) of stock in your company. If you decide to go with an IPO, I can help you set it up."

Mr. Grabner began to redden again, and beads of sweat appeared on his forehead. "I'd offer you excellent terms for venture capital."

Audrey said, "It's a big decision, and I agree with Tensey that we should think about it. It could go either way; we could build our own manufacturing company, or license our solar car to an existing manufacturer."

"Thinking about it would be wise," Jason added.

Bob, Doug and Tensey nodded in agreement.

Bob said, "Well, we'd better get started home. It'll be dark soon, and I don't know how safe the road is these days. We don't have a gun along this time."

CHAPTER 55
BANDITS, DAMAGE AND DECISIONS

Audrey and Tensey decided to sit together in the back seat on the return trip so they could visit about "girl stuff." Doug sat in the front passenger seat. Bob had driven only about half way home when it began getting dark. The road was eerily deserted. A half hour earlier, they had passed one horseback rider, and he was riding in the opposite direction toward Greensville.

"I don't like the feel of this," Bob said, hanging onto the steering wheel so tight his knuckles were white. However, he held the car's speed to only 15 mph so he could slow quickly for rough stretches of road that were harder to see in the twilight. They'd traveled for another five minutes when Bob, who'd been regularly glancing in his rear view mirror, said, "Oh crap. We're being followed by two horsemen coming at a gallop. They have bandannas over their faces, so they must be bandits."

"If they were bandits, wouldn't they have set up a road block to stop us?" Tensey asked.

"No, I don't think so. There are so few cars being driven, it could be weeks before one would pass this way. The bandits probably planned to ambush someone on horseback who could easily ride around a roadblock. I've been driving so slowly that they probably think we'll be easy to catch. Since we are in a car, they probably think we are rich and wearing expensive jewelry."

"Or they may want to steal the car," Doug mused.

Bob pressed the heat exchanger pedal demanding more power from the engine, and the car sped up to 45 mph.

Doug said, "You'll have to go faster than this or they'll catch up with us next time we come to a stretch where we have to slow to 5 mph."

"I know, but if we are going too fast when we come to a rough place in the road, it could break the core supports and disable us."

"Yeah, but I didn't bring my gun. If those guys catch us, we're probably dead anyway."

"I suppose you're right, hold on!" Bob said as he pressed the heat exchanger pedal further down, accelerating to 55 mph.

Occasionally glancing in the rear-view mirror, Bob saw the horsemen follow for a short time while the car got rapidly ahead, then they slowed and turned back. Just as the bandits were out of sight, a rough stretch of road suddenly showed up just ahead. Bob was looking in the rear view mirror to make sure the bandits' apparent reversal wasn't a trick.

Audrey screamed, "Whoa!"

"Watch out," Doug shouted.

Bob slammed on the brakes, but had only slowed to 25 MPH before hitting some bad bumps. The car became airborne for a moment. The passengers were jolted upward, then yanked downward by their seatbelts until the car hit the ground. When the car hit bottom, the springs were compressed to their limit, and the car's body came down with a severe jolt as the stiff neoprene limiters contacted the axels. The seat springs helped cushion the passengers from the severity of the jolt. However, the body of the car received the full force of the jolt, and a sound like breaking glass came from the heat storage core's containment vessel. The bottom of the vessel immediately started radiating more heat than normal.

Doug said, "What was that?"

"I believe one or more of the core supports has broken," Bob said, "And the core is resting on the insulation and crushing it. If I'm right, the elimination of space between the super insulation's foil layers has drastically reduced its insulating capability.

Are you all right, Audrey?" Bob asked. "Being thrown around like that wasn't good for your pregnancy."

Audrey's voice shook as she said, "I guess so, but I'm worried. With a core support gone, the heat will rapidly flow out of the core and the container will get red hot. It's already getting too hot here in the back seat for Tensey and me. Don't stop, but Tensey and I'll climb into the front seat. Drive fast as you can to get us near home before all the heat drains out of the core."

Tensey removed the two front passenger head rests, then climbed over the back of the front seat and sat on Doug's lap. The car was full-sized and had width enough for two passengers and the driver in the bench-style front seat. With Tensey sitting on Doug's lap, there was room for three passengers. Audrey had difficulty climbing over the seatback because of her distended abdomen. She put her right leg over, straddled the seatback in a bent-forward position facing Bob, and got stuck. Bob adjusted the seat to its extreme rear position. Then Audrey folded her left leg to pull her knee past Bob's head, and slide her rear end over the seatback.

"Audrey, get your knee off the steering wheel or we'll go into the ditch," Bob shouted. "Oh crap, we're coming to a rough place."

Bob slammed on the brakes, and this helped Audrey get the rest of the way over the front seatback. She found herself sitting on the front floor, right shoulder against dashboard and no longer contacting the steering wheel, but her knees were against Bob's legs. For a few moments she stuck in that position, then slowly worked herself upward and back with Doug and Tensey pulling on her arms until she was sitting in the seat between Bob and Doug. Tensey had moved so she was facing forward, sitting between Doug's legs.

"Tensey, you're crushing my 'family jewels,'" Doug said in a tense, high voice, his face contorted with pain.

"Oh, I'm sorry, dear," Tensey said as she scooted her butt over onto Doug's right leg.

Bob gripped the steering wheel tightly as he drove through the rough stretch, then sped up to 50.

Doug said, "Don't you think you'd better slow down so you don't hit another rough place at high speed?"

Bob had a grim look on his face, jaw set, lips pressed together, and his eyes squinting as if to penetrate into the darkness past the headlight beam. "I believe we've already sustained about the worst possible damage. I'll watch for rough patches and try to slow before I hit them, but we're going to have a major repair job anyway. The heat gauge is dropping like a rock, so we'll be walking six or seven miles if I don't hurry."

It was now completely dark, and there was no moon. To Bob's surprise, rough patches in the road showed up better in the headlights than they had at dusk. He was able to slow down for each of the remaining bad places. Much to Bob's relief, the car made it all the way to the blacksmith shop before it ran out of useable power. Bob hooked a garden hose onto a faucet in the shop and shot water onto the bottom of the stainless steel containment vessel, producing clouds of steam and quickly cooling the vessel. It had begun to sag because it had gotten too hot while supporting the heavy heat storage core. About 20-minutes later the steam had subsided and Bob turned the water off.

"Well, that does it," Bob said, indicating the end of the day's adventures. Everyone gave a sigh of relief.

As they walked along the road home through the darkness, they visited about the events of the day, and discussed plans for the future.

*   *   *

The next day, Doug helped Bob remove the heat storage assembly from the car with the chain hoist. A prominent bulge was obvious on the bottom side of the horizontal cylindrical containment vessel. Bob built a stand, upended the vessel into a vertical position with its window-end pointed downward, and lowered it onto the stand. Using an acetylene torch, he cut around the side of the containment vessel near the window-end, and lifted the vessel and insulation off the storage core, leaving it standing on the three end-support tubes. Pieces of vitreous carbon from the broken side-support tube dropped out of the vessel onto the floor.

Picking up the pieces, Bob said, "Yep, just as I thought. Looks like a support broke. That was a good test, and it shows us what needs improving. The bottom side-support needs to be stronger."

Doug's forehead wrinkled in disgust as he said, "Damn, that means more orders for materials, and they'll take forever to get here. It'll be months before we have a demonstration prototype to show again."

Bob said, "But this was a blessing in disguise. If the car hadn't been through such a severe test, we wouldn't have known about that weak spot. We might've manufactured a bunch of cars, then had to repair them at our expense. We've learned two important lessons: the support on the downward side of the core must be stronger, and we'd better bolt rather than weld the end onto the containment vessel so it can easily be removed for repairs."

"Could we use a material that's stronger that vitreous carbon for core supports?"

"I don't know of any that have low enough heat conductivity and high strength at the maximum core temperature. Audrey worked for a long time to find this material, and it's the best she could find."

"How about graphite. Its strength actually increases with temperature."

"Audrey said its conductivity's too high."

"Zirconium oxide?"

"She said it's too weak at the maximum core temperature, and it chemically reacts with graphite at high temperatures. I think the best thing to do is increase the diameter of the bottom vitreous carbon support and put up with the consequential larger heat loss through it."

"Okay, I guess we'd better get together in a meeting with the girls to discuss the core supports and decide whether to build a manufacturing plant, or just license the technology for our cars."

*   *   *

The next day, Tensey called a Solar Motor Company board meeting around Bob and Audrey's kitchen table. Audrey read the minutes from the last meeting. Then, Tensey called for old business, and no one responded.

"Since there is no old business, the meeting is open for new business," Tensey said officiously.

Bob said, "Mrs. Chairman."

When he was recognized by Tensey, he said, "I don't see the need for all this formality. If we had 8 or 10-board members that included strangers, I could see the need. But we are good friends, so I move that we just discuss things like we always have."

Doug said, "I second it."

Tensey said, "All in favor say aye."

Four "ayes" rang out, so this and future meetings would be informal.

Bob told of his findings from disassembling the heat storage unit and then summarized the recommended changes. After some discussion, the others approved the core support design changes.

Then, Tensey introduced the need to decide on a method to get funds for the construction of a plant to manufacture solar cars. This brought out a discussion of the tremendous risk of obtaining the 300-million or so credits for this purpose.

Bob said, "Venture capitalists require crippling warrants and excessive returns on their investment. A bank would not be willing to loan enough money, and would want all of the applicants' personal property as well as the company's assets for collateral in case things didn't pan out fast enough to meet payments. An IPO (initial public offering of stock) would be complex, and would take away a large part of the profits as dividends to stockholders."

The four appeared about ready to agree that an IPO was the least objectionable method, but the phone rang.

Audrey smiled at Doug and said, "That's the hard-wired company phone. Tensey and I decided to get one installed both here and at your house. A business listing for Solar Motor Company gives a better impression than just 'Bob Parker' or 'Doug Murphy.' We discussed using wrist phones, but with today's sophisticated spying equipment for grabbing information transmitted on the air, and with the word about our car spreading, those phones are too risky for confidential high-stakes business conversations."

Tensey answered the phone. "Solar Motor Company. Mrs. Murphy, CFO speaking." Then after a pause, she continued, "Oh, okay. We're having a meeting, and all of our executives are present. Let me put you on the speaker. Okay, go ahead."

"As I was saying, I'm President of International Motors. We've heard about your solar powered car, and we may be interested in obtaining a license to manufacture it."

"How did you hear about it?"

"There was a news broadcast last night interviewing an attorney seen riding in the car in Greensville. He told how impressed he was with the car's comfort, speed and convenience, and that it doesn't require expensive batteries or fuel. We had an executive meeting this morning, decided to look into it, and perhaps obtain a license to manufacture it."

Tensey said, "What might you offer for a license?"

"If the car is as good as the news broadcast indicated, we would be pleased to offer fifty million credits up front, and 4% of the selling price for each car sold."

"That's not nearly enough. You should see the reaction of the people who have seen our car. It's much less expensive than an electric, and it doesn't incorporate any scarce materials. Since the car will be relatively inexpensive, and is inexpensive to run, it should sell like crazy. The profits will be huge. We're planning to manufacture it ourselves."

"Mrs. Murphy, I'm sure you are aware of the huge expense and high risk of setting up a manufacturing plant on that scale. We're already set up for manufacturing cars and, in addition, have all the advertising and distribution facilities that will be needed. Let me confer with my colleagues They're here in the office with me and have been listening on a speaker phone. I'm going to mute our phone so we can confer privately. I'll un-mute it when we are ready to talk to you."

"Fine, and I'll do the same."

For about 10-minutes the executives of the Solar Motor Company conferred while waiting for International Motors.

Bob opened the discussion, saying, "Tensey, 50-million credits is a lot. Don't you think we should grab it rather than risking losing the deal?"

"No, Bob. I've estimated the world market for our car, and I think the time is right for billions to be sold, with hundreds of billions in net profit during the first few years. International Motors should be willing to give us at least 100-million credits up front. That's less than 0.1% of profits I estimated for the first couple of years."

Audrey and Doug both agreed with Tensey.

Bob said, "But, we haven't even finished shaking down the design yet."

"That doesn't matter. We'll have it . . . "

Tensey's response was interrupted by the speaker phone. A different man's voice said, "Hello, are you there?"

Tensey released "Mute" on her phone and responded, "Yes."

" I'm Chief Executive Officer of International Motors. We may be willing to offer you 150-million credits up front, and

12% of the profit on each car sold. However, we will require a demonstration of the car and its solar charging equipment before we offer to purchase the license. We will also require that the license be exclusive."

Tensey said, "That sounds like a fairly good offer. How soon do you plan to get here for a demonstration."

"We are located in the middle part of the continent, so it will take about 18 days to get there in one of our gasoline powered vans. I'm sure you know how bad the roads are these days."

"Yes, we sure do," Tensey said, casting a knowing glance at Bob, then she continued, "We're in the process of improving our design, and our demonstration car has been disassembled for the changes. Because of the time required for materials we;ve ordered to get here, we can't be ready for you in 18 days. It may be a month or two. I'll call you when have a firm date for demonstrating the car"

"Okay, Mrs. Murphy. We're looking forward to seeing your demonstration. I'll await your call."

* * *

Doug and Audrey calculated the optimum size and wall thickness of vitreous carbon tubes required to give twice the strength of the original tubes. Tubes would have good side-flexural strength without too much heat leakage, but would require foil insulation inside their bore to avoid excessive radiation loss of heat. Audrey ordered six, and the vendor promised delivery within three weeks.

Bob surveyed the damage done to the super-insulation when the core supports collapsed, and decided to replace the graphite foil. Audrey ordered the foil, and was able to get a promised delivery of four weeks.

While waiting for the special materials to arrive, Bob and Doug repaired the containment vessel. designed and installed an improved shock absorbing spring suspension system and universal joints in the drive shaft from the Solar Propulsion Module to reduce shock on the engine, transmission and heat storage unit on rough roads.

* * *

Finally, the new core-support tubes and graphite foil arrived, and Bob decided the car would be ready for demonstration in less than 18 days. Tensey called the CEO of IM (International Motors). Eighteen days later, the CEO and three of his top executives arrived and got rooms in the hotel. A demonstration was planned for the next day, which was predicted to be cloudy. This was unfortunate since it would emphasize the main weakness of a solar powered car. The IM and Solar Motor Company executives met at Bob and Audrey's house. After polite introductions and coffee, Doug described the car's features and the solar charging method to the IM executives, then nervously explained that the car had been designed to allow electrical charging to supplement solar charging on cloudy days.

The CEO said, "Of course. We realize the sun doesn't shine all the time, and we expected a supplementary charging method." This relieved Doug's anxiety, and he continued explaining the car's performance and specifications. The executives returned to the hotel to rest from their long trip and prepare for the next day's demonstration.

Bob electrically charged the heat storage core during the night, so it was ready for the big demonstration in the morning. To give an impression of the car's solar capability, Bob parked the car near the solar mirror and waited there the next morning. Doug, Tensey and Audrey greeted the IM executives when they arrived, and took them to the mirror to examine the car. Bob, Doug and Audrey explained the various features of the solar mirror charging system.

The car had room for the driver and five passengers, so Doug invited the four executives to take a ride. Audrey, Doug and Tensey went to Bob's house and sat on the front steps. Bob took the executives for a ride around Stoneville, then out onto the road to Greensville, hitting 55 MPH at times, but slowing down for rough places in the road. Doug hadn't gone along since the car would perform better without the load of an added passenger. Even though stronger core support tubes and a shock absorbing suspension had been installed on the storage unit, the new arrangement had not been severely tested. Bob decided that slowing down would make a better impression than going too fast over bumps, causing a core support to break and overheat the three men in the back seat. After driving a few miles out of town, Bob turned the car around as he explained how he had "easily" outrun bandits on this same road. (He left out the part about the core support failing.) However, one of the executives said, "I don't see how you outran anyone when you have to slow down for bumps. Why do you slow down so much?"

Bob realized he'd have to explain, and his mind was racing trying to think of how to spin the answer without making it sound too bad. He wished Doug were there to quickly come up with a good answer. He considered putting off the answer until getting back to Doug, but he felt that the delay would put too much emphasis on the problem, so he answered the question.

"First of all, we outran the robbers because they were on horseback. I drove 55 MPH on the smooth parts of the road, so slowing for the short, rough patches didn't give them a chance to catch up. The reason I have slowed so much now is that we just modified the core supports, and I haven't had a chance to thoroughly test the new design."

"Why did you change the design?"

Bob had to suppress a gasp when he heard this question. A complete answer telling about the supports failing would reveal what he feared might be a deal-breaker. Then he remembered how Doug always put a positive spin on answers like this. It was almost as if Doug were there whispering into his ear.

"The first design was 'quick and dirty' to demonstrate the first design as quickly as possible. We all agreed that the new design would be more reliable."

The car was now on a smooth section of road, so Bob pressed the pedal to insert the heat exchanger further into the core, and the car quickly accelerated to 65 MPH. The executives all let out remarks such as "Holy Jupiter," "Explosive," and "Wow," as they were briefly pressed against the back of their seats. Even at high speed, the car was almost silent, except for road noise from the tires.

When they got back to Stoneville, Bob said, "I heard someone say, 'Wow.' That's the same reaction we've heard from almost everyone who has seen the car. If you don't mind, I'd like to demonstrate the public's 'wow factor' for you."

IM's CEO said, "Yes, we'd like that."

Almost immediately, Bob regretted the offer he'd just made in the heat of success. In his mind he heard his inner voice say,

"Oh God, what if people here are so used to seeing this car now that they won't be that interested. You fool, you may have just blown the deal." But it was too late, he had already offered to show off the marketing advantage of this new kind of car. He pulled up in front of a grocery store, next to a bank office, and got out of the car. In a few minutes, people began to gather around the car to look it over, much to Bob's relief. Then, much to his delight, they showed intense interest by asking many questions about the car. Such a large crowd gathered that a short time later, Bob had trouble driving away. When the carload of executives arrived back in Bob's driveway near the front steps, where he'd left Audrey, Tensey and Doug, Audrey wasn't there.

"Where's Audrey?" Bob asked.

"Don't worry, she's in the house lying down. She's in labor," Tensey said. "We called the ambulance wagon ten minutes ago, and they will probably have the horses hitched up in another five minutes or so."

Bob's face reddened as he said, "To hell with the ambulance wagon. It rides so rough that it'll probably pop the kid out before they even get Audrey to the hospital. It might even cause her to hemorrhage. I'll take her in the car.

Bob drove the car into his driveway, went into the house, and came out with Audrey. After helping her into the car, he sped off toward the hospital, with Doug riding along in the back seat to bring the car back for any further demonstrations that might be required.

On the way to the hospital, Bob told Doug about the demonstration of the car, including the "Wow" factor of the crowd, and how well it went. Before following the nurse who wheeled Audrey into the hospital, Bob described in more detail the reaction of the executives, and suggested that they might be willing to either pay more "up-front" for an exclusive license, or accept a license without exclusive rights.

*   *   *

The IM executives stayed for another night, hoping for a sunny day on which the solar charging mirror could be demonstrated. In the morning, the sun shone brightly in a cloudless, azure sky. Bob wanted to go to Audrey at the hospital, but he knew she was in good hands. When he phoned her earlier that morning, she told him she was fine, and insisted that he stick with the IM deal. Audrey said it was more important for him to be available for the solar mirror demonstration since it could make or break this important deal. Doug and Tensey arrived, and thoroughly discussed the day's marketing strategy with Bob over coffee.

Later, when the IM people drove into the driveway, Doug, Tensey and Bob greeted them, and they all went to the solar mirror for the demonstration. Bob had already backed the car into position for extraction of the Solar Propulsion Module using the mirror's arms. He had also connected a long extension cable, from the heat storage unit's instrument cable to the charge (temperature) gauge on the car's instrument panel, so the IM executives could see the amount of heat stored in the core as it was being charged. Before removing the Solar Propulsion Module from the car, Bob showed the IM executives the charge gauge on the car's instrument panel. It indicated that the storage core's energy level was at about 30% of full charge.

Bob and Doug had installed automatic motorized systems to extract the motor/heat storage assembly from the car, and continuously adjust the mirror's azimuth and elevation to track the sun, so Bob had only to press a button, stand back, and watch the system perform. As heat energy built up in the core, the IM people saw the progress on the charge indicator in the car. They were visibly impressed. By mid morning everything was still going well, so Bob got on his horse and left for the hospital. A short time later, Tensey and Doug could see the executives were getting tired of standing around watching the solar charging process, so they invited them in for coffee and discussions about the deal.

When Bob got to the hospital, Audrey was still in labor. What's wrong, Doctor? I thought the baby would have been born by now."

The doctor looked grim as he said, "Bob, you and Audrey have a decision to make."

CHAPTER 56
OH BABY!

The doctor said, "I hate to tell you this, Bob, but Audrey has been in labor too long. I'm afraid we may have to take the baby by Cesarean Section if she doesn't manage to give birth in the next hour or so. She's strong and healthy or I wouldn't have let it go this long."

"Is a Cesarean bad, Doc? What are the risks?"

The doctor described the risks of both letting the labor go on too much longer, and the Cesarean.

"Okay Doc. I'll discuss it with Audrey. May I see her now."

"Sure. But I want to warn you, she's going to be in a bad mood after almost 24 hours of labor."

Bob went in to see Audrey in her labor room. When he walked into the room, he said, "Hi, honey, how are you doing?" Suddenly, a labor pain hit Audrey and she let out a shriek that made Bob's ears ring.

When the pain passed, Audrey shouted, "Tell them to get this damn thing out of me!"

Bob thought, the doc's description of her being in a bad mood was a gross under-statement. Then he said, "The doc said he might have to do a Cesarean. Is that okay with you?"

"Yes, for God's sake, anything. Just get it out of me."

"Okay, dear, I'll tell the doc not to wait any longer."

"Yes, yes. Just shut up and go get the doctor. Hurry. Get it done!"

Bob found the doctor and told him to go ahead immediately with the Cesarean.

The doctor said, "Let's give her another hour or so to try birthing normally."

"But she's in such pain. I want you to go ahead with the Cesarean now."

The doctor argued a little more, but Bob insisted on an immediate Cesarean in accord with Audrey's wishes. However, by the time Bob and the doctor got to the labor room, Audrey had made progress, and the anesthetist had given her a "Spinal" to block the pain. Audrey was so quiet that Bob was worried she might be unconscious.

"Are you all right, Dear?" he asked in a quiet, quavering voice.

"Yes. Thank you for getting the doctor," she said in a strong, confident tone.

Bob thought, thank God she's in her right mind again.

An orderly began pushing Audrey's gurney to the delivery room, and the doctor said, "Mr. Parker, you may come and watch the birth if you wish, but you'll have to put on a sterile gown, hat, gloves, and mask."

Hearing this, Audrey said, "I'm not feeling any pain now, Dear, and I don't need you to hold my hand. Why don't you just wait in the waiting room."

Bob thought about how gallant it would be for him to comfort Audrey during her final birthing process, but then he remembered his aversion to blood, and Audrey's statement that she was no longer in pain, so he went to the waiting room.

Half an hour later, the doctor came into the waiting room and said, "Mr. Parker, you have a fine, healthy son."

"Thank you, Doc. How's my wife. May I see her now?"

"Yes, of course. She's fine, but very tired after being in labor so long. If she's asleep, please don't wake her. She's been through an ordeal, and she needs her rest. If you wish to see your son, you may go down to the newborn's nursery and have the nurse hold him up to the window."

Bob went to Audrey's room, but she was fast asleep. He kissed her forehead, then went to the nursery. The nurse was there and he pointed to the crib that had a tag that said, "Boy, Parker, 9 lb 4 oz, 19-1/2 in." The nurse held up a tiny, red-faced baby snuggled in a blanket. Blue eyes opened momentarily, blinked sleepily, then closed.

Bob said to himself, "Poor little guy, I guess it was an ordeal for you too."

*   *   *

When Bob got back to the solar mirror, he was surprised that no one was there. The past two hours had been so intense, that he hadn't experienced the passage of time. It seemed to him as if he'd just left a few minutes ago. It worried him that the IM executives' van wasn't anywhere to be seen. The solar mirror was still charging the heat storage core, and the instrument panel indicated that it was nearly at full charge. Bob thought, damn, I hope the deal didn't fall through. With a new baby, Audrey and I are going to need a good income.

Then he looked up to see Doug and Tensey rapidly walking across the field toward him.

CHAPTER 57
WOW!

As Doug and Tensey approached, Bob could see they were smiling. They asked him about Audrey. He proudly gave them a brief description of the birth and the baby, including his size, weight and length. Then, as soon as he could, without seeming too terse, he anxiously asked, "Tell me what happened with the IM executives. Why did they leave? Did they buy?"

Doug said, "Guess."

"Oh, c'mon, I'm dying with curiosity."

"Just make a guess."

"Damn it, Doug. Oh, okay. Something went wrong with the demonstration, and they picked up their marbles and went home."

"What makes you think that?"

"Their car is gone, and it's still early, so there must not have been the usual haggling that goes on in a deal."

"Yup, you're right."

"Oh my God, did the deal really fall through?"

"No. I meant you're right, there wasn't any haggling. They made us an offer we couldn't refuse."

Bob's face flushed as he was suddenly released from anxiety that had built up during Audrey's ordeal, and from worry about possible failure of the IM deal. He said, "Quit teasing me and give me the facts."

"Okay, don't blow a gasket. You did such a good job of demonstrating the car that the IM executives agreed to 200-million credits up front, plus 15% of the profit on each car, provided we'll give them an exclusive license. We felt that it was enough, so we didn't haggle any further. It's all subject to approval by you and Audrey, of course."

"Wow, that's really a good deal! Where do I sign?"

"The contract will have to be signed by the four of us and the IM executives in front of witnesses and a notary. The executives are going to stay at the hotel until their legal department can put the contract together and send it to them electronically. They brought a computer and printer along, so they can print copies of the contract without waiting a couple of weeks for them to get here by express mail. They said it would take about three days to have their attorney get it ready."

"That's good. By then, Audrey should be recovered enough that she'll able to go with us to a notary public to sign the papers."

"It's not a problem if she can't. We could take the notary to her. I think we should be able to get the judge and sheriff to sign as witnesses on a deal this big."

Tensey asked, "Do you think Audrey would feel like having visitors now?"

"No. She's absolutely worn out after struggling hard with the birth for almost 24 hours. The doctor said she'll feel much better after a good night's sleep, so tomorrow she should be okay."

The next morning, Tensey and Doug accompanied Bob to the hospital. Audrey was nursing the baby when they arrived.

"My God, he's half grown!" Doug said as he looked admiringly at the nine-pound baby.

Bob grinned and stood tall with his shoulders back and his chest pushed out farther than usual.

Tensey looked adoringly at the baby and said, "Oh, he's beautiful."

Audrey grinned, but Bob frowned and said, "What do you mean by 'beautiful?' He's not a girl."

"I'm sorry. I miss-spoke. I meant handsome," Tensey said, looking into Bob's eyes and smiling. Bob's frown instantly disappeared and morphed into a smile.

The four friends enjoyed visiting in the warm, sterile comfort of the hospital room, admiring the new little life and speculating about what he'd be like when he grew up.

*　　　*　　　*

Three days later, the contract arrived. Doug and Bob drove the solar powered car to Greensville to have Jason Bright look the contract over. They could have transmitted it electronically, but thought there might be a need for discussion that could more easily be done in person. Besides, in this new age of rapid motor transportation, it was a quick trip. It didn't take long for Jason to determine that the contract was acceptable.

Bob and Doug left Greeensville on the one-hour trip home at 11 o'clock. They'd only traveled about ten miles when they rounded a corner and, in the road about 200-feet ahead of them, was a group of four men sitting on horses, in the middle of the road, guns drawn, bandannas over their faces. Bob slammed on the brakes, and stopped about 25 feet from the first horse. The rider said, "We are taking your car. You, passenger, get out. We only need the driver. We don't want to kill anyone we don't have to, so don't try anything."

Ambush! Bob and Doug looked stunned. Then, Bob leaned on the horn. The horses weren't used to hearing the loud blare of a car horn, and they bucked and bolted in spite of their riders' efforts to control them. An opening momentarily appeared between the horses, and Bob charged through it at full power, blaring the horn all the way. The riders had set their ambush location around a curve just before a straight, smooth stretch of road. Bob was able to get a head start in the confusion, and got up to 55 mph before the startled horses and riders recovered. However, about a mile down the road, the car suddenly came to a rough patch of road, and Bob could only slow to 20-mph before hitting it. This time, the stronger core support tubes and special shock absorbing system prevented damage. The men arrived safely at home and enjoyed horrifying their wives with the story of their narrow escape from the attempted ambush by armed car thieves.

Doug said, "From now on, I'm going to carry my rifle on all my trips out of town."

Bob added, "Yeah. And I'll get some buckshot shells for my 8-guage semi-automatic shotgun. It's bigger than a 12 guage, and kicks so hard it almost breaks my shoulder, but it'll be perfect for self defense."

"I'll bet that when law officers are using our solar cars to patrol the road to Greensville, there won't many bandits on it," Audrey said.

Two hours later the sheriff, Bob (who was carrying the baby), Audrey, Doug, Tensey, and the International Motors executives met in front of the courthouse. Inside, they went to the tribal notary's office and were joined by the judge. Tensey had arranged for the judge and sheriff, in addition to the notary, to sign as witnesses to the transaction.

When all copies had been signed and witnessed, IM's financial officer electronically transferred 200-million credits into the Solar Motor Company's account, Tensey deposited 99 million credits into Bob and Audrey's account, and the same amount into hers and Doug's account. She left 2 million credits in the Solar Motor Company's account to cover future legal fees and other contingencies that might arise.

Afterward, the four friends merrily visited together in the local restaurant about their narrow escapes and spectacular good fortune.

Tensey said, "I didn't want to be a distraction during the deal, so I didn't say anything earlier. I have some more good news: I'm pregnant!"

Bob and Audrey laughed and congratulated the new parents-to-be.

Doug said, "I must be in heaven."

Bob, Audrey, Doug and Tensy became famous worldwide as people with modest incomes reaped the benefits of being released from the slow, exposed mode of horse travel and farming. However, most people had little or no concept of the risks and hard scientific work, engineering, construction of prototypes, and manufacturing that provided this improvement in their lives.

THE END

Made in the USA
Coppell, TX
21 December 2020

46869192R00167